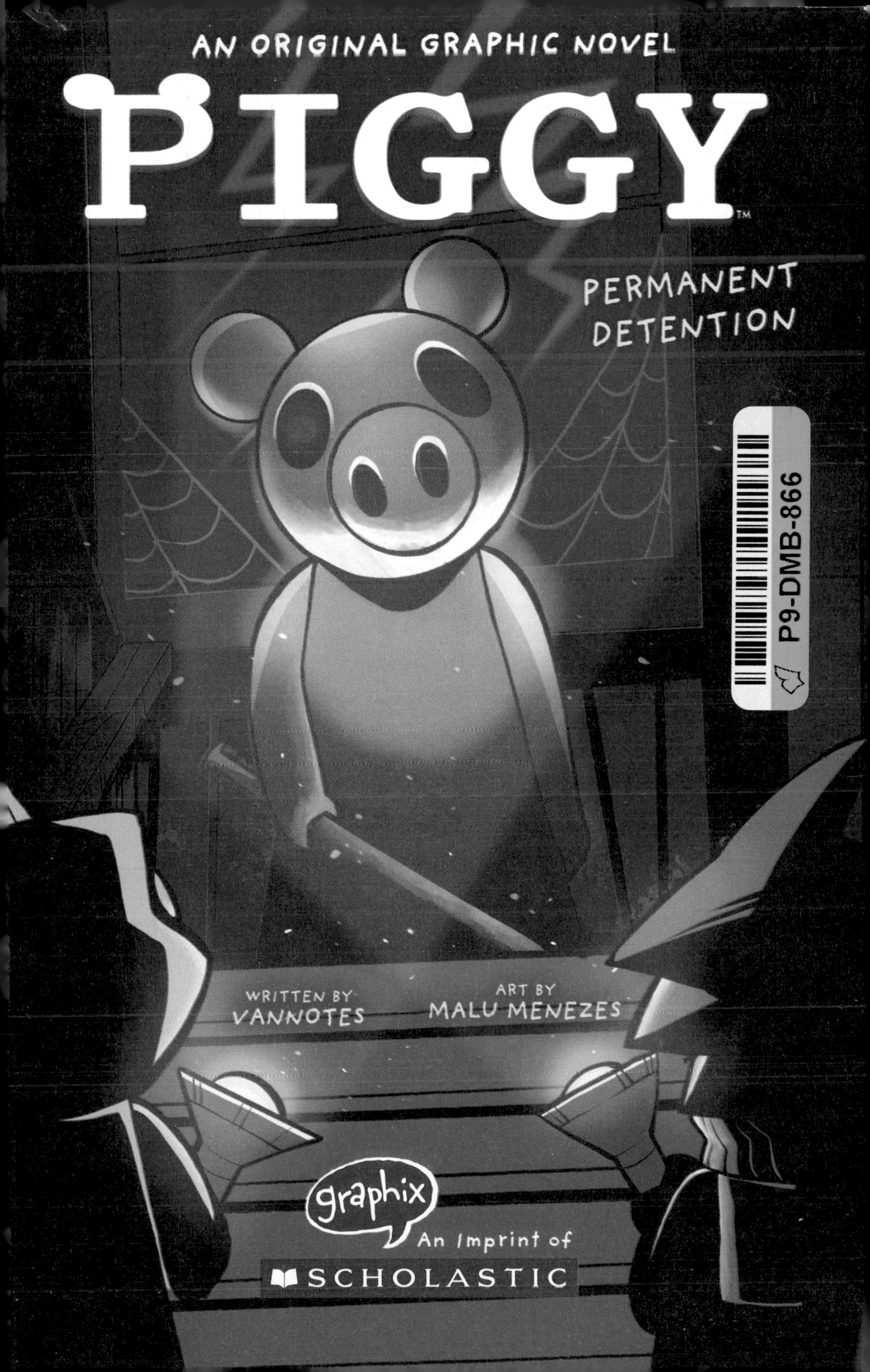
AN ORIGINAL GRAPHIC NOVEL
PIGGY™
PERMANENT DETENTION
WRITTEN BY VANNOTES
ART BY MALU MENEZES
graphix
An Imprint of SCHOLASTIC

All rights reserved. Published by Graphix, an imprint of Scholastic Inc., *Publishers since 1920*. SCHOLASTIC, GRAPHIX, and associated logos are trademarks and/or registered trademarks of Scholastic Inc.

ISBN 978-1-338-84824-3

10 9 8 7 6 5 4 3 2

23 24 25 26 27

Printed in the U.S.A.

40

First edition, September 2023

Edited by Michael Petranek

Lettering by Patrick Brosseau

Book design by Jeff Shake

Color by Astronym

Layouts by Dawn Guzzo

CHAPTER: 1

AFTER AN OUTBREAK THAT'S TURNED THE WORLD UPSIDE DOWN, WILLOW AND HER TEAM OF SURVIVORS, THE SILVER PAW, DO ALL THEY CAN TO STAY ALIVE. IT'S DIFFICULT WHEN THERE'S INFECTED ROAMING EVERYWHERE AND DANGER LURKS AROUND EVERY CORNER. IT'S EASIER WHEN YOU'RE WITH YOUR CREW . . . BUT WHAT IF YOU GET SPLIT UP?

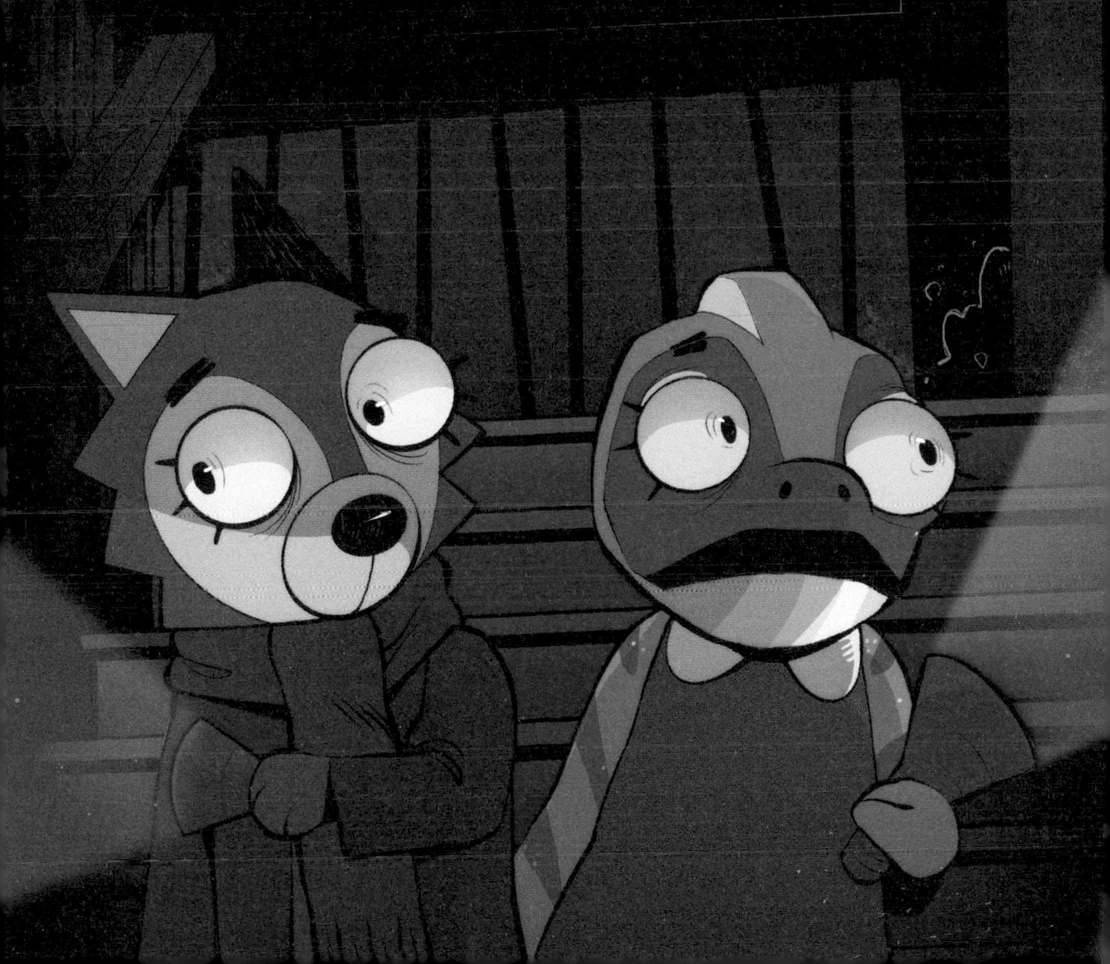

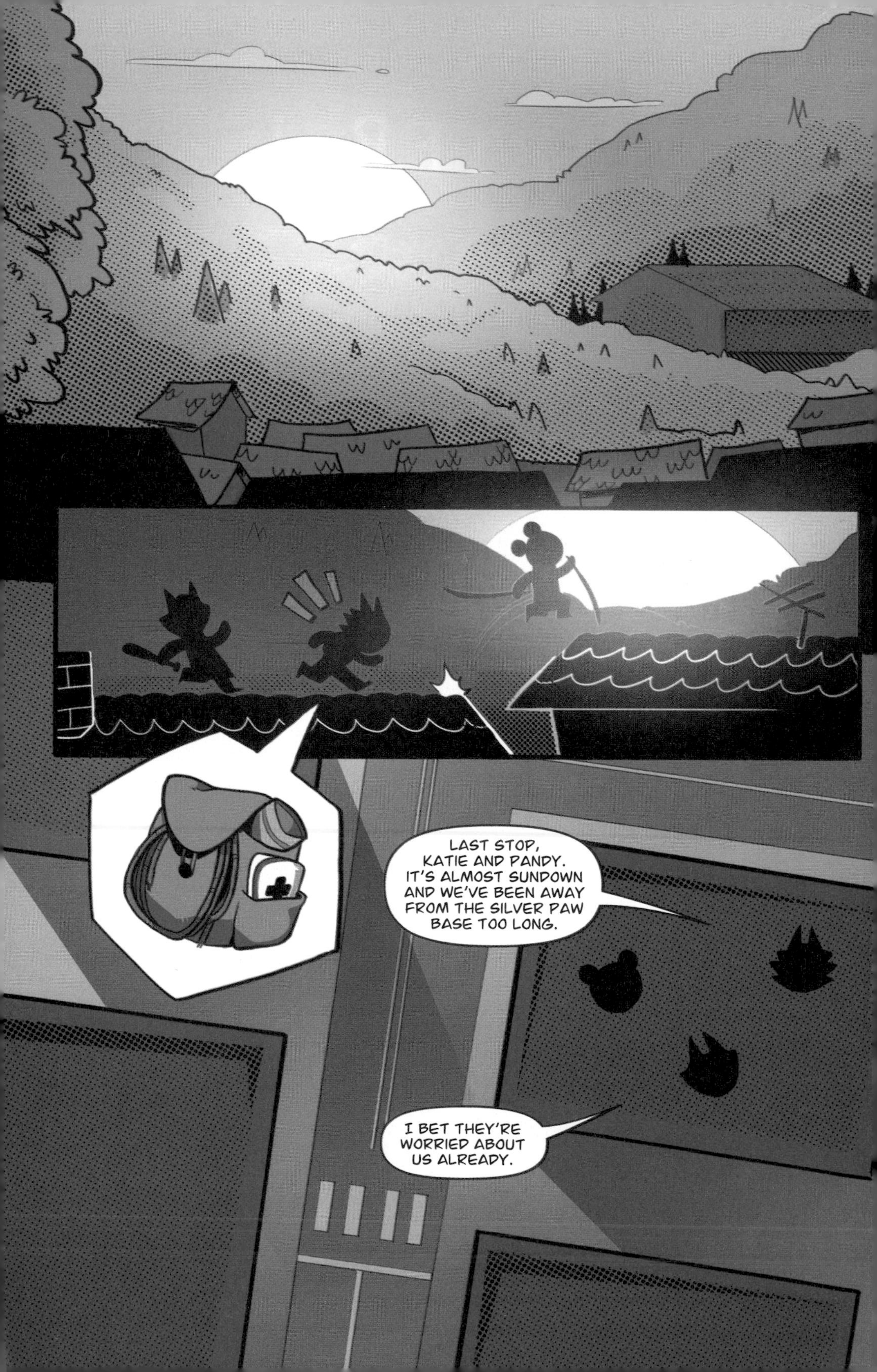
LAST STOP, KATIE AND PANDY. IT'S ALMOST SUNDOWN AND WE'VE BEEN AWAY FROM THE SILVER PAW BASE TOO LONG.
I BET THEY'RE WORRIED ABOUT US ALREADY.

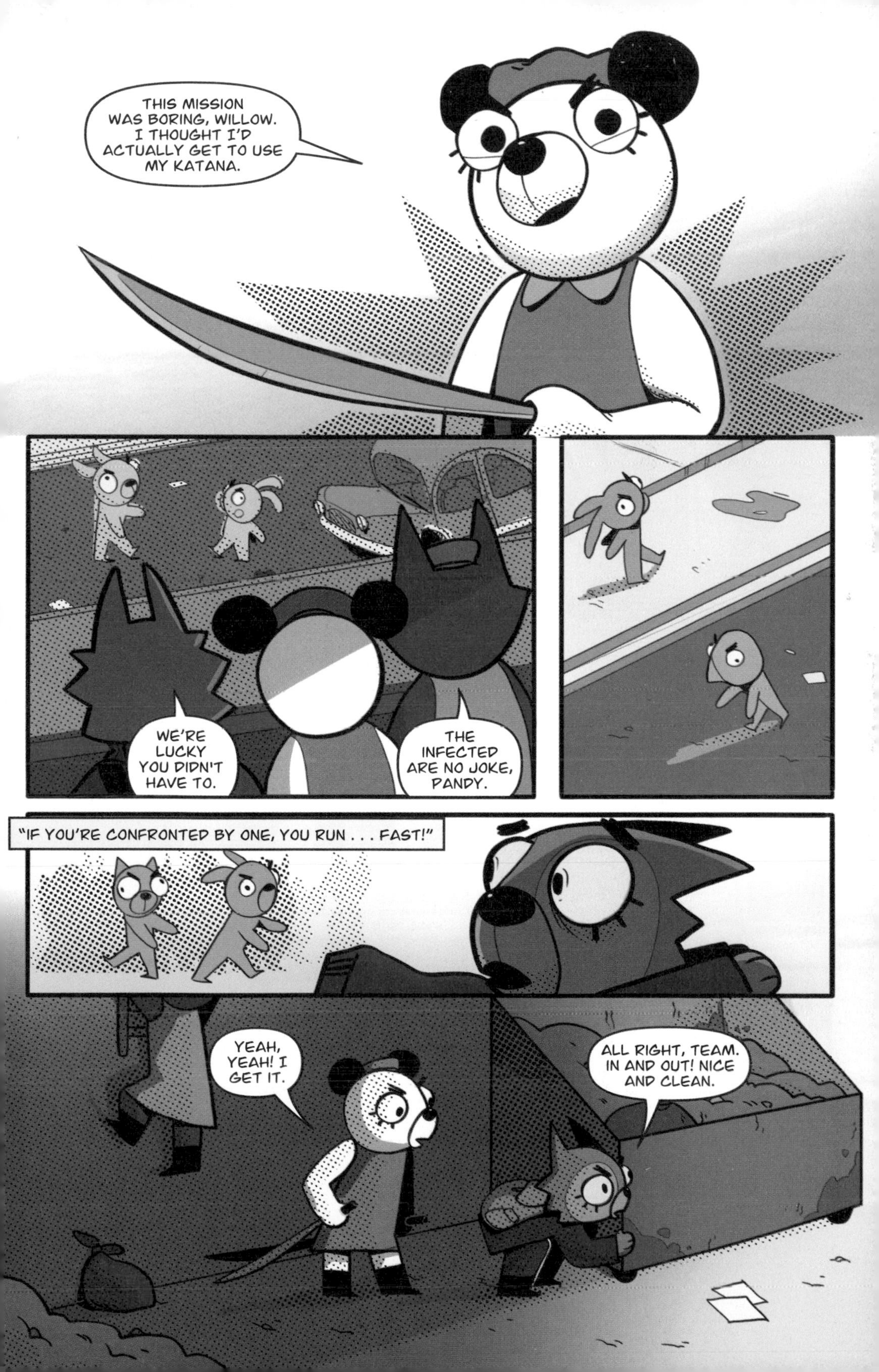
THIS MISSION WAS BORING, WILLOW. I THOUGHT I'D ACTUALLY GET TO USE MY KATANA.
WE'RE LUCKY YOU DIDN'T HAVE TO.
THE INFECTED ARE NO JOKE, PANDY.
"IF YOU'RE CONFRONTED BY ONE, YOU RUN . . . FAST!"
YEAH, YEAH! I GET IT.
ALL RIGHT, TEAM. IN AND OUT! NICE AND CLEAN.

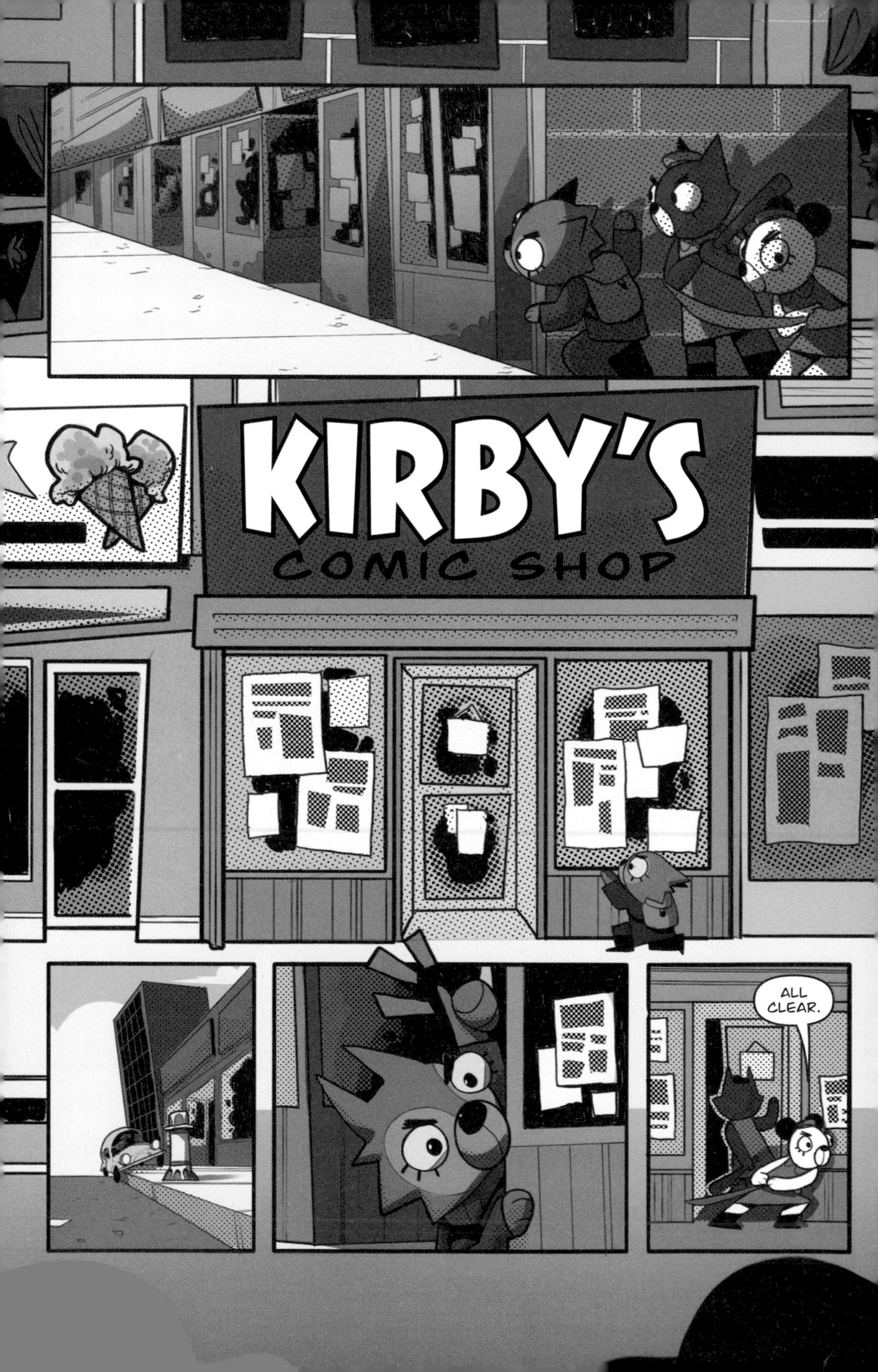
KIRBY'S
COMIC SHOP
ALL CLEAR.

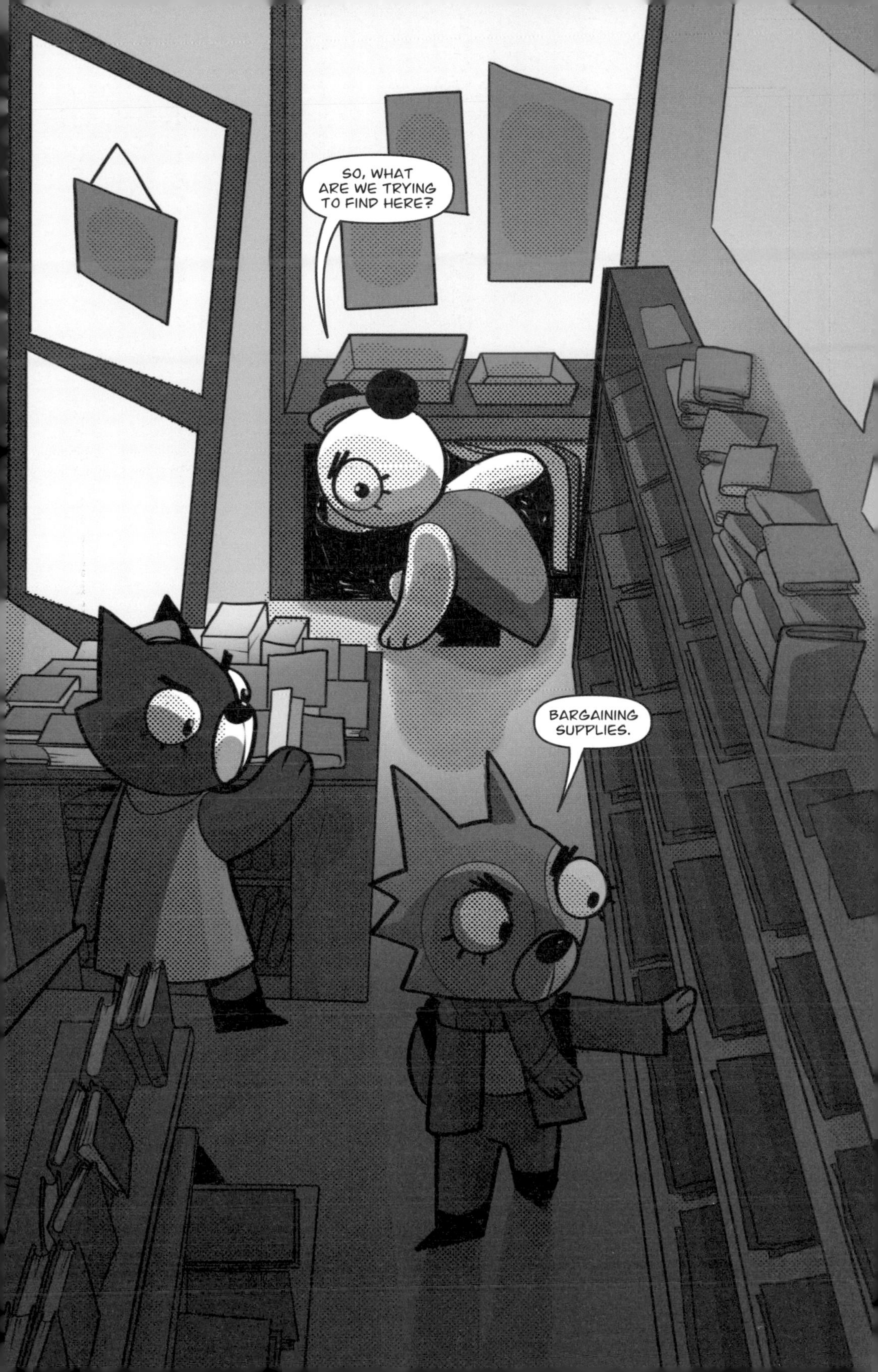
SO, WHAT ARE WE TRYING TO FIND HERE?
BARGAINING SUPPLIES.

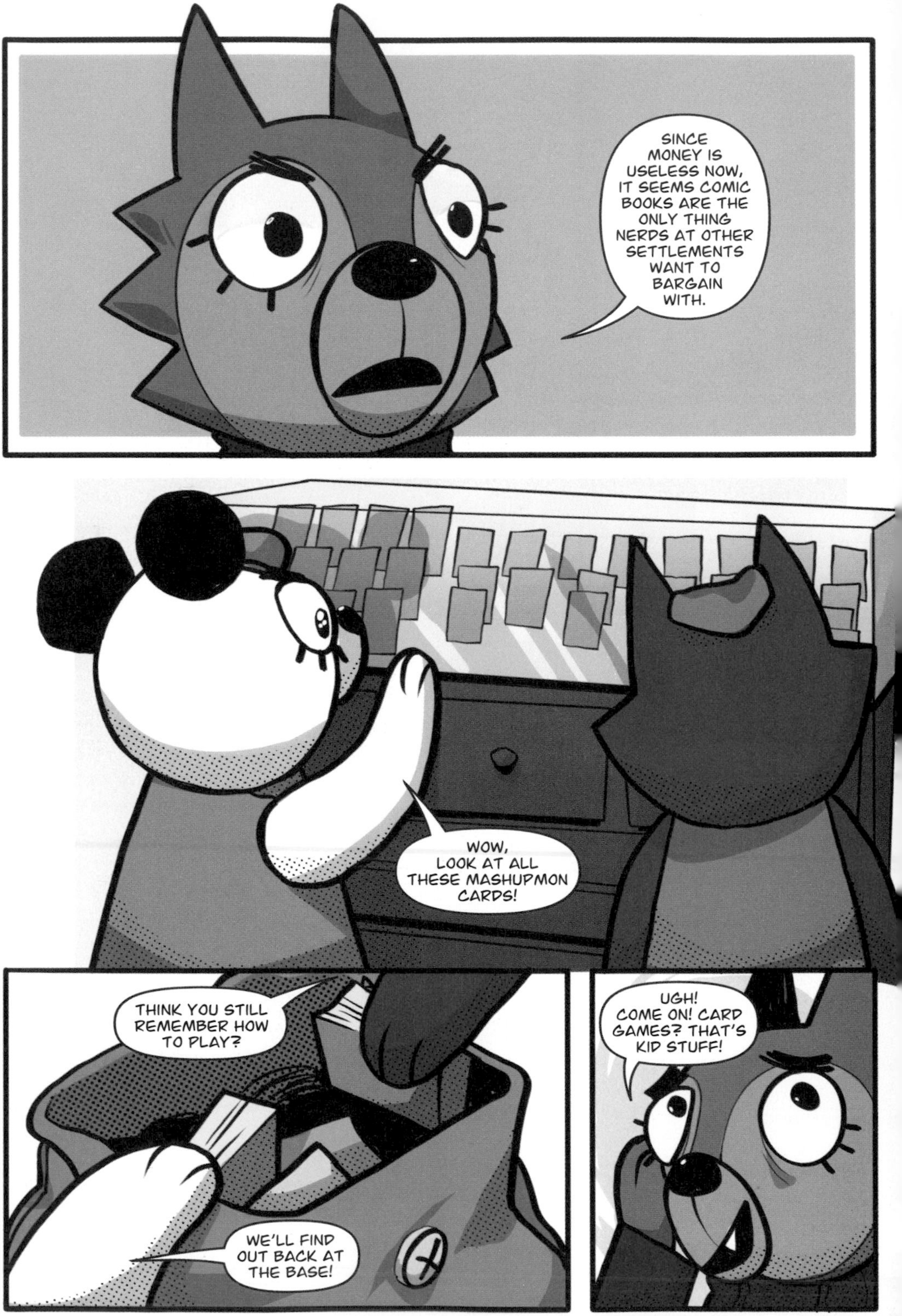
SINCE MONEY IS USELESS NOW, IT SEEMS COMIC BOOKS ARE THE ONLY THING NERDS AT OTHER SETTLEMENTS WANT TO BARGAIN WITH.
WOW, LOOK AT ALL THESE MASHUPMON CARDS!
THINK YOU STILL REMEMBER HOW TO PLAY?
WE'LL FIND OUT BACK AT THE BASE!
UGH! COME ON! CARD GAMES? THAT'S KID STUFF!

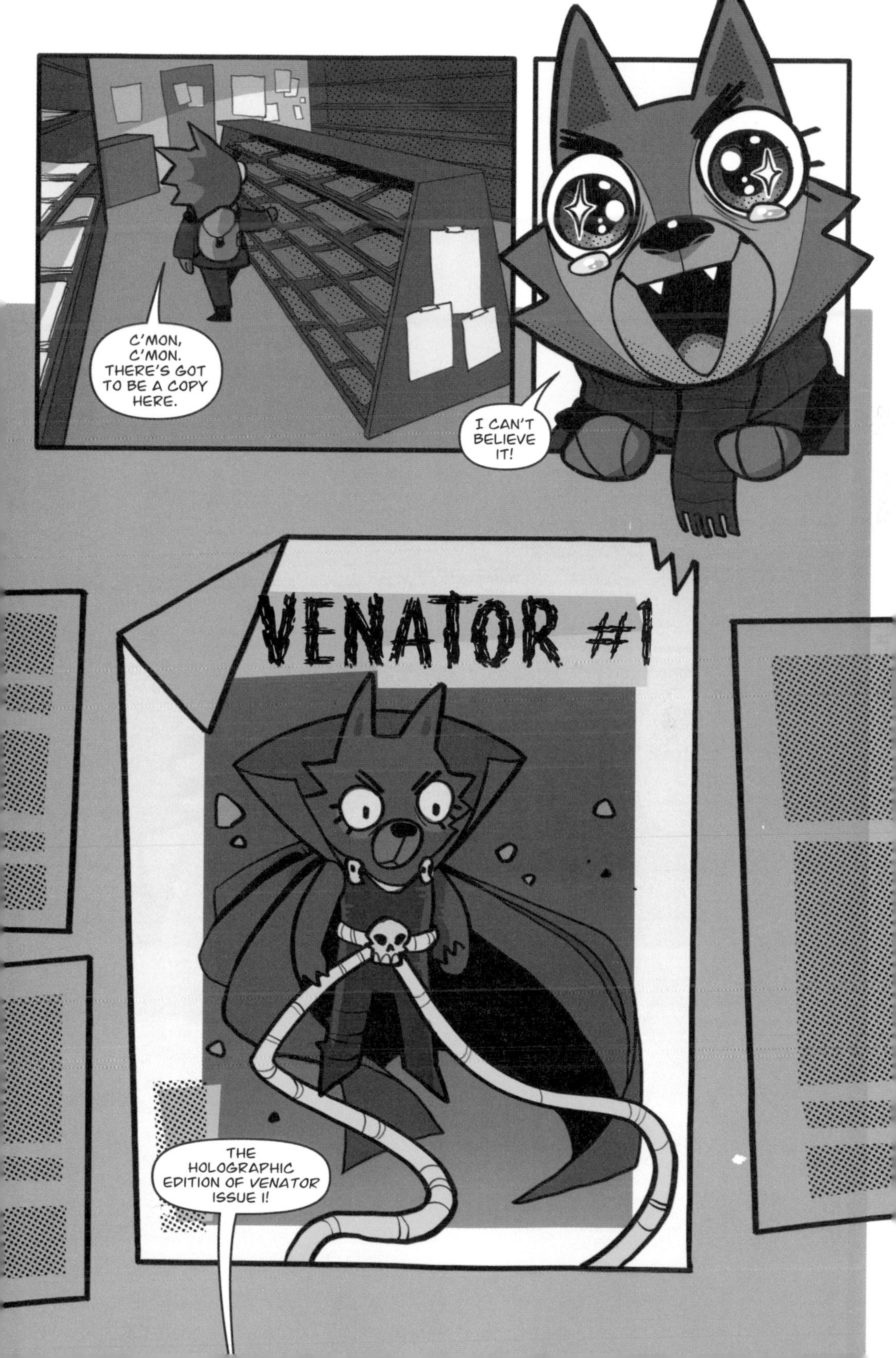
C'MON, C'MON. THERE'S GOT TO BE A COPY HERE.
I CAN'T BELIEVE IT!
VENATOR #1
THE HOLOGRAPHIC EDITION OF VENATOR ISSUE 1!

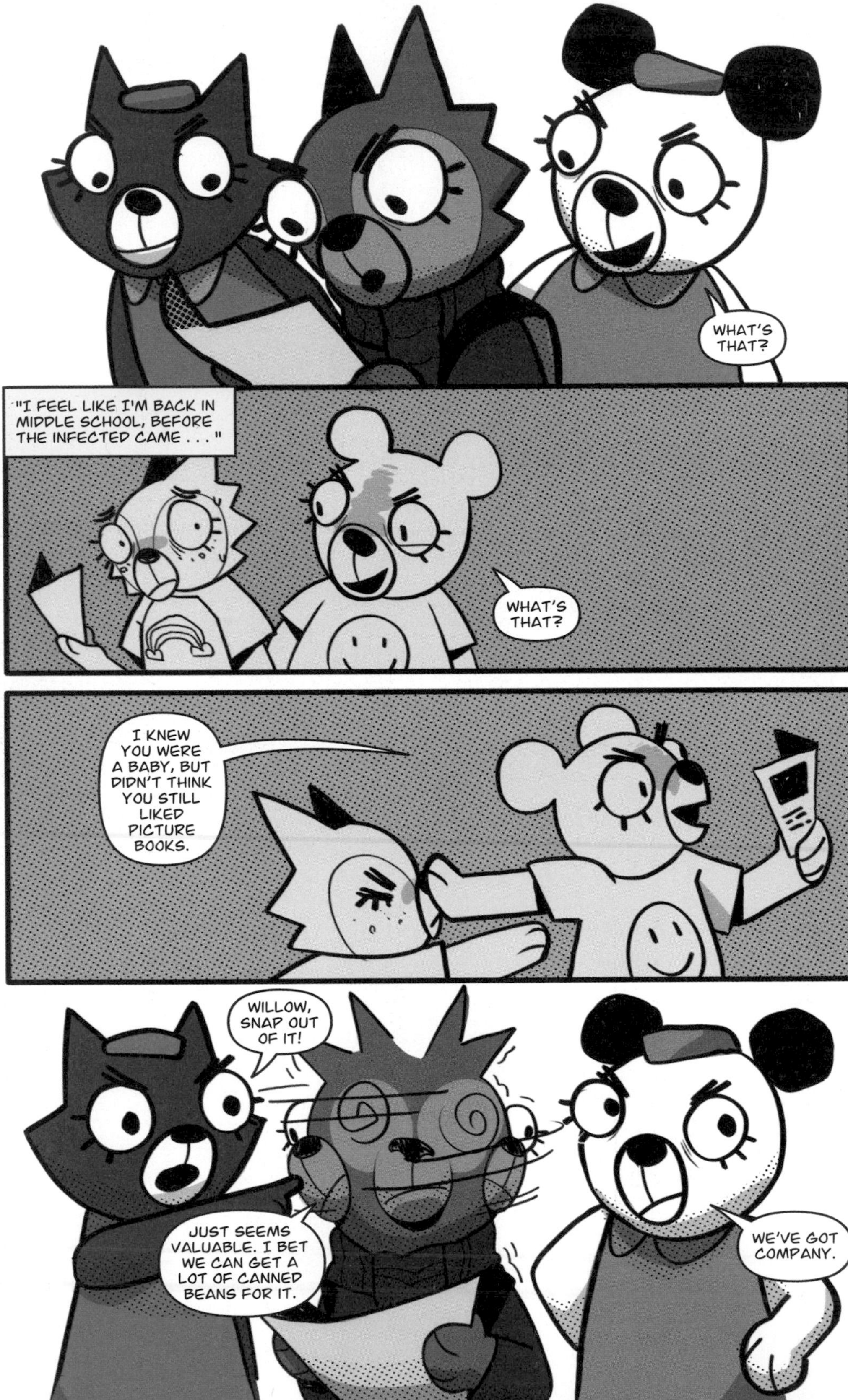
WHAT'S THAT?
"I FEEL LIKE I'M BACK IN MIDDLE SCHOOL, BEFORE THE INFECTED CAME . . ."
WHAT'S THAT?
I KNEW YOU WERE A BABY, BUT DIDN'T THINK YOU STILL LIKED PICTURE BOOKS.
WILLOW, SNAP OUT OF IT!
JUST SEEMS VALUABLE. I BET WE CAN GET A LOT OF CANNED BEANS FOR IT.
WE'VE GOT COMPANY.

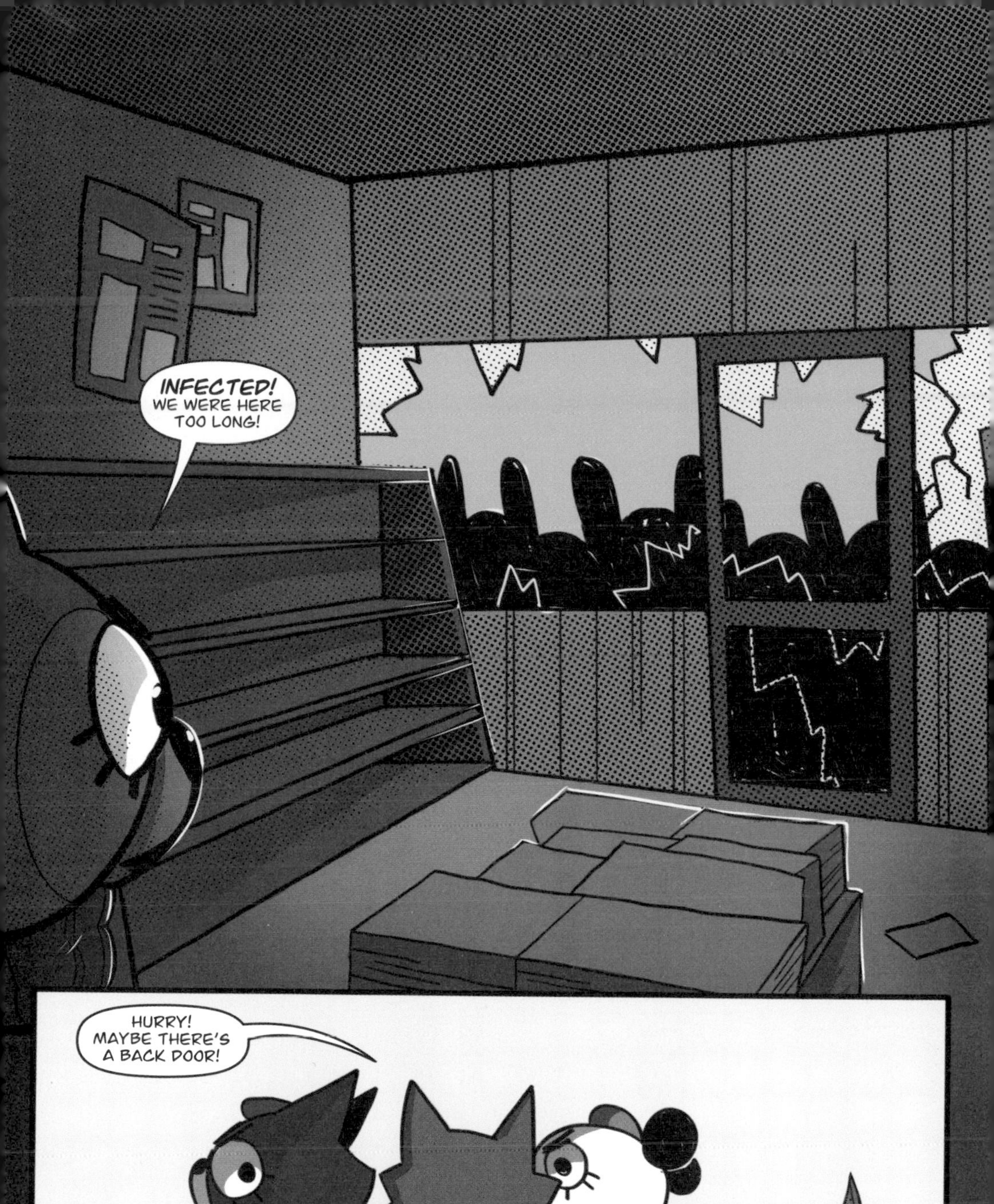
INFECTED! WE WERE HERE TOO LONG!

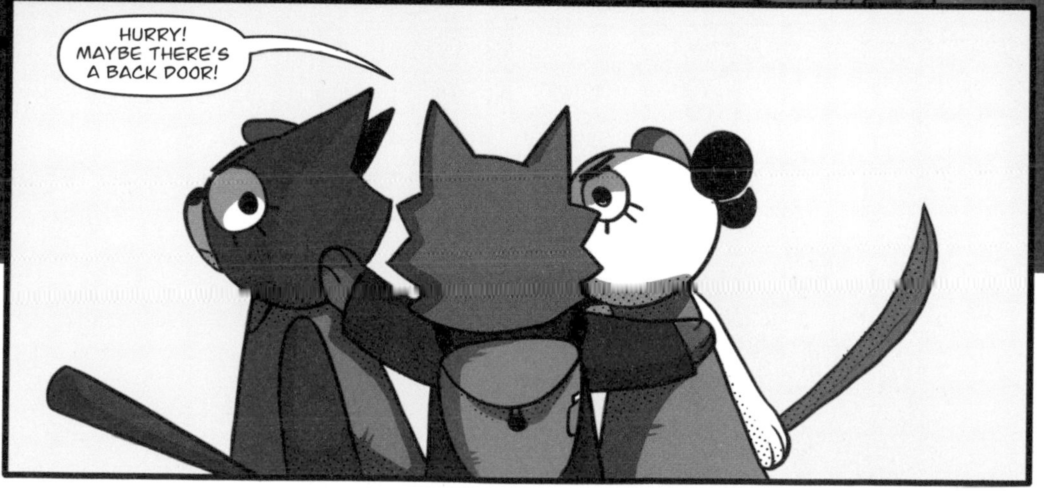
HURRY! MAYBE THERE'S A BACK DOOR!

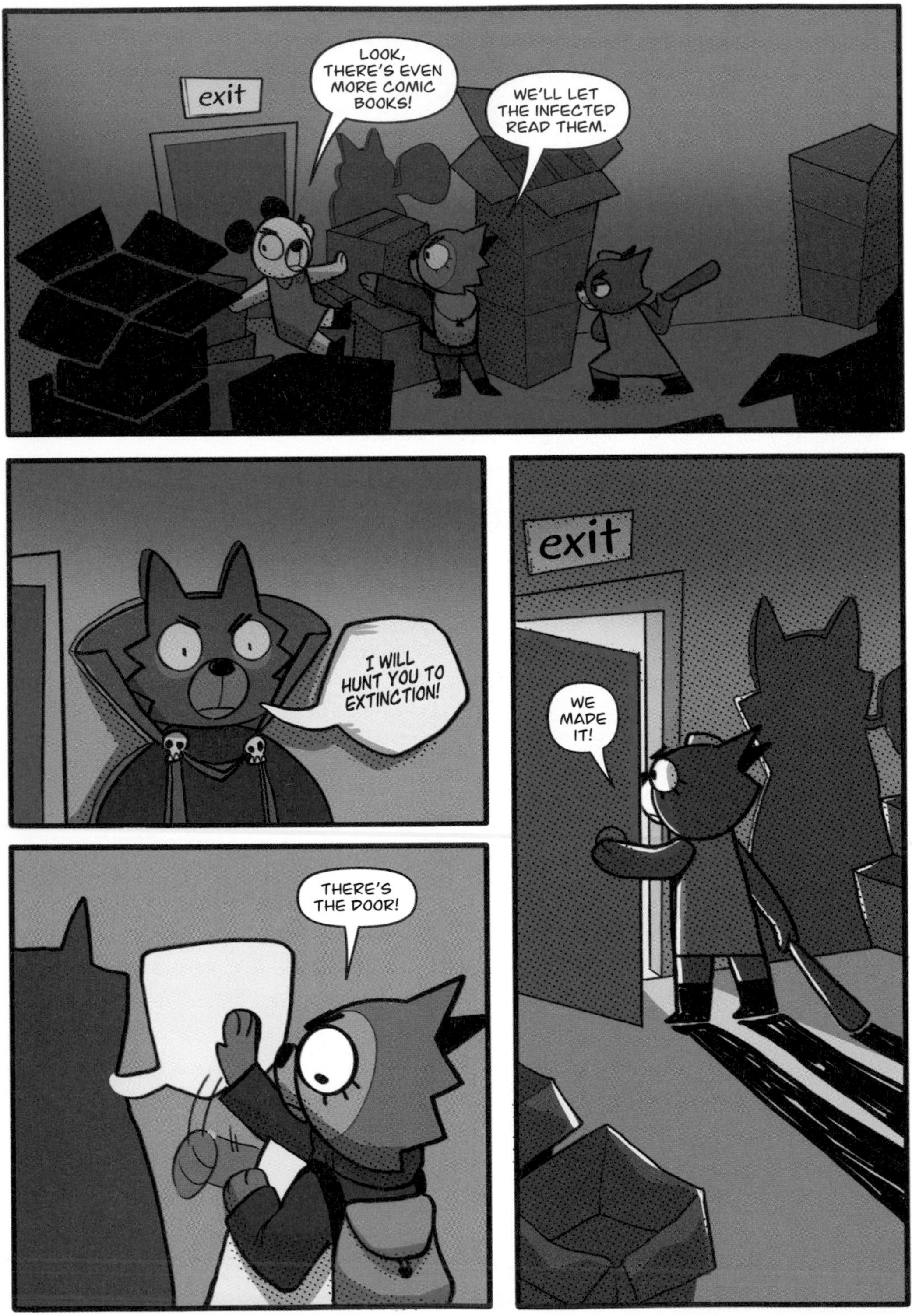
exit
LOOK, THERE'S EVEN MORE COMIC BOOKS!
WE'LL LET THE INFECTED READ THEM.
I WILL HUNT YOU TO EXTINCTION!
THERE'S THE DOOR!
exit
WE MADE IT!

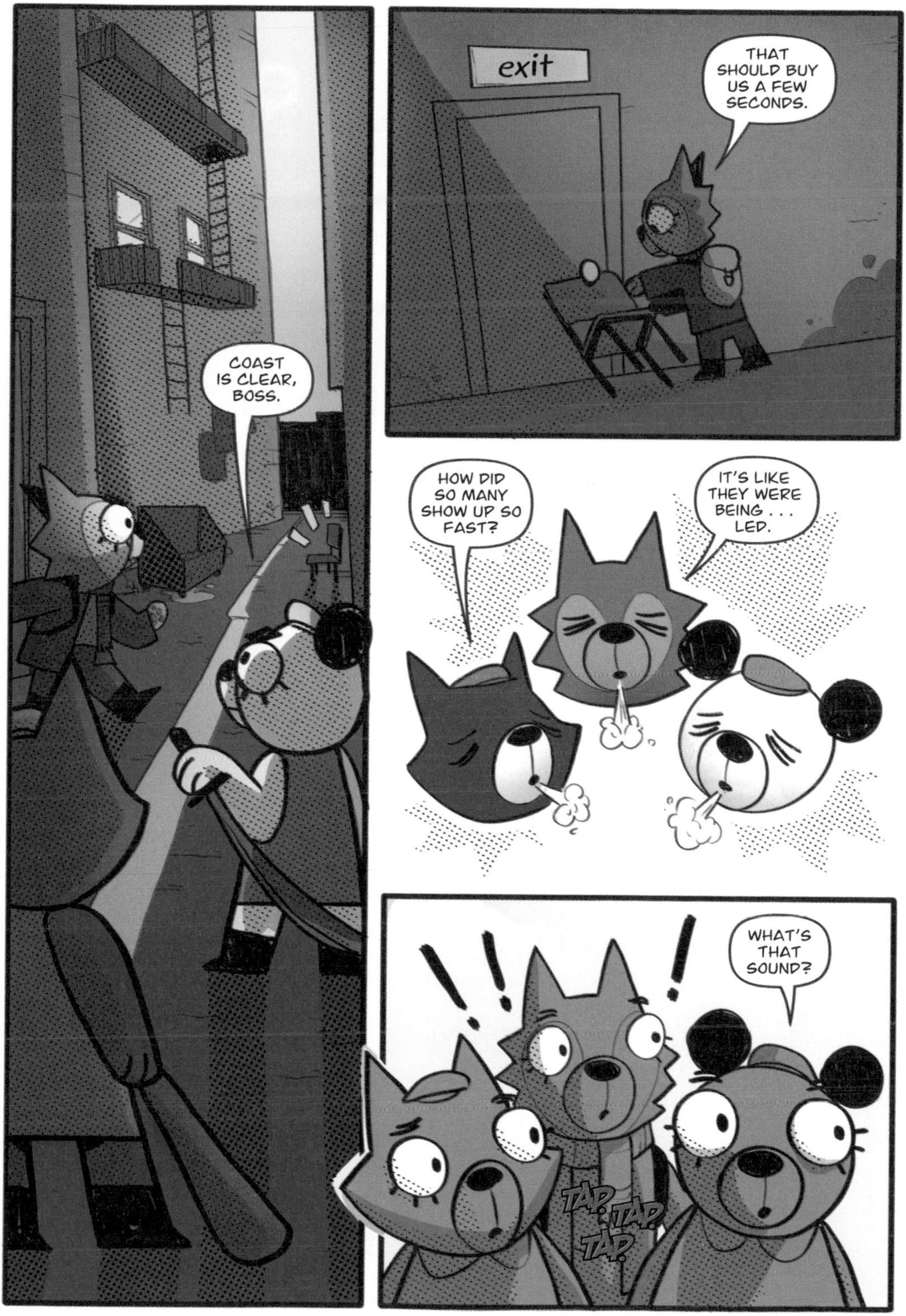
COAST IS CLEAR, BOSS.
exit
THAT SHOULD BUY US A FEW SECONDS.
HOW DID SO MANY SHOW UP SO FAST?
IT'S LIKE THEY WERE BEING . . . LED.
WHAT'S THAT SOUND?
TAP. TAP. TAP.

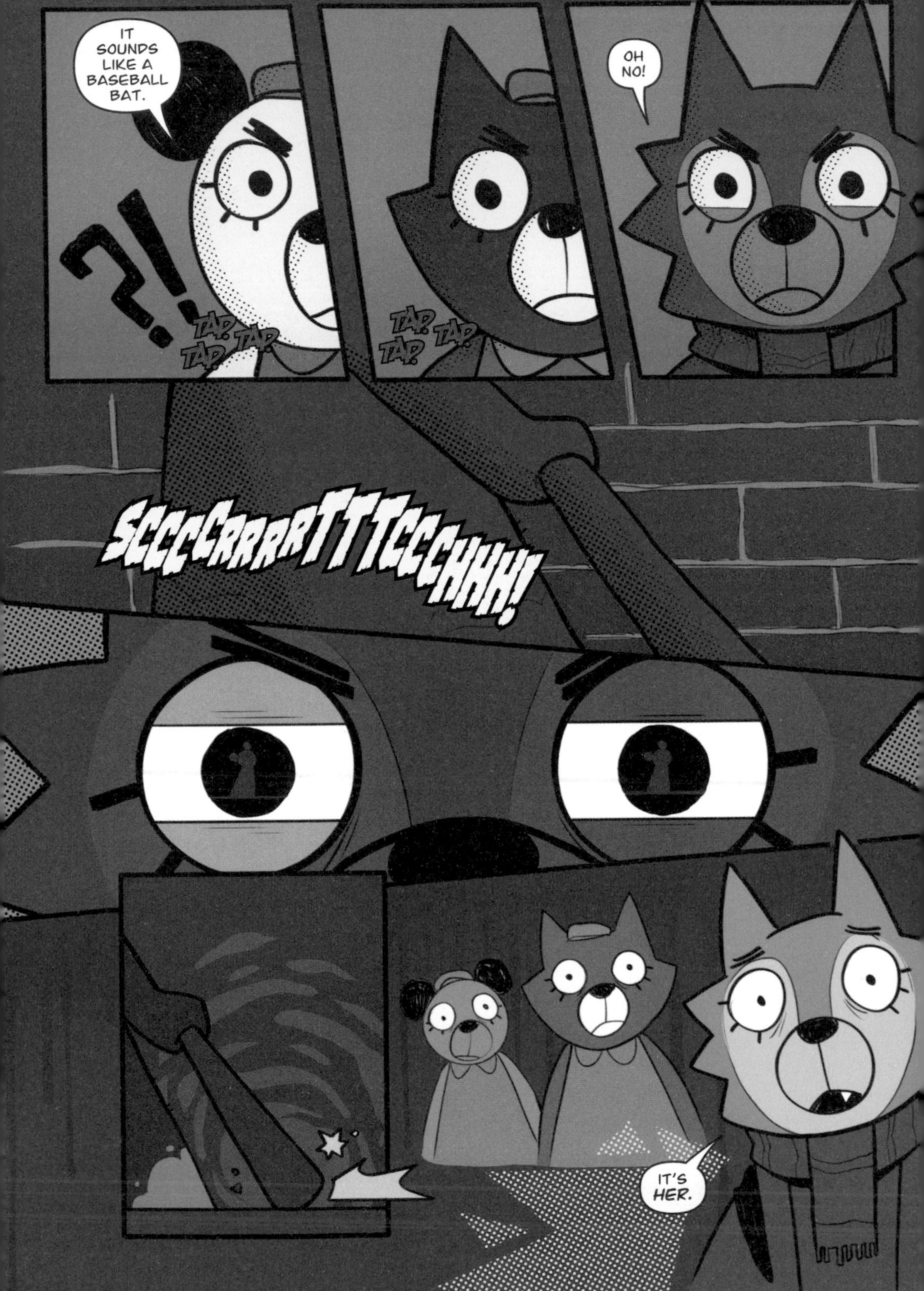
IT SOUNDS LIKE A BASEBALL BAT.
?!
TAP TAP TAP
TAP TAP TAP
OH NO!
SCCCCRRRRRTTTTCCCHHH!
IT'S HER.

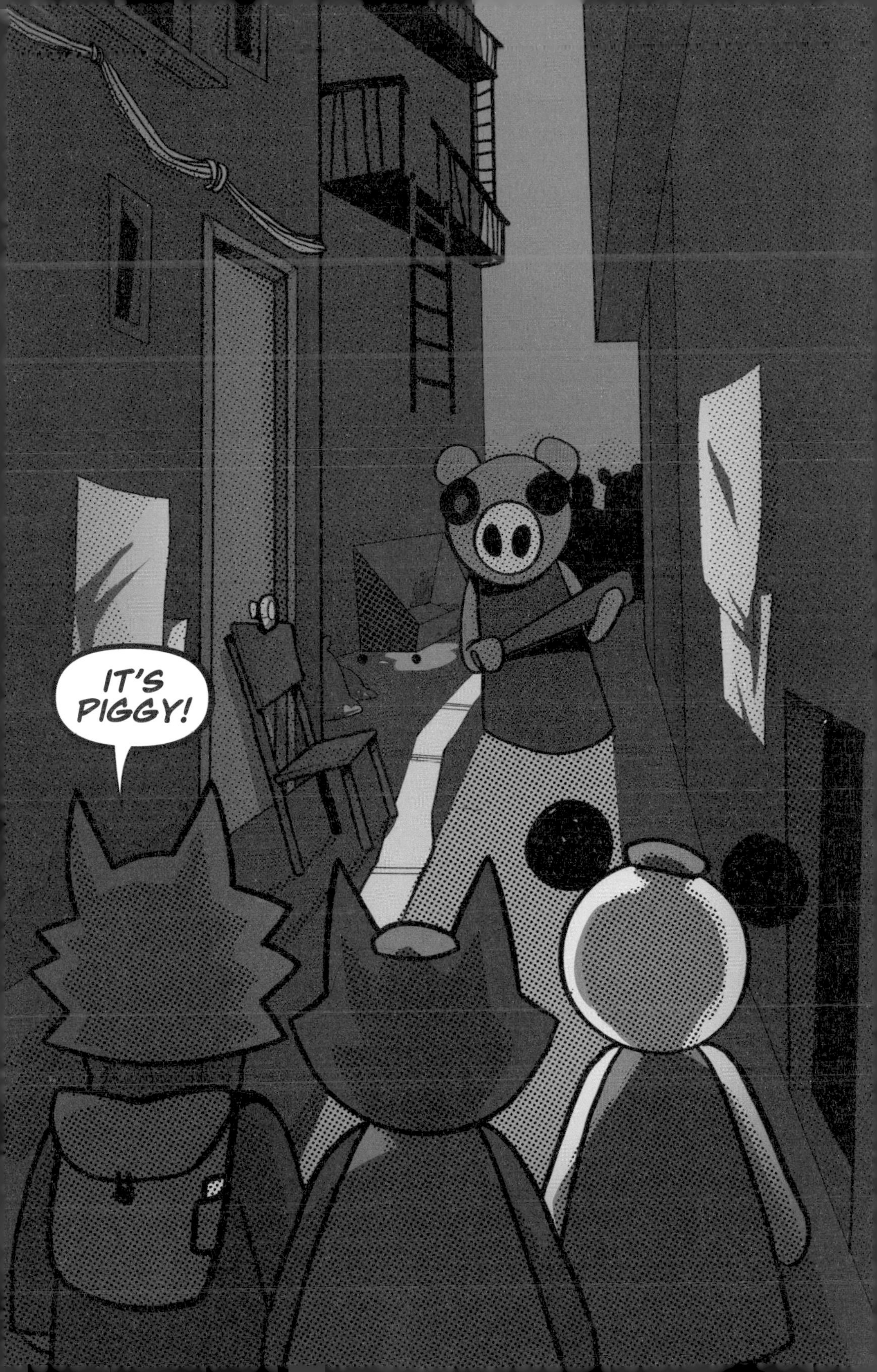
IT'S PIGGY!

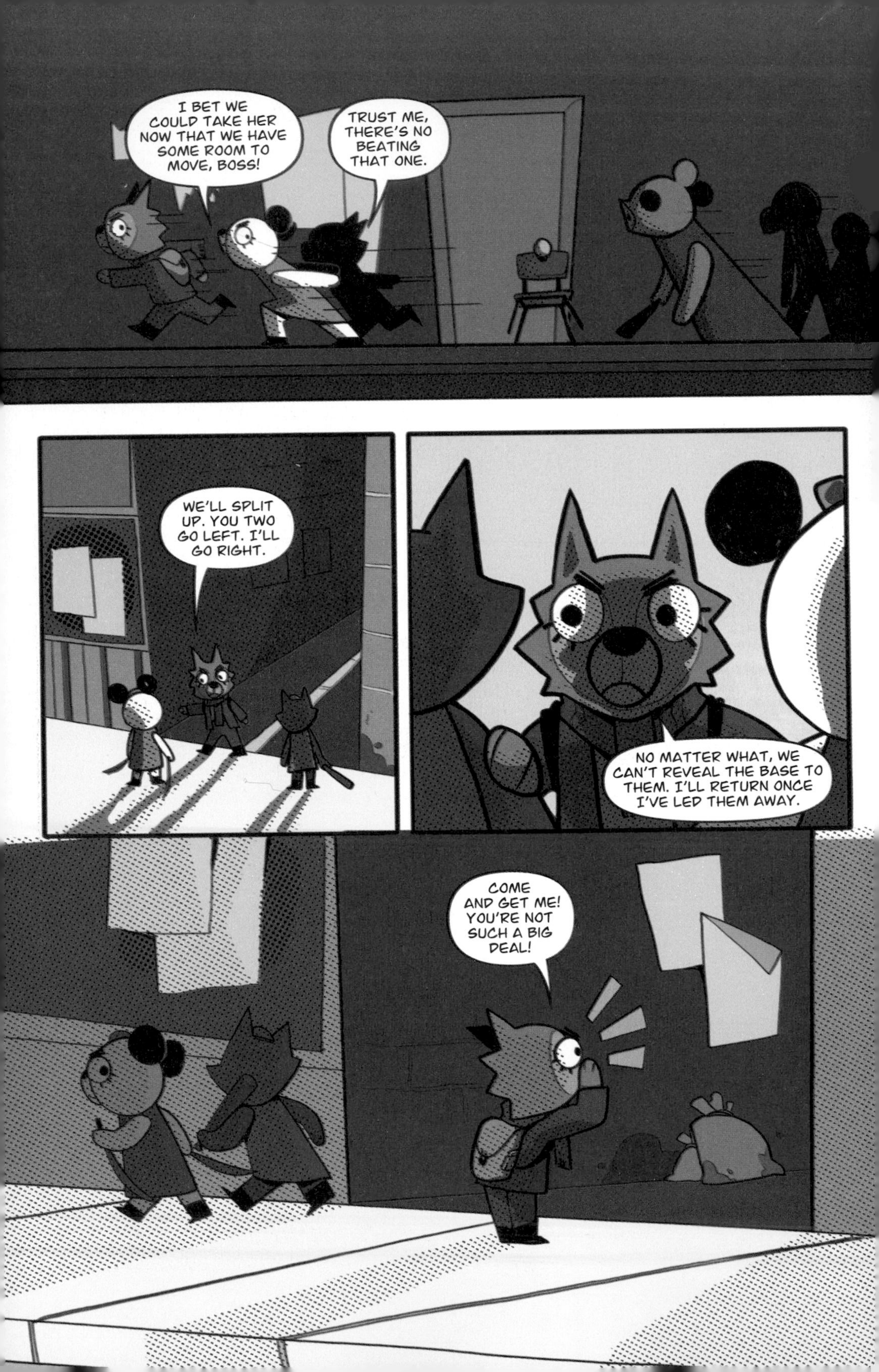
I BET WE COULD TAKE HER NOW THAT WE HAVE SOME ROOM TO MOVE, BOSS!
TRUST ME, THERE'S NO BEATING THAT ONE.
WE'LL SPLIT UP. YOU TWO GO LEFT. I'LL GO RIGHT.
NO MATTER WHAT, WE CAN'T REVEAL THE BASE TO THEM. I'LL RETURN ONCE I'VE LED THEM AWAY.
COME AND GET ME! YOU'RE NOT SUCH A BIG DEAL!

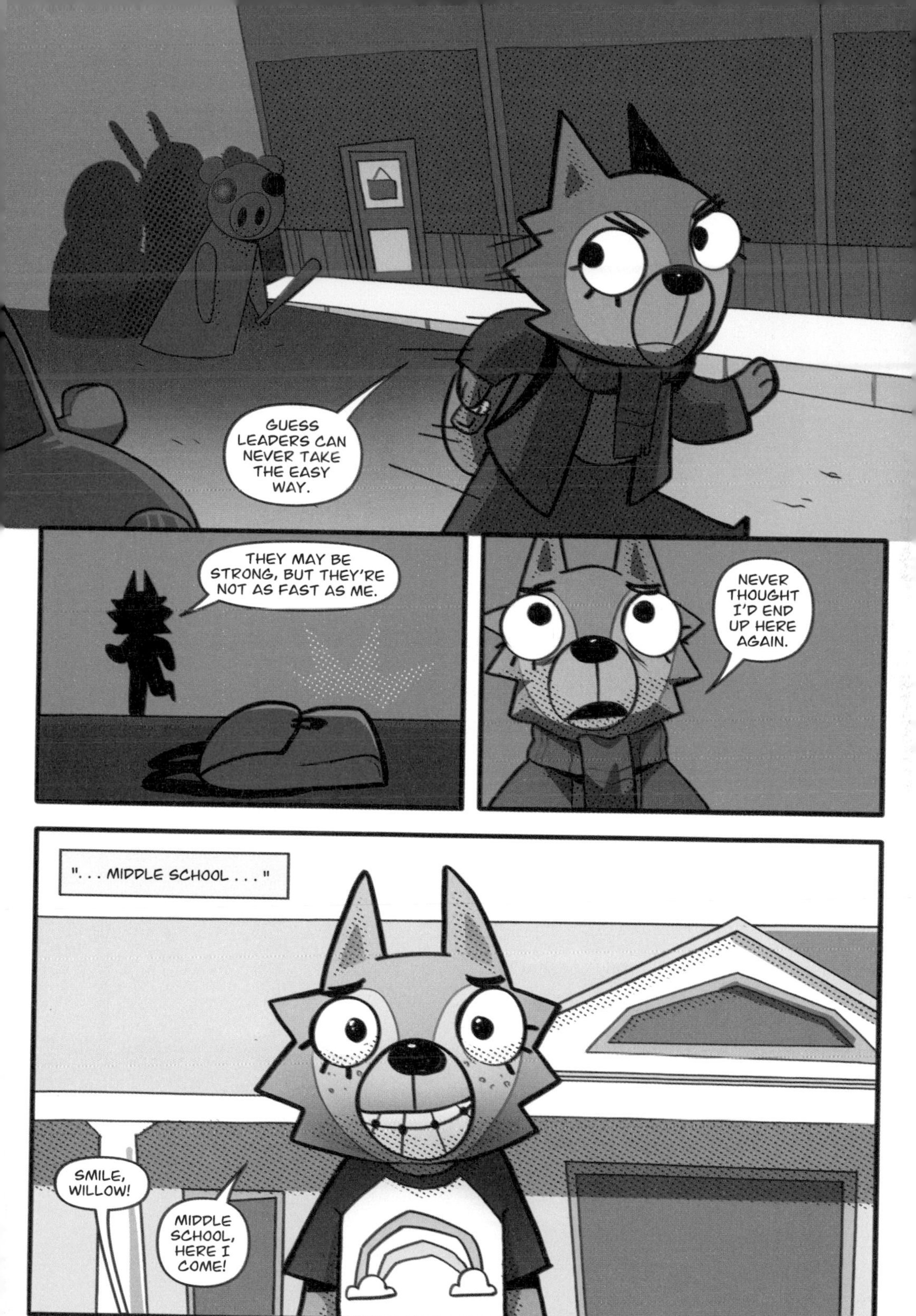
GUESS LEADERS CAN NEVER TAKE THE EASY WAY.
THEY MAY BE STRONG, BUT THEY'RE NOT AS FAST AS ME.
NEVER THOUGHT I'D END UP HERE AGAIN.
". . . MIDDLE SCHOOL . . ."
SMILE, WILLOW!
MIDDLE SCHOOL, HERE I COME!

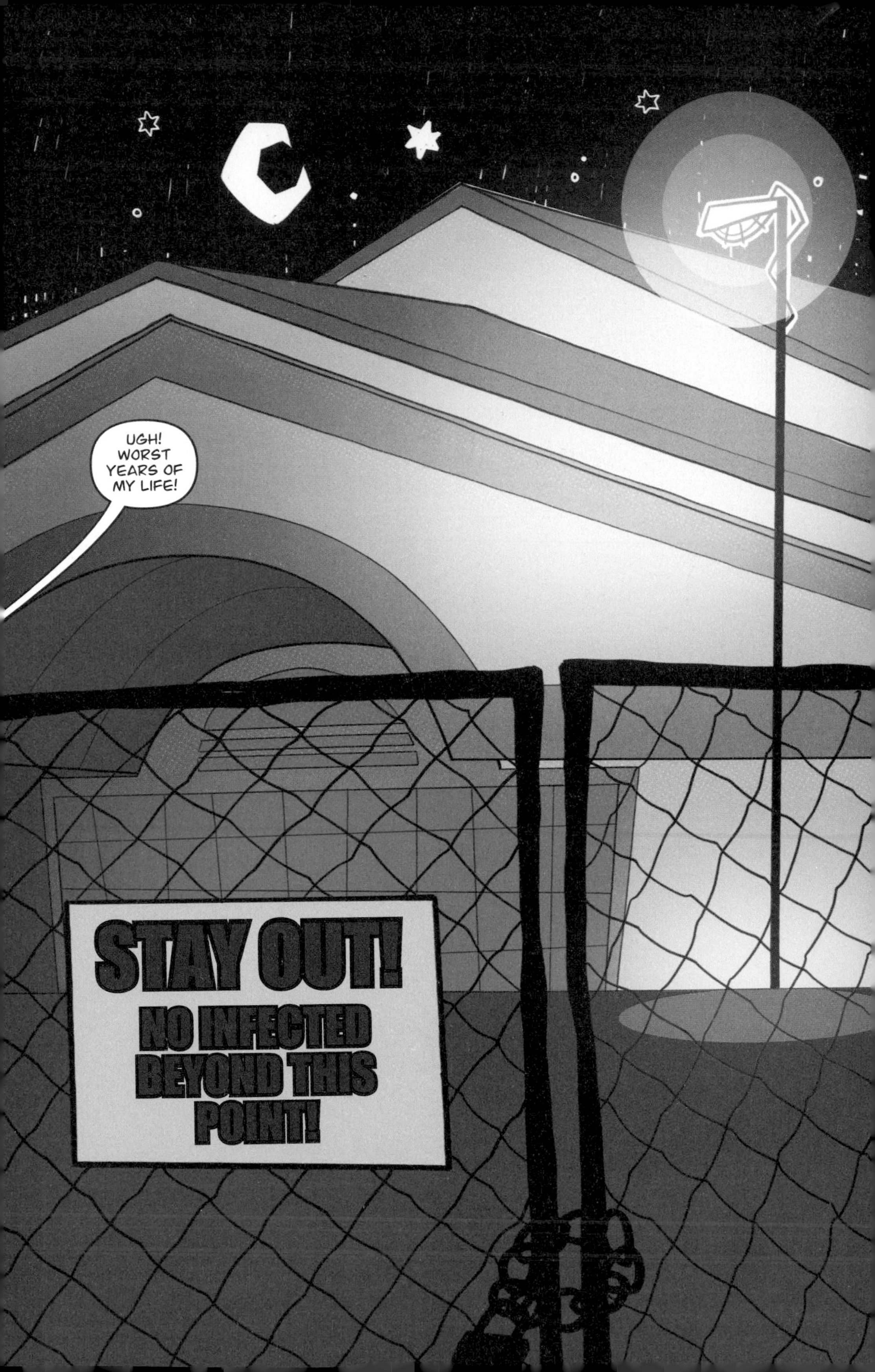
UGH! WORST YEARS OF MY LIFE!
STAY OUT!
NO INFECTED BEYOND THIS POINT!

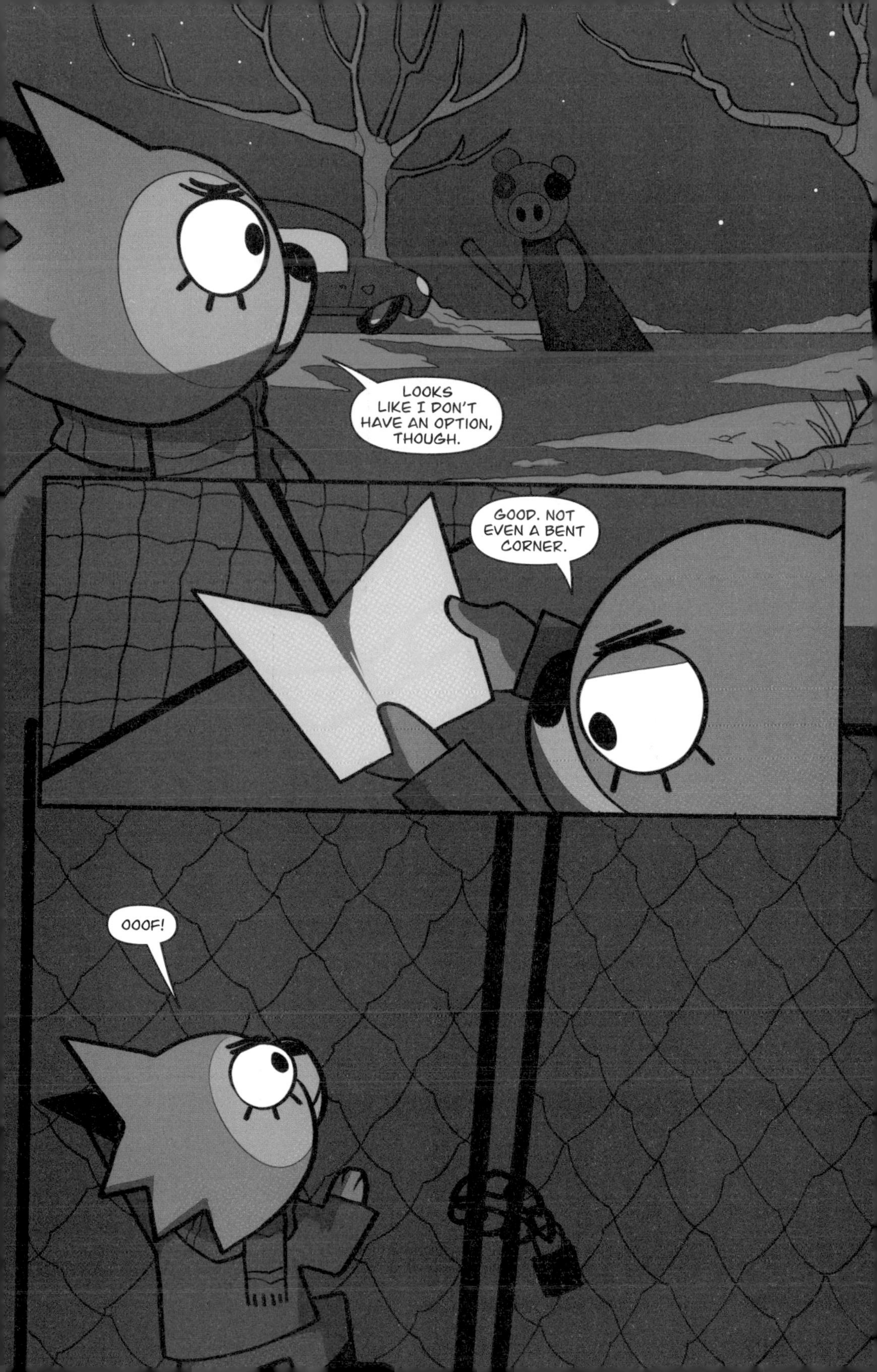
LOOKS LIKE I DON'T HAVE AN OPTION, THOUGH.
GOOD. NOT EVEN A BENT CORNER.
OOOF!

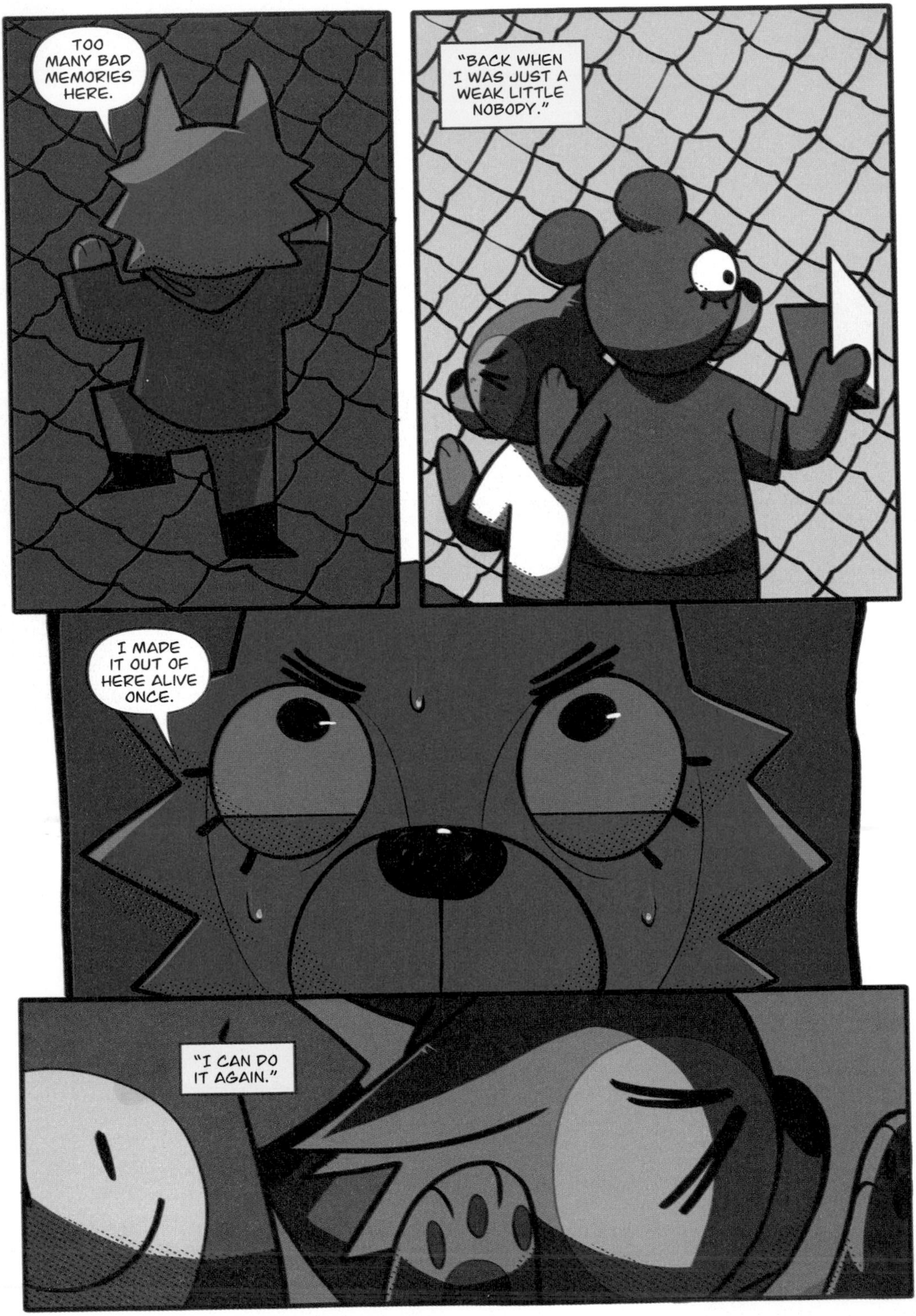
TOO MANY BAD MEMORIES HERE.
"BACK WHEN I WAS JUST A WEAK LITTLE NOBODY."
I MADE IT OUT OF HERE ALIVE ONCE.
"I CAN DO IT AGAIN."

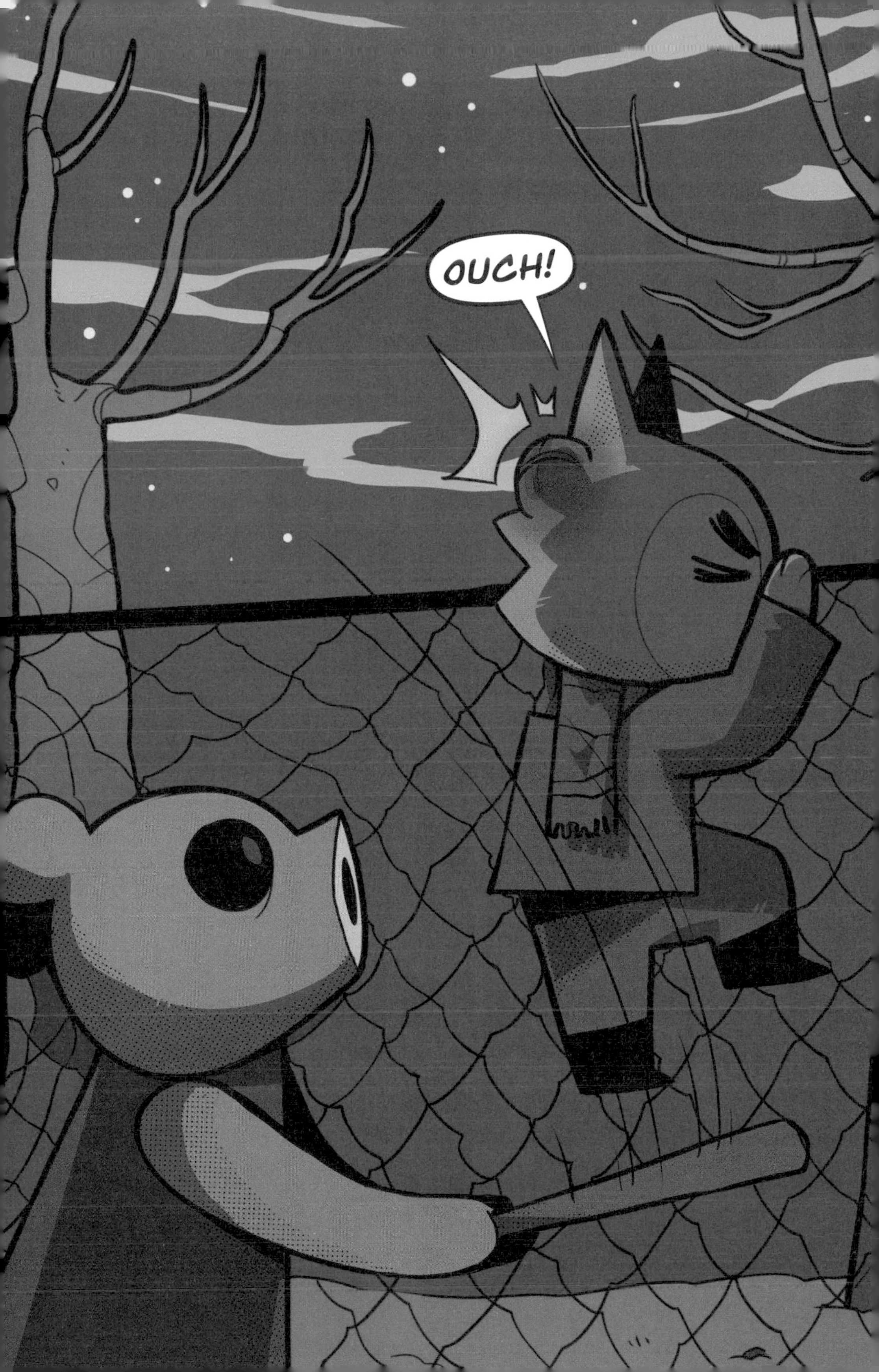
OUCH!

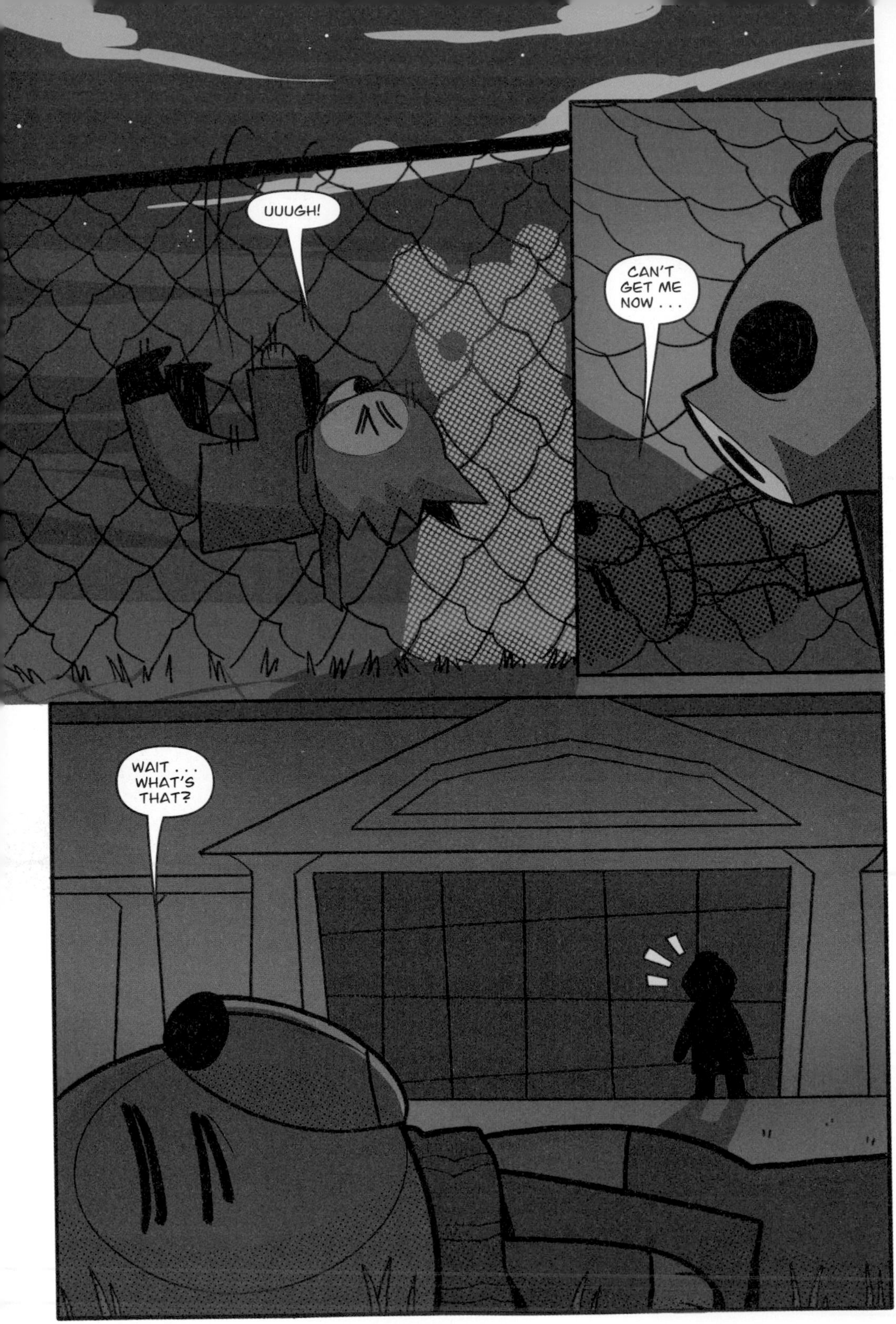
UUUGH!
CAN'T GET ME NOW . . .
WAIT . . . WHAT'S THAT?

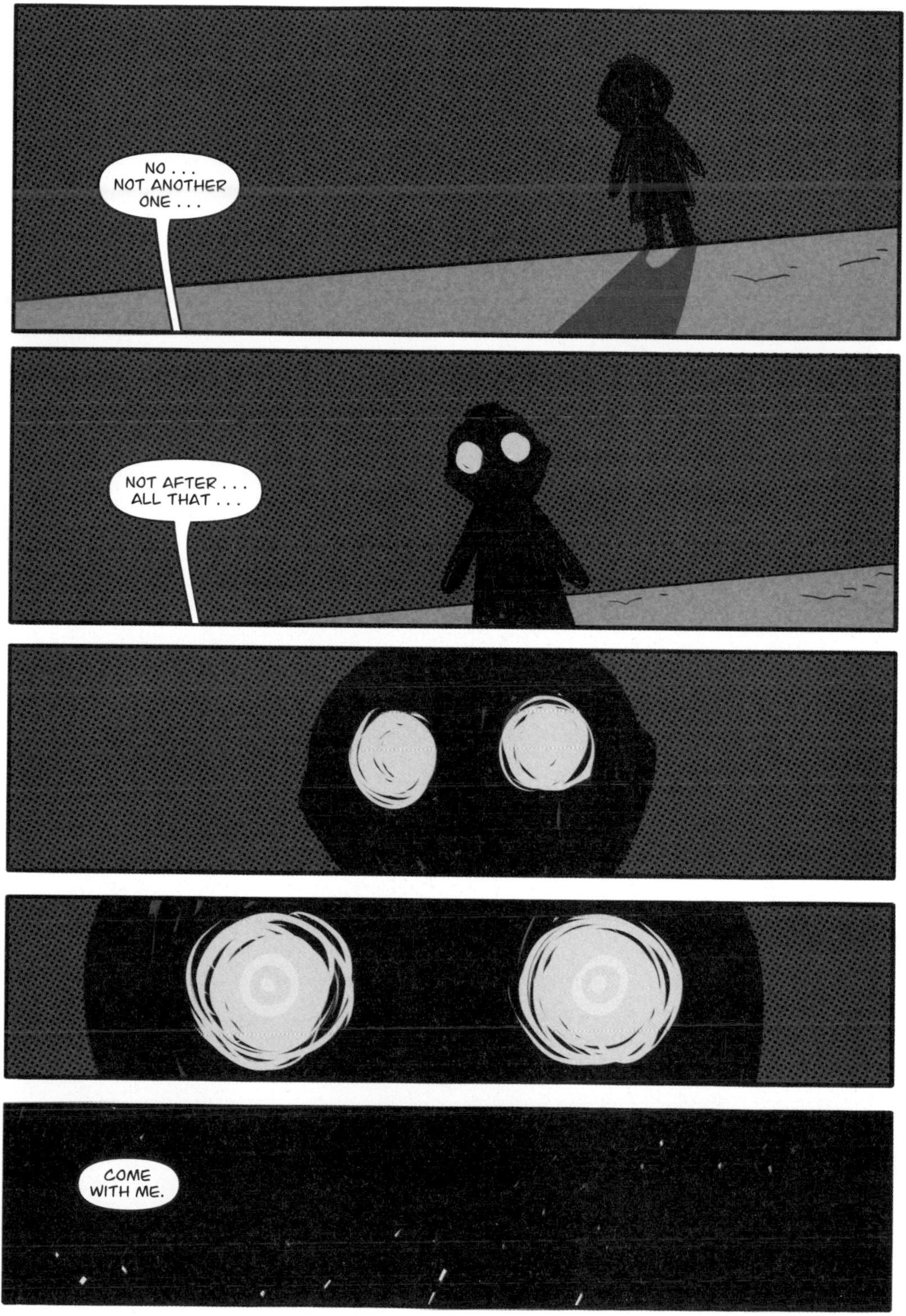
NO . . . NOT ANOTHER ONE . . .
NOT AFTER . . . ALL THAT . . .
COME WITH ME.

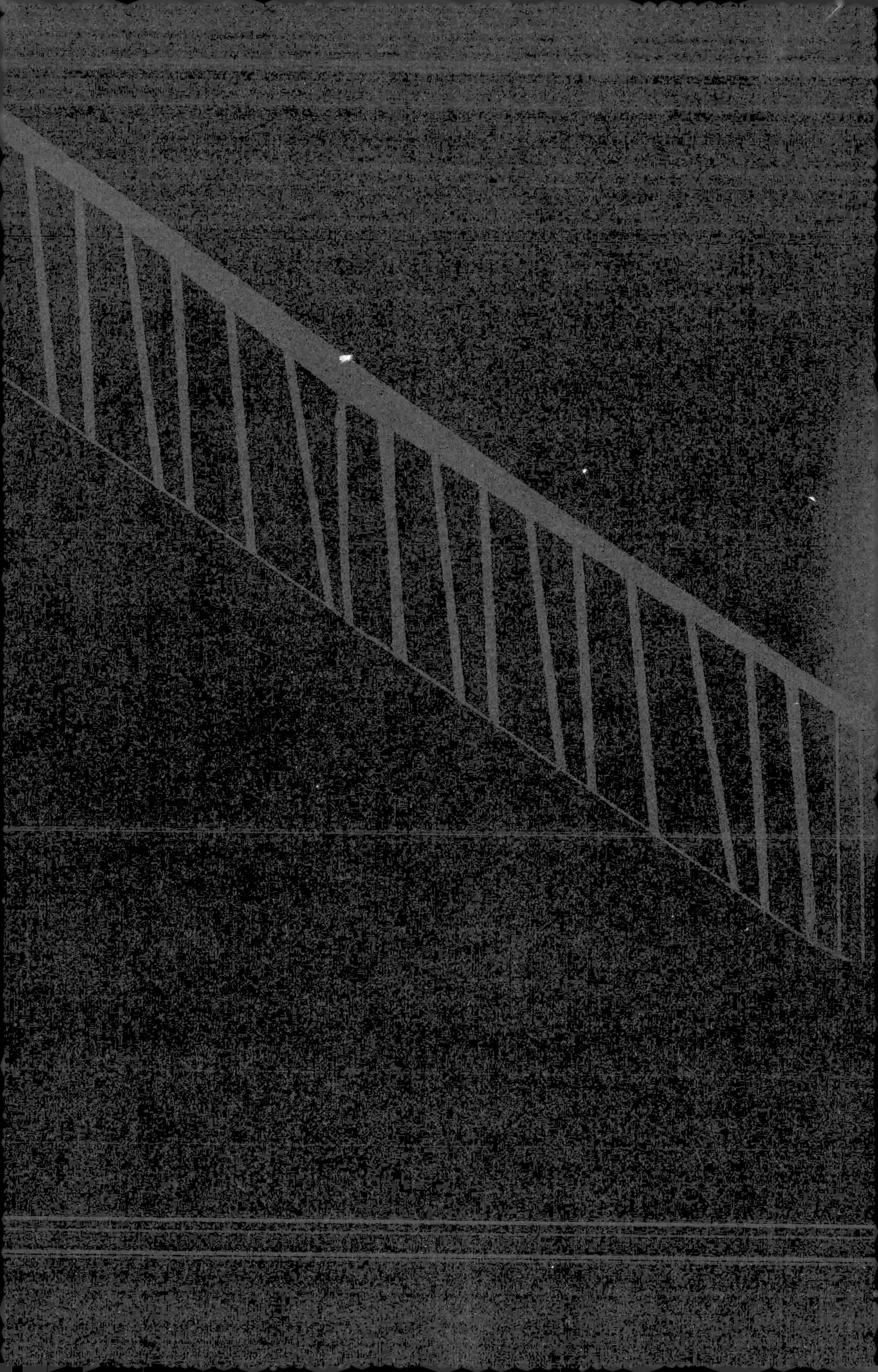

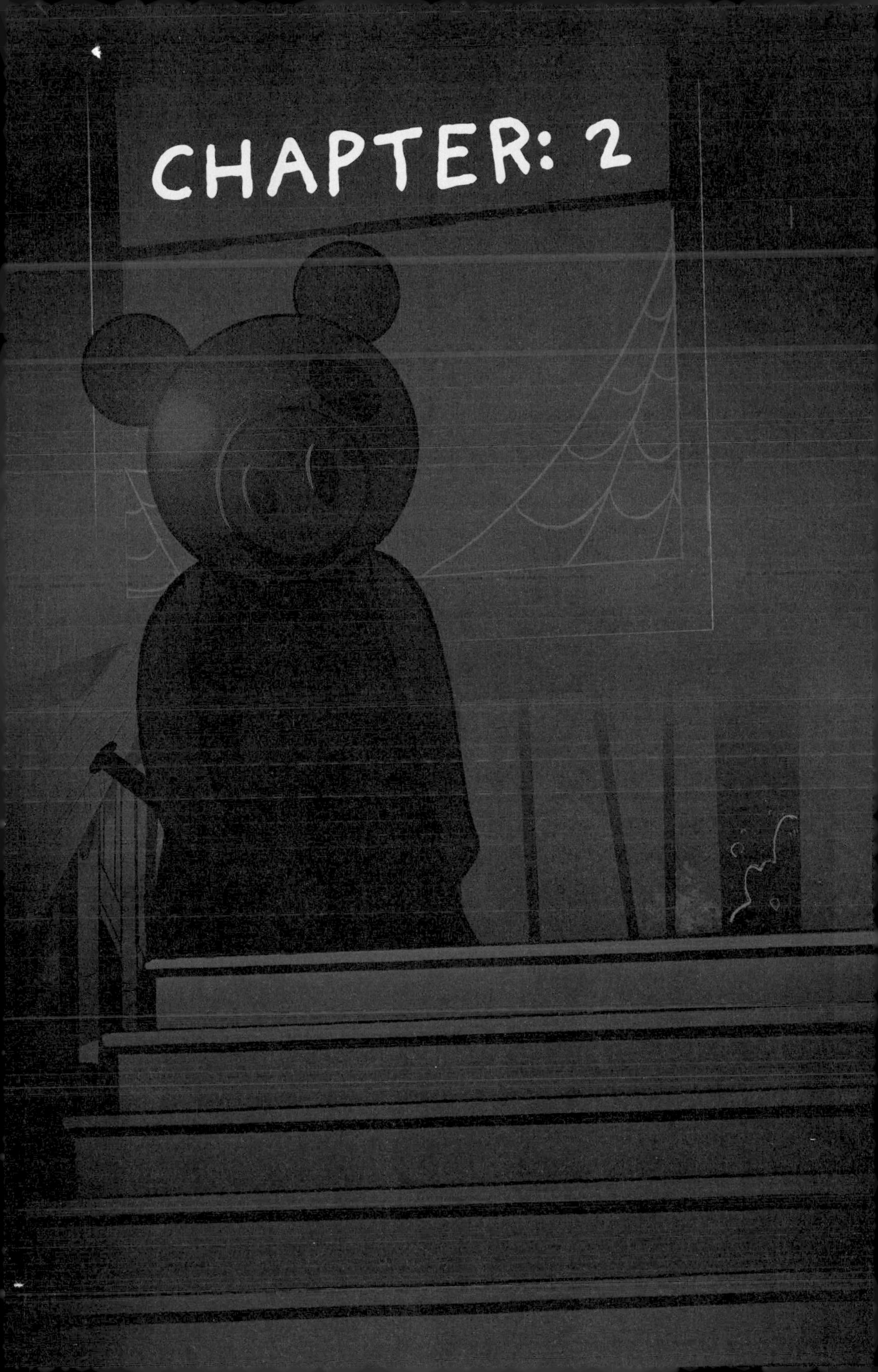
CHAPTER: 2

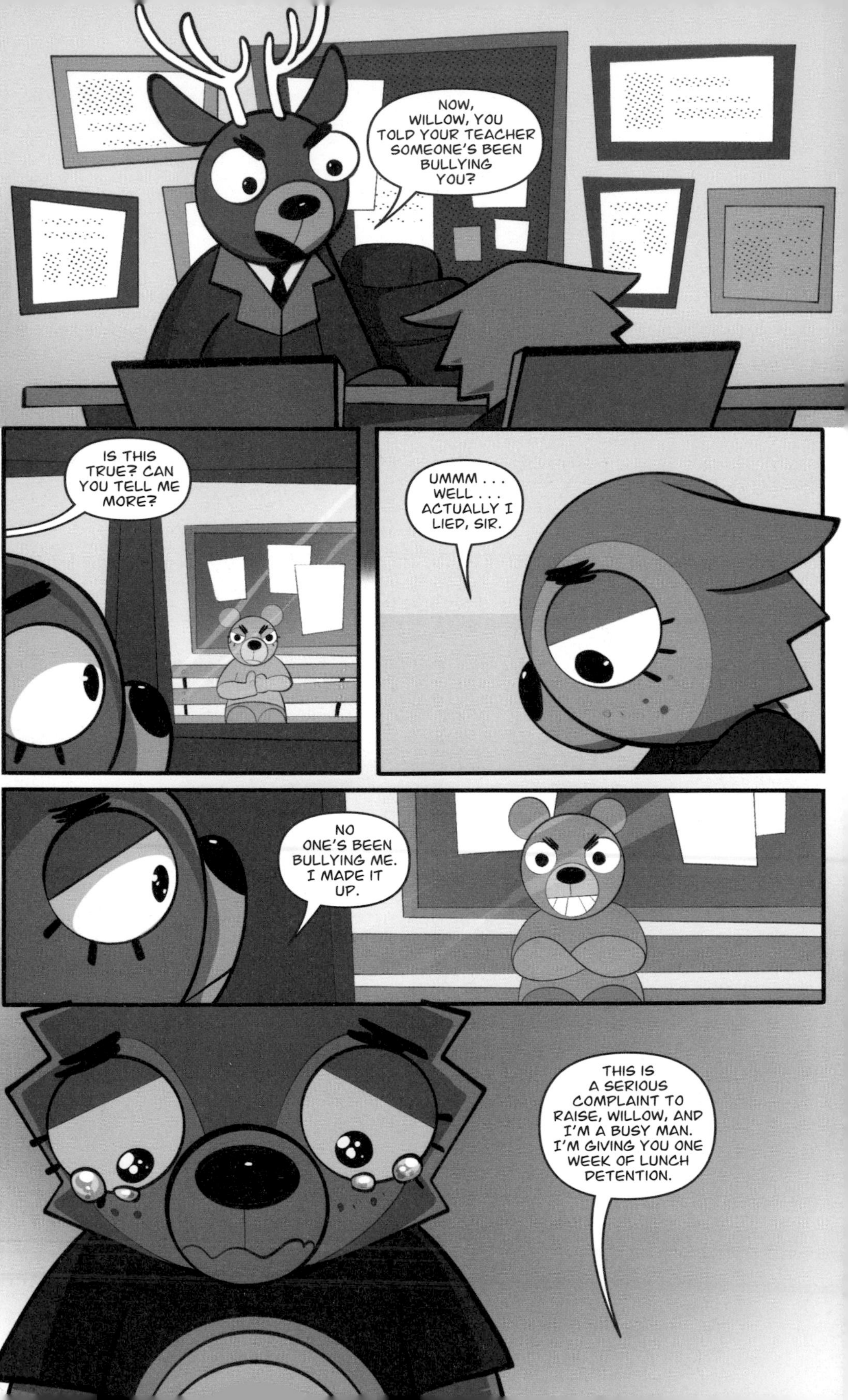
NOW, WILLOW, YOU TOLD YOUR TEACHER SOMEONE'S BEEN BULLYING YOU?
IS THIS TRUE? CAN YOU TELL ME MORE?
UMMM . . . WELL . . . ACTUALLY I LIED, SIR.
NO ONE'S BEEN BULLYING ME. I MADE IT UP.
THIS IS A SERIOUS COMPLAINT TO RAISE, WILLOW, AND I'M A BUSY MAN. I'M GIVING YOU ONE WEEK OF LUNCH DETENTION.

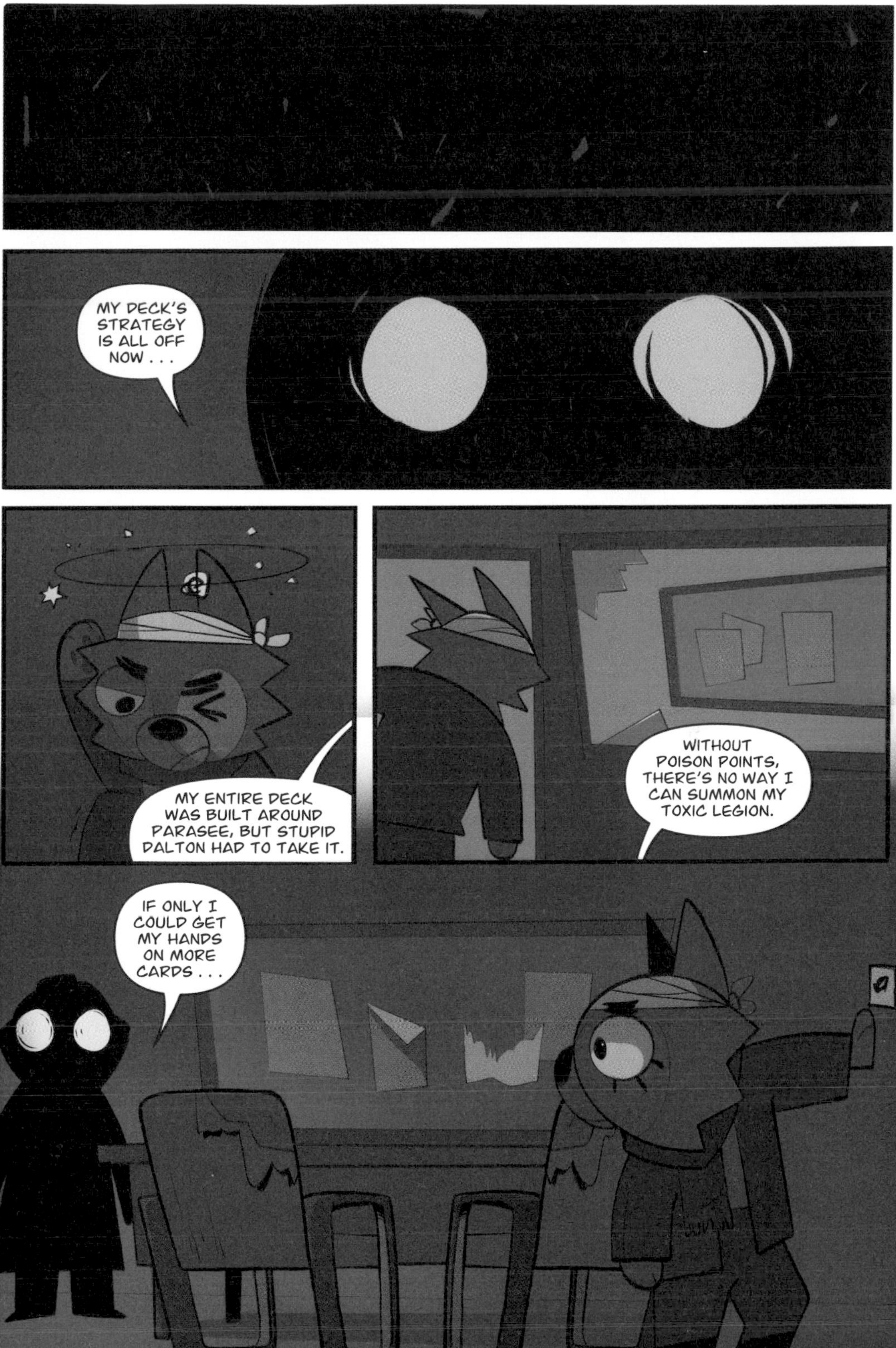
MY DECK'S STRATEGY IS ALL OFF NOW . . .
MY ENTIRE DECK WAS BUILT AROUND PARASEE, BUT STUPID DALTON HAD TO TAKE IT.
WITHOUT POISON POINTS, THERE'S NO WAY I CAN SUMMON MY TOXIC LEGION.
IF ONLY I COULD GET MY HANDS ON MORE CARDS . . .

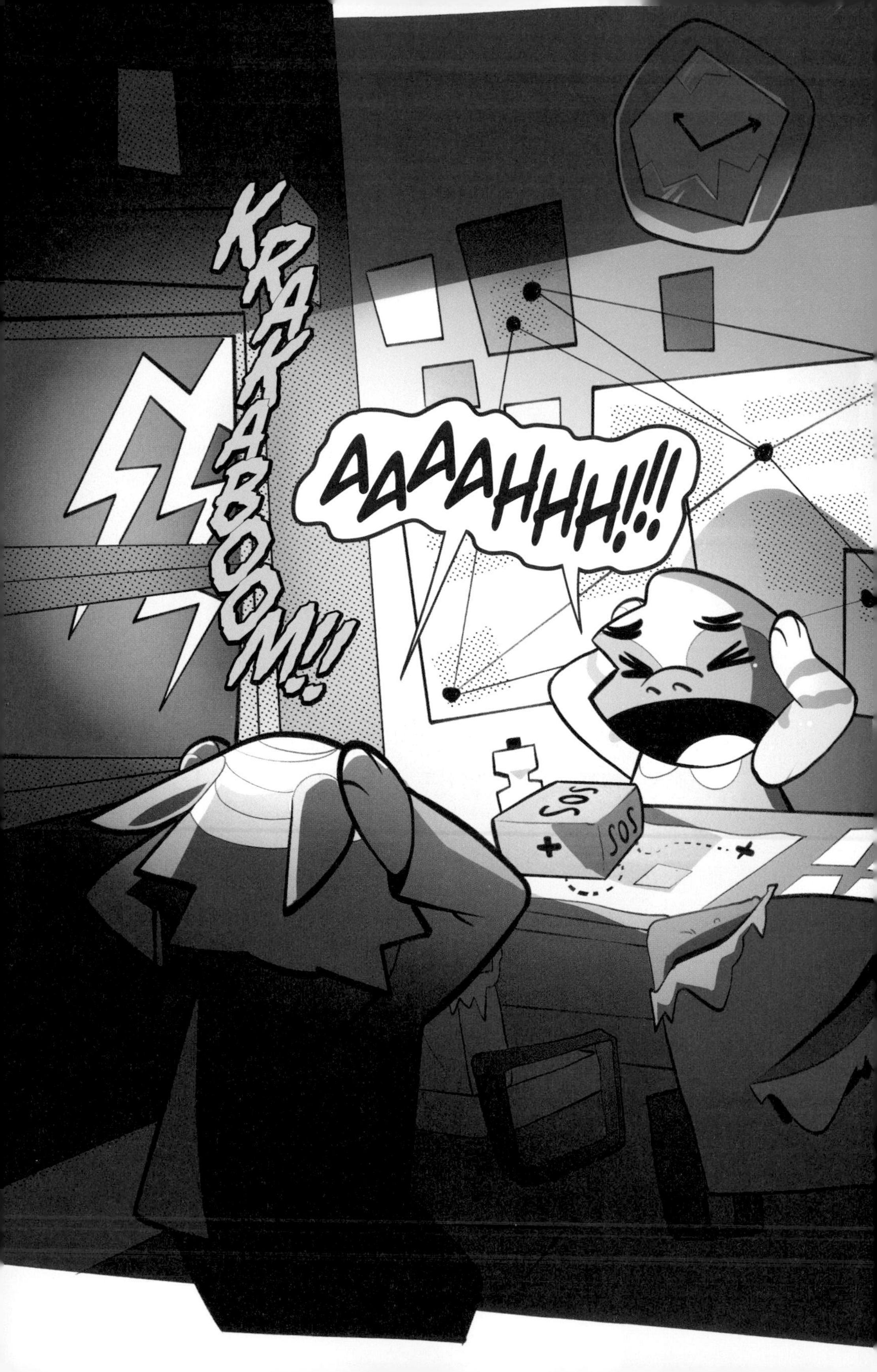
KRAKABOOM!!
AAAAHHH!!!
SOS
SOS

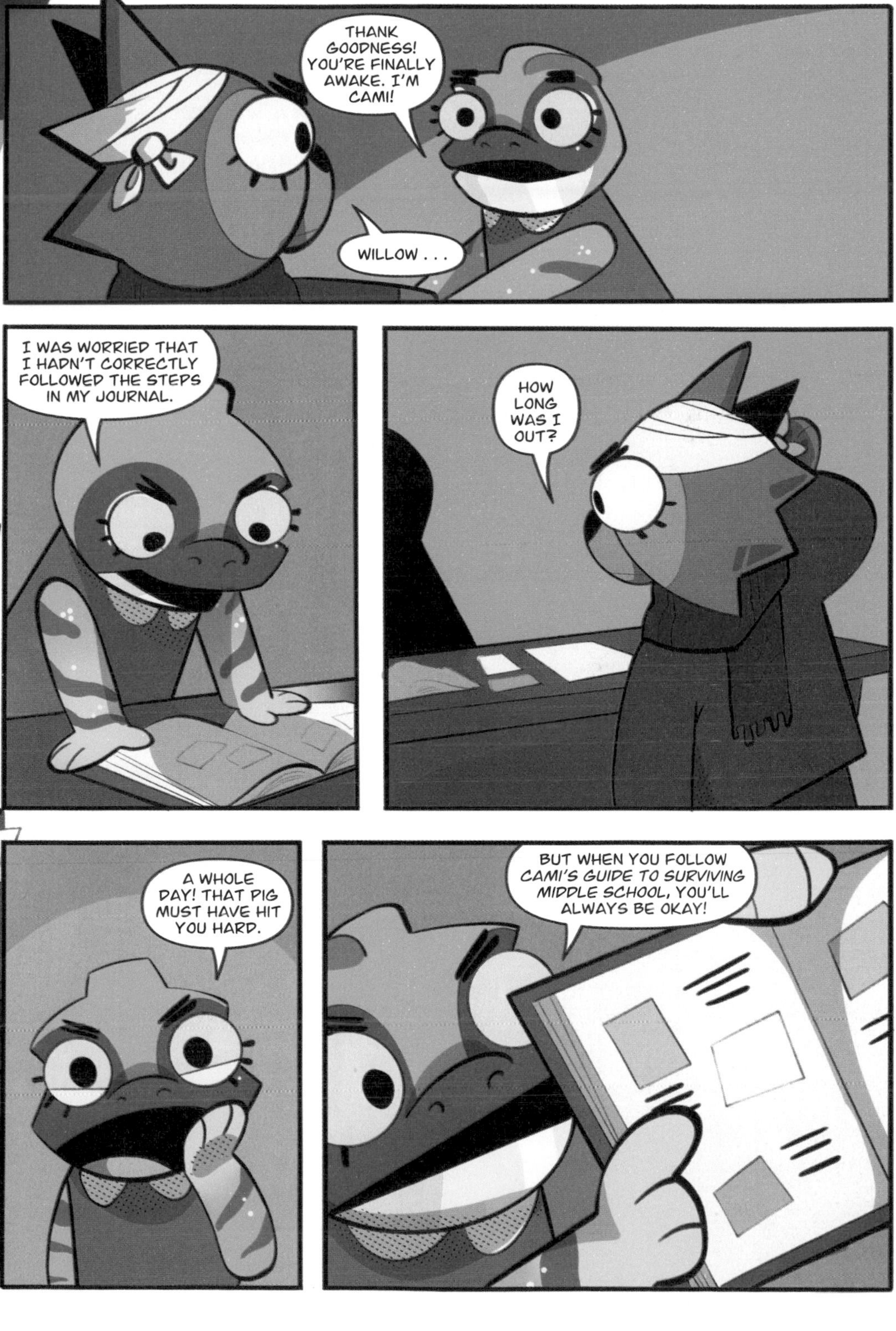
THANK GOODNESS! YOU'RE FINALLY AWAKE. I'M CAMI!
WILLOW . . .
I WAS WORRIED THAT I HADN'T CORRECTLY FOLLOWED THE STEPS IN MY JOURNAL.
HOW LONG WAS I OUT?
A WHOLE DAY! THAT PIG MUST HAVE HIT YOU HARD.
BUT WHEN YOU FOLLOW CAMI'S GUIDE TO SURVIVING MIDDLE SCHOOL, YOU'LL ALWAYS BE OKAY!

Survival Tip for Middle School #1 - Emergency First Aid

In the event of an emergency, call for help (see more in later entries). In the meantime, you can save someone's life by making sure they receive first aid. Every emergency is different, though, which is why it's important to learn how to handle different situations.

Step 1 - Remove the individual from immediate dangers such as fire, gas leaks, or scary infected pigs with bats.

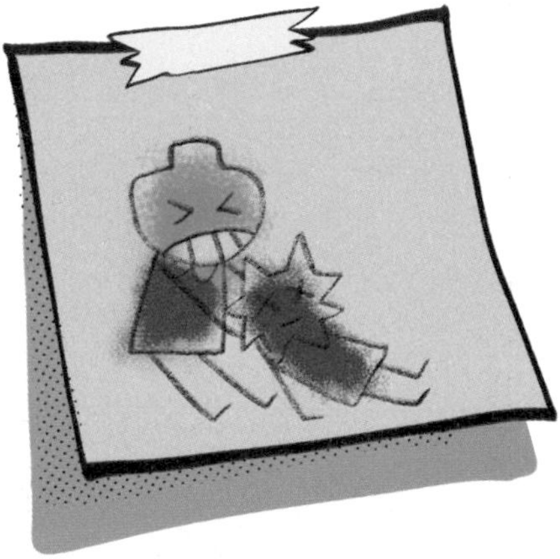

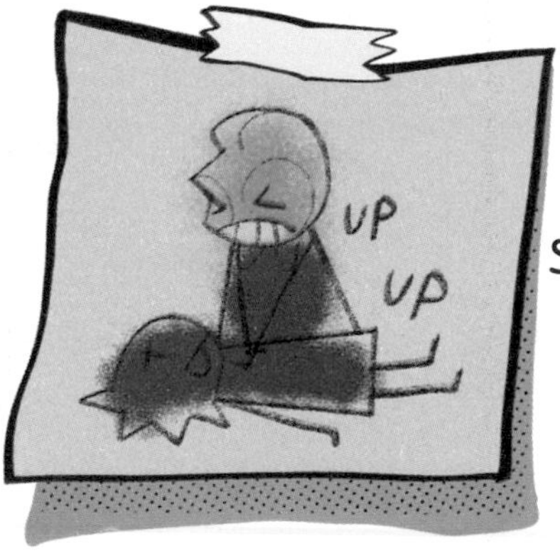
UP
UP

Step 2 - Make sure the injured person is kept still. If you can, elevate their legs a few inches off the ground in case they are in shock.

Step 3 - If the person is wounded, apply bandages or use available sterile materials. Apply steady pressure to stop bleeding.

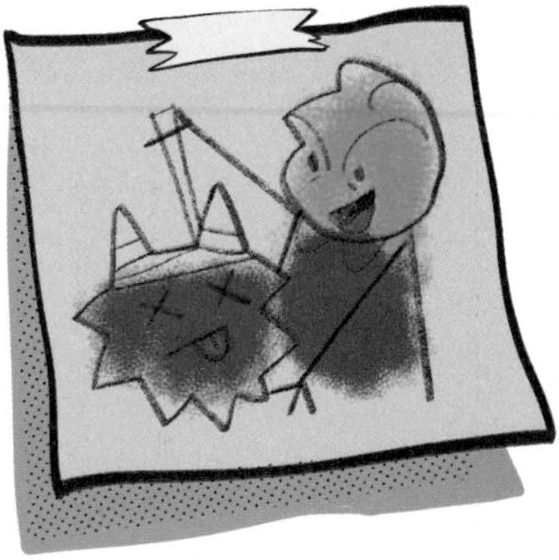

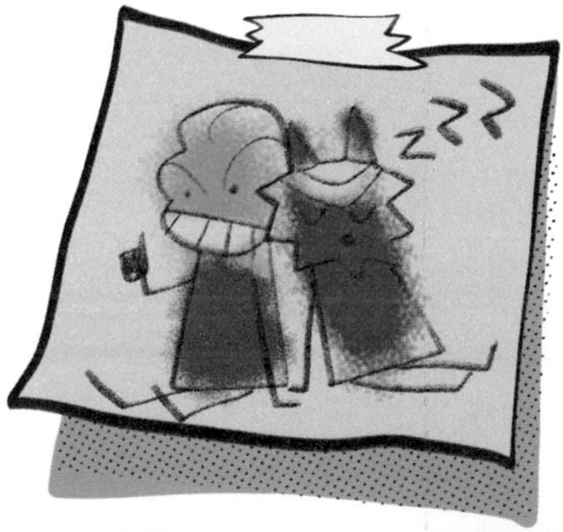
ZZZ

Step 4 - Keep your eye on the injured person for changes in condition until help arrives.

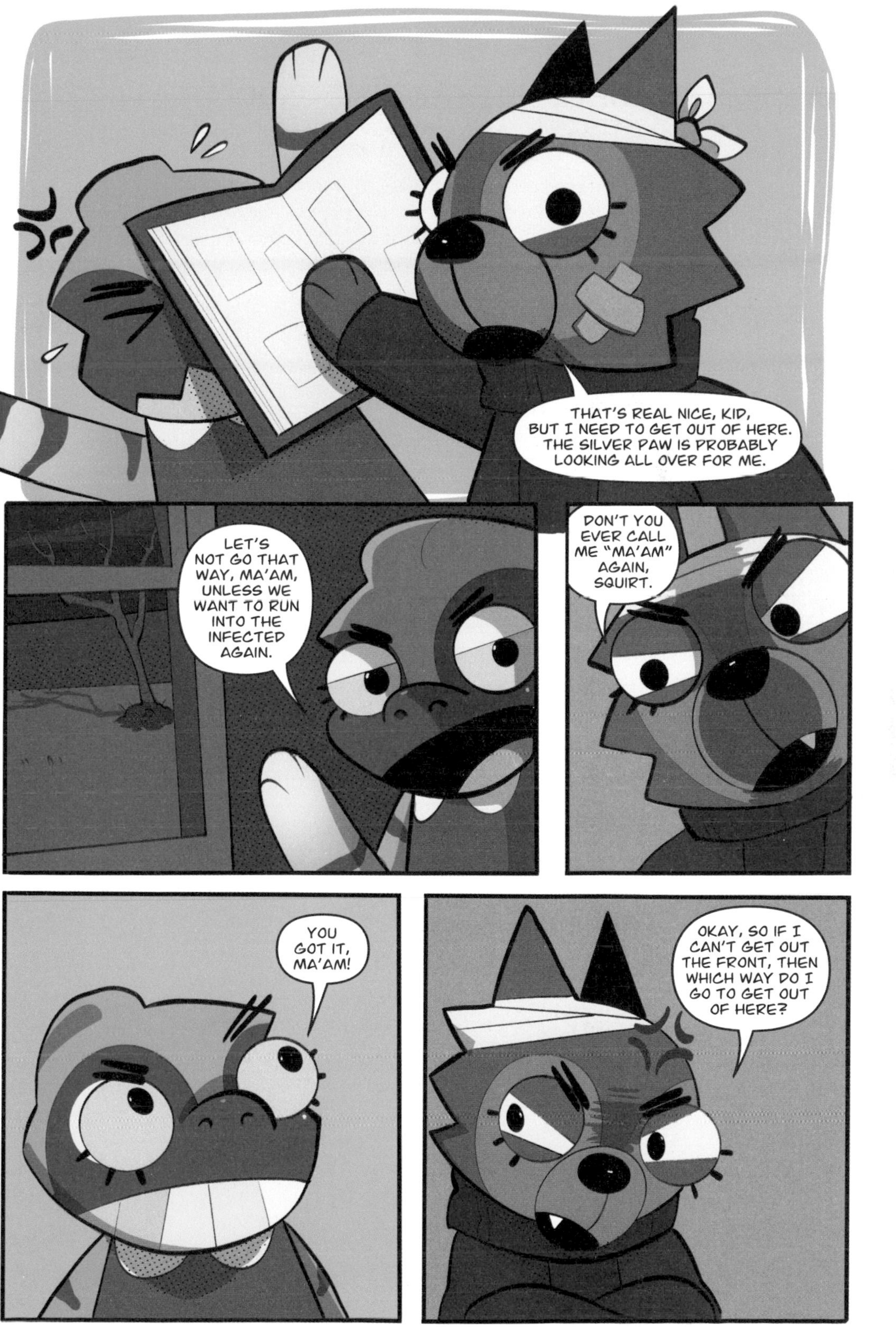
THAT'S REAL NICE, KID, BUT I NEED TO GET OUT OF HERE. THE SILVER PAW IS PROBABLY LOOKING ALL OVER FOR ME.
LET'S NOT GO THAT WAY, MA'AM, UNLESS WE WANT TO RUN INTO THE INFECTED AGAIN.
DON'T YOU EVER CALL ME "MA'AM" AGAIN, SQUIRT.
YOU GOT IT, MA'AM!
OKAY, SO IF I CAN'T GET OUT THE FRONT, THEN WHICH WAY DO I GO TO GET OUT OF HERE?

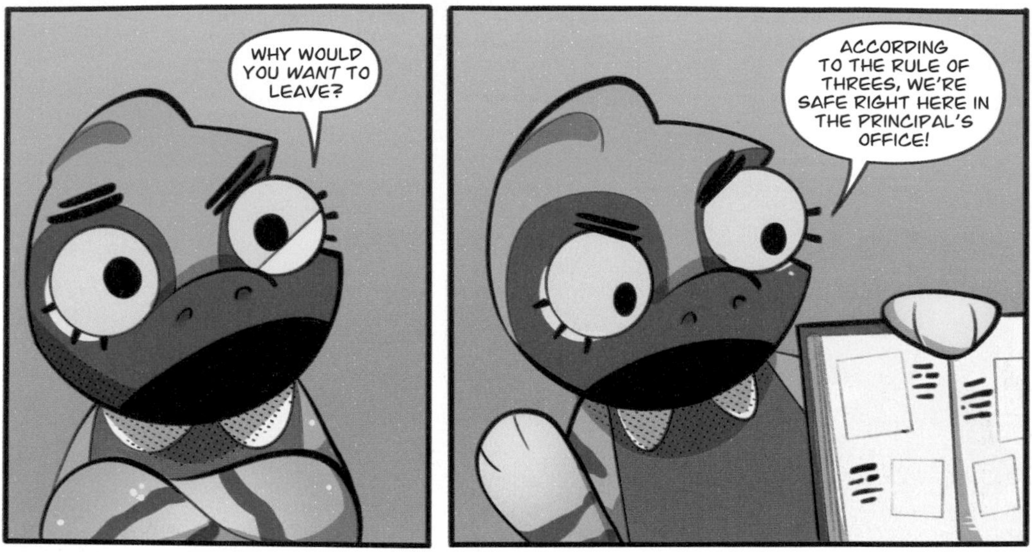
WHY WOULD YOU WANT TO LEAVE?
ACCORDING TO THE RULE OF THREES, WE'RE SAFE RIGHT HERE IN THE PRINCIPAL'S OFFICE!

Survival Tip for Middle School #2 - Rule of Threes

The body is resilient, but in an emergency situation, follow the rule of threes.

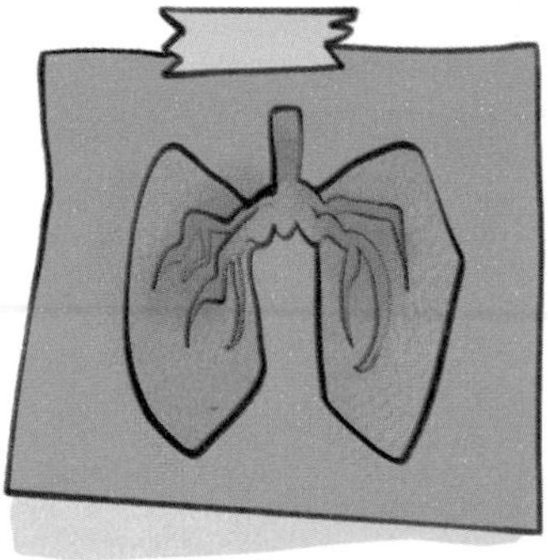

You can survive three minutes without oxygen.

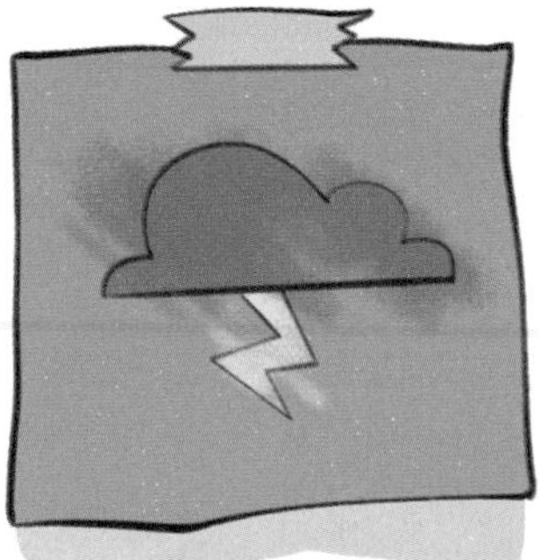

Three hours without shelter in extreme weather.

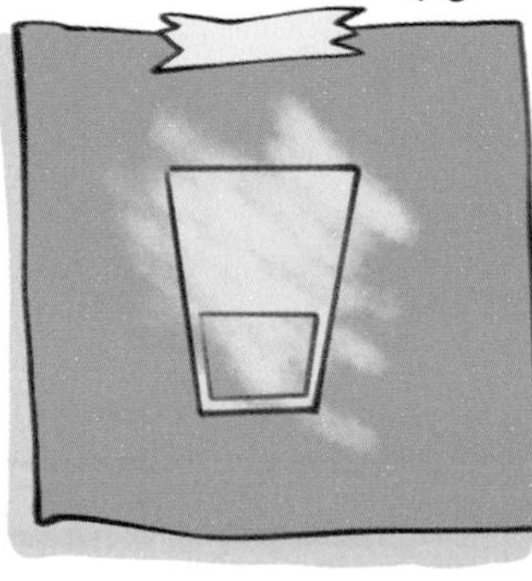

Three days without water.

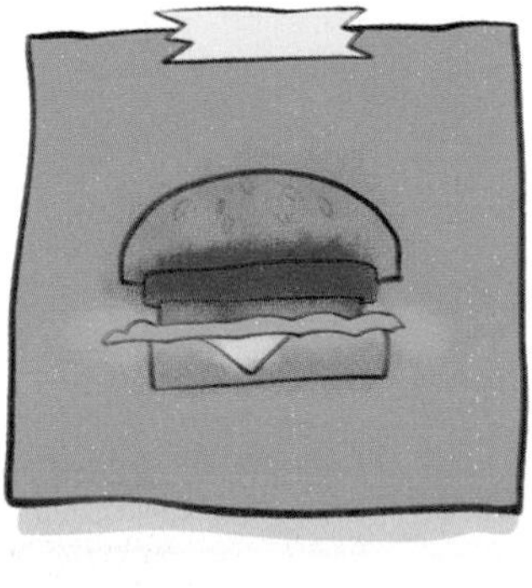

Three weeks without food.

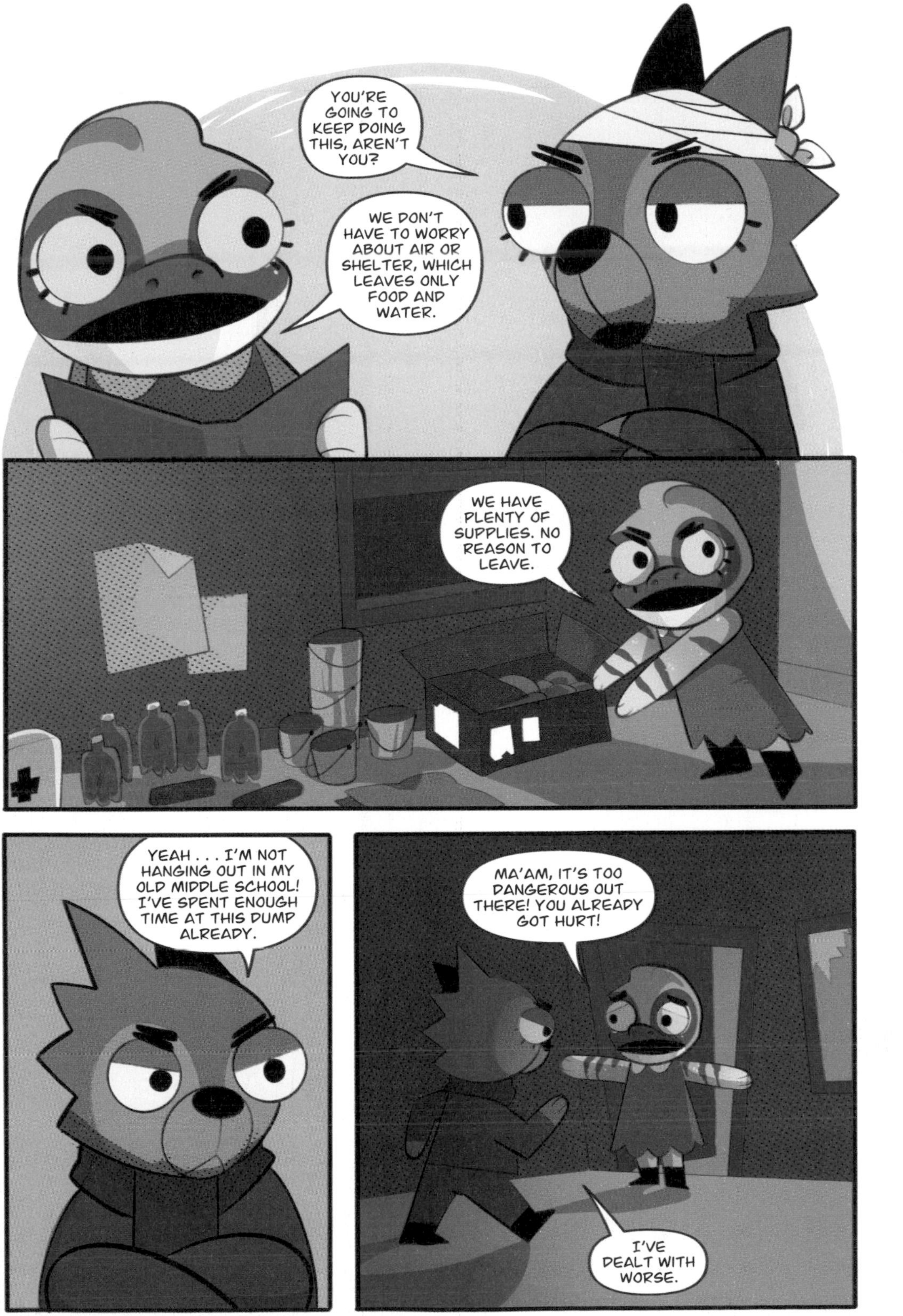
YOU'RE GOING TO KEEP DOING THIS, AREN'T YOU?
WE DON'T HAVE TO WORRY ABOUT AIR OR SHELTER, WHICH LEAVES ONLY FOOD AND WATER.
WE HAVE PLENTY OF SUPPLIES. NO REASON TO LEAVE.
YEAH . . . I'M NOT HANGING OUT IN MY OLD MIDDLE SCHOOL! I'VE SPENT ENOUGH TIME AT THIS DUMP ALREADY.
MA'AM, IT'S TOO DANGEROUS OUT THERE! YOU ALREADY GOT HURT!
I'VE DEALT WITH WORSE.

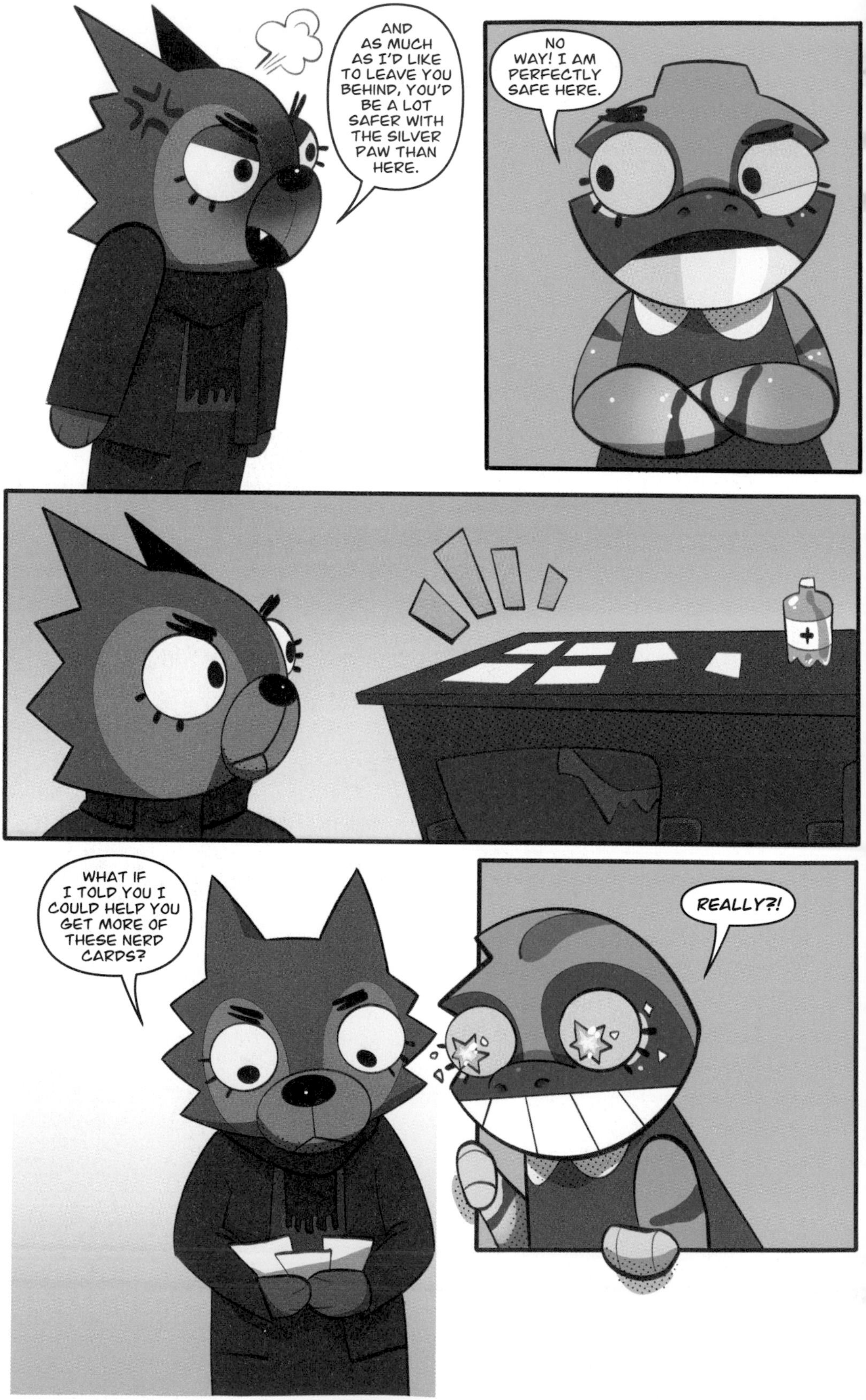
AND AS MUCH AS I'D LIKE TO LEAVE YOU BEHIND, YOU'D BE A LOT SAFER WITH THE SILVER PAW THAN HERE.
NO WAY! I AM PERFECTLY SAFE HERE.
WHAT IF I TOLD YOU I COULD HELP YOU GET MORE OF THESE NERD CARDS?
REALLY?!

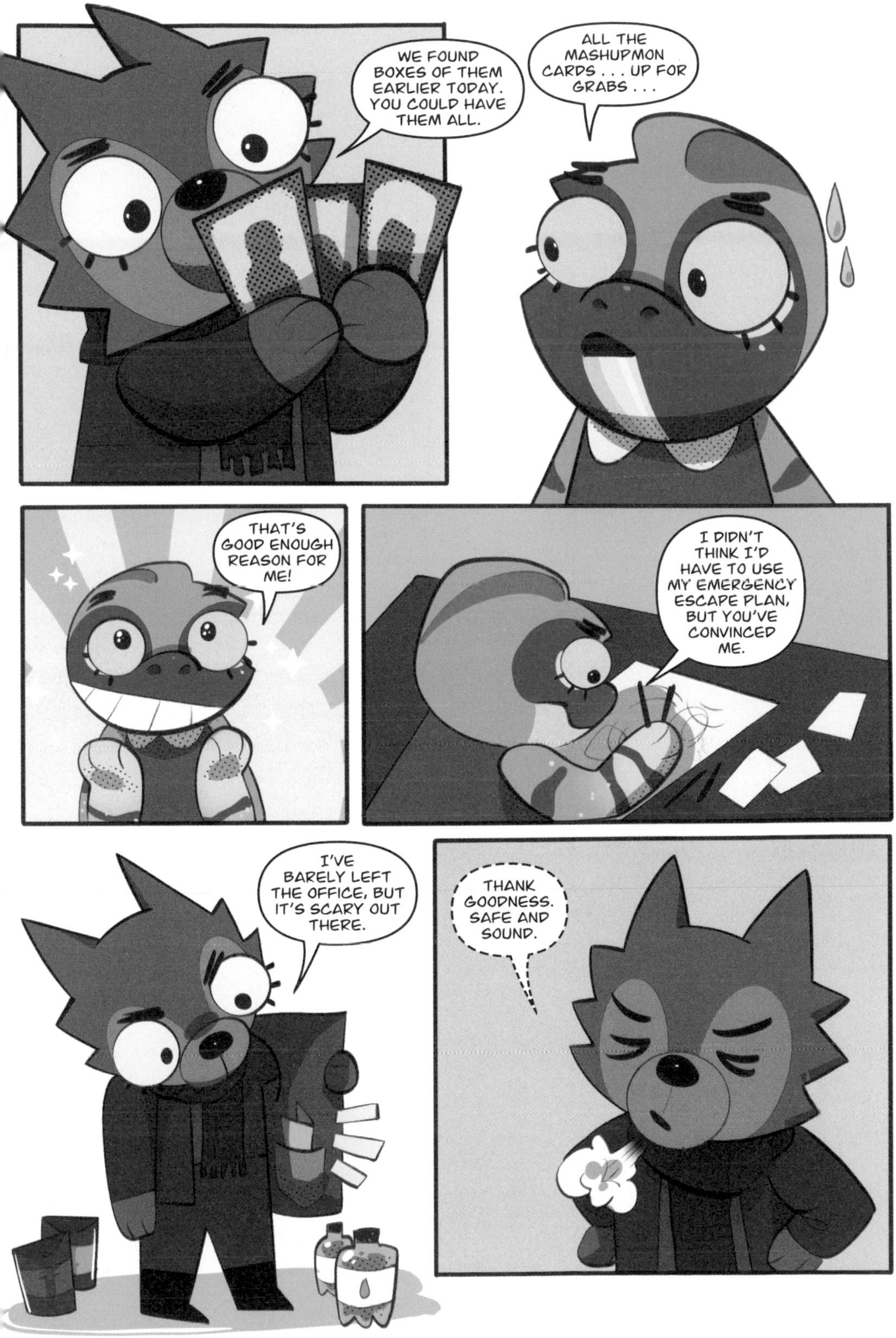
WE FOUND BOXES OF THEM EARLIER TODAY. YOU COULD HAVE THEM ALL.
ALL THE MASHUPMON CARDS . . . UP FOR GRABS . . .
THAT'S GOOD ENOUGH REASON FOR ME!
I DIDN'T THINK I'D HAVE TO USE MY EMERGENCY ESCAPE PLAN, BUT YOU'VE CONVINCED ME.
I'VE BARELY LEFT THE OFFICE, BUT IT'S SCARY OUT THERE.
THANK GOODNESS. SAFE AND SOUND.

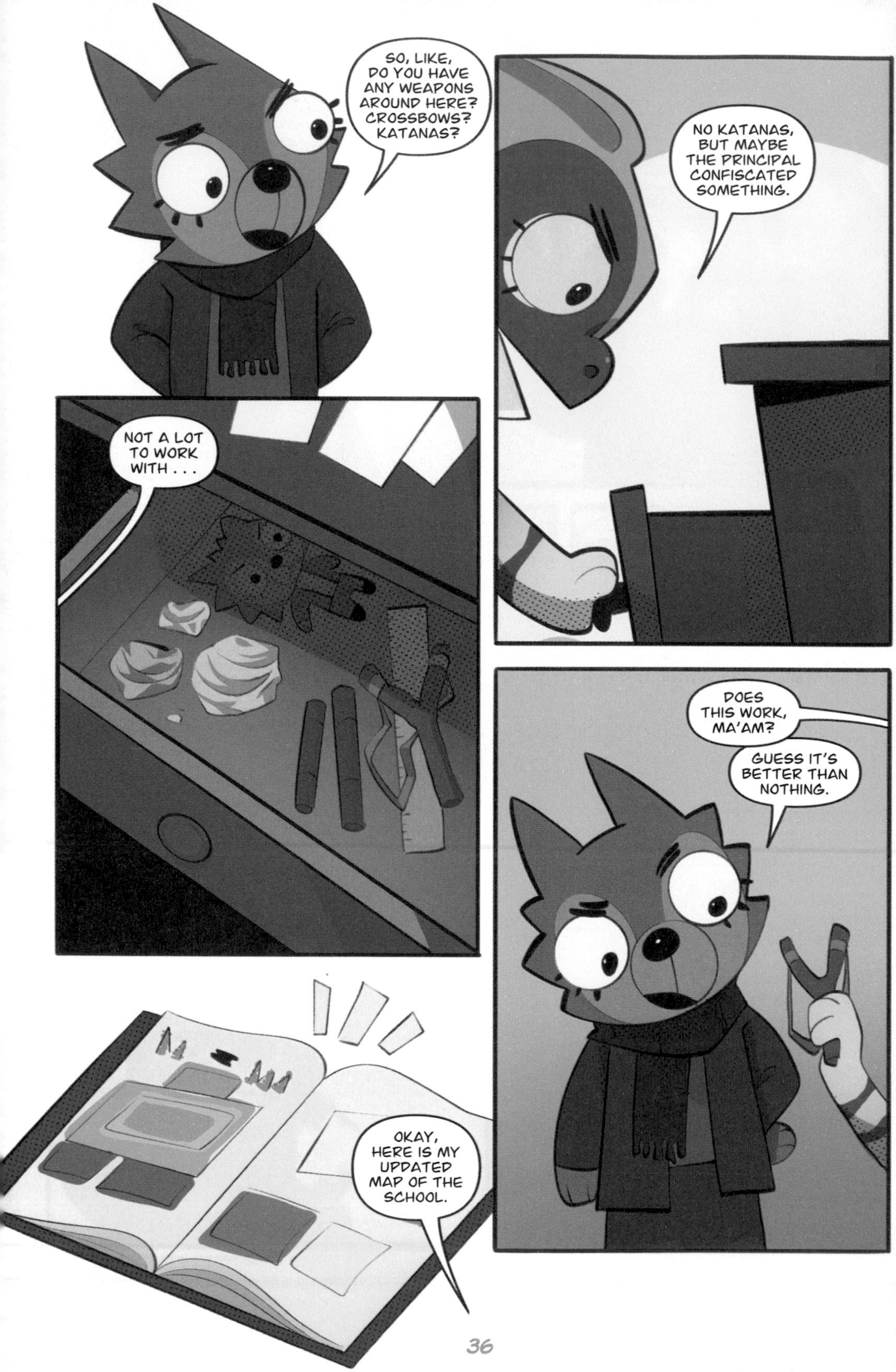
SO, LIKE, DO YOU HAVE ANY WEAPONS AROUND HERE? CROSSBOWS? KATANAS?
NO KATANAS, BUT MAYBE THE PRINCIPAL CONFISCATED SOMETHING.
NOT A LOT TO WORK WITH . . .
DOES THIS WORK, MA'AM?
GUESS IT'S BETTER THAN NOTHING.
OKAY, HERE IS MY UPDATED MAP OF THE SCHOOL.

Survival Tip for Middle School #3 - Map of the Terrain

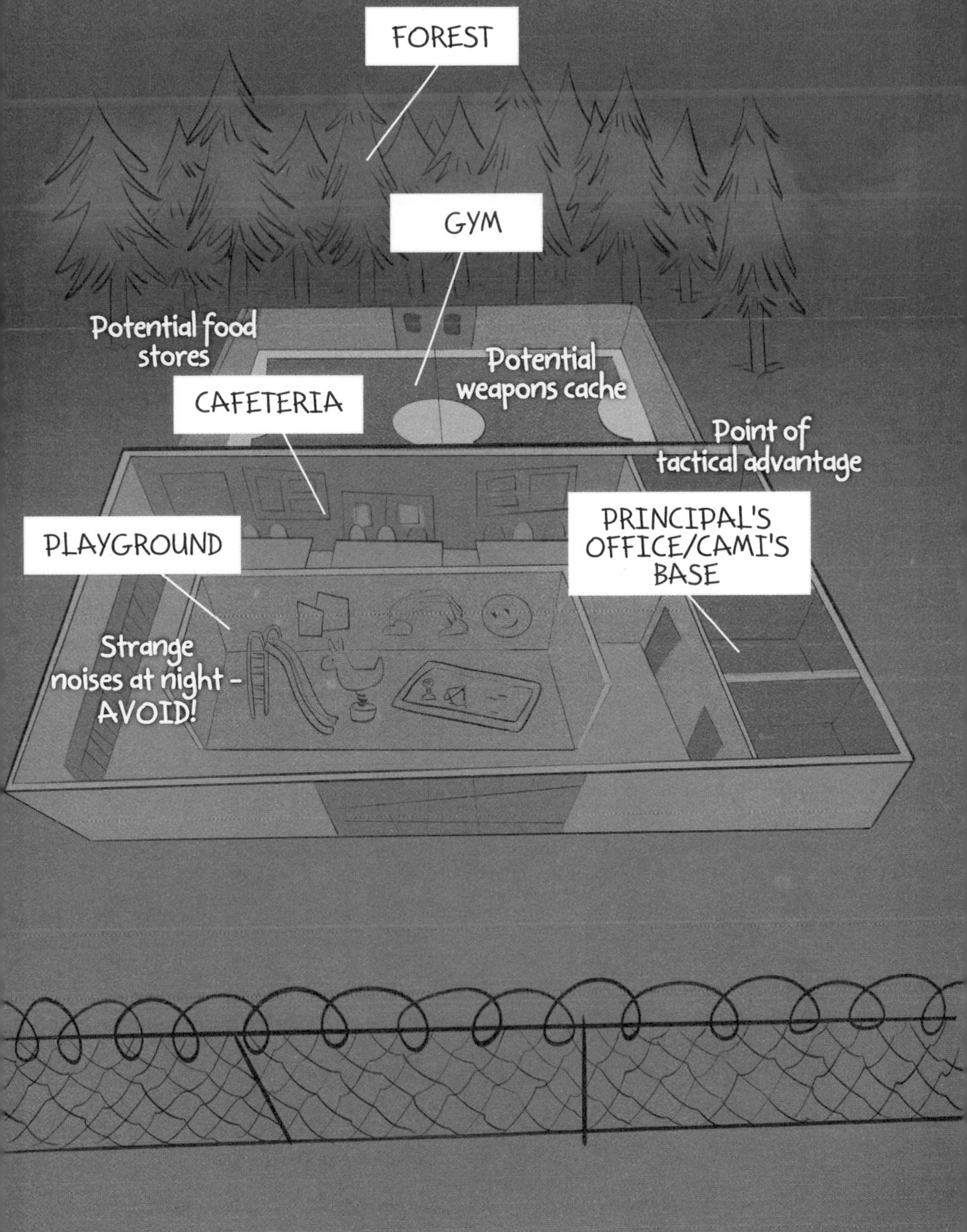
FOREST
GYM
Potential food stores
Potential weapons cache
CAFETERIA
Point of tactical advantage
PRINCIPAL'S OFFICE/CAMI'S BASE
PLAYGROUND
Strange noises at night - AVOID!

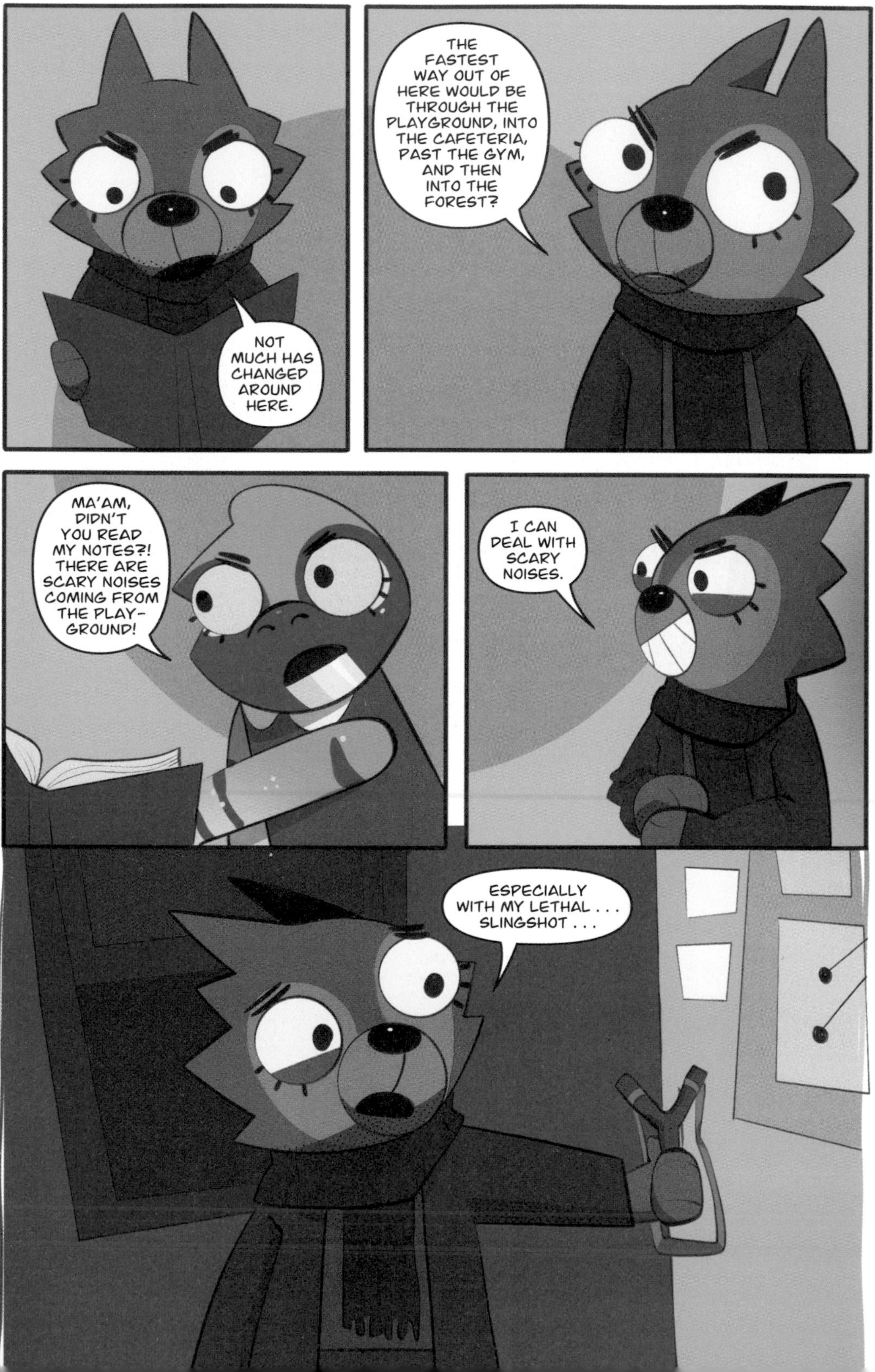
NOT MUCH HAS CHANGED AROUND HERE.
THE FASTEST WAY OUT OF HERE WOULD BE THROUGH THE PLAYGROUND, INTO THE CAFETERIA, PAST THE GYM, AND THEN INTO THE FOREST?
MA'AM, DIDN'T YOU READ MY NOTES?! THERE ARE SCARY NOISES COMING FROM THE PLAY-GROUND!
I CAN DEAL WITH SCARY NOISES.
ESPECIALLY WITH MY LETHAL . . . SLINGSHOT . . .

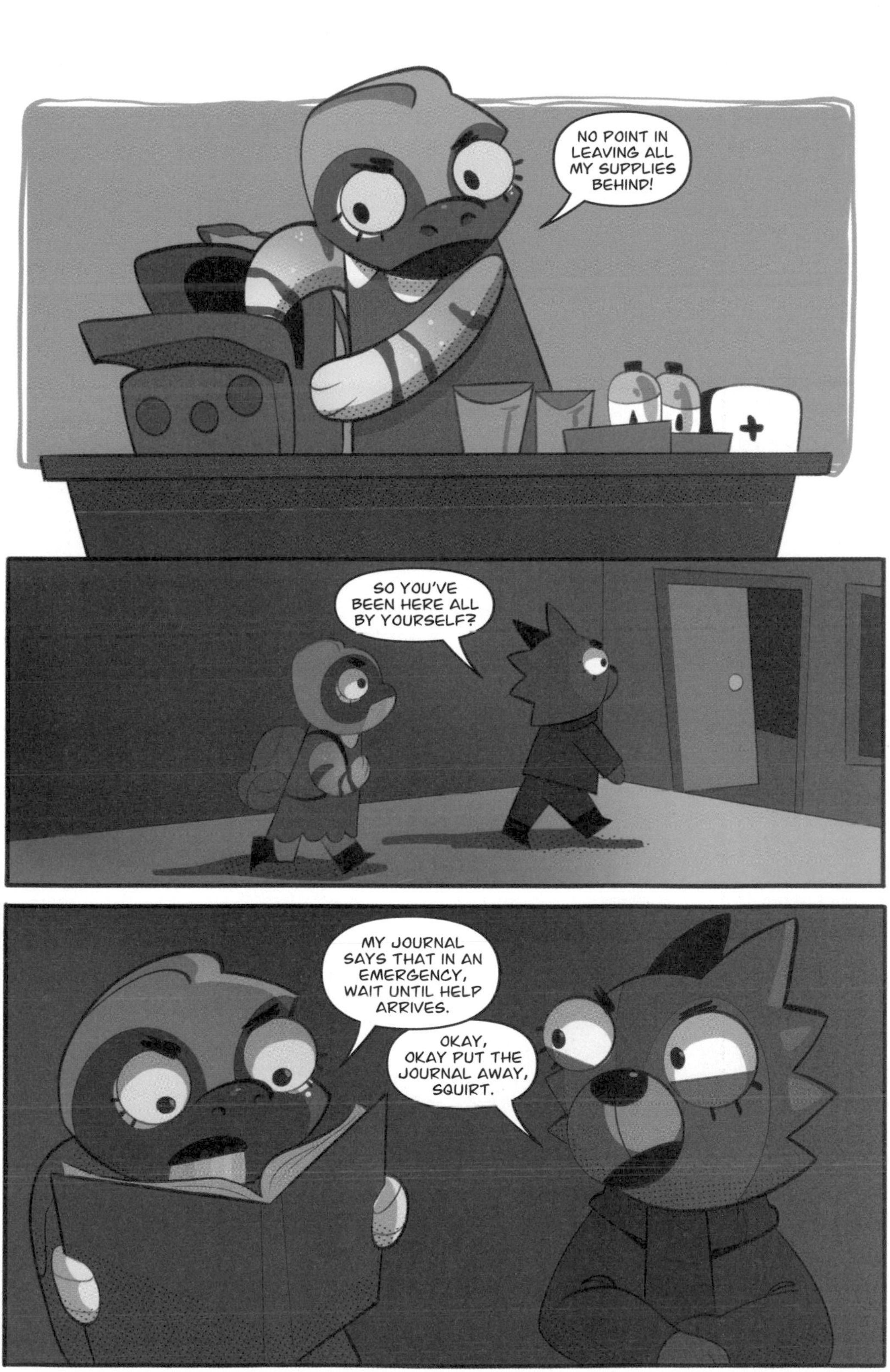
NO POINT IN LEAVING ALL MY SUPPLIES BEHIND!
SO YOU'VE BEEN HERE ALL BY YOURSELF?
MY JOURNAL SAYS THAT IN AN EMERGENCY, WAIT UNTIL HELP ARRIVES.
OKAY, OKAY PUT THE JOURNAL AWAY, SQUIRT.

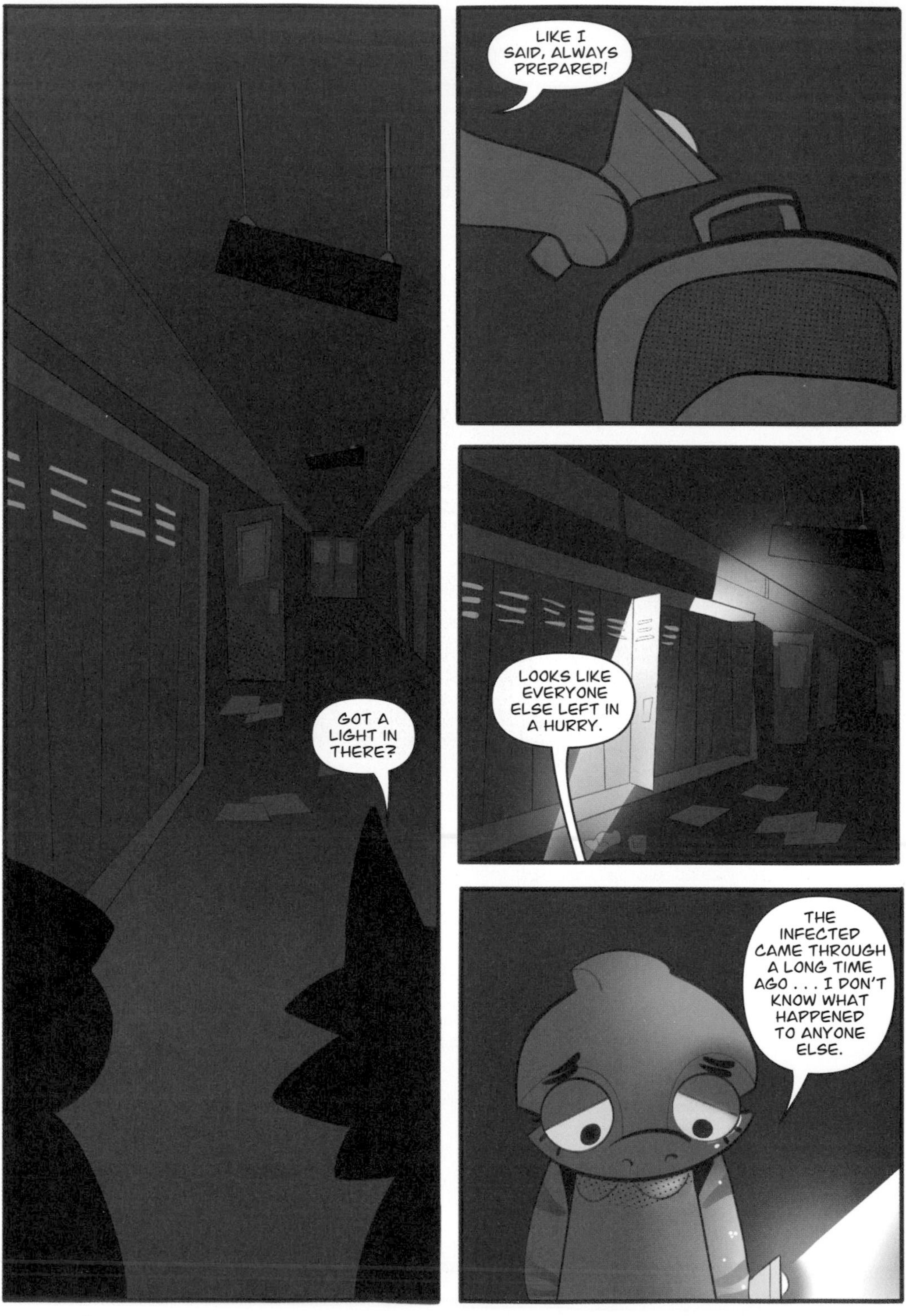
GOT A LIGHT IN THERE?
LIKE I SAID, ALWAYS PREPARED!
LOOKS LIKE EVERYONE ELSE LEFT IN A HURRY.
THE INFECTED CAME THROUGH A LONG TIME AGO . . . I DON'T KNOW WHAT HAPPENED TO ANYONE ELSE.

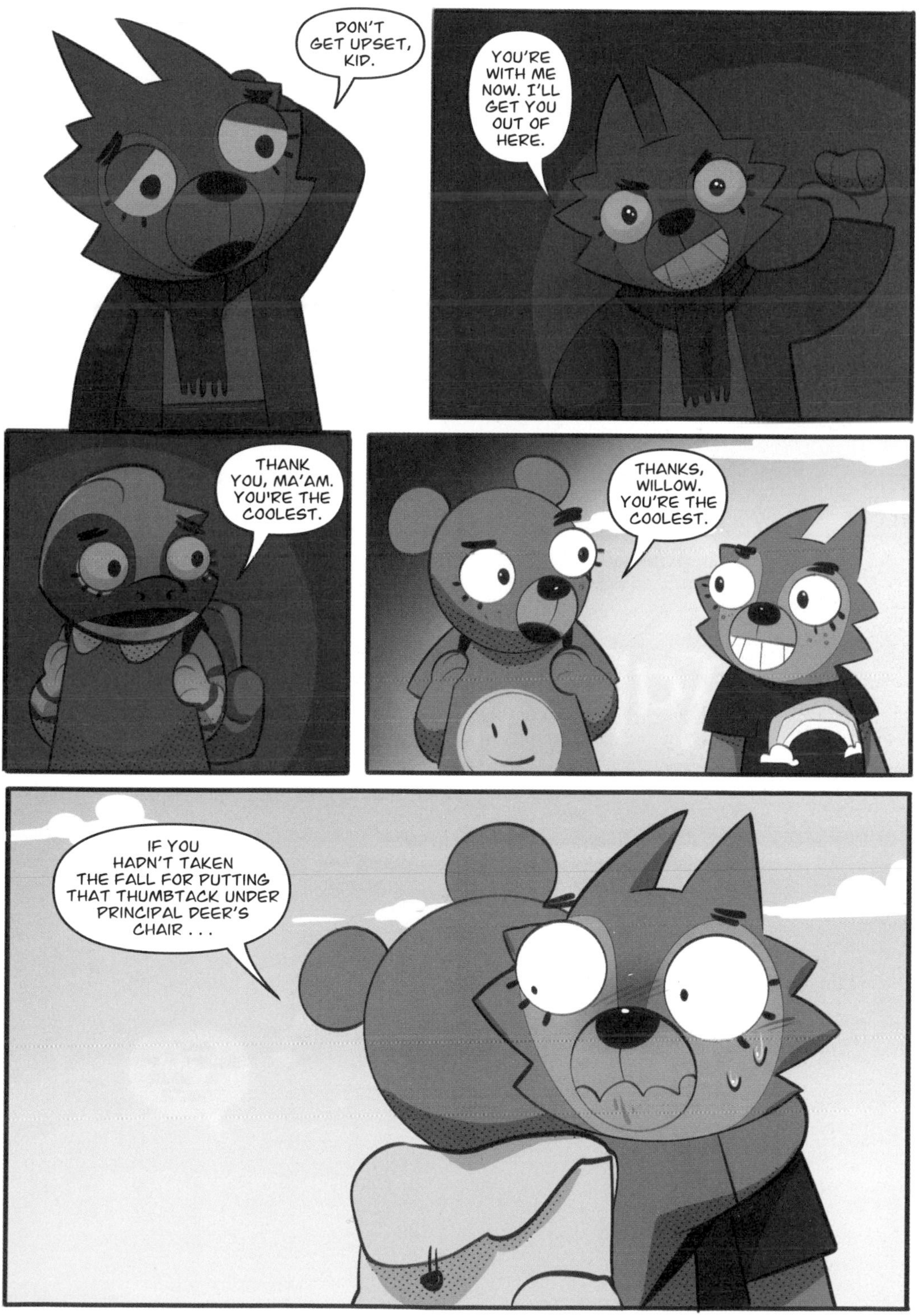
DON'T GET UPSET, KID.
YOU'RE WITH ME NOW. I'LL GET YOU OUT OF HERE.
THANK YOU, MA'AM. YOU'RE THE COOLEST.
THANKS, WILLOW. YOU'RE THE COOLEST.
IF YOU HADN'T TAKEN THE FALL FOR PUTTING THAT THUMBTACK UNDER PRINCIPAL DEER'S CHAIR . . .

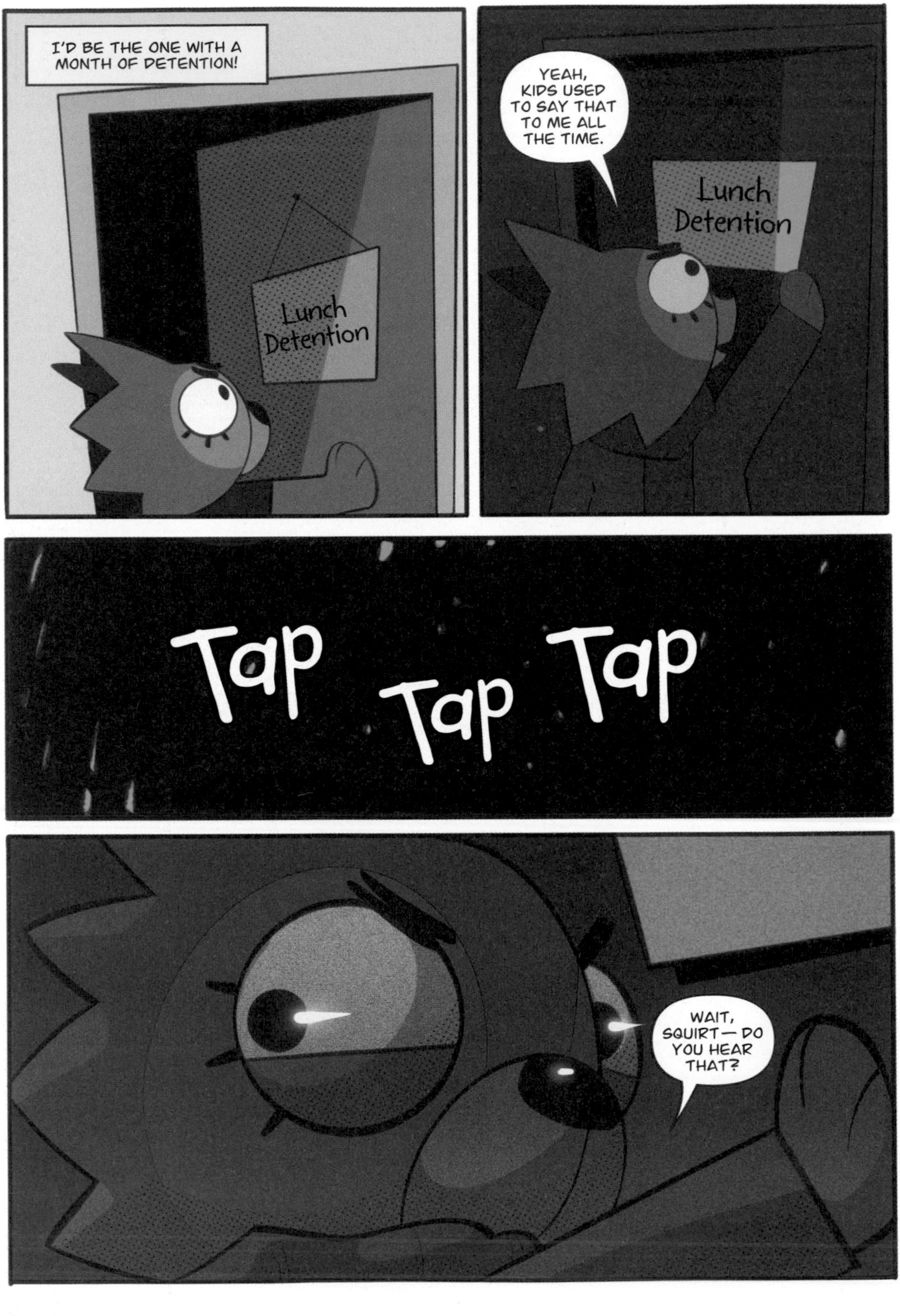
I'D BE THE ONE WITH A MONTH OF DETENTION!
Lunch Detention
YEAH, KIDS USED TO SAY THAT TO ME ALL THE TIME.
Lunch Detention
Tap Tap Tap
WAIT, SQUIRT— DO YOU HEAR THAT?

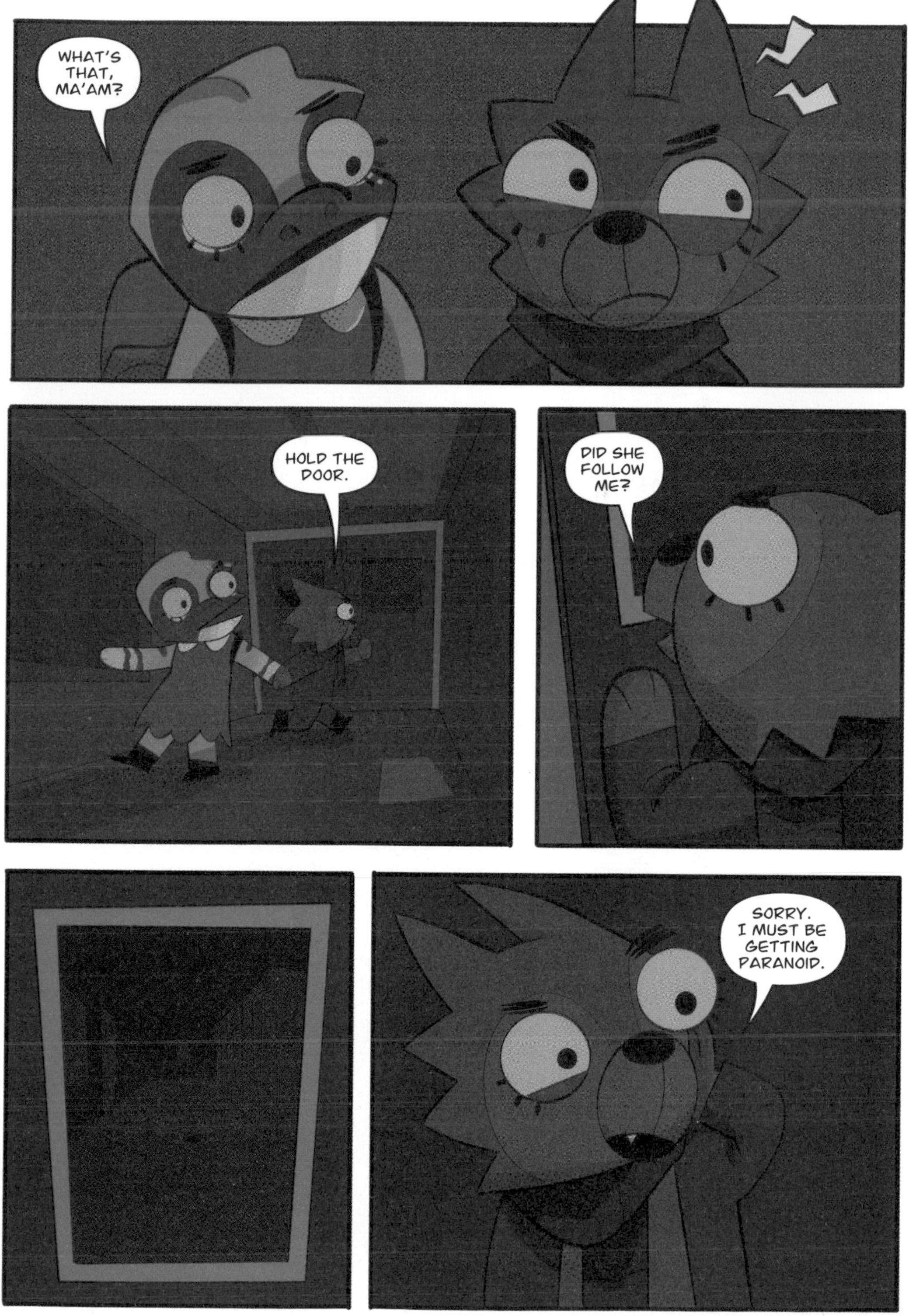
WHAT'S THAT, MA'AM?
HOLD THE DOOR.
DID SHE FOLLOW ME?
SORRY. I MUST BE GETTING PARANOID.

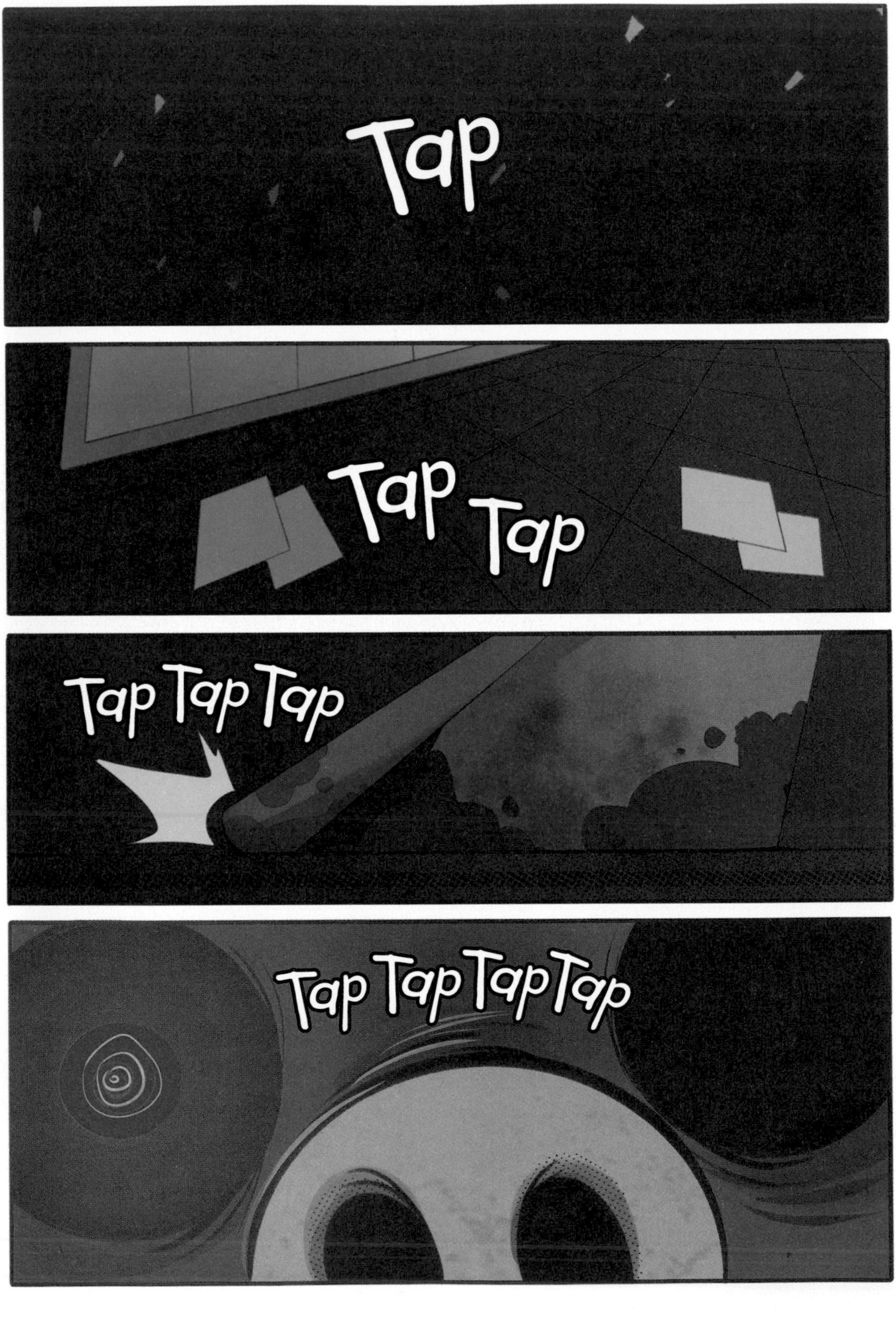
Tap
Tap
Tap
Tap Tap Tap
Tap Tap Tap Tap

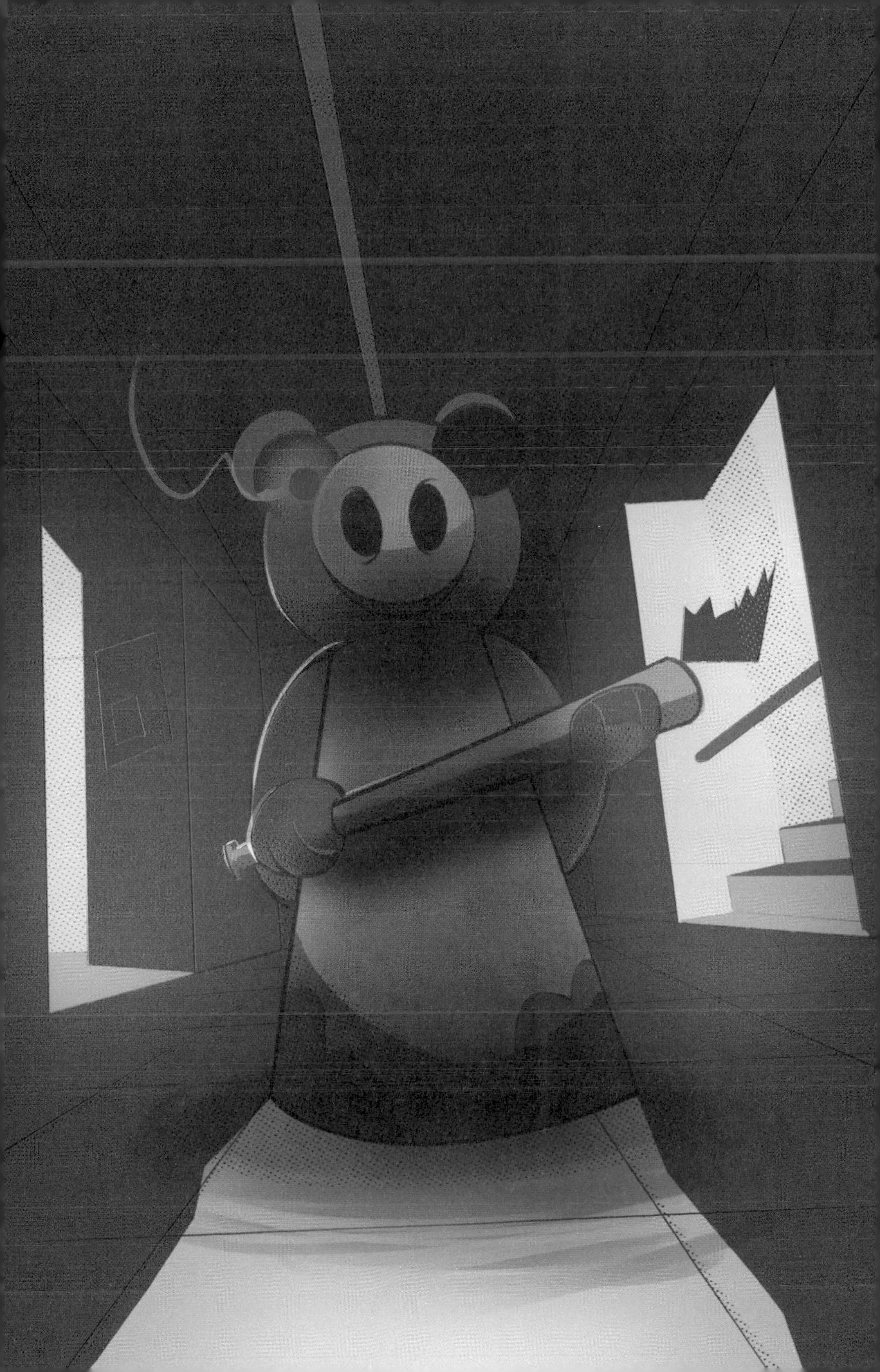

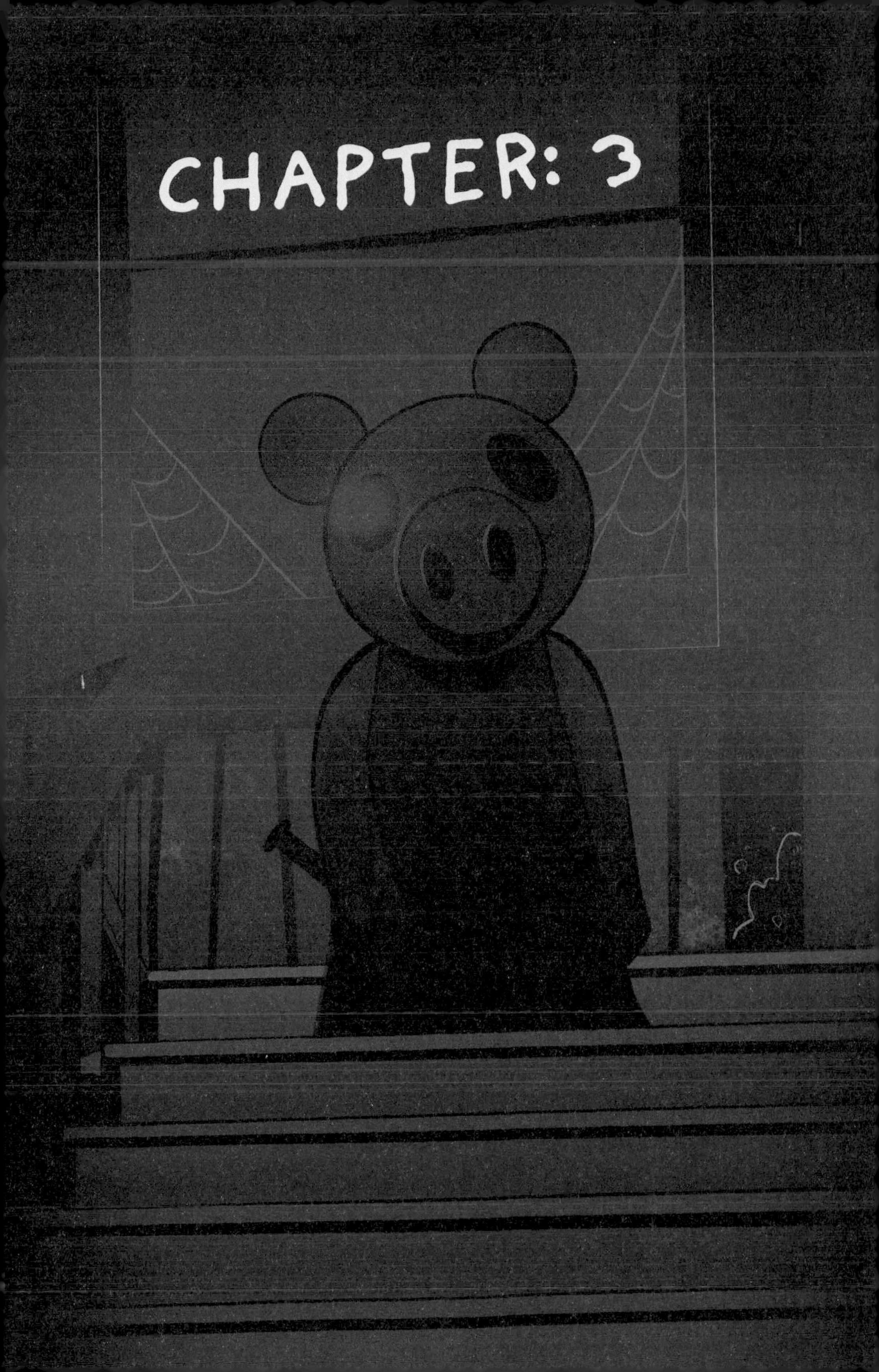
CHAPTER: 3

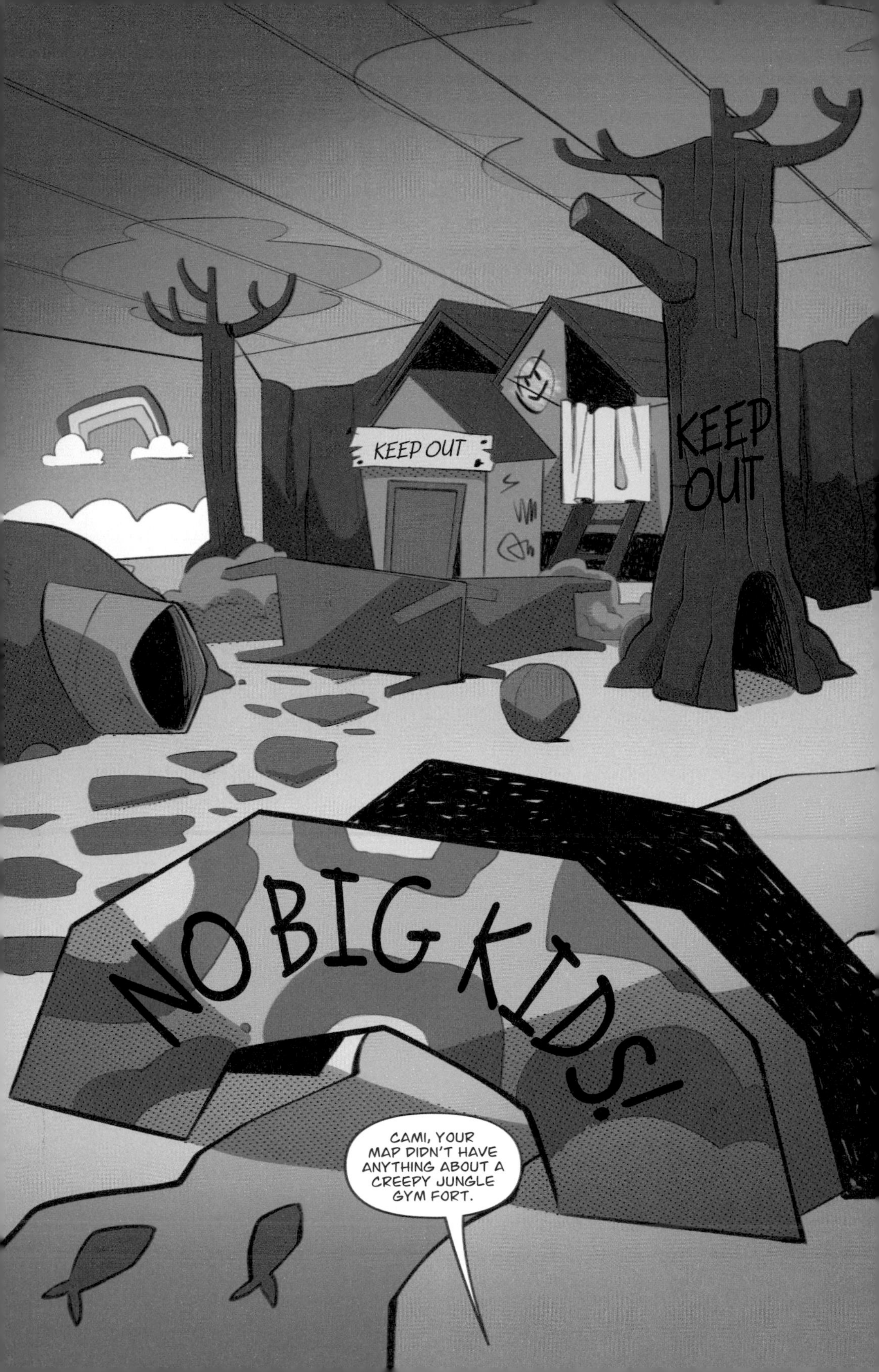
KEEP OUT
KEEP OUT
NO BIG KIDS!
CAMI, YOUR MAP DIDN'T HAVE ANYTHING ABOUT A CREEPY JUNGLE GYM FORT.

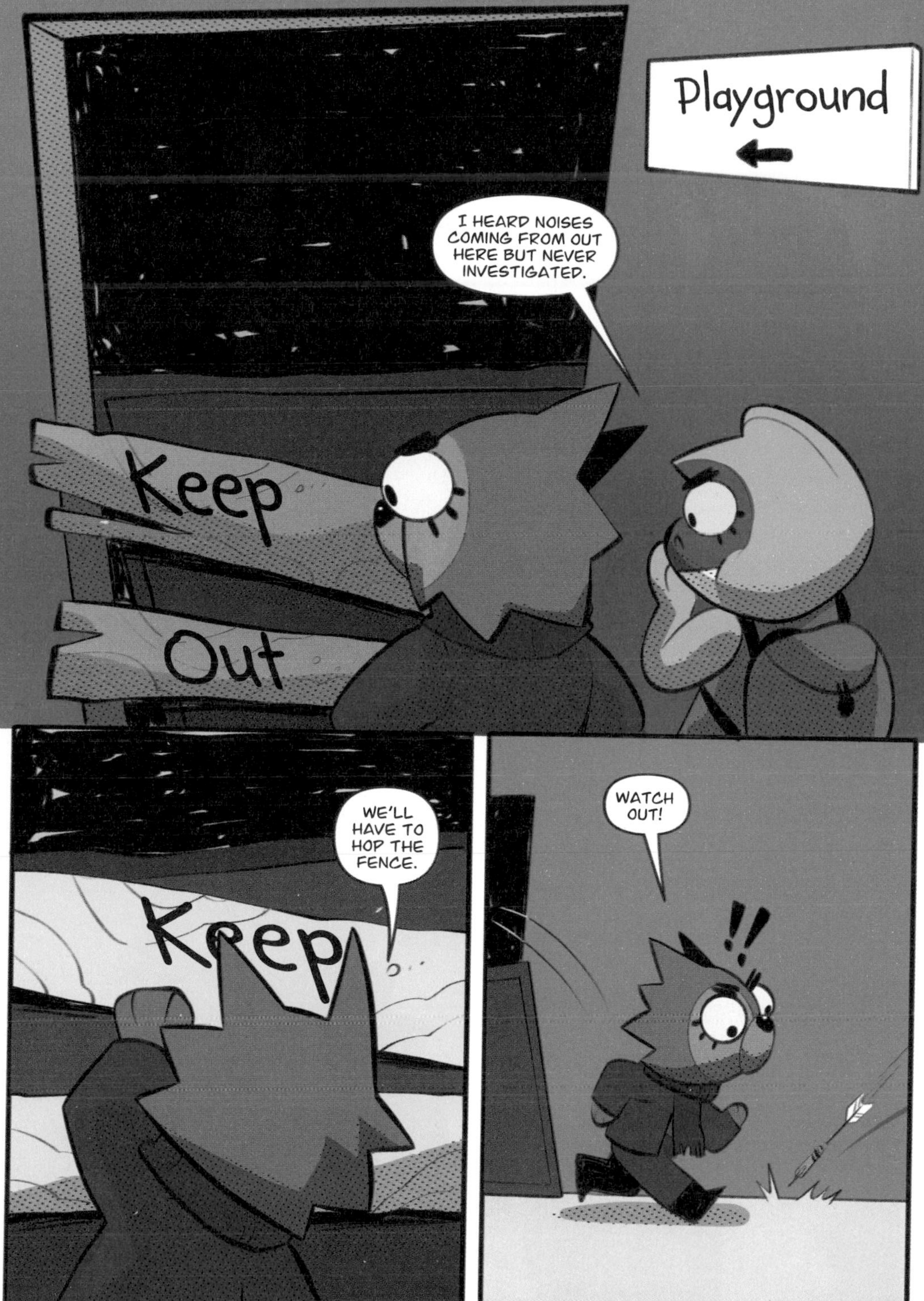
Playground
I HEARD NOISES COMING FROM OUT HERE BUT NEVER INVESTIGATED.
Keep
Out
WE'LL HAVE TO HOP THE FENCE.
Keep
WATCH OUT!
!!

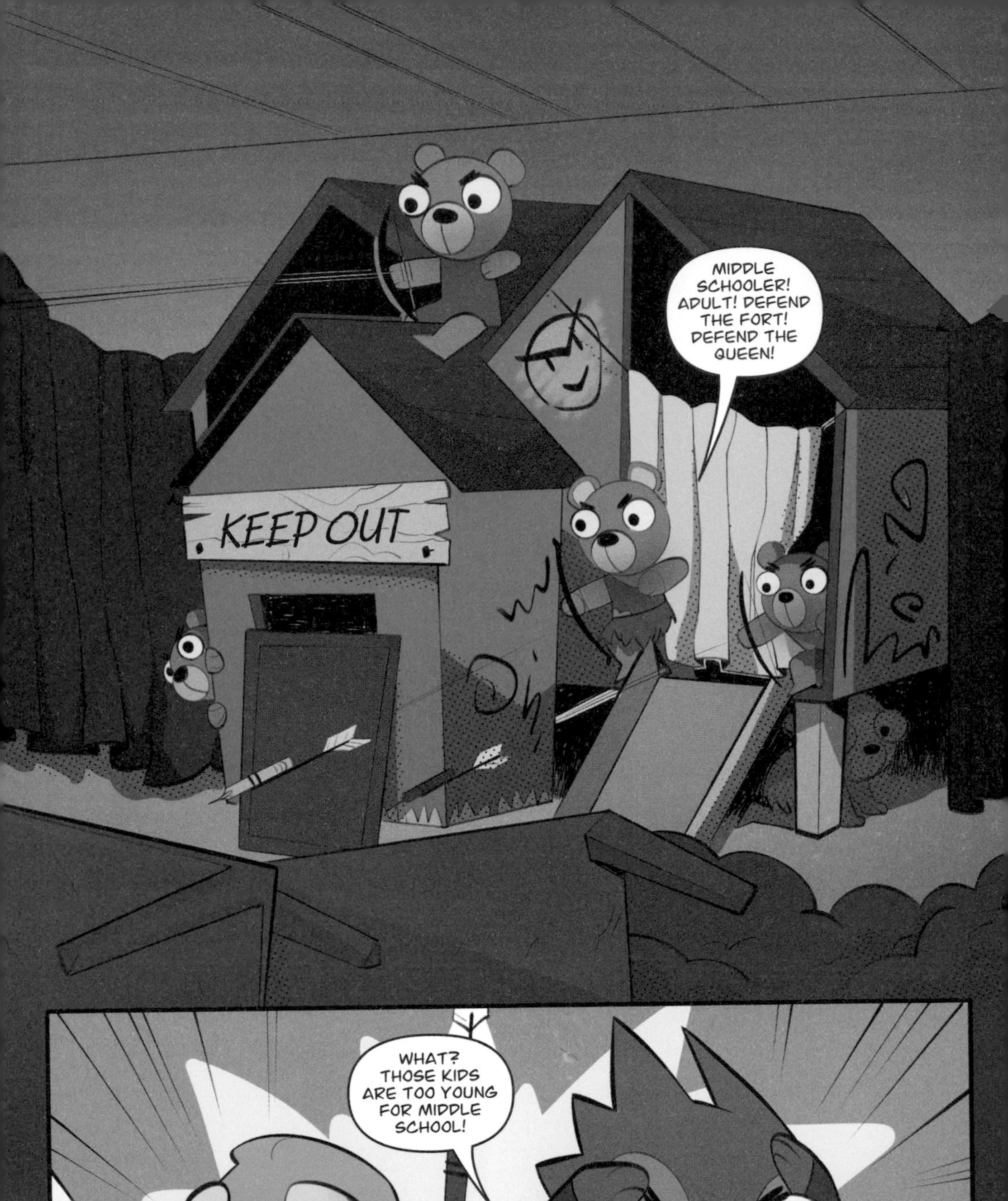
KEEP OUT
MIDDLE SCHOOLER! ADULT! DEFEND THE FORT! DEFEND THE QUEEN!

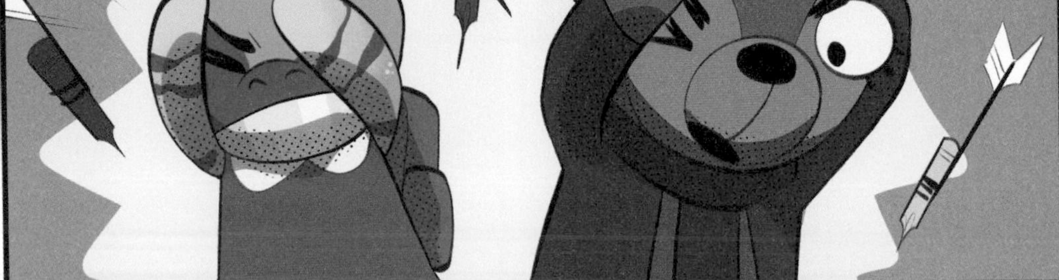
WHAT? THOSE KIDS ARE TOO YOUNG FOR MIDDLE SCHOOL!

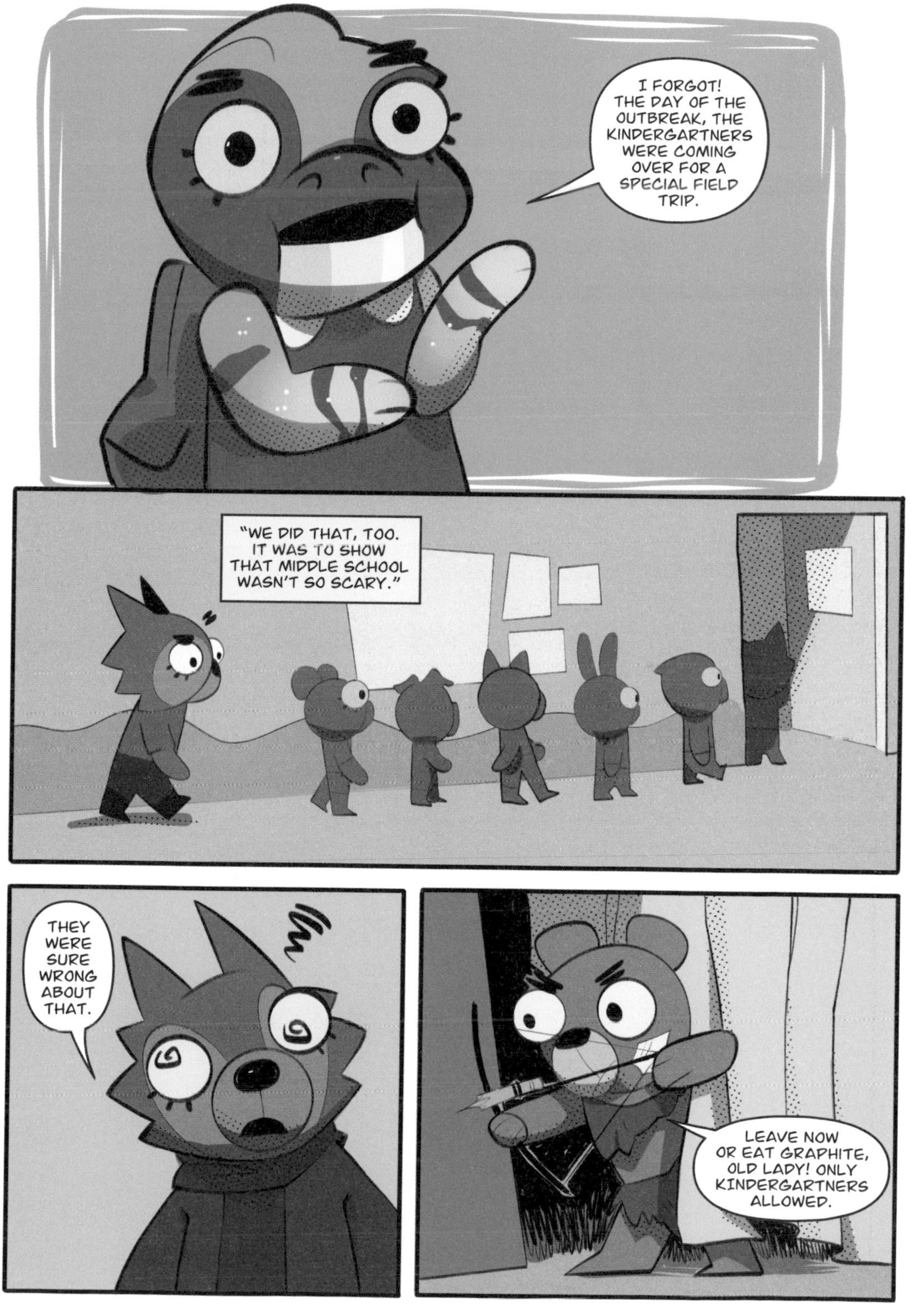
I FORGOT! THE DAY OF THE OUTBREAK, THE KINDERGARTNERS WERE COMING OVER FOR A SPECIAL FIELD TRIP.
"WE DID THAT, TOO. IT WAS TO SHOW THAT MIDDLE SCHOOL WASN'T SO SCARY."
THEY WERE SURE WRONG ABOUT THAT.
LEAVE NOW OR EAT GRAPHITE, OLD LADY! ONLY KINDERGARTNERS ALLOWED.

WHO ARE YOU CALLING OLD, YOU TWERP?!

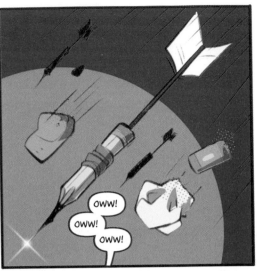

OWW!

OWW!

OWW!

I REQUEST A RETREAT, MA'AM!

REQUEST GRANTED!

KEEP OUT

HOW DID THEY GET THOSE PENCILS SO SHARP?

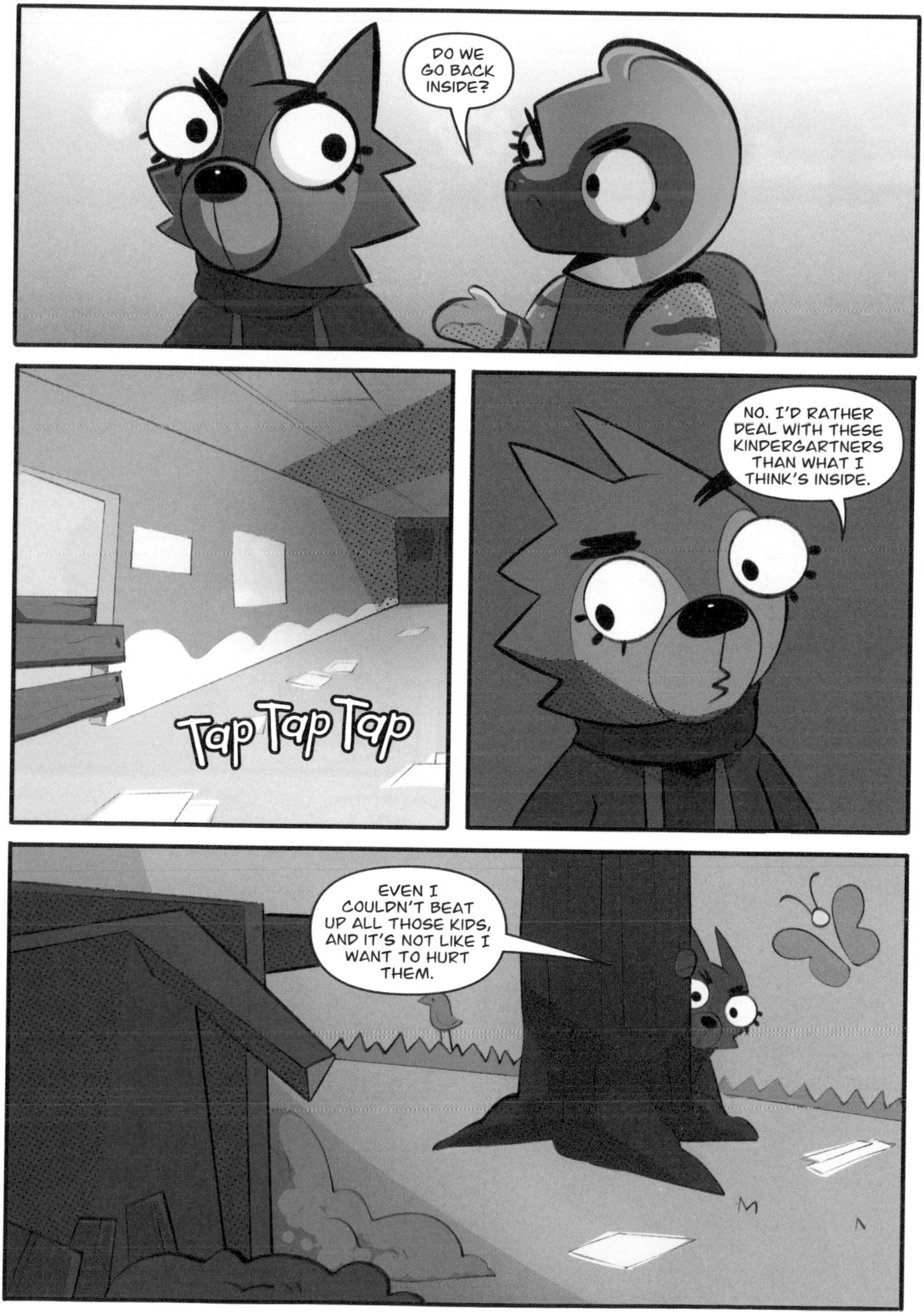
DO WE GO BACK INSIDE?
Tap Tap Tap
NO. I'D RATHER DEAL WITH THESE KINDERGARTNERS THAN WHAT I THINK'S INSIDE.
EVEN I COULDN'T BEAT UP ALL THOSE KIDS, AND IT'S NOT LIKE I WANT TO HURT THEM.

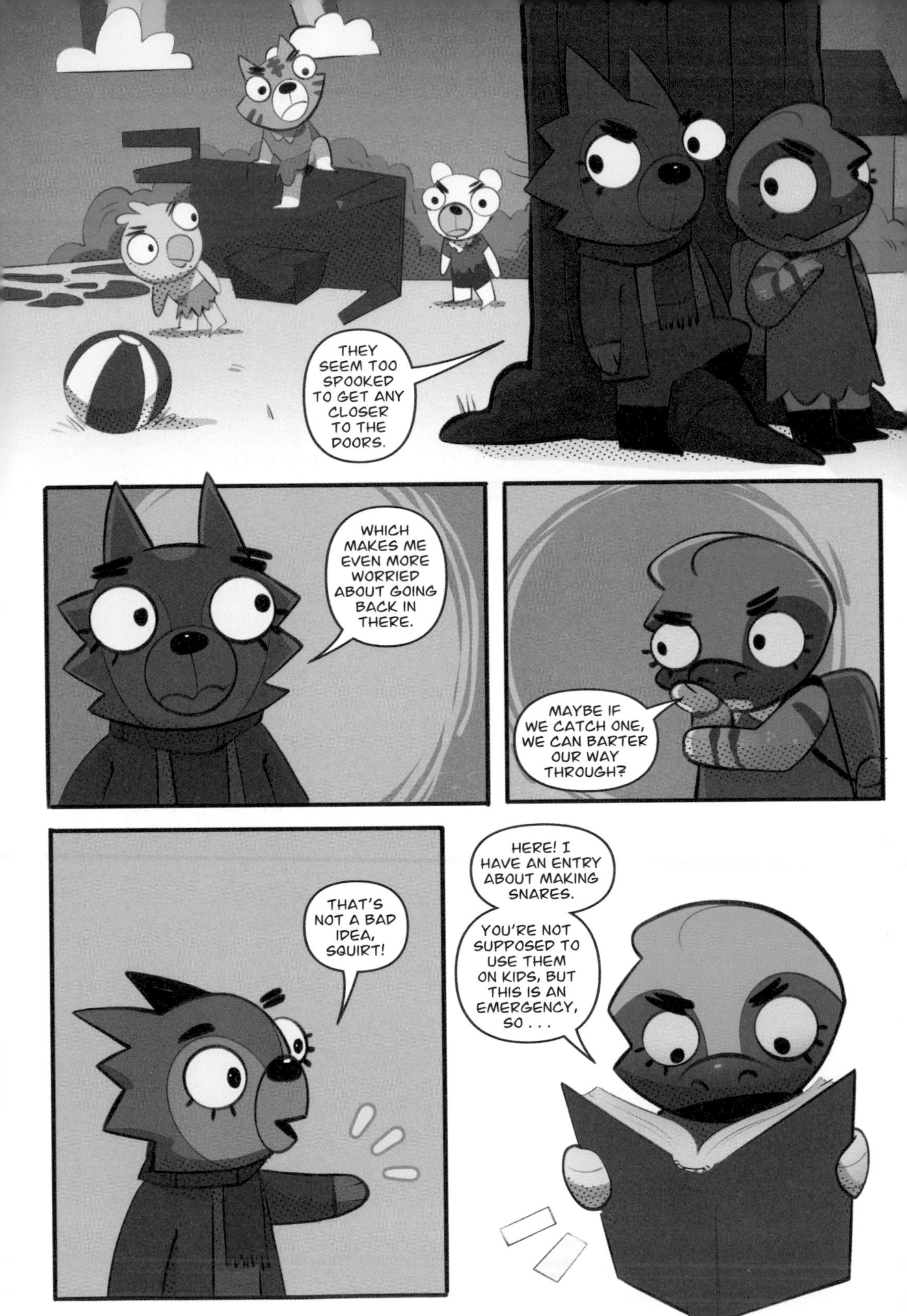
THEY SEEM TOO SPOOKED TO GET ANY CLOSER TO THE DOORS.
WHICH MAKES ME EVEN MORE WORRIED ABOUT GOING BACK IN THERE.
MAYBE IF WE CATCH ONE, WE CAN BARTER OUR WAY THROUGH?
THAT'S NOT A BAD IDEA, SQUIRT!
HERE! I HAVE AN ENTRY ABOUT MAKING SNARES.
YOU'RE NOT SUPPOSED TO USE THEM ON KIDS, BUT THIS IS AN EMERGENCY, SO . . .

Survival Tip for Middle School #4 – Making Snares

Snares are useful tools for any survivalist and only require a piece of metal wire or rope. Snares should not be used on other kids.

Take your metal wire and wrap it around a stick.

Take out the stick.

Take the ends of your wire and twist them together.

Take the end of your wire and thread it through your loop. Now you have a simple snare!

Either you can pull on the loop to tighten it, or anything caught will tighten it, too!

WE'LL HAVE TO THROW IT AROUND THAT HOLE TO CATCH THEIR FOOT. AND WE'LL NEED BAIT.

WE'LL ALSO NEED A DISTRACTION.

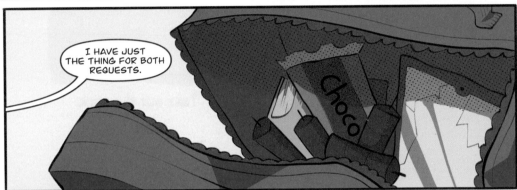

I HAVE JUST THE THING FOR BOTH REQUESTS.

YOU DIDN'T TELL ME YOU HAD FIRECRACKERS AND CANDY BARS!

I DIDN'T THINK YOU'D BE RESPONSIBLE WITH EITHER OF THEM.

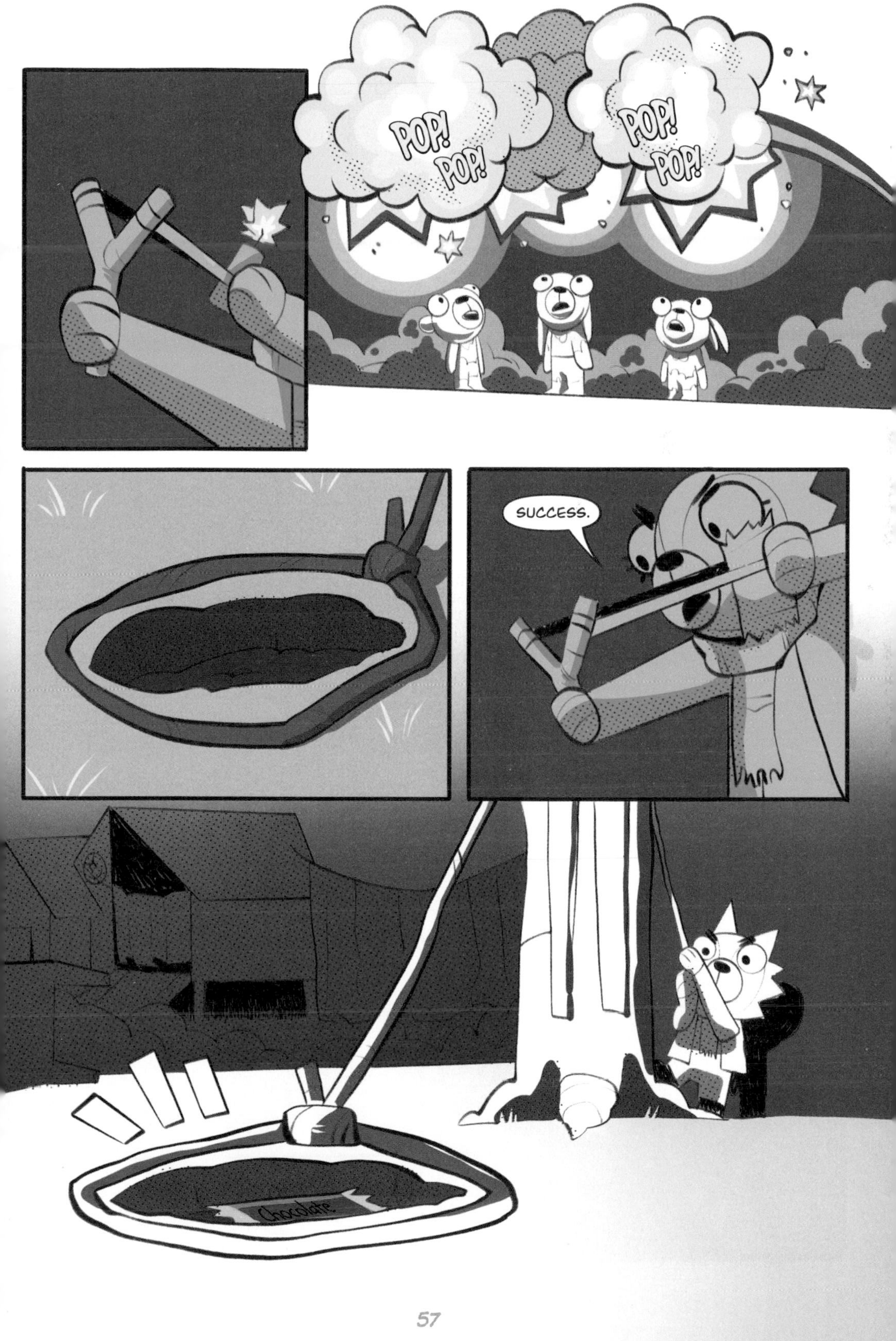
POP! POP!
POP! POP!
SUCCESS.
Chocolate

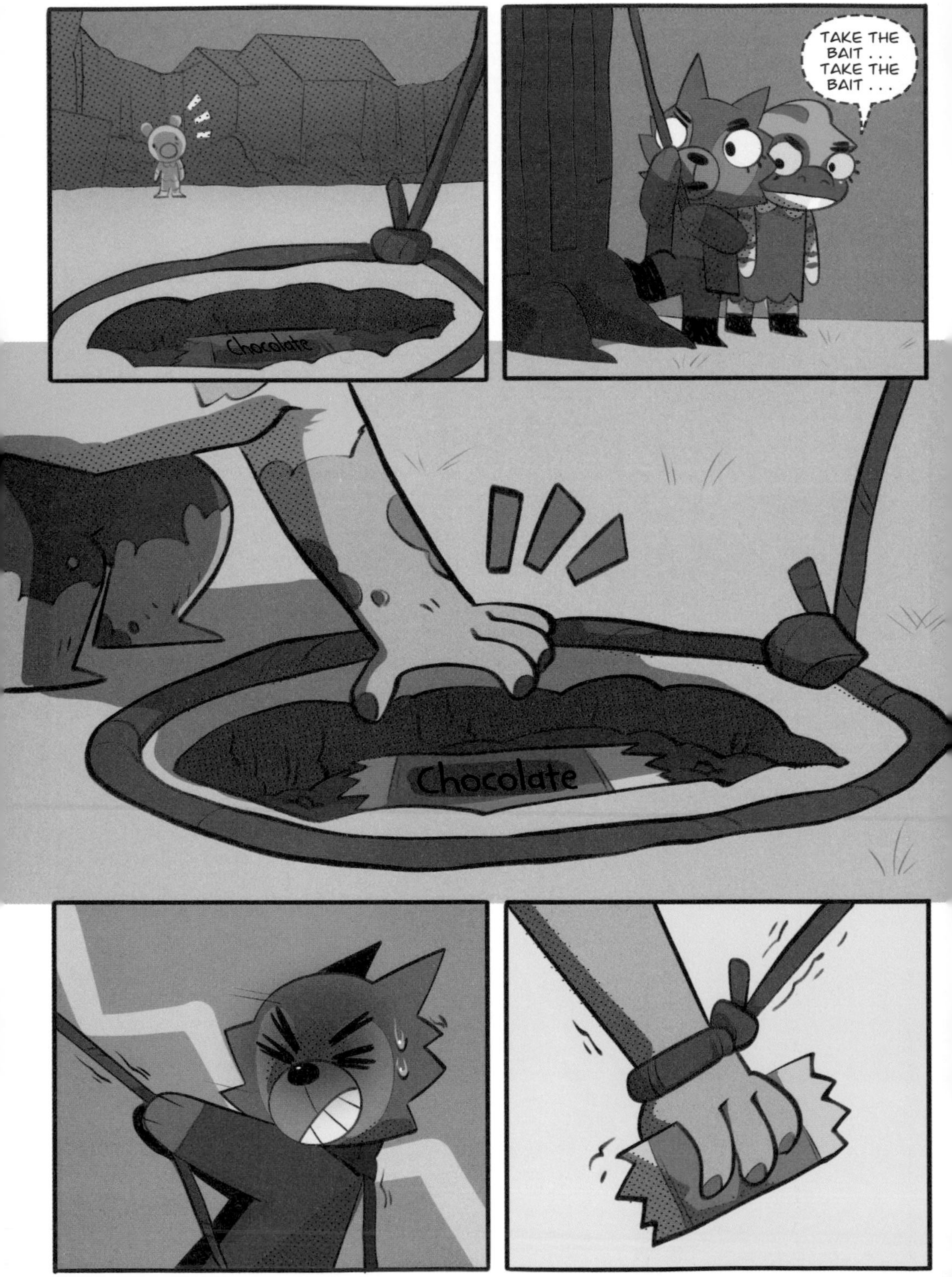
Chocolate
TAKE THE BAIT . . . TAKE THE BAIT . . .
Chocolate

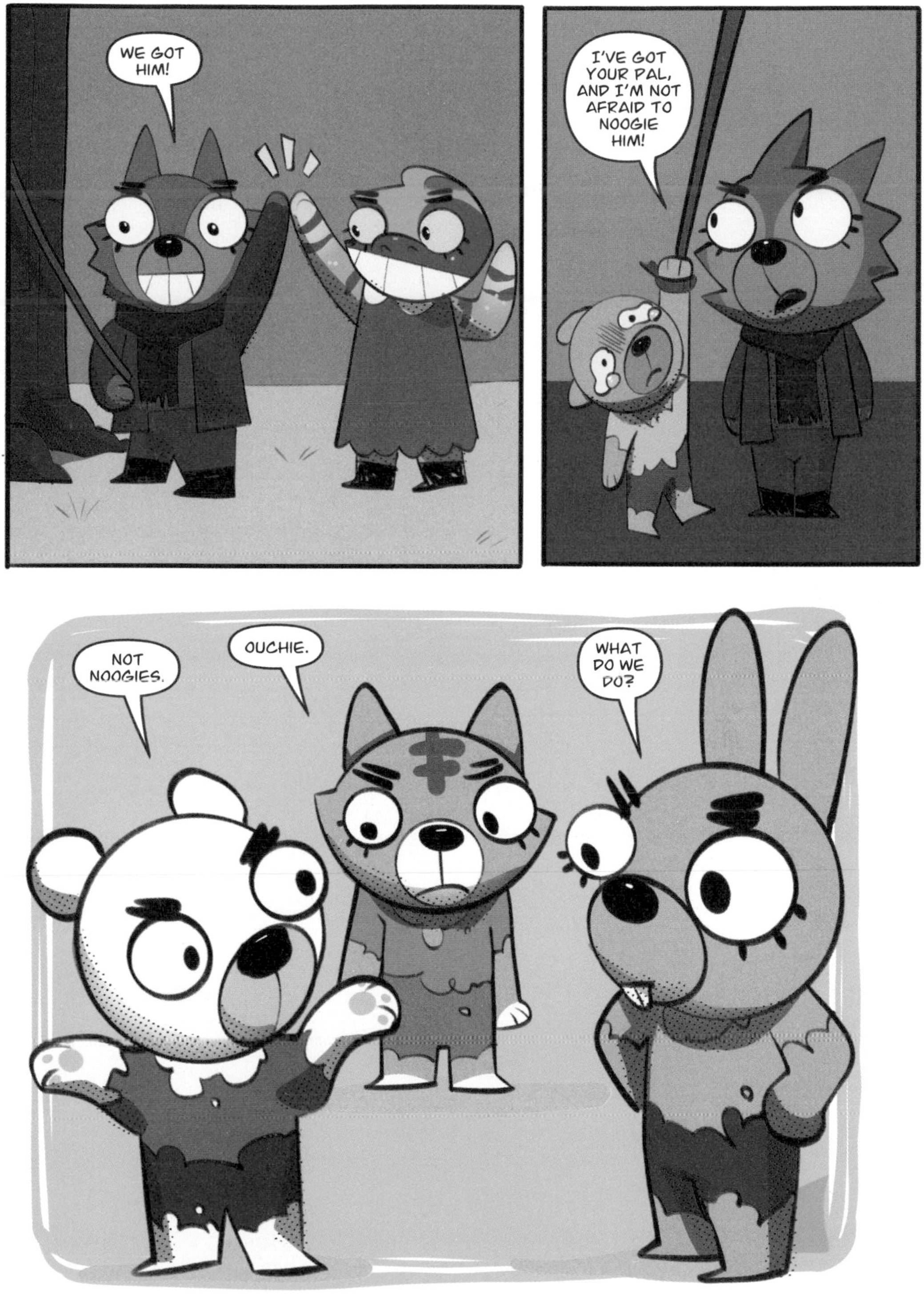
WE GOT HIM!
I'VE GOT YOUR PAL, AND I'M NOT AFRAID TO NOOGIE HIM!
NOT NOOGIES.
OUCHIE.
WHAT DO WE DO?

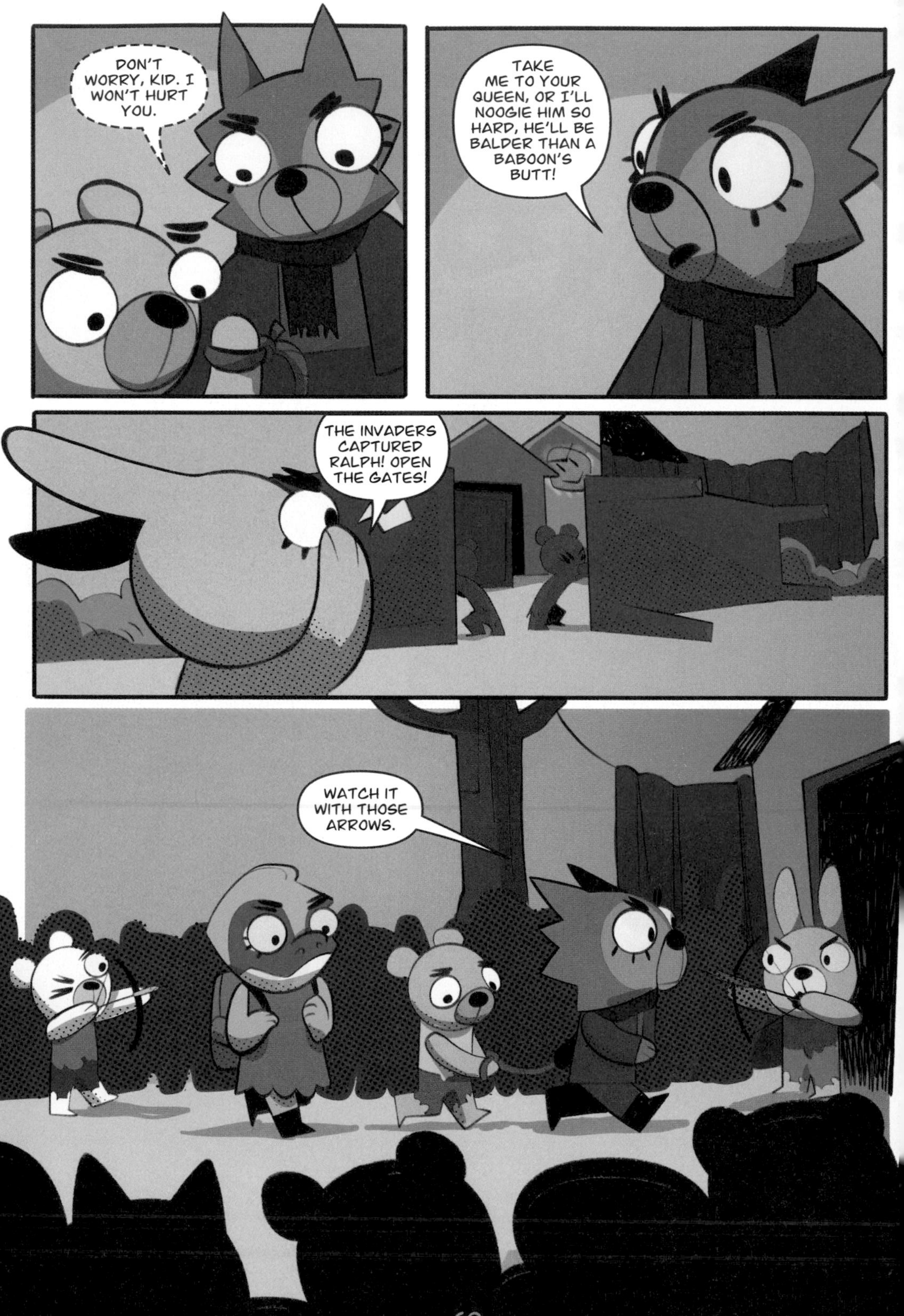
DON'T WORRY, KID. I WON'T HURT YOU.
TAKE ME TO YOUR QUEEN, OR I'LL NOOGIE HIM SO HARD, HE'LL BE BALDER THAN A BABOON'S BUTT!
THE INVADERS CAPTURED RALPH! OPEN THE GATES!
WATCH IT WITH THOSE ARROWS.

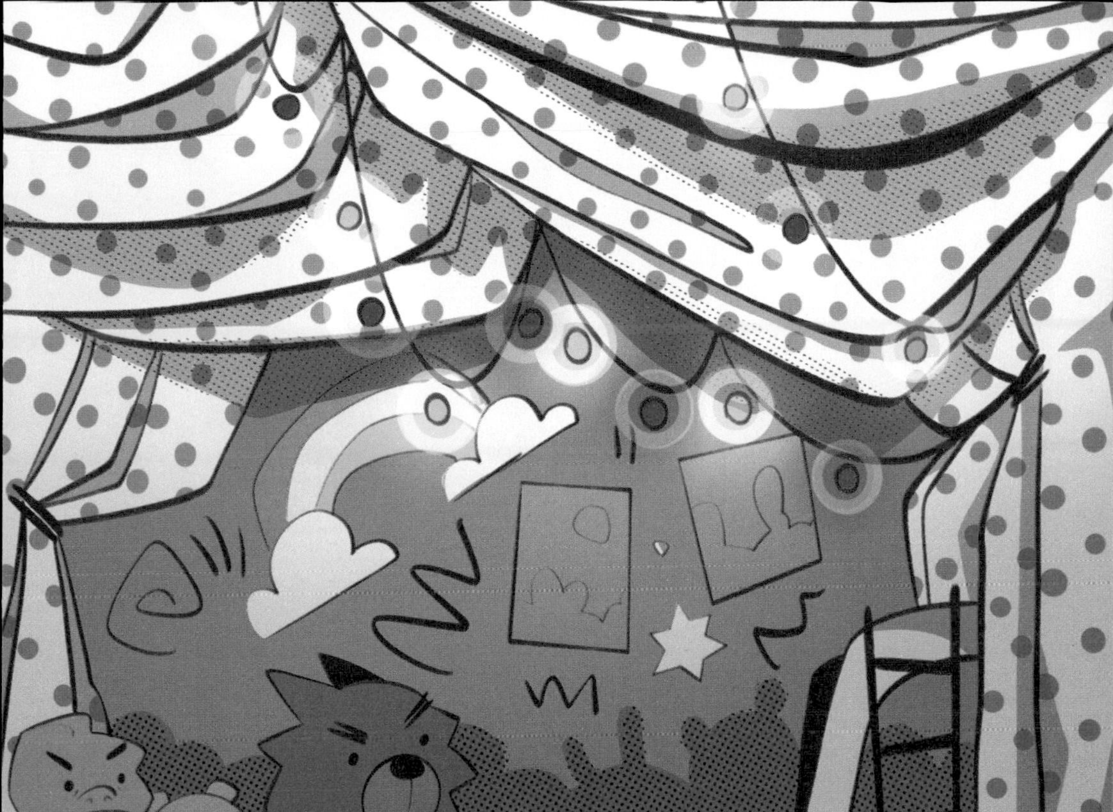

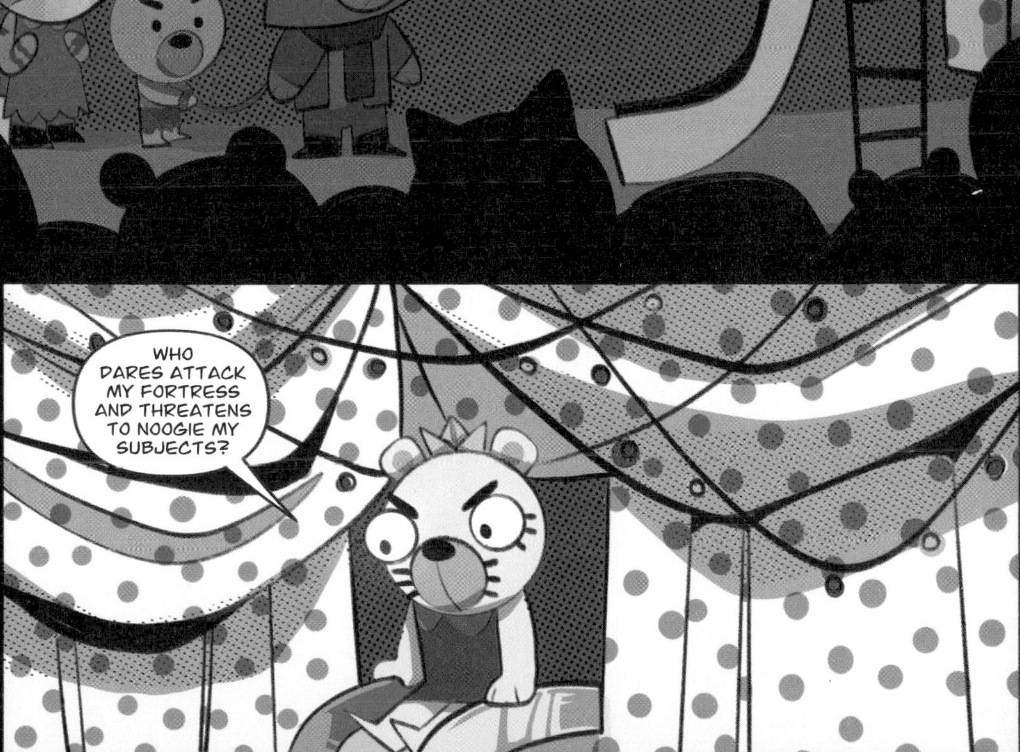
WHO DARES ATTACK MY FORTRESS AND THREATENS TO NOOGIE MY SUBJECTS?

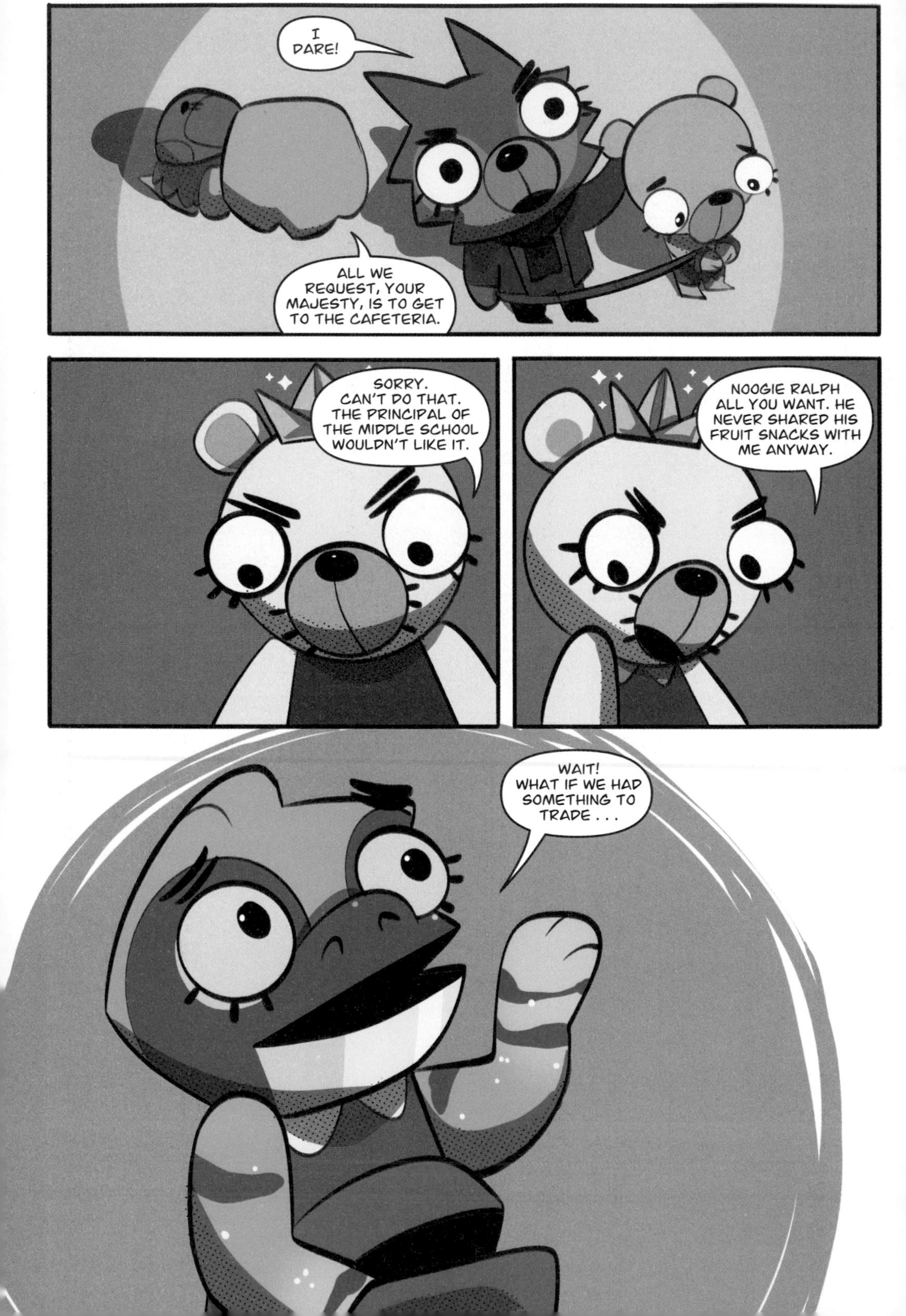
I DARE!
ALL WE REQUEST, YOUR MAJESTY, IS TO GET TO THE CAFETERIA.
SORRY. CAN'T DO THAT. THE PRINCIPAL OF THE MIDDLE SCHOOL WOULDN'T LIKE IT.
NOOGIE RALPH ALL YOU WANT. HE NEVER SHARED HIS FRUIT SNACKS WITH ME ANYWAY.
WAIT! WHAT IF WE HAD SOMETHING TO TRADE . . .

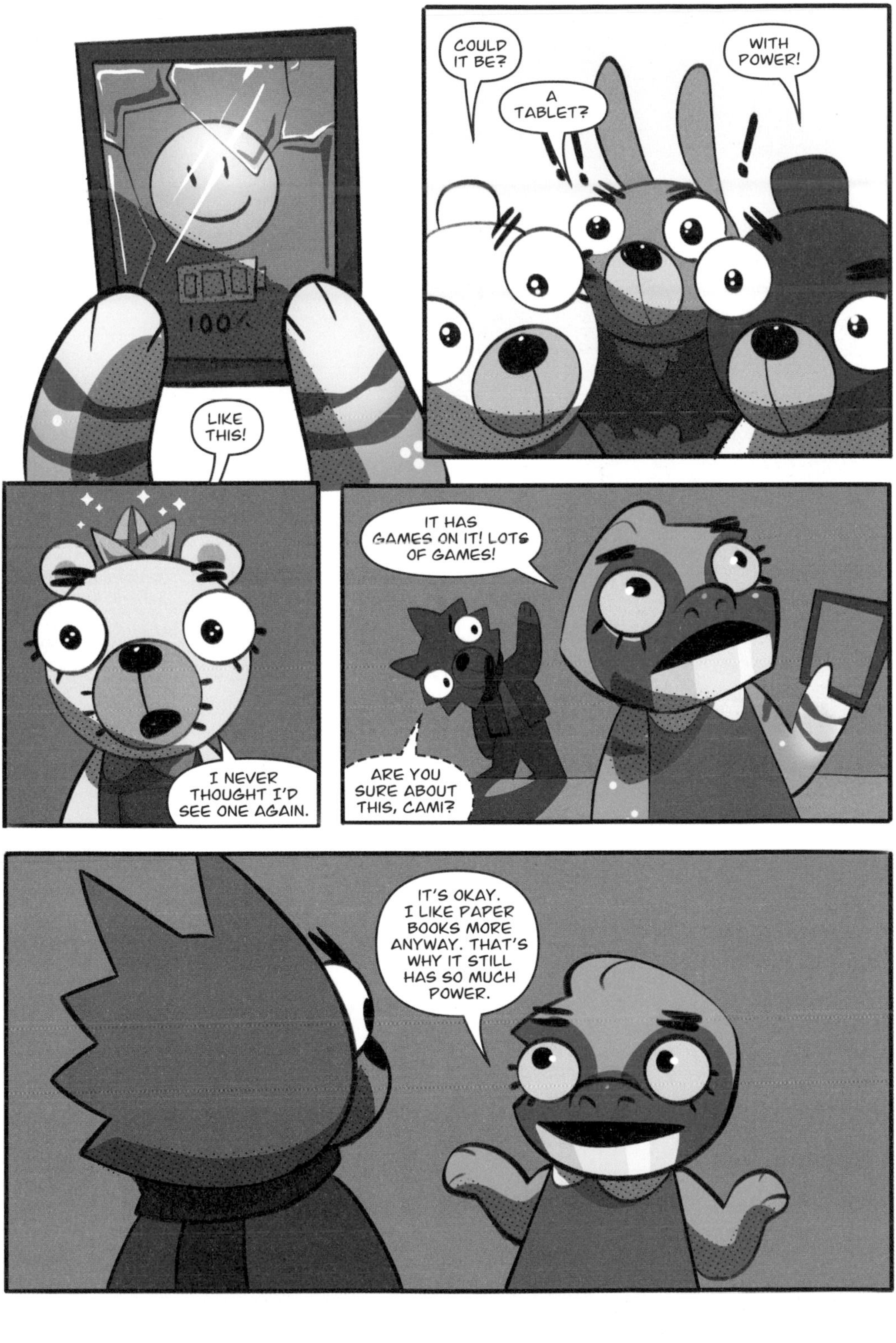
LIKE THIS!
COULD IT BE?
A TABLET?
WITH POWER!
I NEVER THOUGHT I'D SEE ONE AGAIN.
IT HAS GAMES ON IT! LOTS OF GAMES!
ARE YOU SURE ABOUT THIS, CAMI?
IT'S OKAY. I LIKE PAPER BOOKS MORE ANYWAY. THAT'S WHY IT STILL HAS SO MUCH POWER.

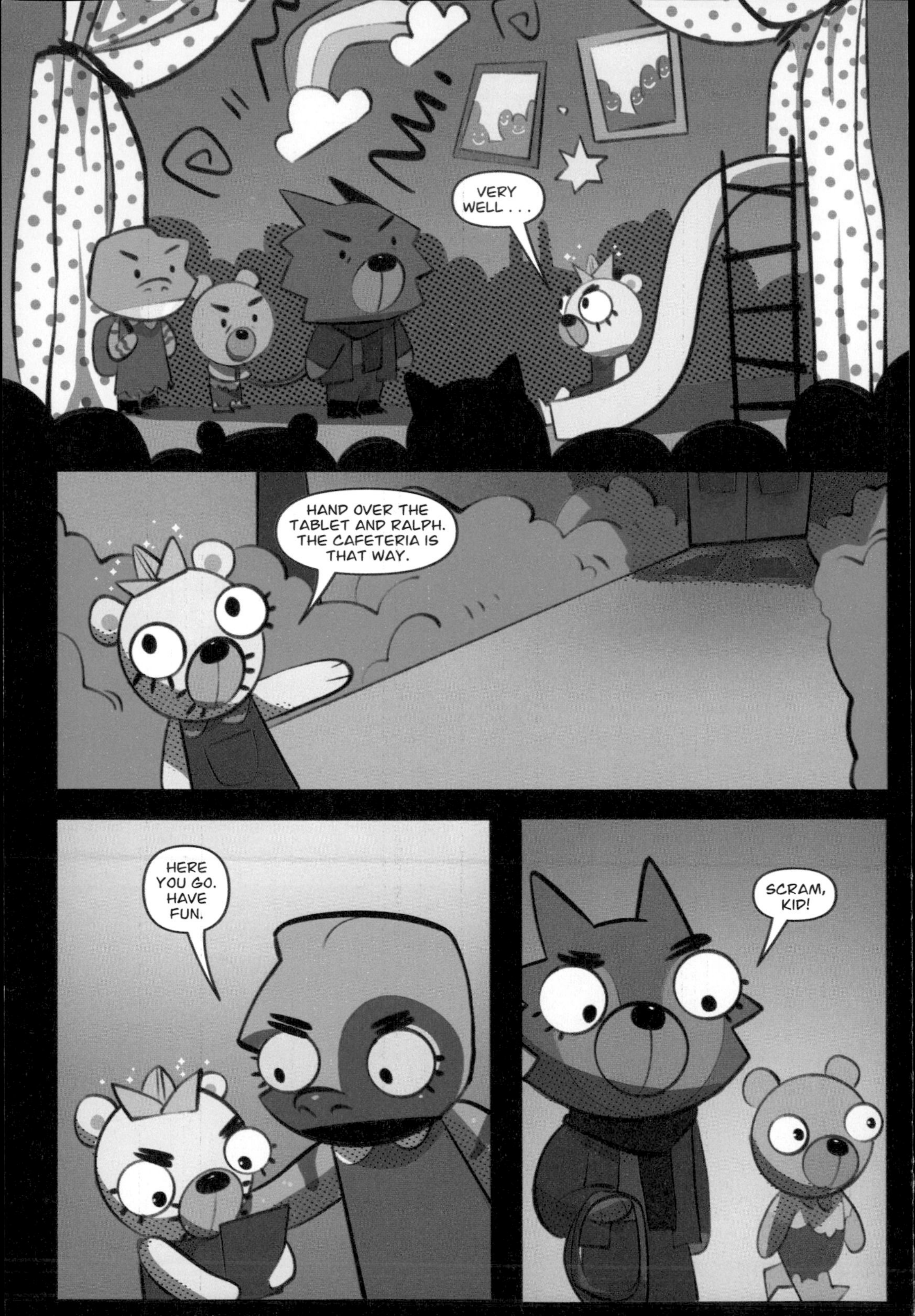
VERY WELL . . .
HAND OVER THE TABLET AND RALPH. THE CAFETERIA IS THAT WAY.
HERE YOU GO. HAVE FUN.
SCRAM, KID!

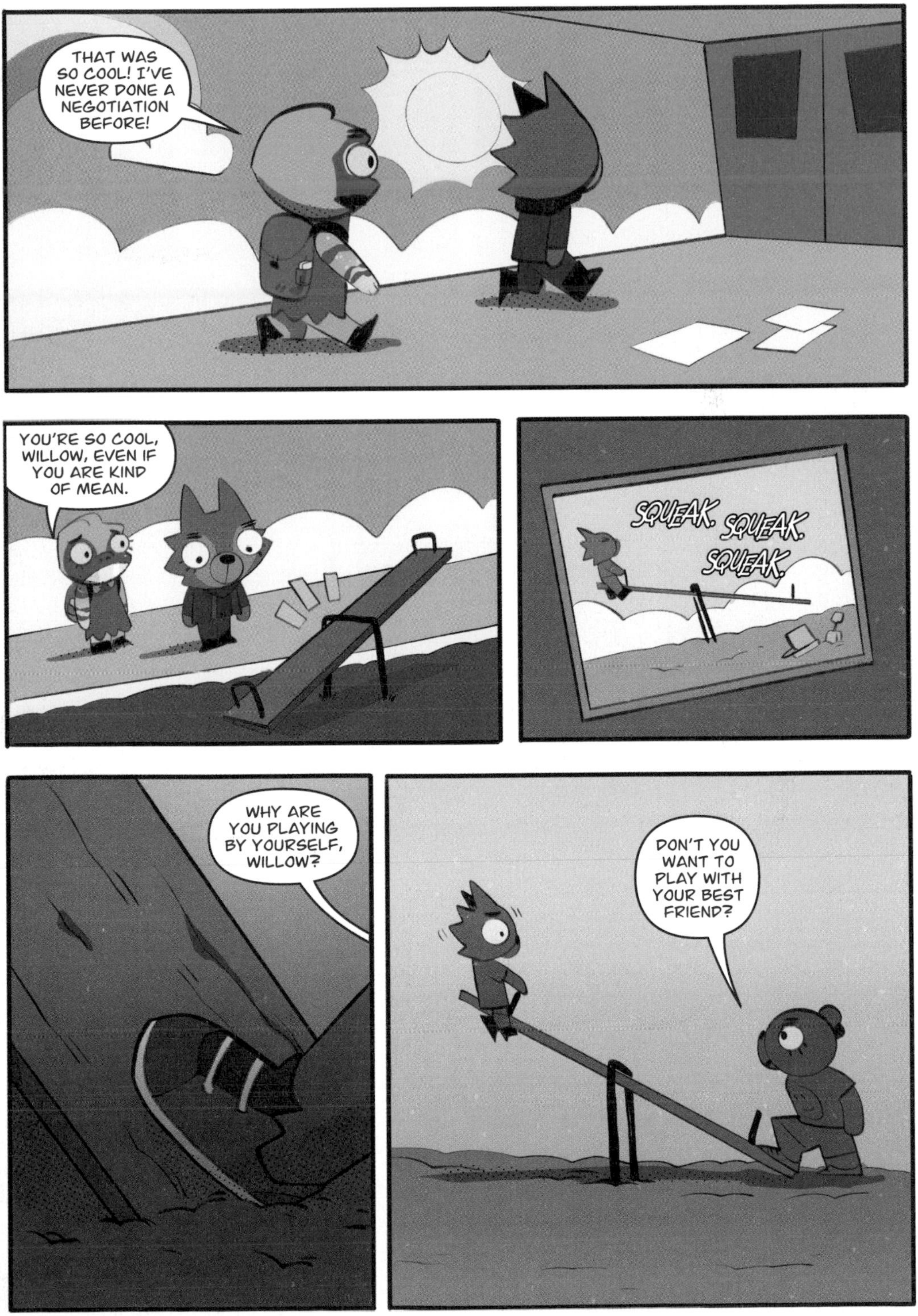

THAT WAS SO COOL! I'VE NEVER DONE A NEGOTIATION BEFORE!
YOU'RE SO COOL, WILLOW, EVEN IF YOU ARE KIND OF MEAN.
SQUEAK. SQUEAK. SQUEAK.
WHY ARE YOU PLAYING BY YOURSELF, WILLOW?
DON'T YOU WANT TO PLAY WITH YOUR BEST FRIEND?

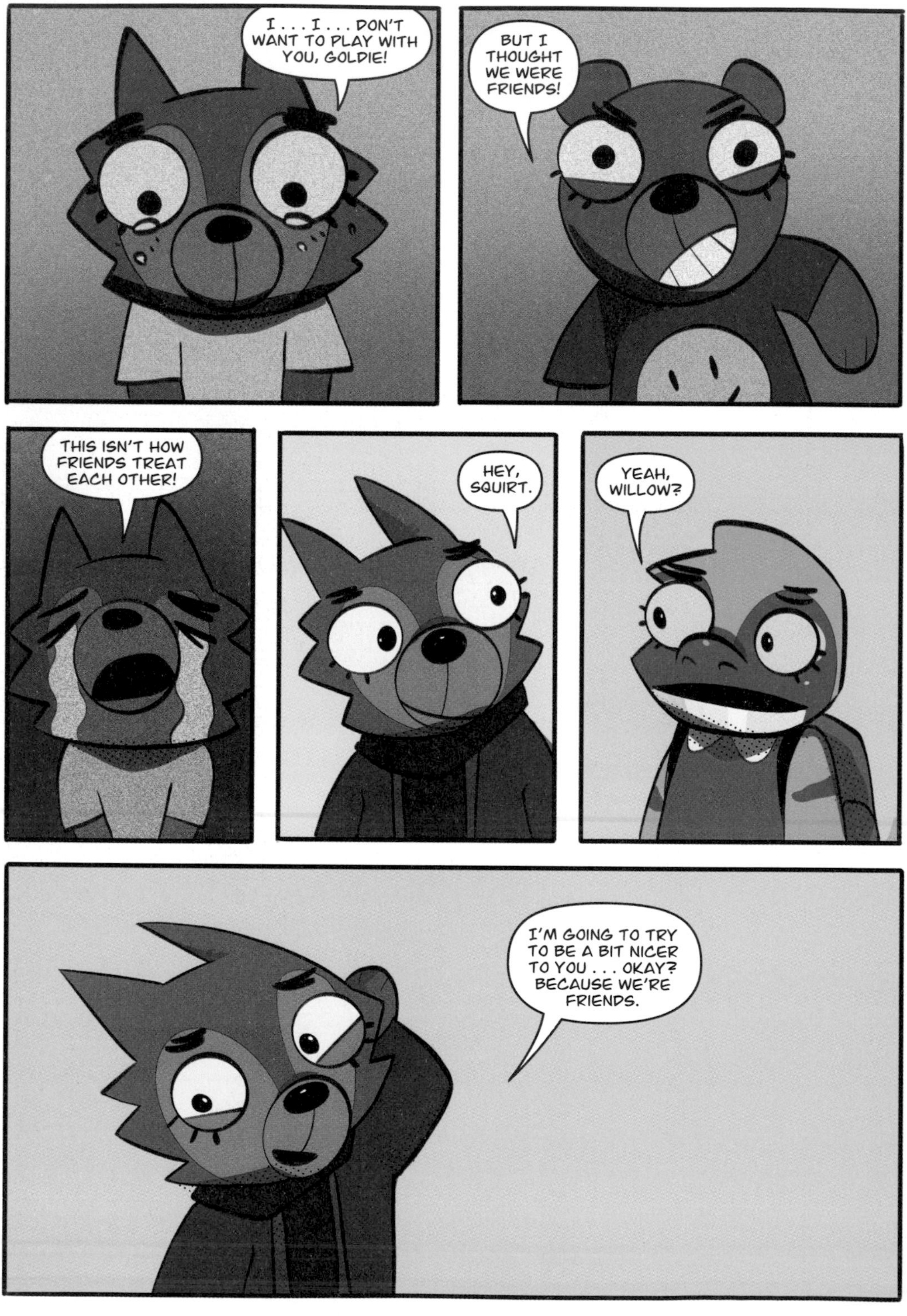
I . . . I . . . DON'T WANT TO PLAY WITH YOU, GOLDIE!
BUT I THOUGHT WE WERE FRIENDS!
THIS ISN'T HOW FRIENDS TREAT EACH OTHER!
HEY, SQUIRT.
YEAH, WILLOW?
I'M GOING TO TRY TO BE A BIT NICER TO YOU . . . OKAY? BECAUSE WE'RE FRIENDS.

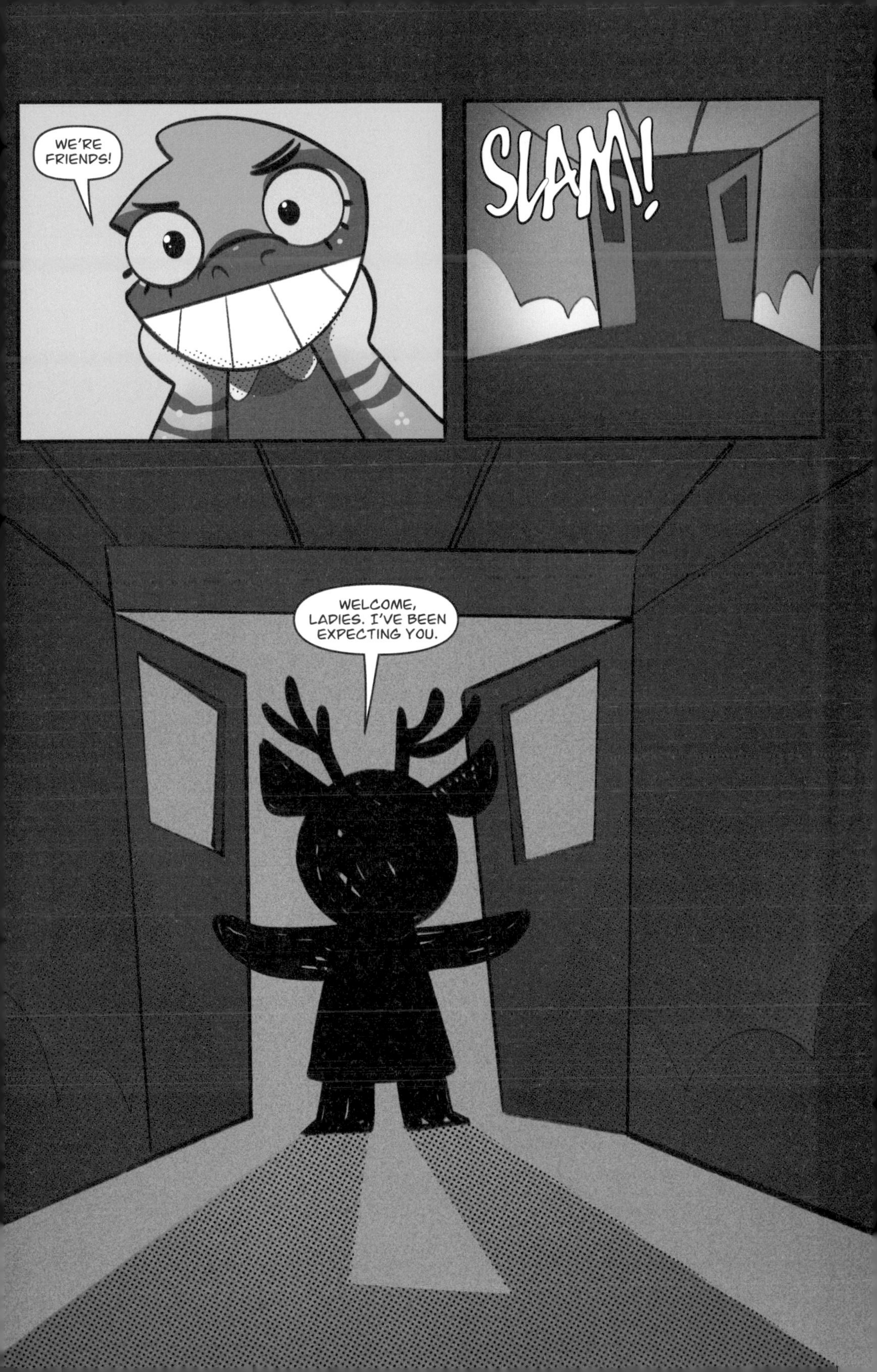
WE'RE FRIENDS!
SLAM!
WELCOME, LADIES. I'VE BEEN EXPECTING YOU.

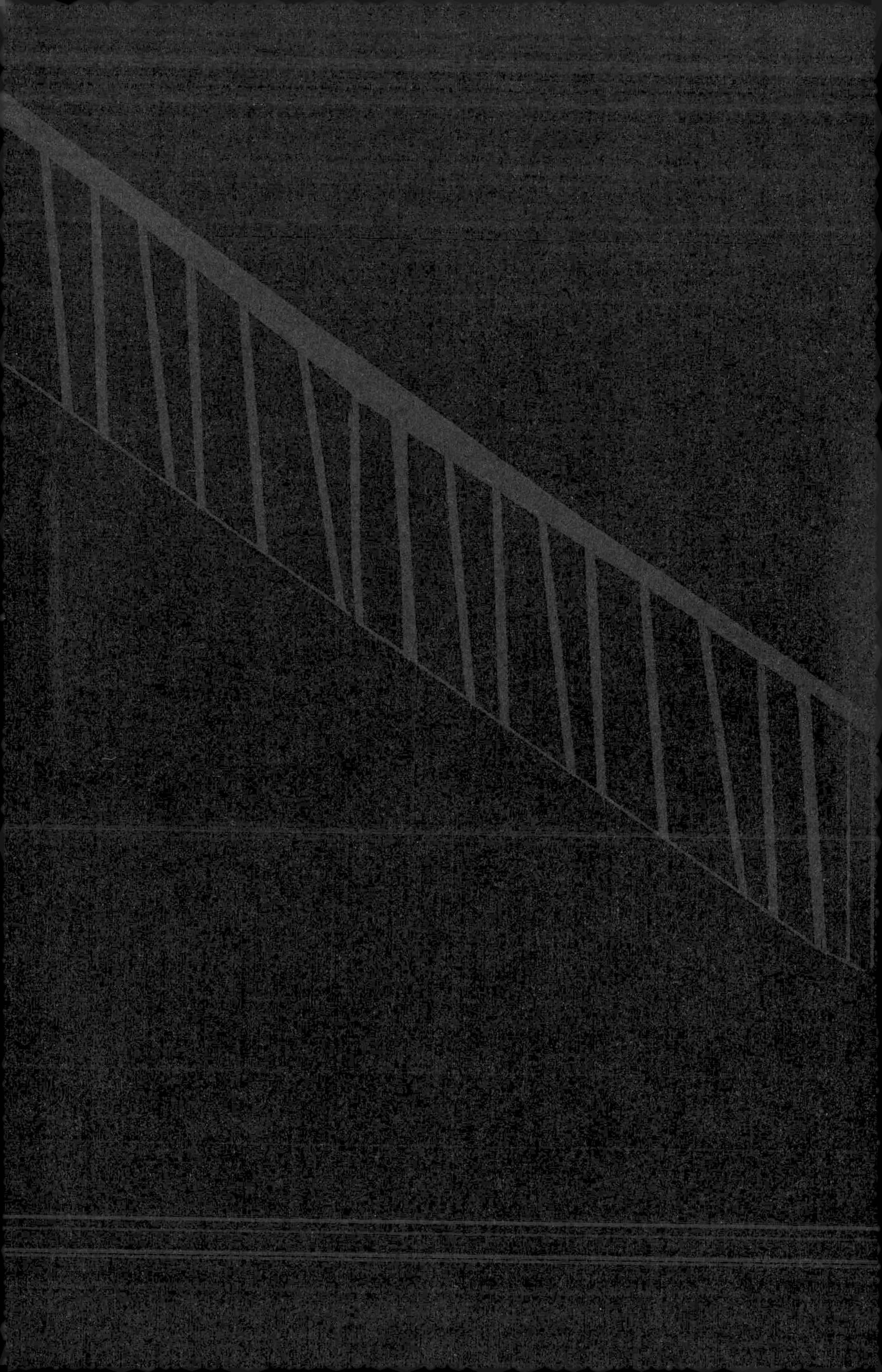

CHAPTER: 4

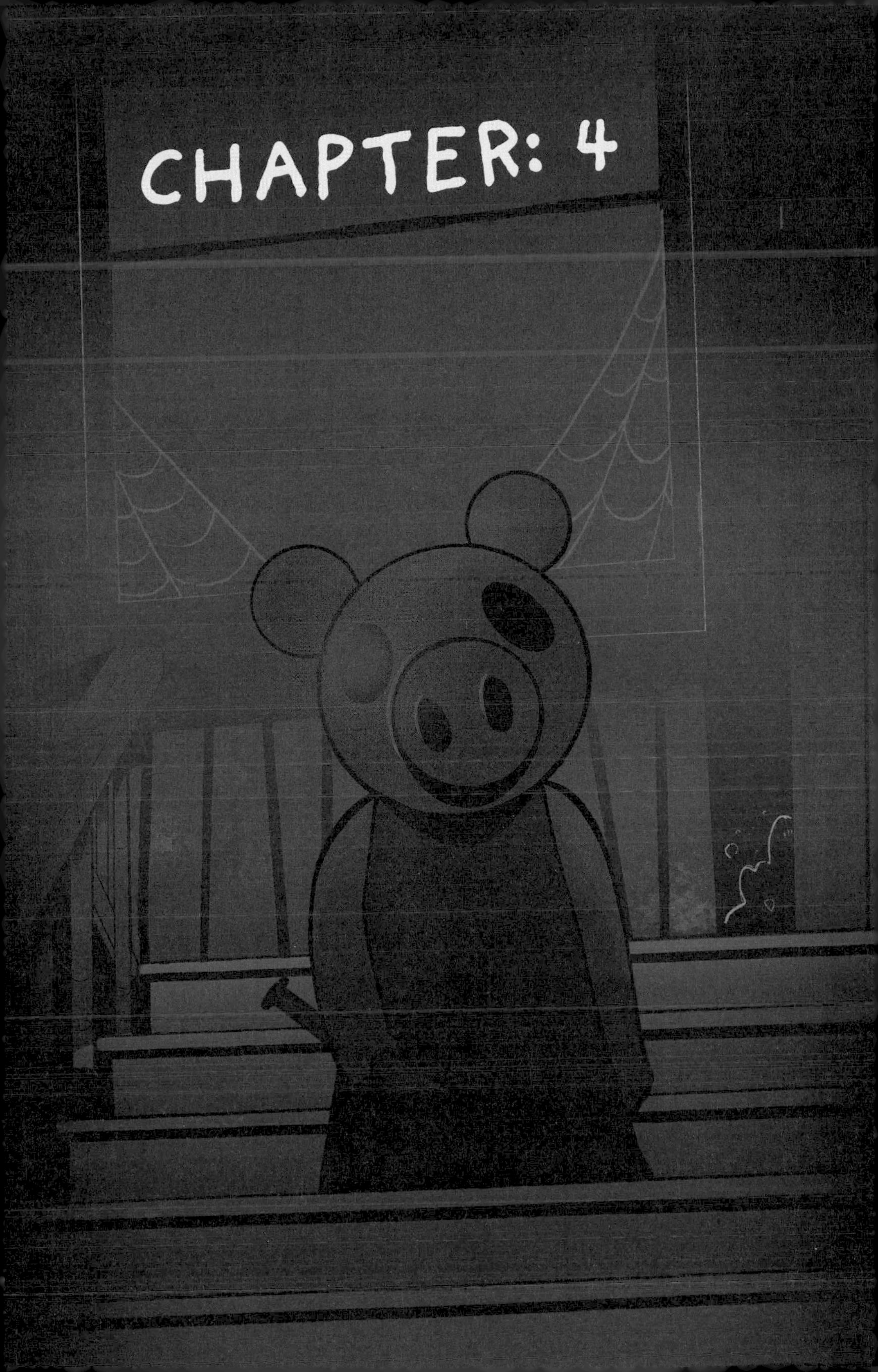

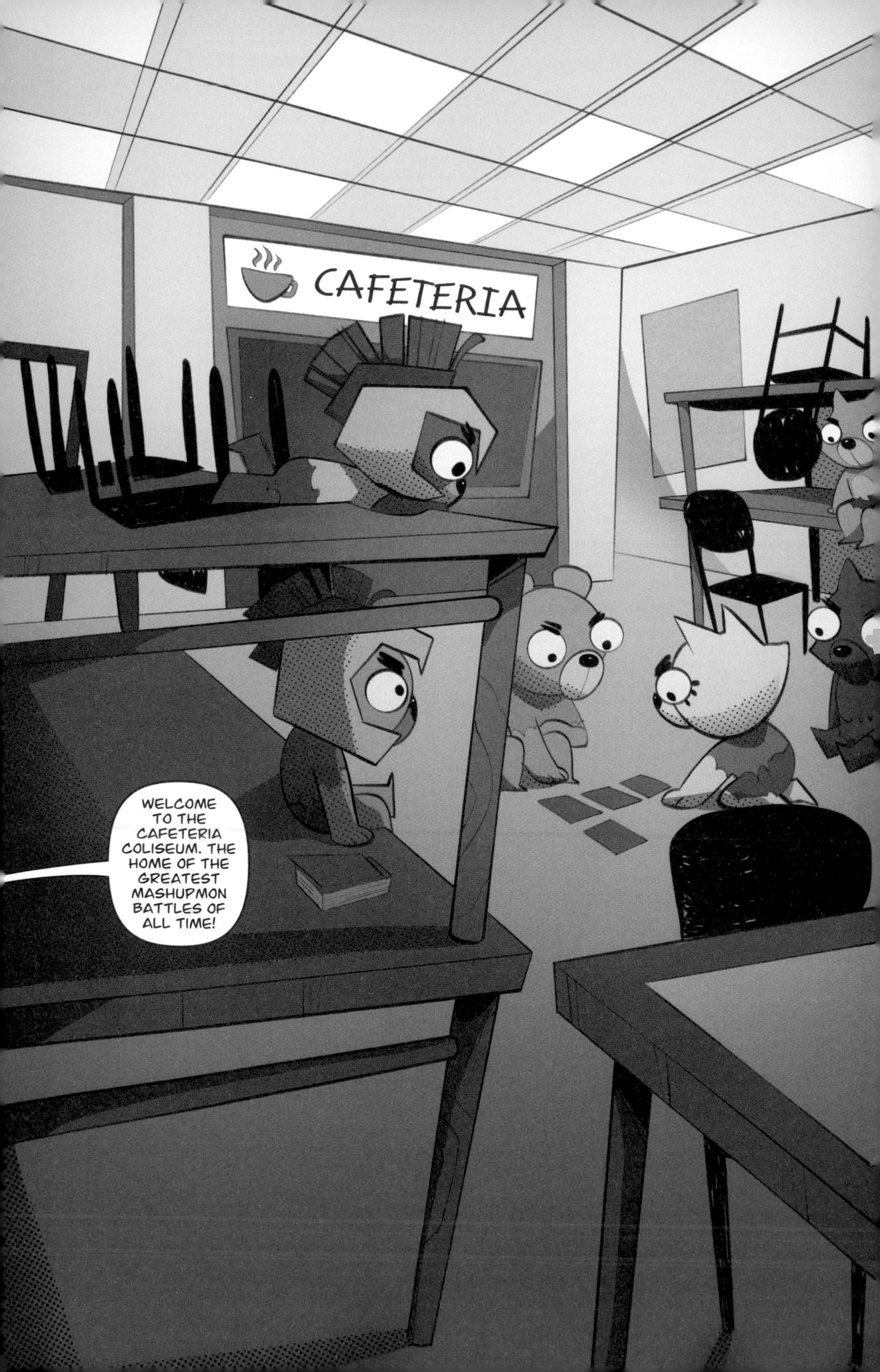
CAFETERIA
WELCOME TO THE CAFETERIA COLISEUM. THE HOME OF THE GREATEST MASHUPMON BATTLES OF ALL TIME!

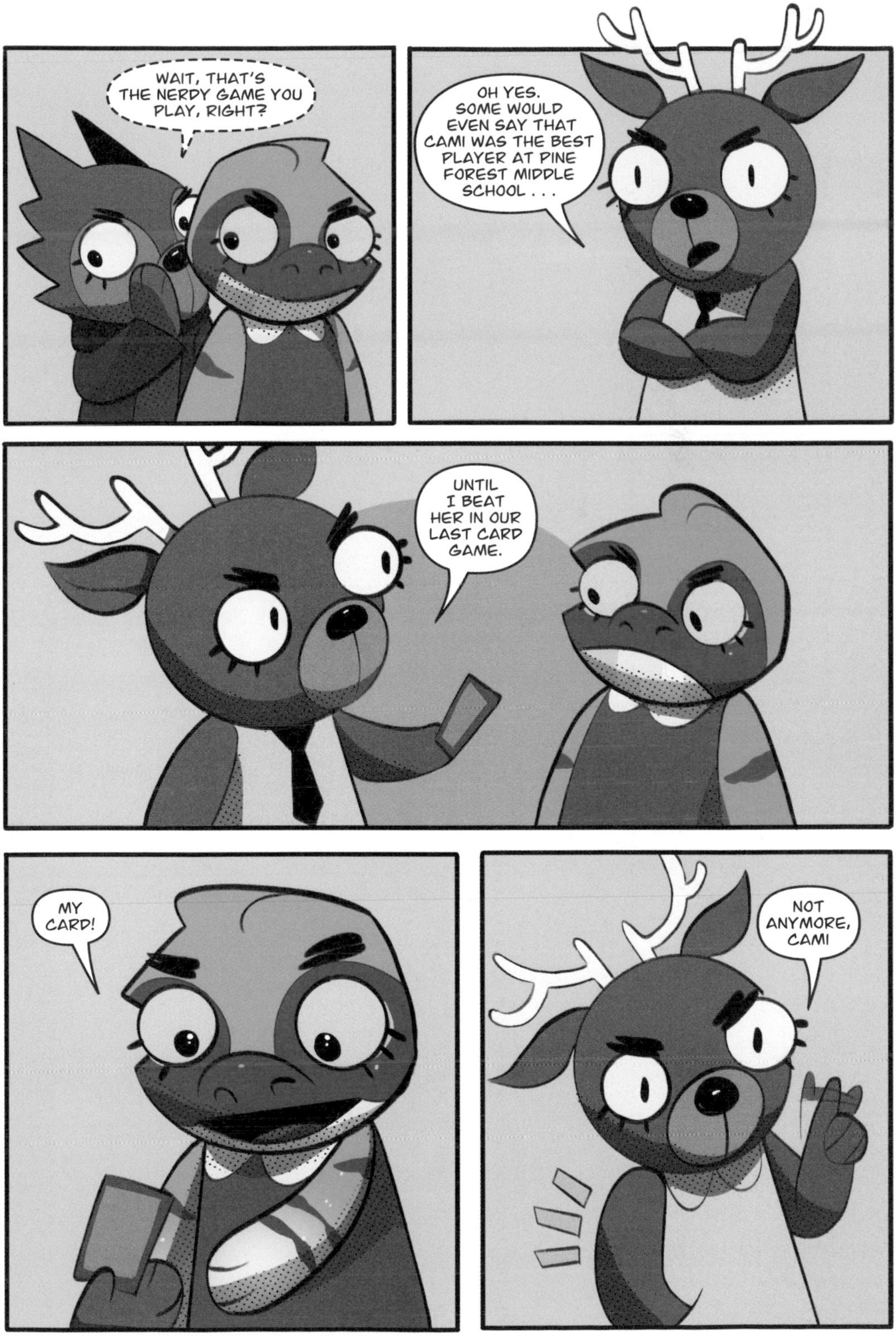
WAIT, THAT'S THE NERDY GAME YOU PLAY, RIGHT?
OH YES. SOME WOULD EVEN SAY THAT CAMI WAS THE BEST PLAYER AT PINE FOREST MIDDLE SCHOOL . . .
UNTIL I BEAT HER IN OUR LAST CARD GAME.
MY CARD!
NOT ANYMORE, CAMI

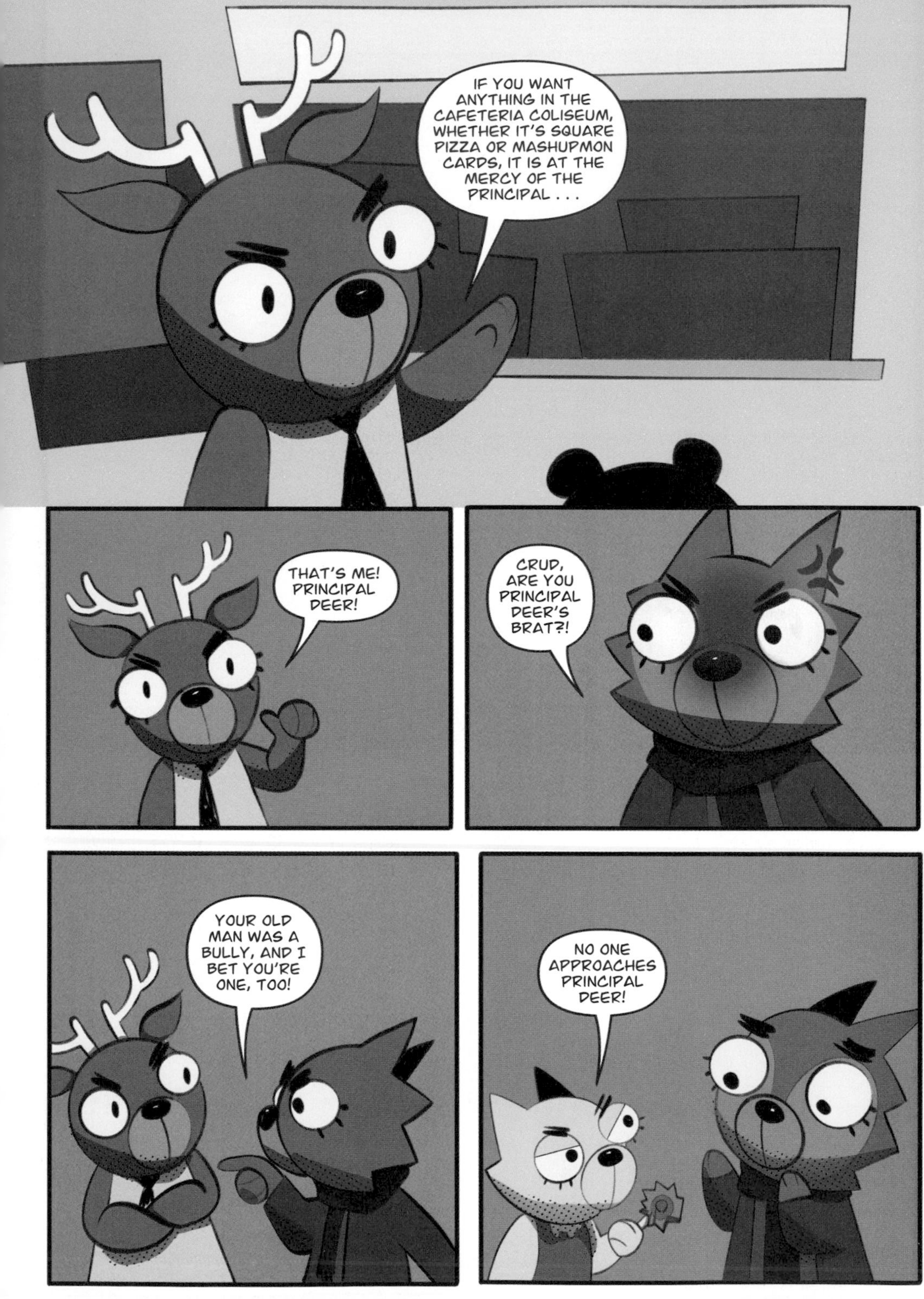
IF YOU WANT ANYTHING IN THE CAFETERIA COLISEUM, WHETHER IT'S SQUARE PIZZA OR MASHUPMON CARDS, IT IS AT THE MERCY OF THE PRINCIPAL . . .
THAT'S ME! PRINCIPAL DEER!
CRUD, ARE YOU PRINCIPAL DEER'S BRAT?!
YOUR OLD MAN WAS A BULLY, AND I BET YOU'RE ONE, TOO!
NO ONE APPROACHES PRINCIPAL DEER!

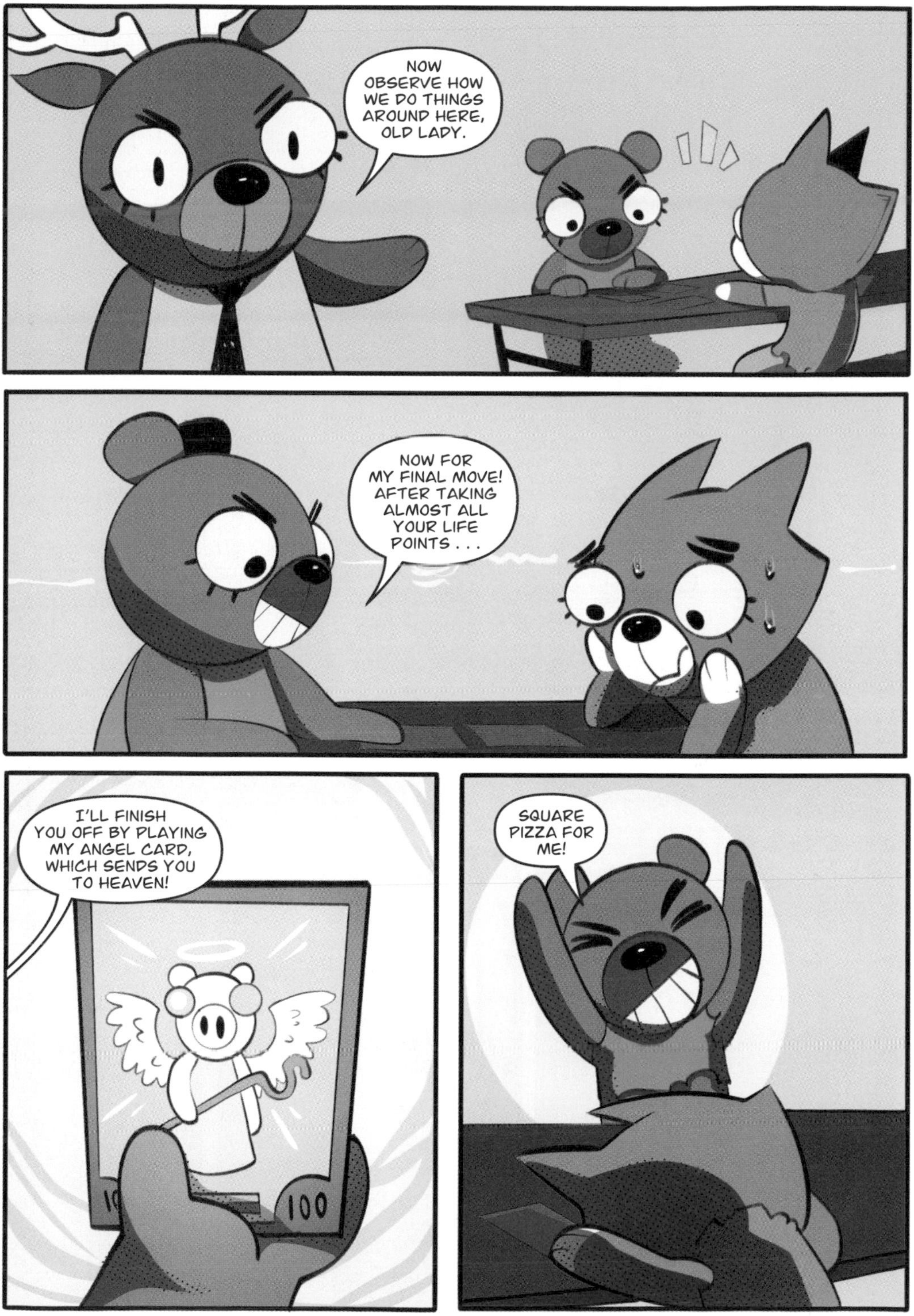
NOW OBSERVE HOW WE DO THINGS AROUND HERE, OLD LADY.
NOW FOR MY FINAL MOVE! AFTER TAKING ALMOST ALL YOUR LIFE POINTS . . .
I'LL FINISH YOU OFF BY PLAYING MY ANGEL CARD, WHICH SENDS YOU TO HEAVEN!
100
SQUARE PIZZA FOR ME!

YOU LOST.

YOU KNOW THE PUNISHMENT FOR LOSING.

NO! PLEASE! HAVE MERCY, PRINCIPAL DEER!

CAFETERIA

OOF!

LET ME OUT! PLEASE, PRINCIPAL DEER!

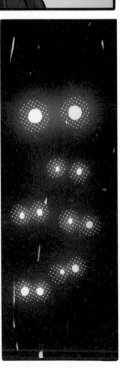

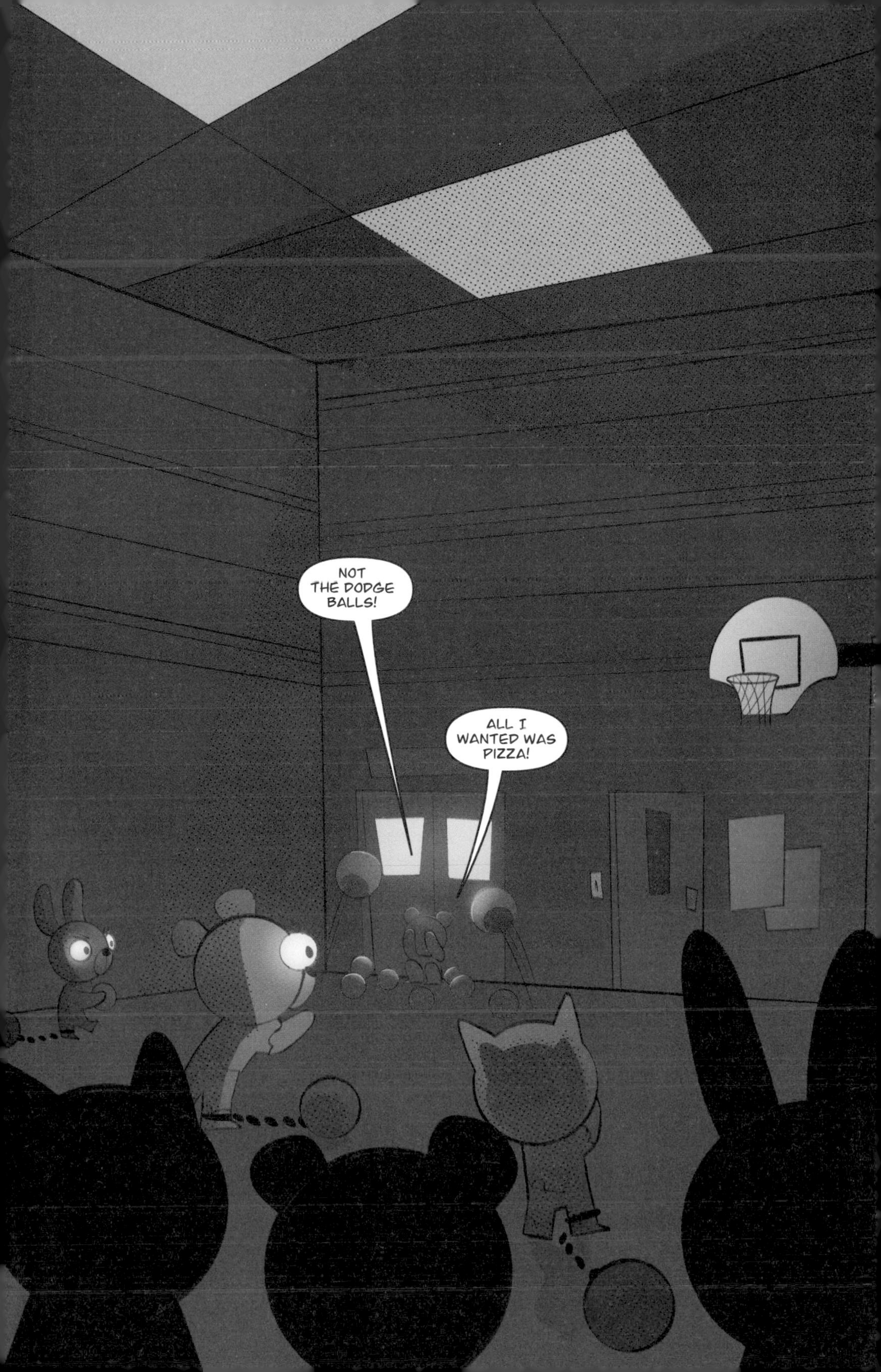
NOT THE DODGE BALLS!
ALL I WANTED WAS PIZZA!

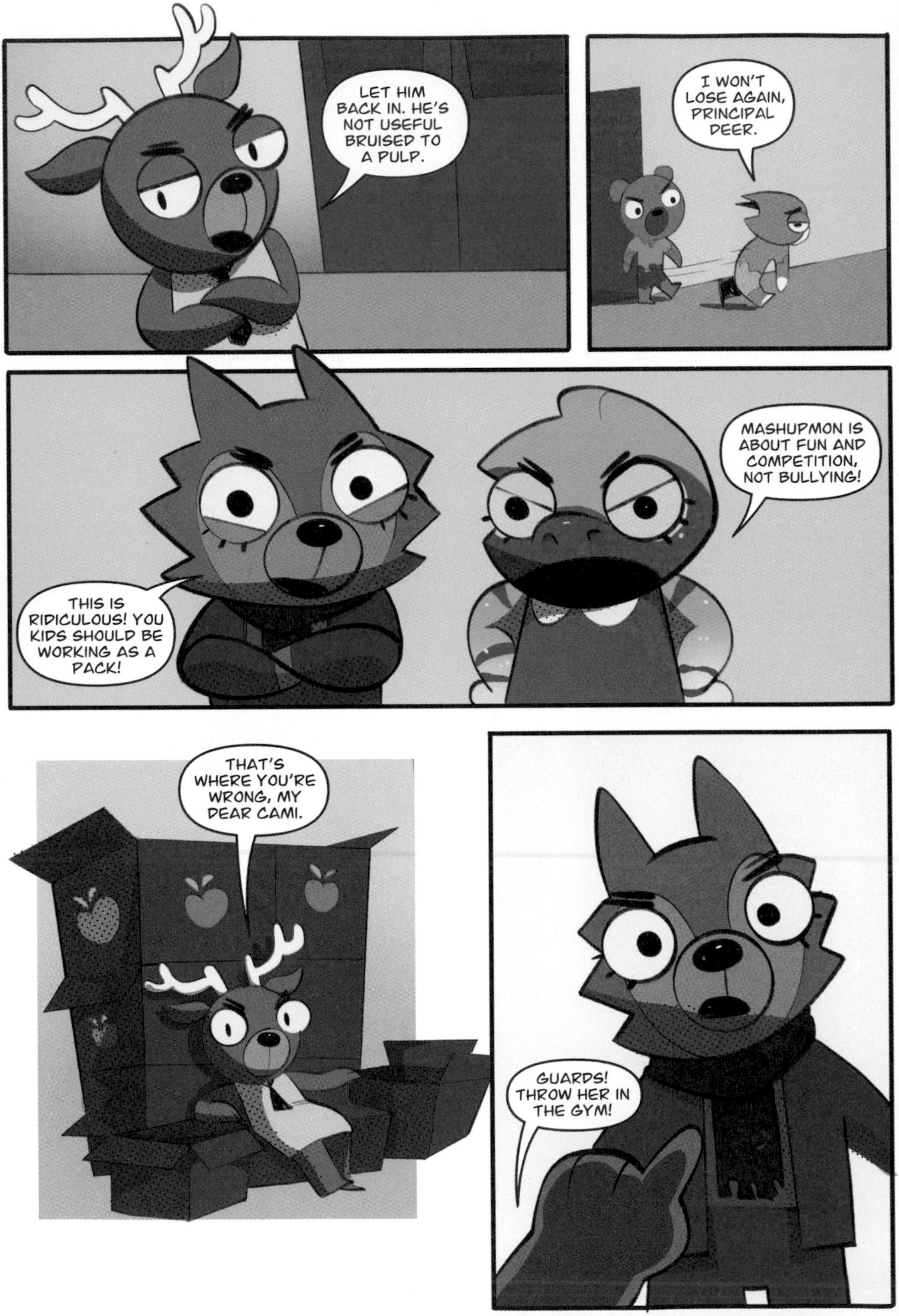
LET HIM BACK IN. HE'S NOT USEFUL BRUISED TO A PULP.
I WON'T LOSE AGAIN, PRINCIPAL DEER.
MASHUPMON IS ABOUT FUN AND COMPETITION, NOT BULLYING!
THIS IS RIDICULOUS! YOU KIDS SHOULD BE WORKING AS A PACK!
THAT'S WHERE YOU'RE WRONG, MY DEAR CAMI.
GUARDS! THROW HER IN THE GYM!

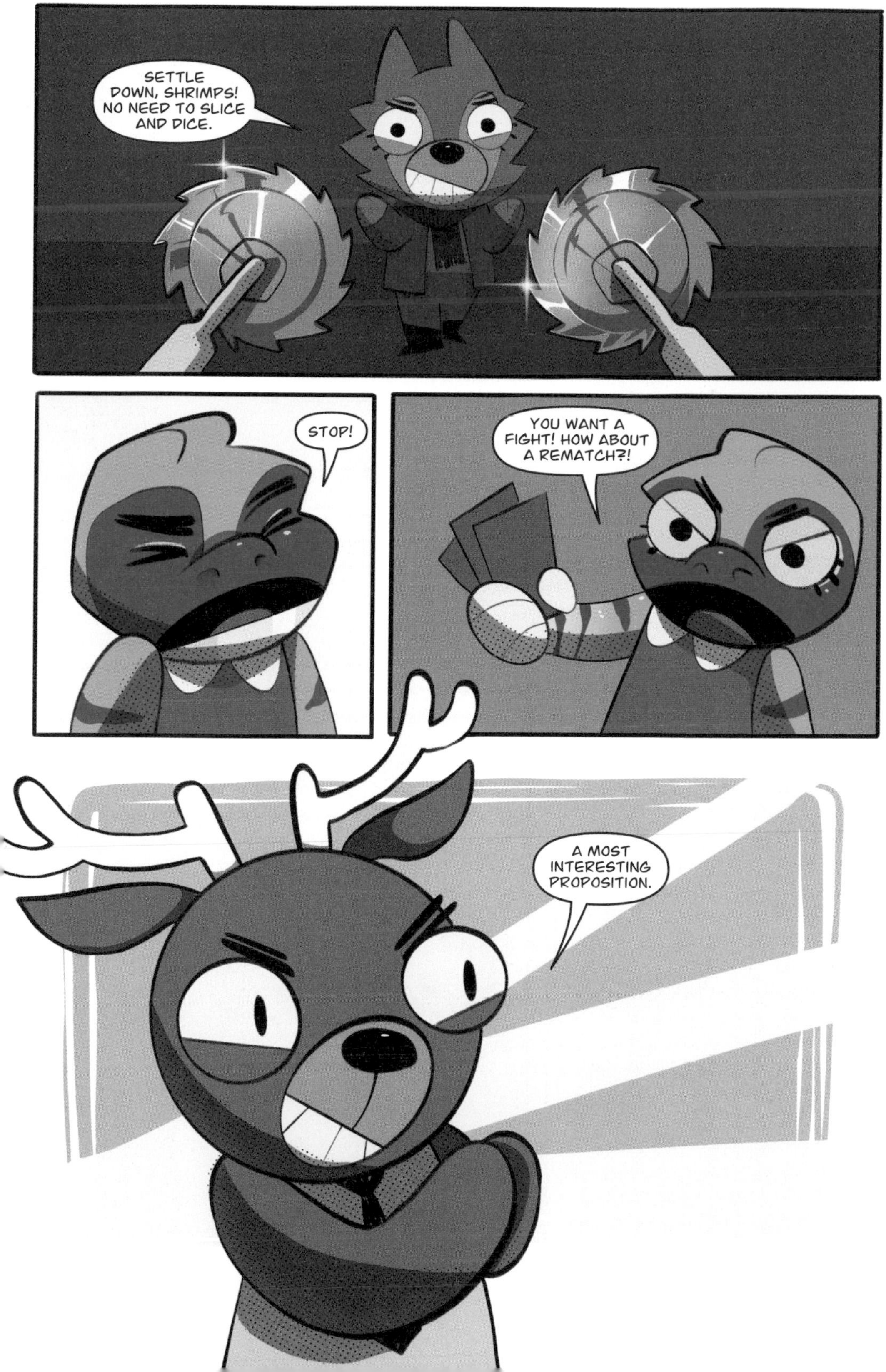
SETTLE DOWN, SHRIMPS! NO NEED TO SLICE AND DICE.
STOP!
YOU WANT A FIGHT! HOW ABOUT A REMATCH?!
A MOST INTERESTING PROPOSITION.

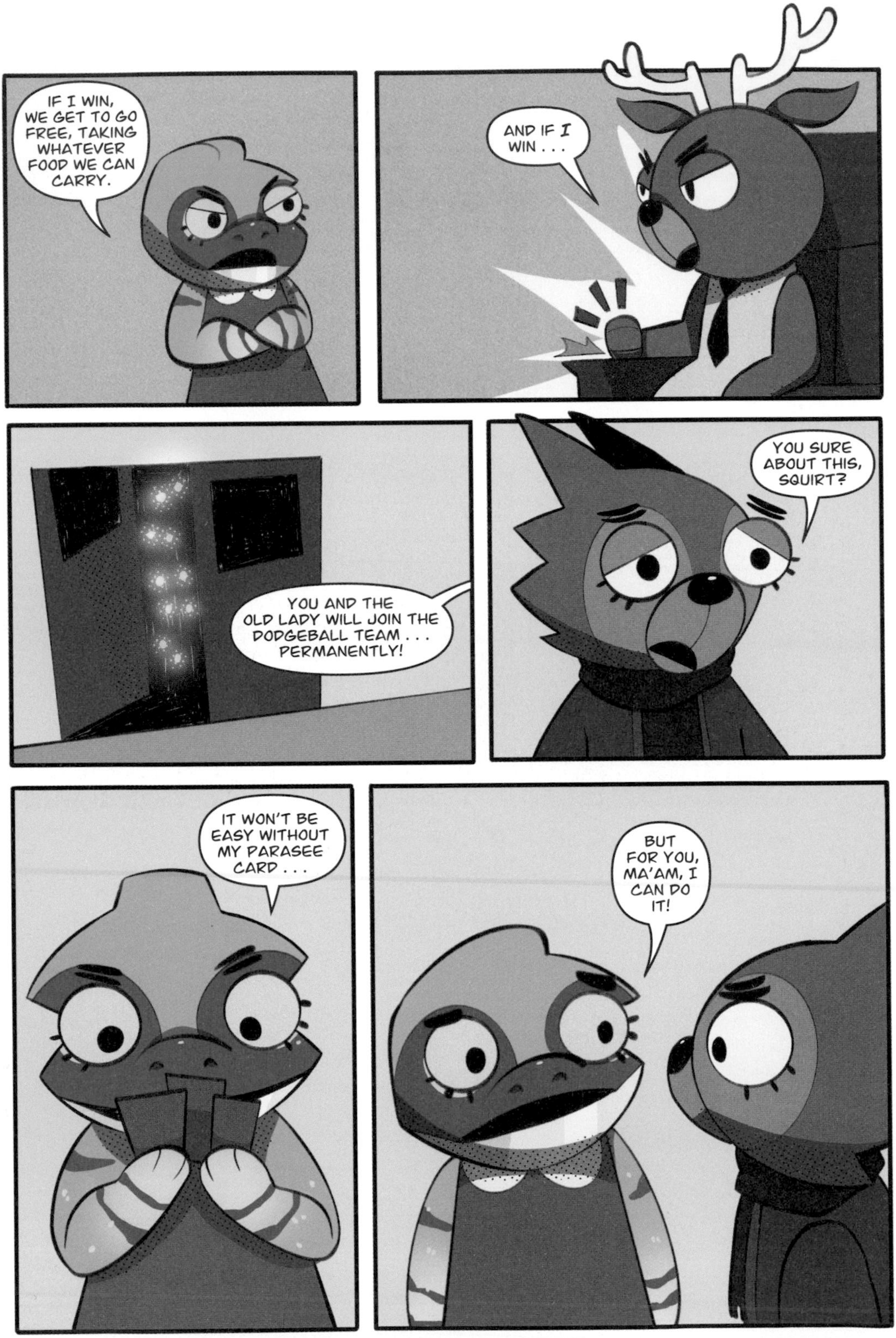
IF I WIN, WE GET TO GO FREE, TAKING WHATEVER FOOD WE CAN CARRY.
AND IF I WIN . . .
YOU AND THE OLD LADY WILL JOIN THE DODGEBALL TEAM . . . PERMANENTLY!
YOU SURE ABOUT THIS, SQUIRT?
IT WON'T BE EASY WITHOUT MY PARASEE CARD . . .
BUT FOR YOU, MA'AM, I CAN DO IT!

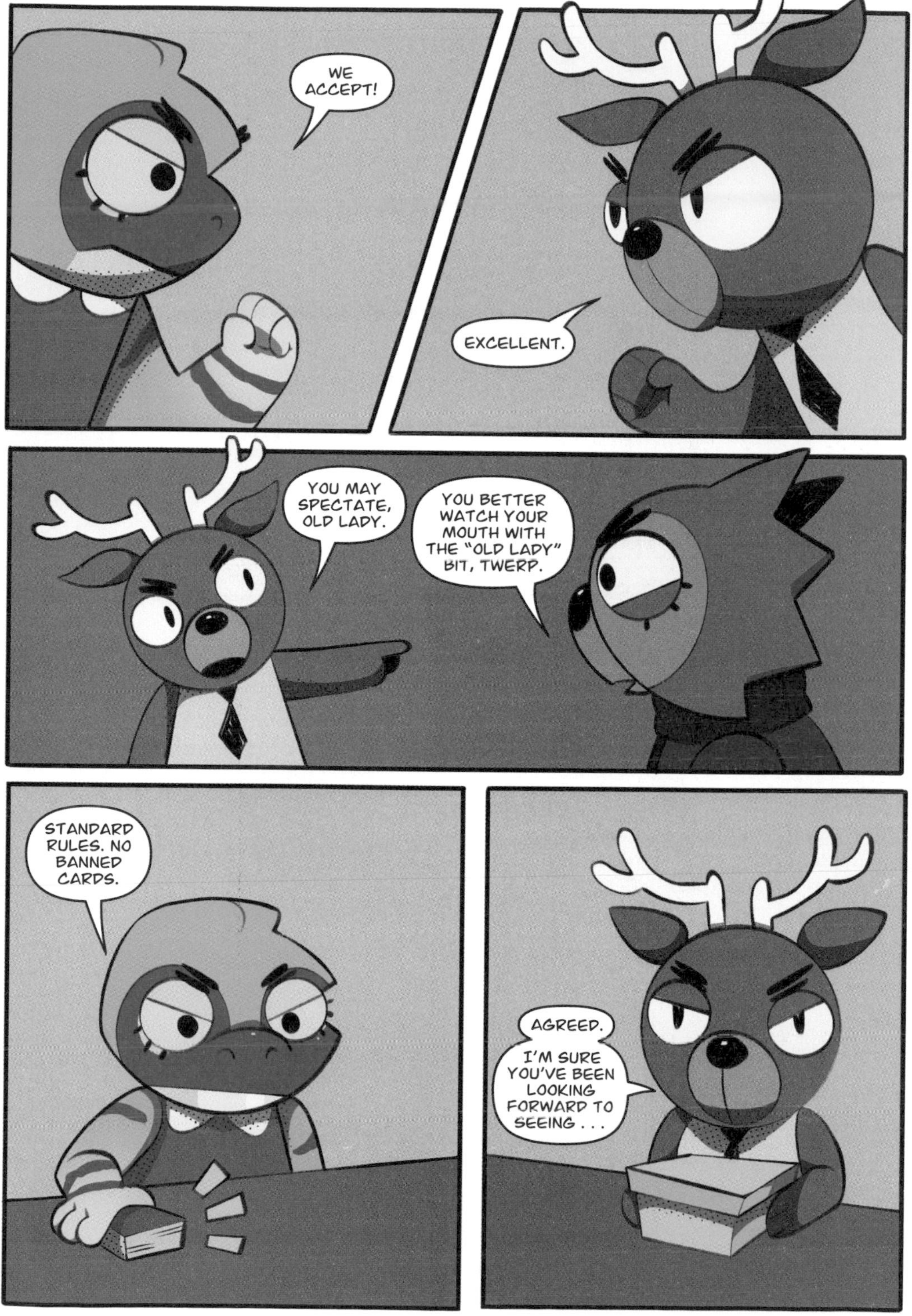
WE ACCEPT!
EXCELLENT.
YOU MAY SPECTATE, OLD LADY.
YOU BETTER WATCH YOUR MOUTH WITH THE "OLD LADY" BIT, TWERP.
STANDARD RULES. NO BANNED CARDS.
AGREED.
I'M SURE YOU'VE BEEN LOOKING FORWARD TO SEEING . . .

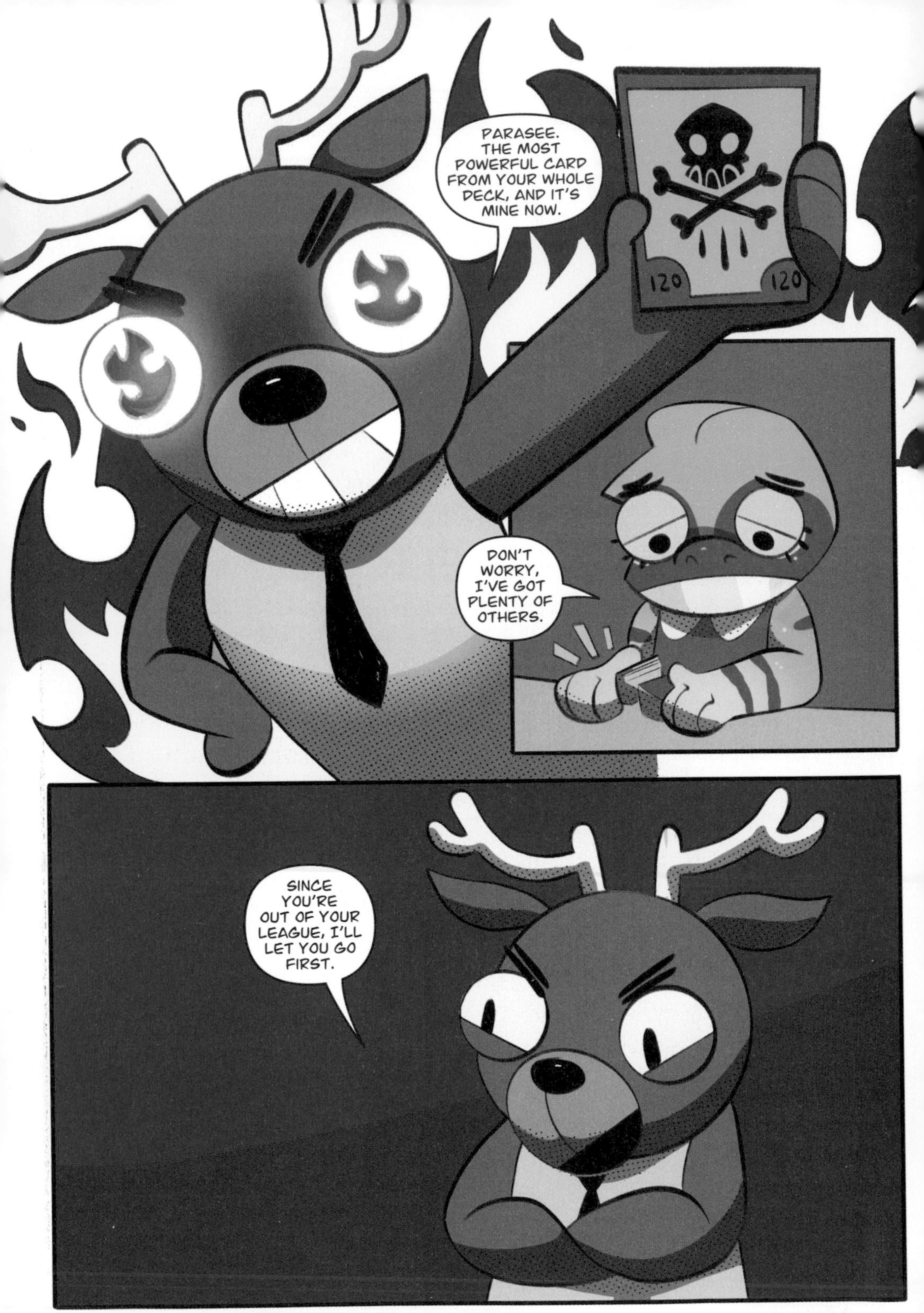
PARASEE. THE MOST POWERFUL CARD FROM YOUR WHOLE DECK, AND IT'S MINE NOW.
120
120
DON'T WORRY, I'VE GOT PLENTY OF OTHERS.
SINCE YOU'RE OUT OF YOUR LEAGUE, I'LL LET YOU GO FIRST.

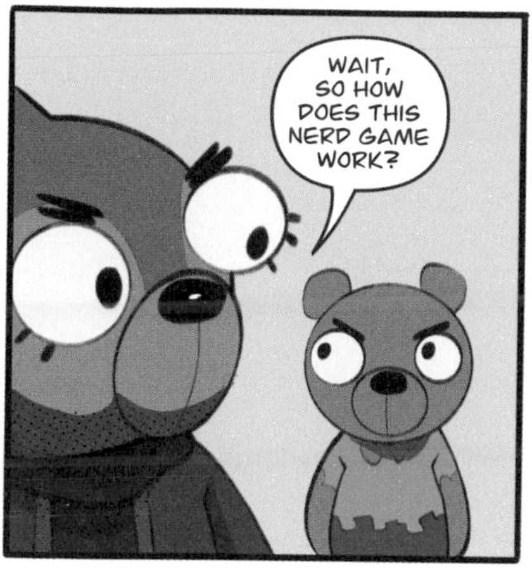
WAIT, SO HOW DOES THIS NERD GAME WORK?

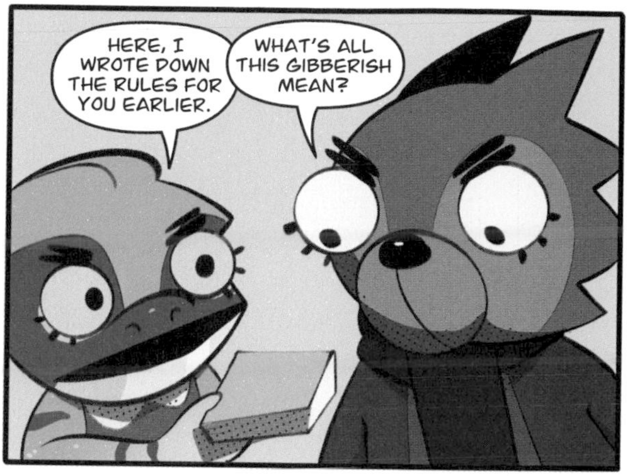
HERE, I WROTE DOWN THE RULES FOR YOU EARLIER.
WHAT'S ALL THIS GIBBERISH MEAN?

Survival Tip for Middle School #5 - How to Play MashUpMon

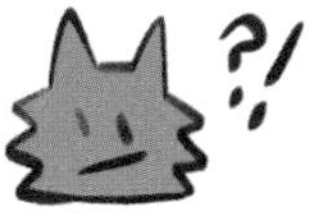
?!

MashUpMon is the greatest game ever! There are over 10,000 different cards and you can build your deck in all sorts of ways. I mainly use poison type cards, because you can use long-term status effects to slowly wear down your opponent, even if you aren't the most powerful player. I can't do that without my Parasee card, though. The important thing in MashUpMon is that powerful cards are cool, but they are easily trumped by trap cards. Trap cards have status effects that can totally change the way the game is played, like the Pot of Weeds. Each attack takes energy cards.

The more powerful the attack, the more energy needed. Individual cards are important, but players need to have a strong deck to win.

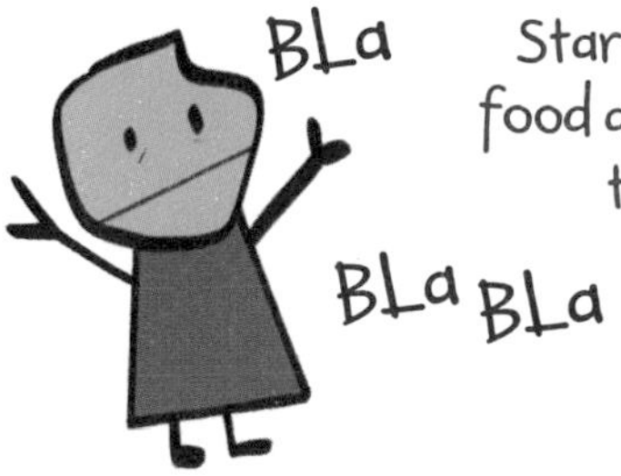
BLa
BLa BLa

Start grabbing food and be ready to run!

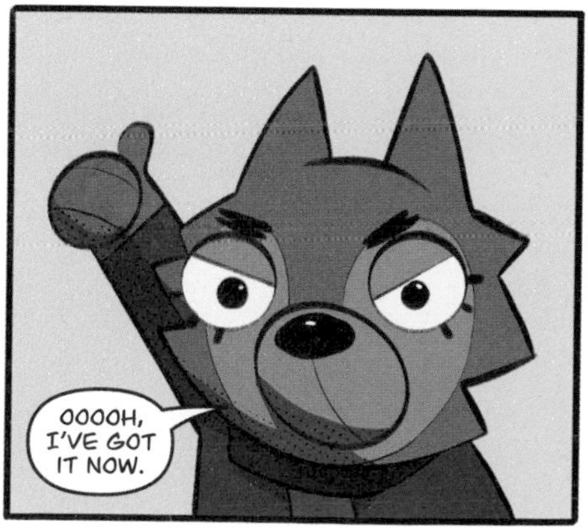
OOOOH, I'VE GOT IT NOW.

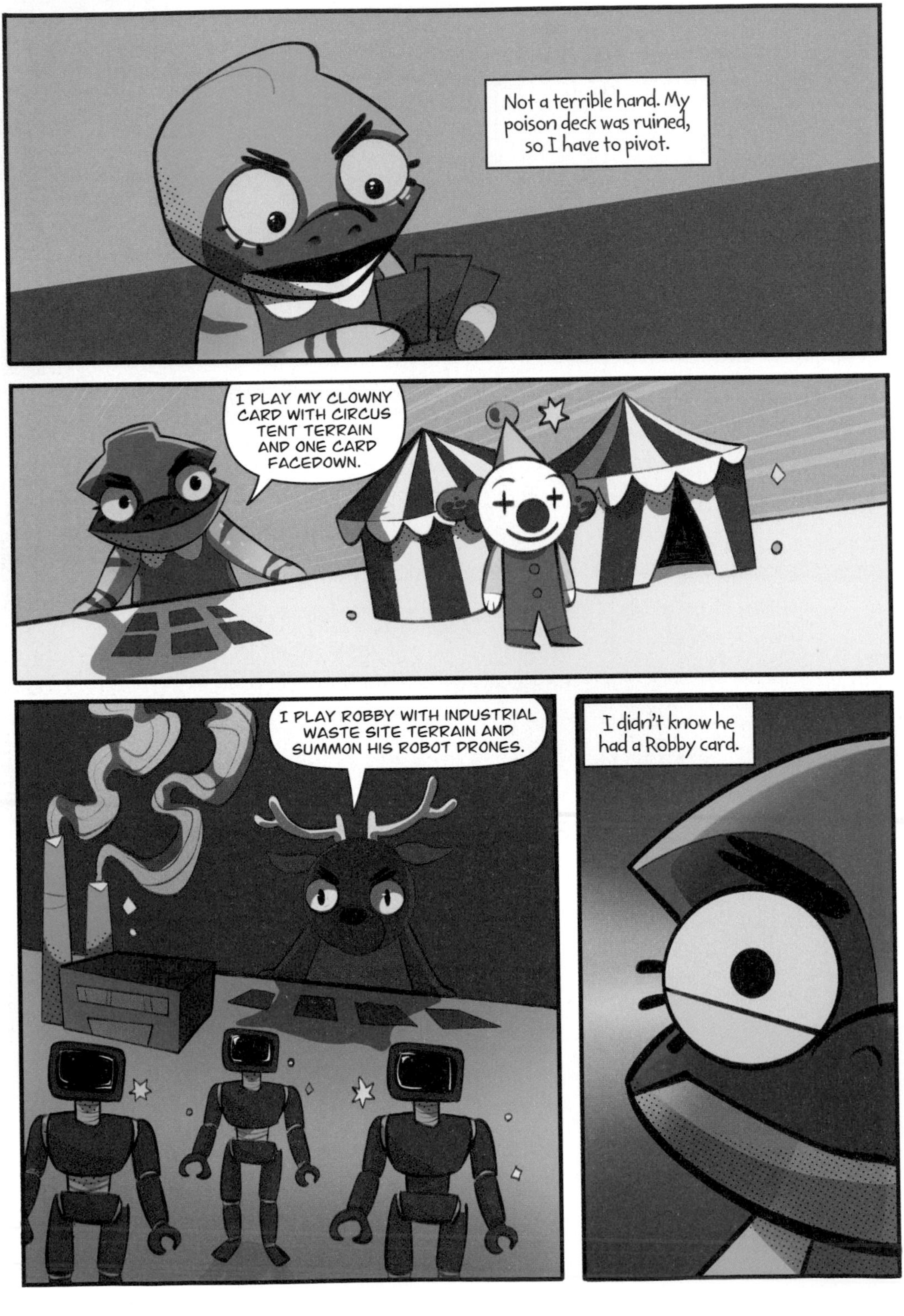

Not a terrible hand. My poison deck was ruined, so I have to pivot.
I PLAY MY CLOWNY CARD WITH CIRCUS TENT TERRAIN AND ONE CARD FACEDOWN.
I PLAY ROBBY WITH INDUSTRIAL WASTE SITE TERRAIN AND SUMMON HIS ROBOT DRONES.
I didn't know he had a Robby card.

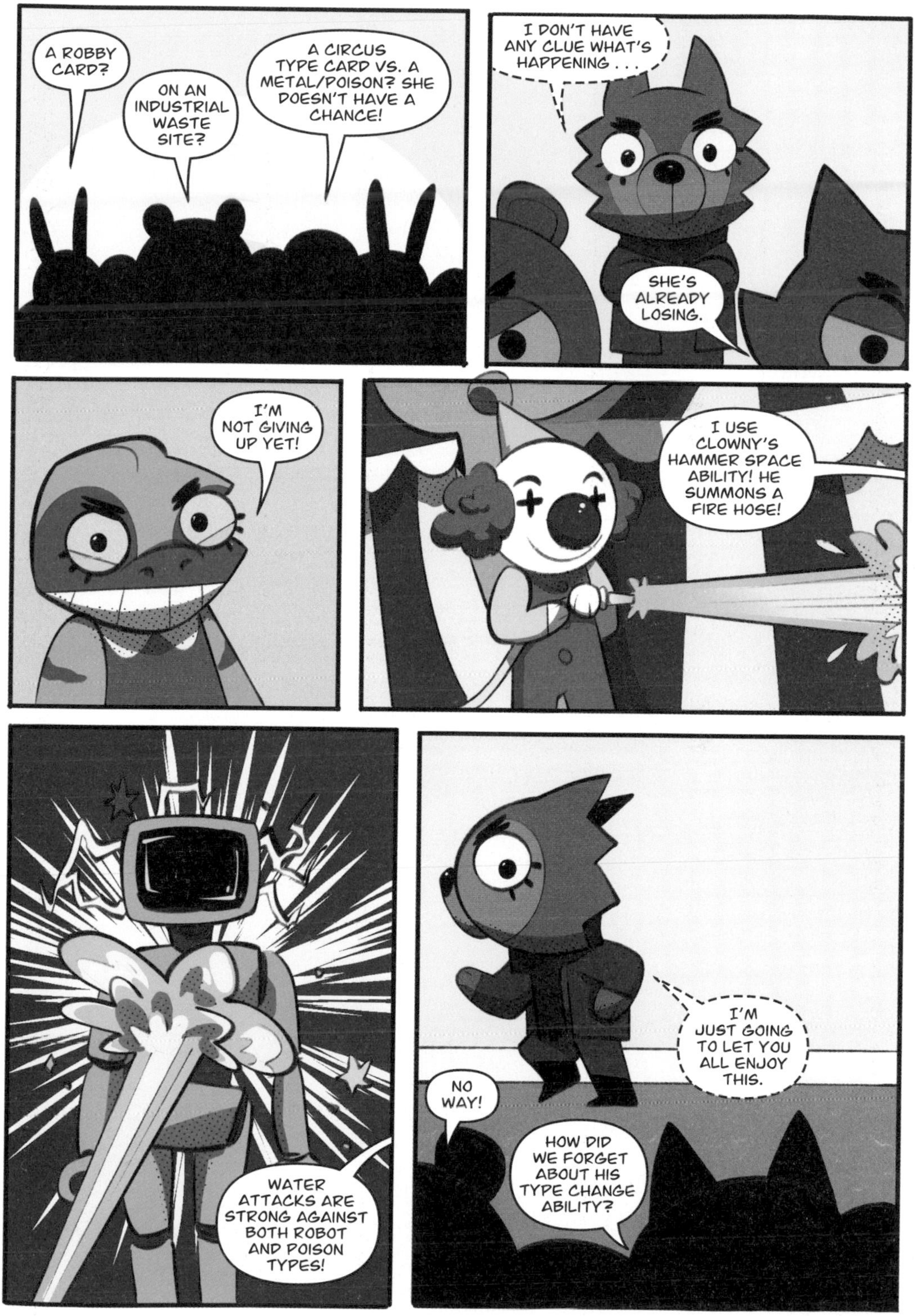
A ROBBY CARD?
ON AN INDUSTRIAL WASTE SITE?
A CIRCUS TYPE CARD VS. A METAL/POISON? SHE DOESN'T HAVE A CHANCE!
I DON'T HAVE ANY CLUE WHAT'S HAPPENING . . .
SHE'S ALREADY LOSING.
I'M NOT GIVING UP YET!
I USE CLOWNY'S HAMMER SPACE ABILITY! HE SUMMONS A FIRE HOSE!
WATER ATTACKS ARE STRONG AGAINST BOTH ROBOT AND POISON TYPES!
I'M JUST GOING TO LET YOU ALL ENJOY THIS.
NO WAY!
HOW DID WE FORGET ABOUT HIS TYPE CHANGE ABILITY?

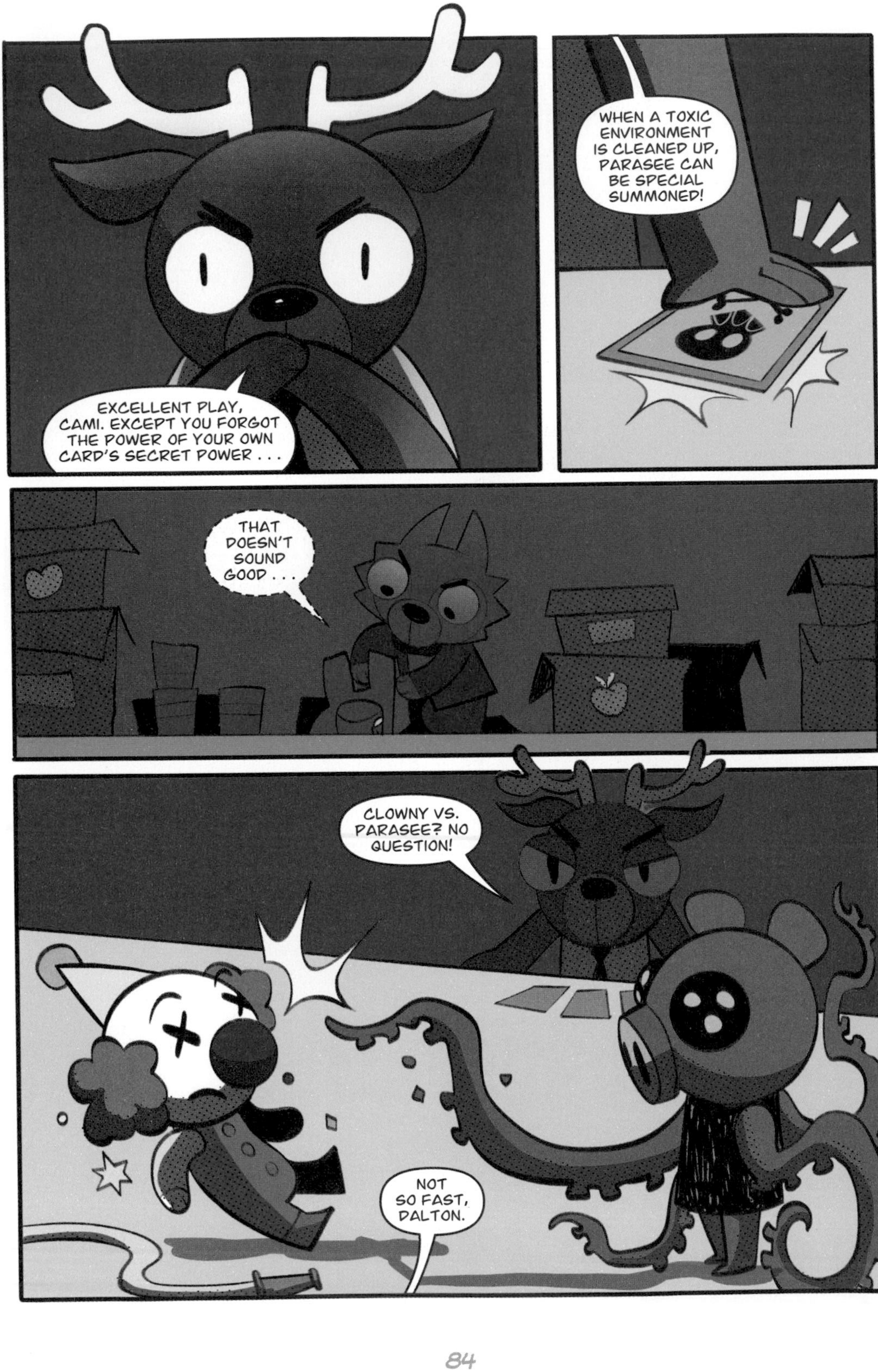
EXCELLENT PLAY, CAMI. EXCEPT YOU FORGOT THE POWER OF YOUR OWN CARD'S SECRET POWER . . .
WHEN A TOXIC ENVIRONMENT IS CLEANED UP, PARASEE CAN BE SPECIAL SUMMONED!
THAT DOESN'T SOUND GOOD . . .
CLOWNY VS. PARASEE? NO QUESTION!
NOT SO FAST, DALTON.

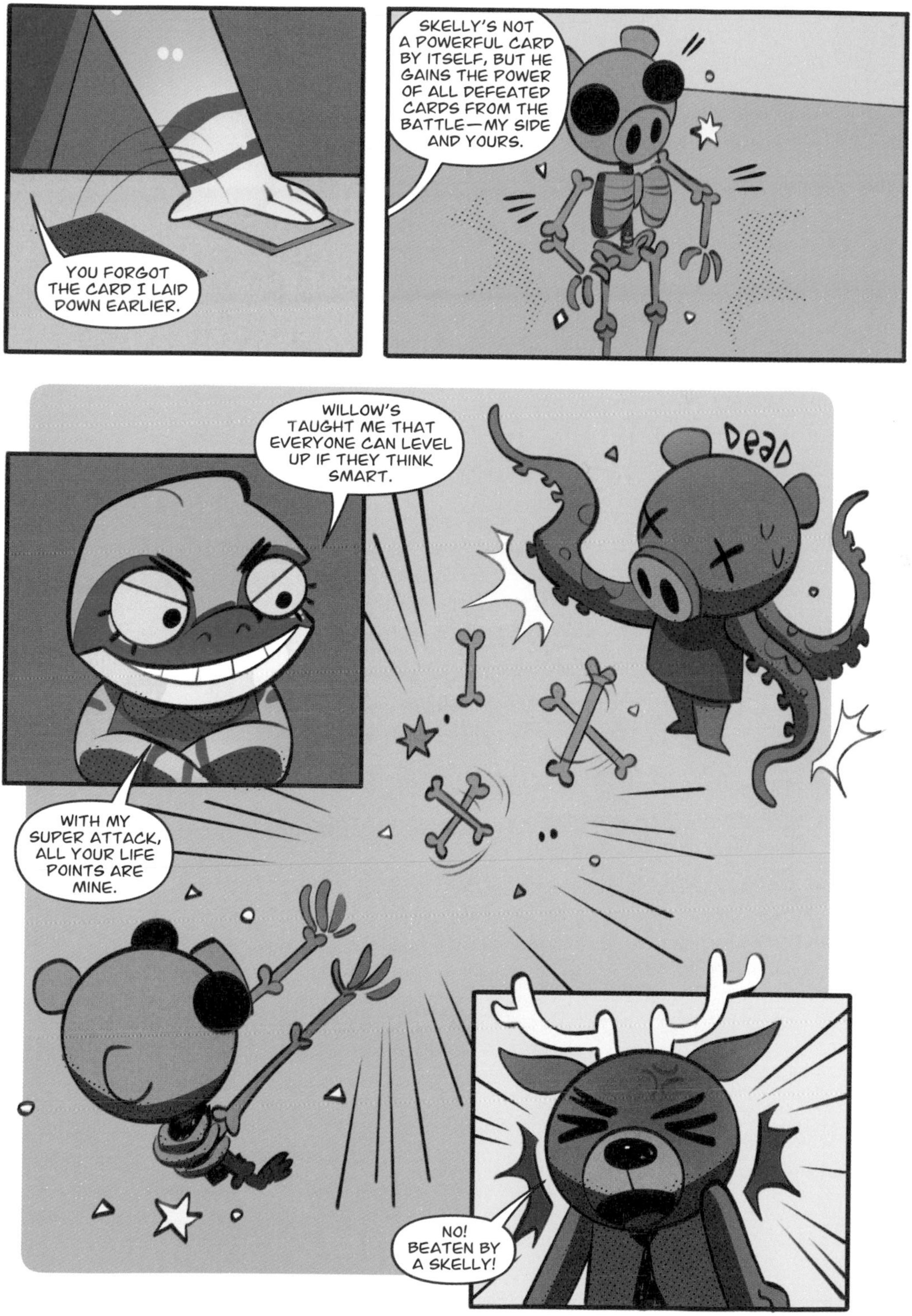
YOU FORGOT THE CARD I LAID DOWN EARLIER.
SKELLY'S NOT A POWERFUL CARD BY ITSELF, BUT HE GAINS THE POWER OF ALL DEFEATED CARDS FROM THE BATTLE—MY SIDE AND YOURS.
WILLOW'S TAUGHT ME THAT EVERYONE CAN LEVEL UP IF THEY THINK SMART.
DEAD
WITH MY SUPER ATTACK, ALL YOUR LIFE POINTS ARE MINE.
NO! BEATEN BY A SKELLY!

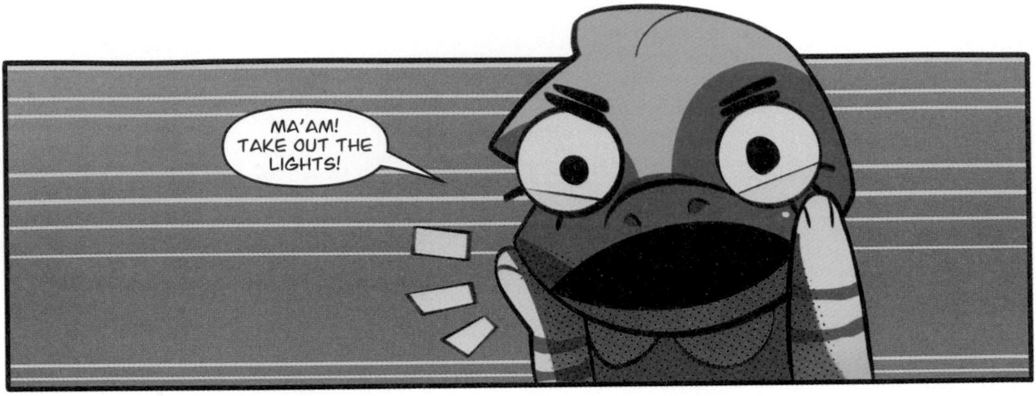
MA'AM!
TAKE OUT THE
LIGHTS!

Survival Tip for Middle School #6 - Slingshots

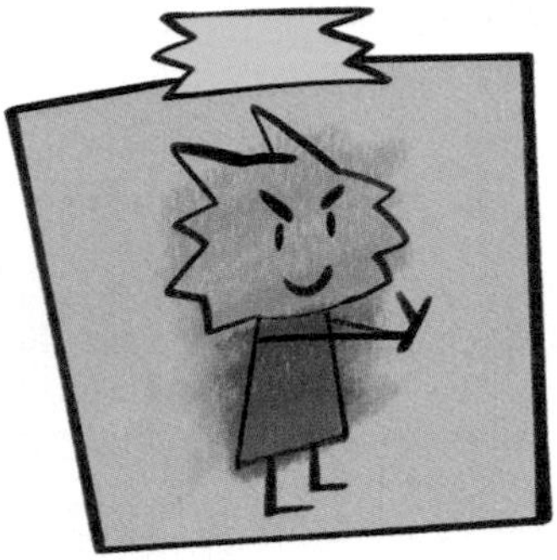

In a survival situation, slingshots are great projectile weapons due to their accuracy and because they don't require special ammo.

Hold the handle of the slingshot with your dominant hand. Make your shot more accurate by holding the slingshot vertically rather than horizontally. Hold your wrist and forearm so they're aligned.

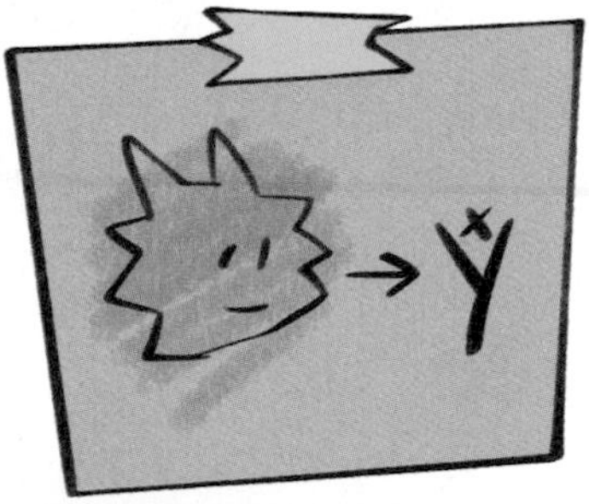

Slingshots are best fired with both eyes open, looking straight through the Y.

Don't aim your slingshot at other people (even Dalton Deer). Practice your slingshot skills in a wide open place in case of ricochet.

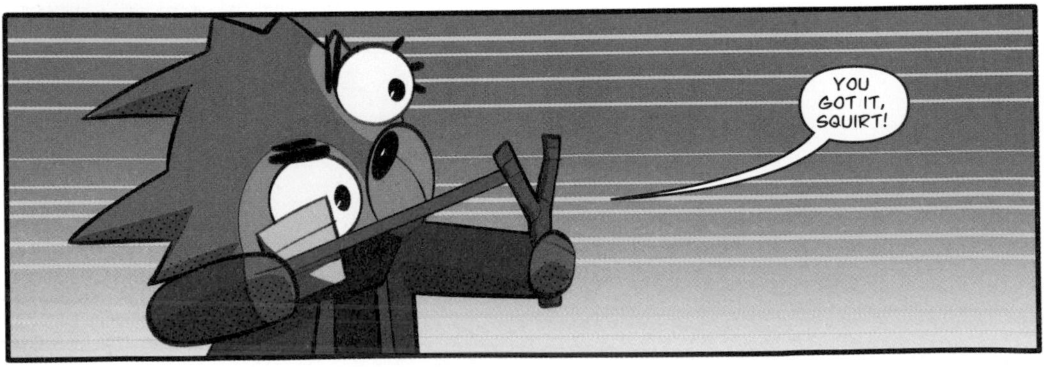
YOU
GOT IT,
SQUIRT!

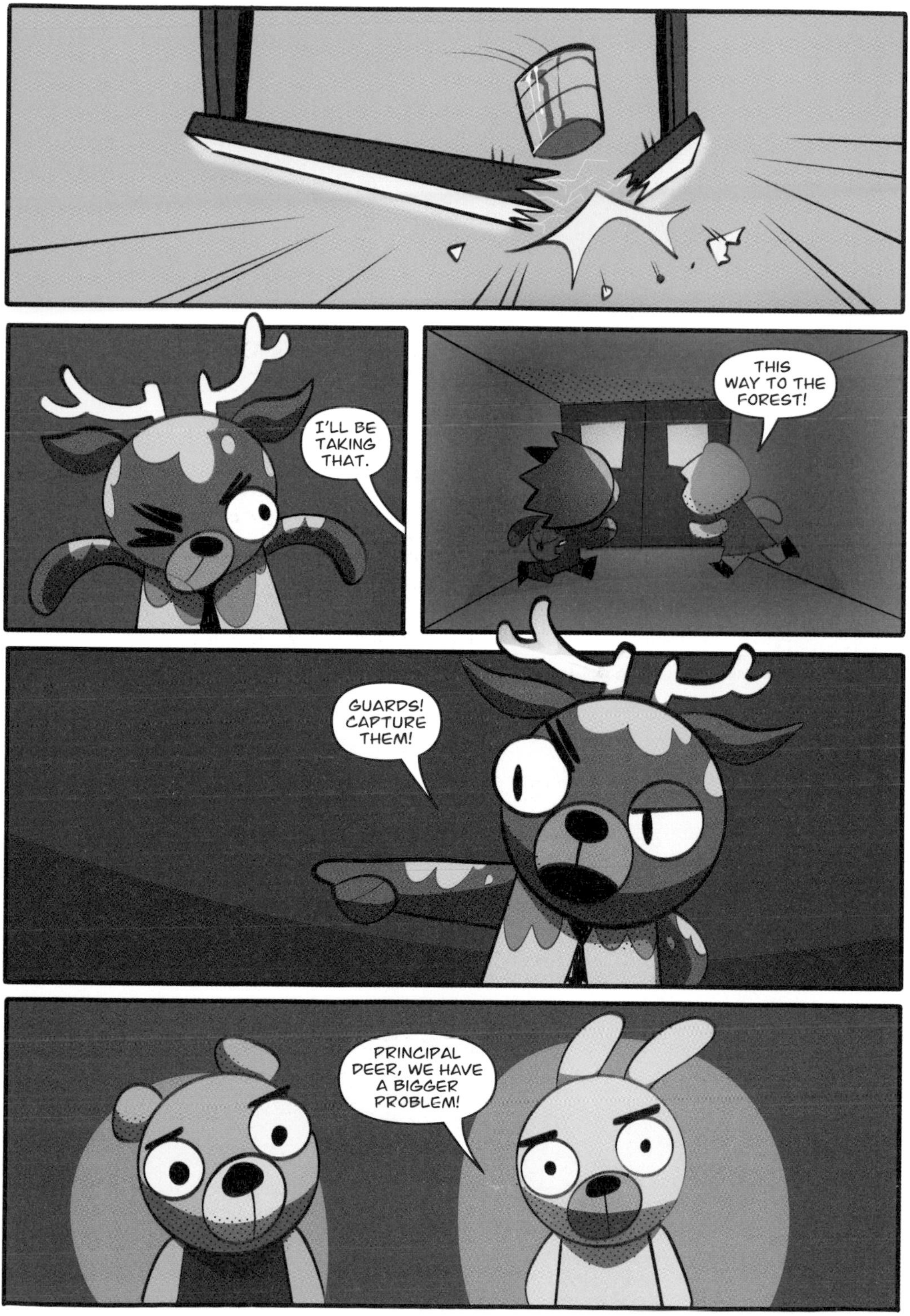
I'LL BE TAKING THAT.
THIS WAY TO THE FOREST!
GUARDS! CAPTURE THEM!
PRINCIPAL DEER, WE HAVE A BIGGER PROBLEM!

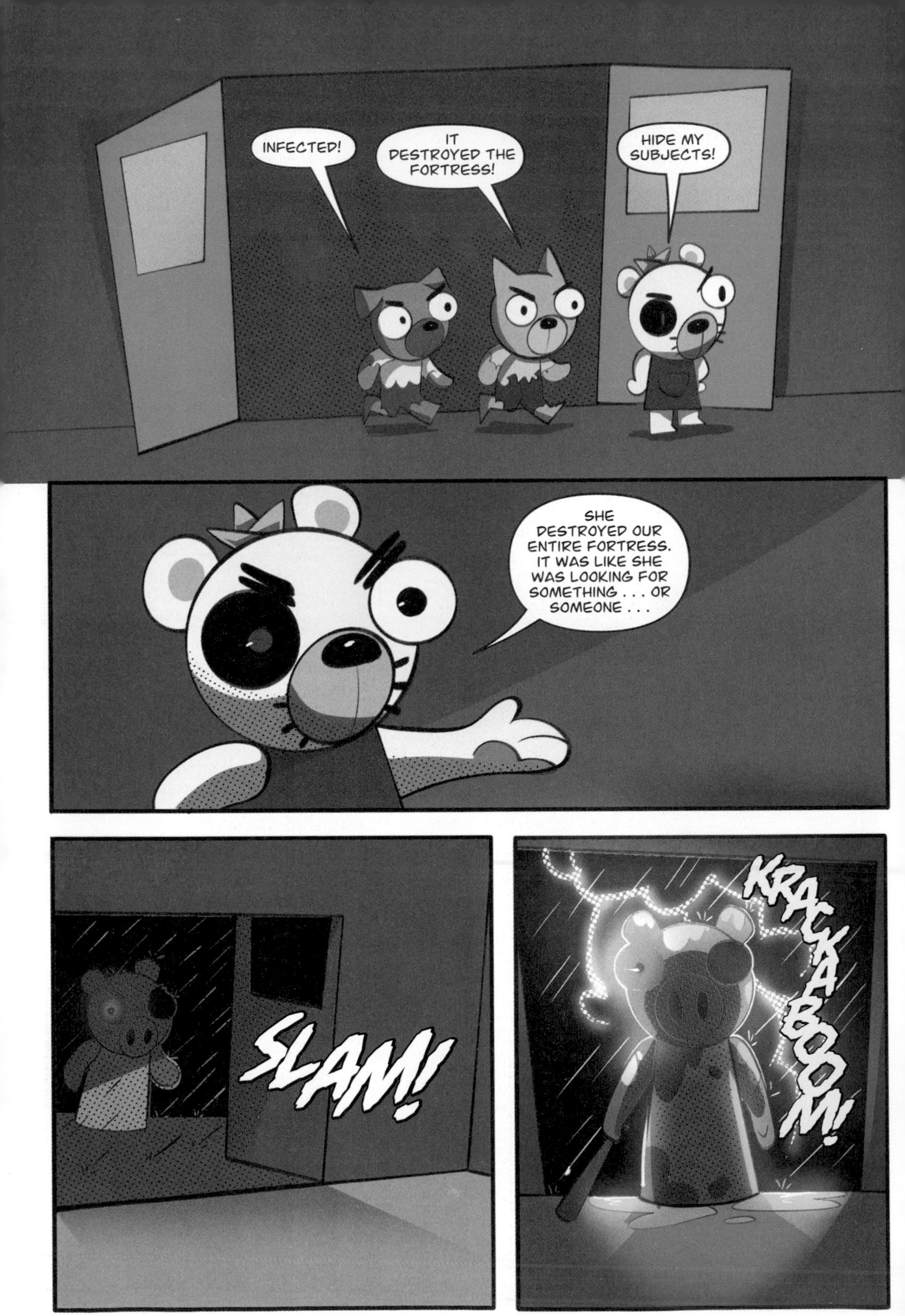
INFECTED!
IT DESTROYED THE FORTRESS!
HIDE MY SUBJECTS!
SHE DESTROYED OUR ENTIRE FORTRESS. IT WAS LIKE SHE WAS LOOKING FOR SOMETHING . . . OR SOMEONE . . .
SLAM!
KRACKABOOM!

Drip.

Drip.

Drip.

SNIFFLE . . . SNIFFLE . . .

BE QUIET!

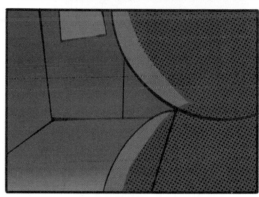

THOSE TWO DON'T STAND A CHANCE.

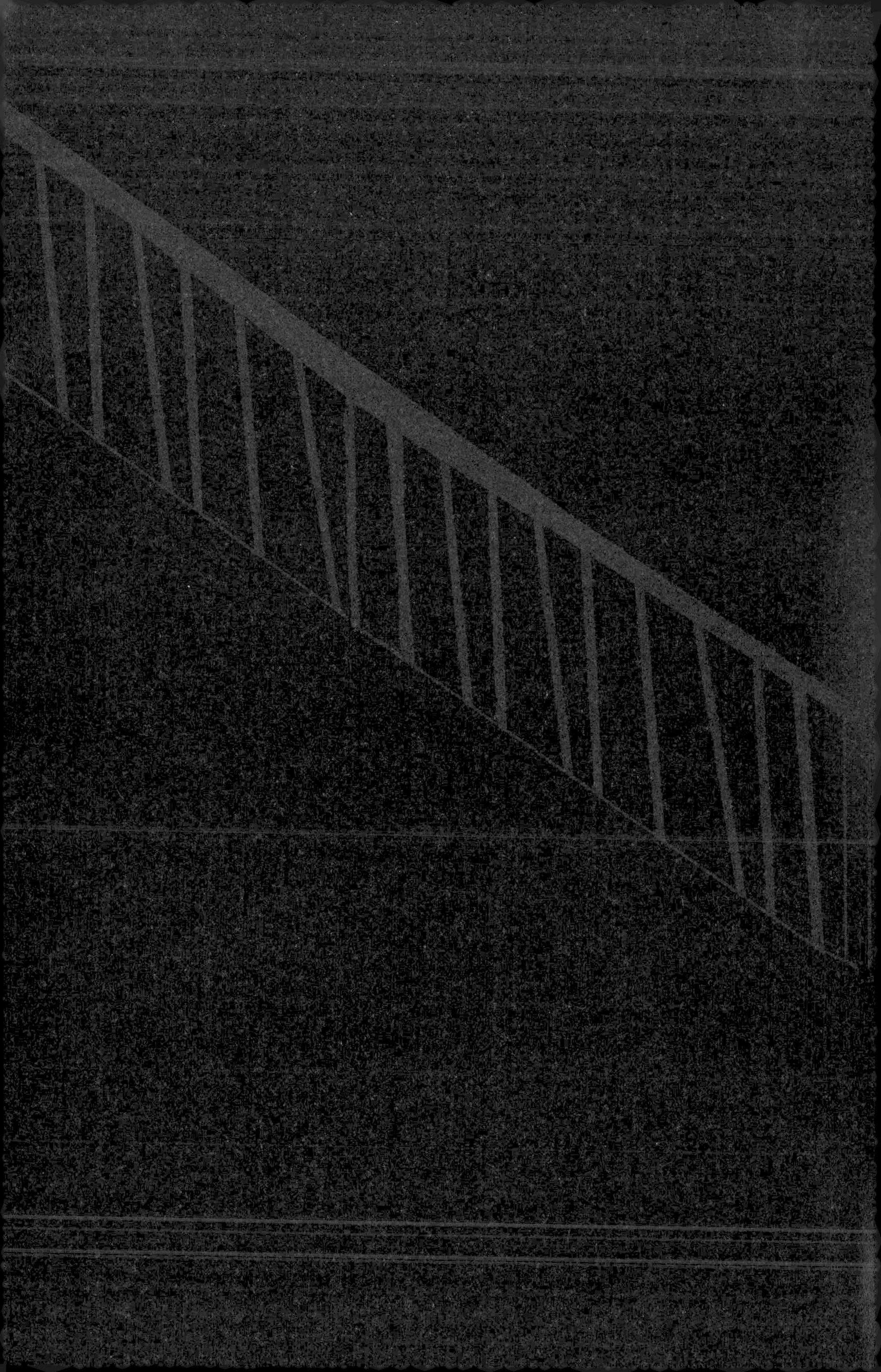

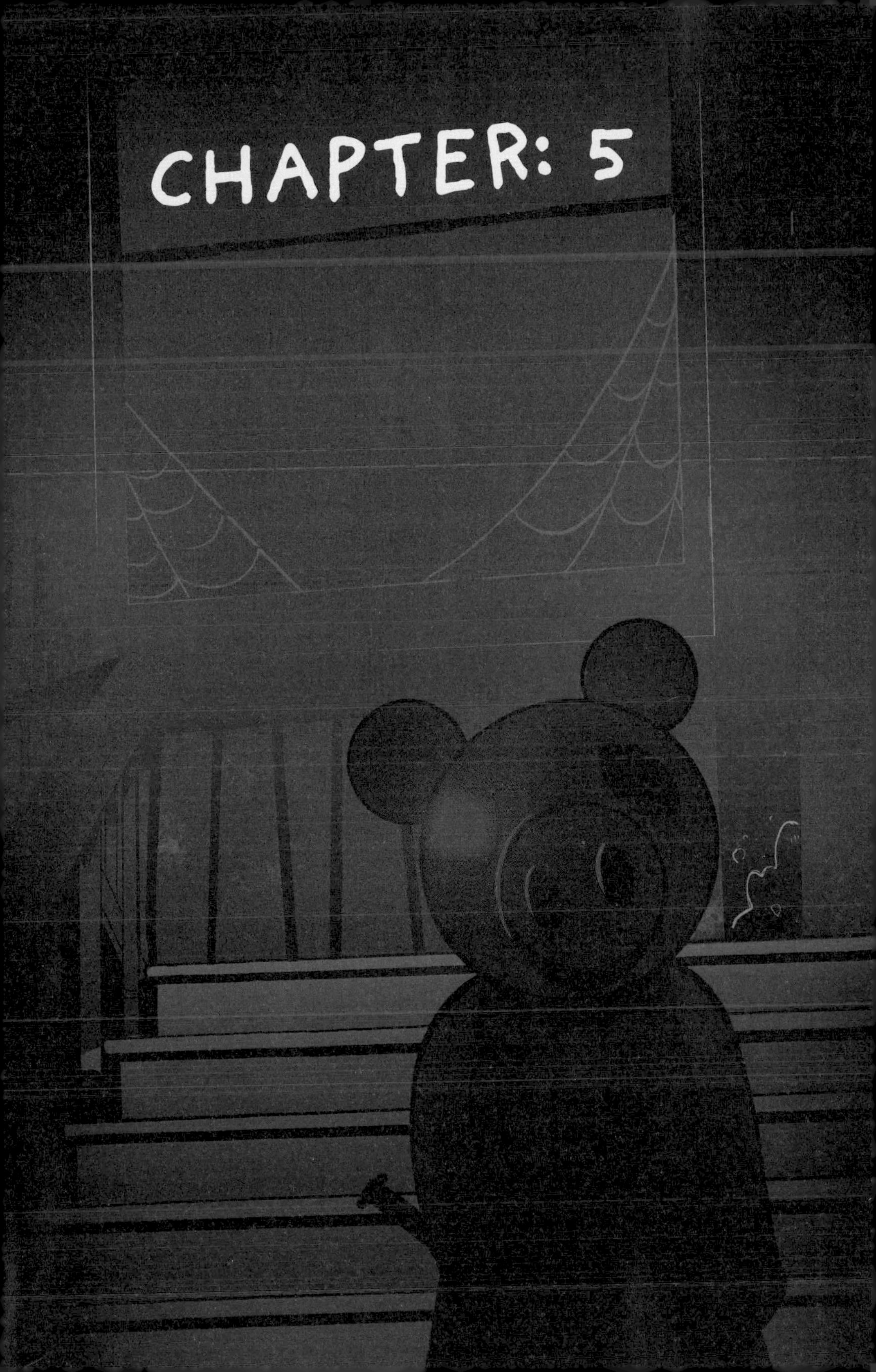
CHAPTER: 5

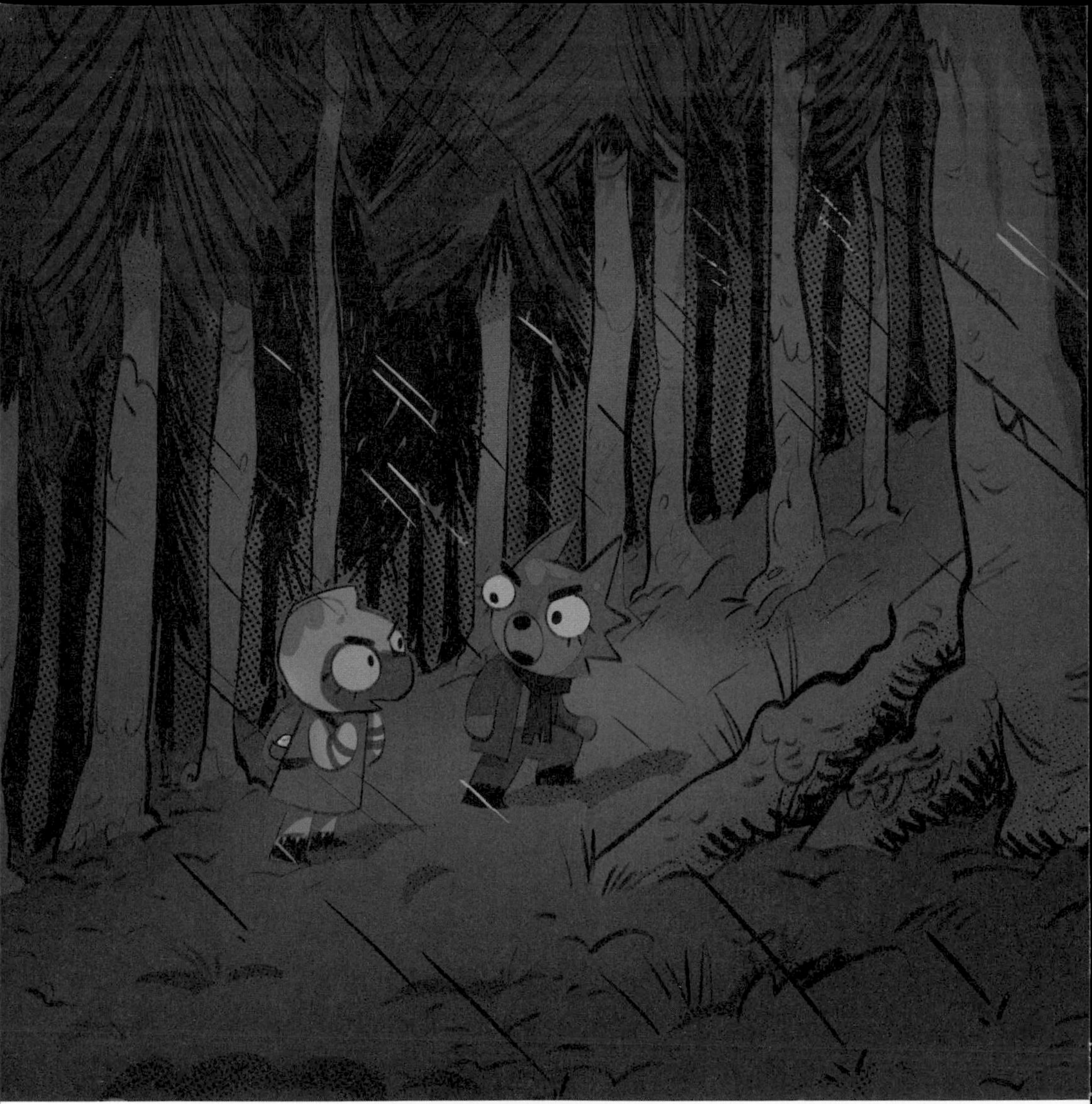

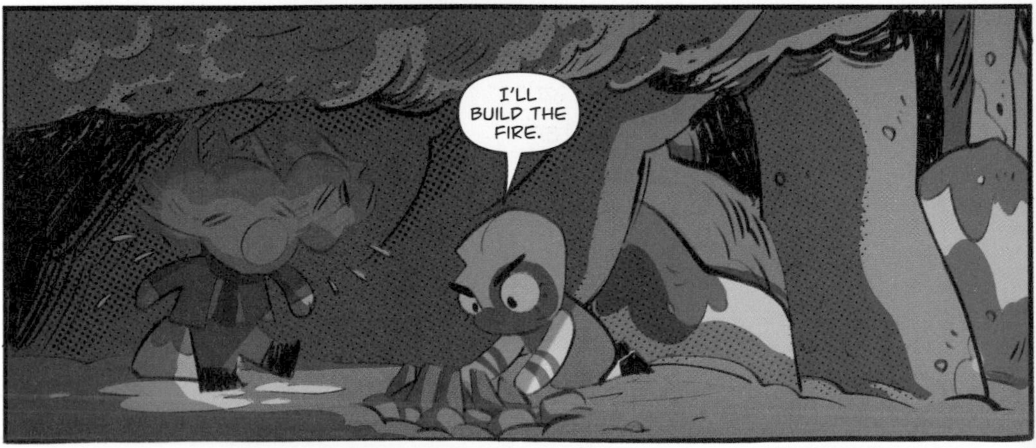
I'LL BUILD THE FIRE.

Survival Tip for Middle School #7 – Building a Campfire (Adult supervision required)

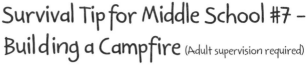

Note: Don't build a campfire *inside* the middle school.

To build a campfire, you need three types of material: tinder, kindling, and firewood.

Fires need plenty of fuel and oxygen.

Put your loose kindling in the middle of a pyramid of sticks.

If you don't have a lighter or string to make a bow, you can use your hands and a stick to drill and light the fire.

Once you have a good fire going, gradually add larger and larger materials.

Put out your fire with sand or dirt. Water won't deprive your fire of oxygen as effectively. Instead, use water to cool the hot sand so it doesn't heat up again.

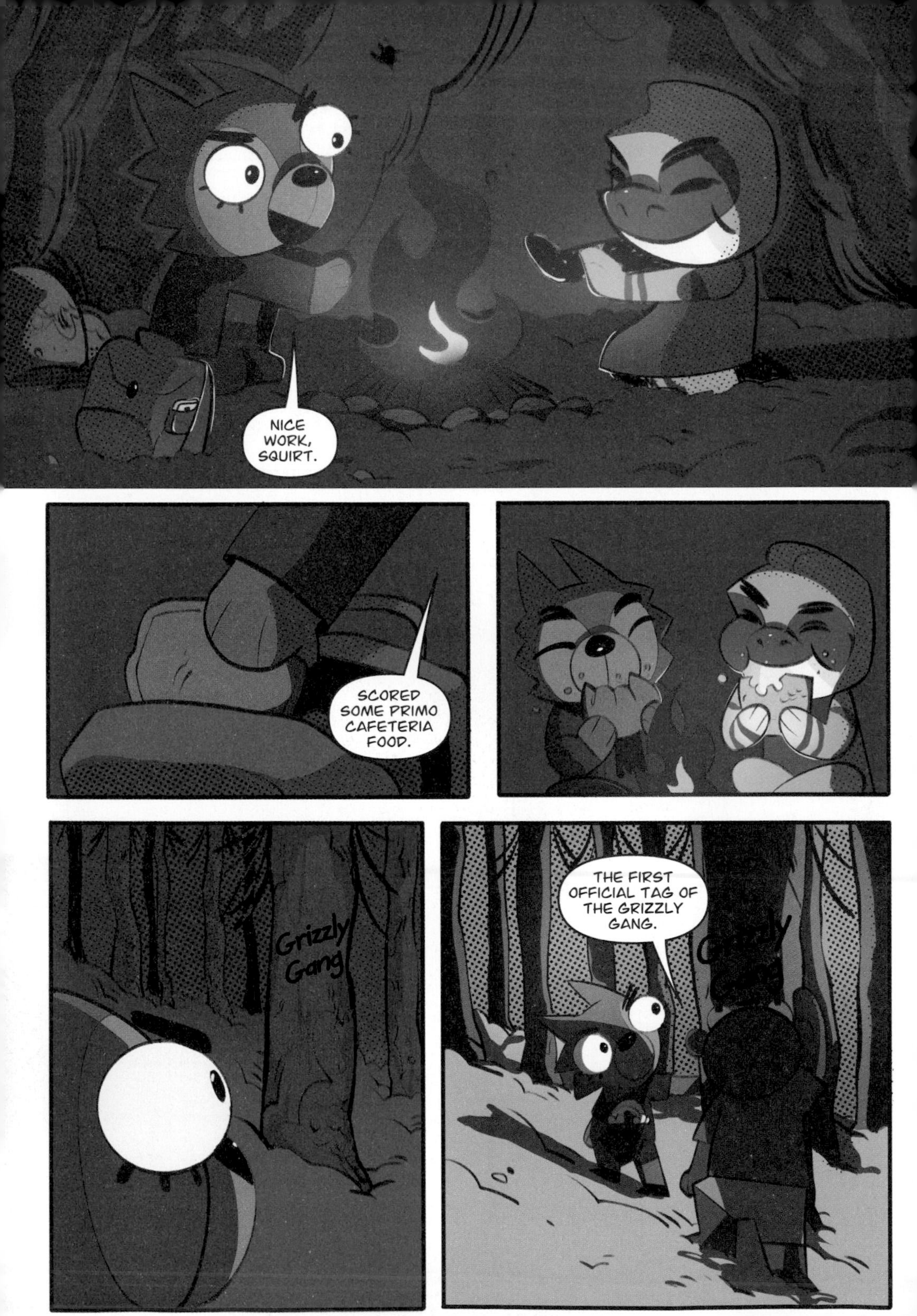
NICE WORK, SQUIRT.
SCORED SOME PRIMO CAFETERIA FOOD.
Grizzly Gang
THE FIRST OFFICIAL TAG OF THE GRIZZLY GANG.

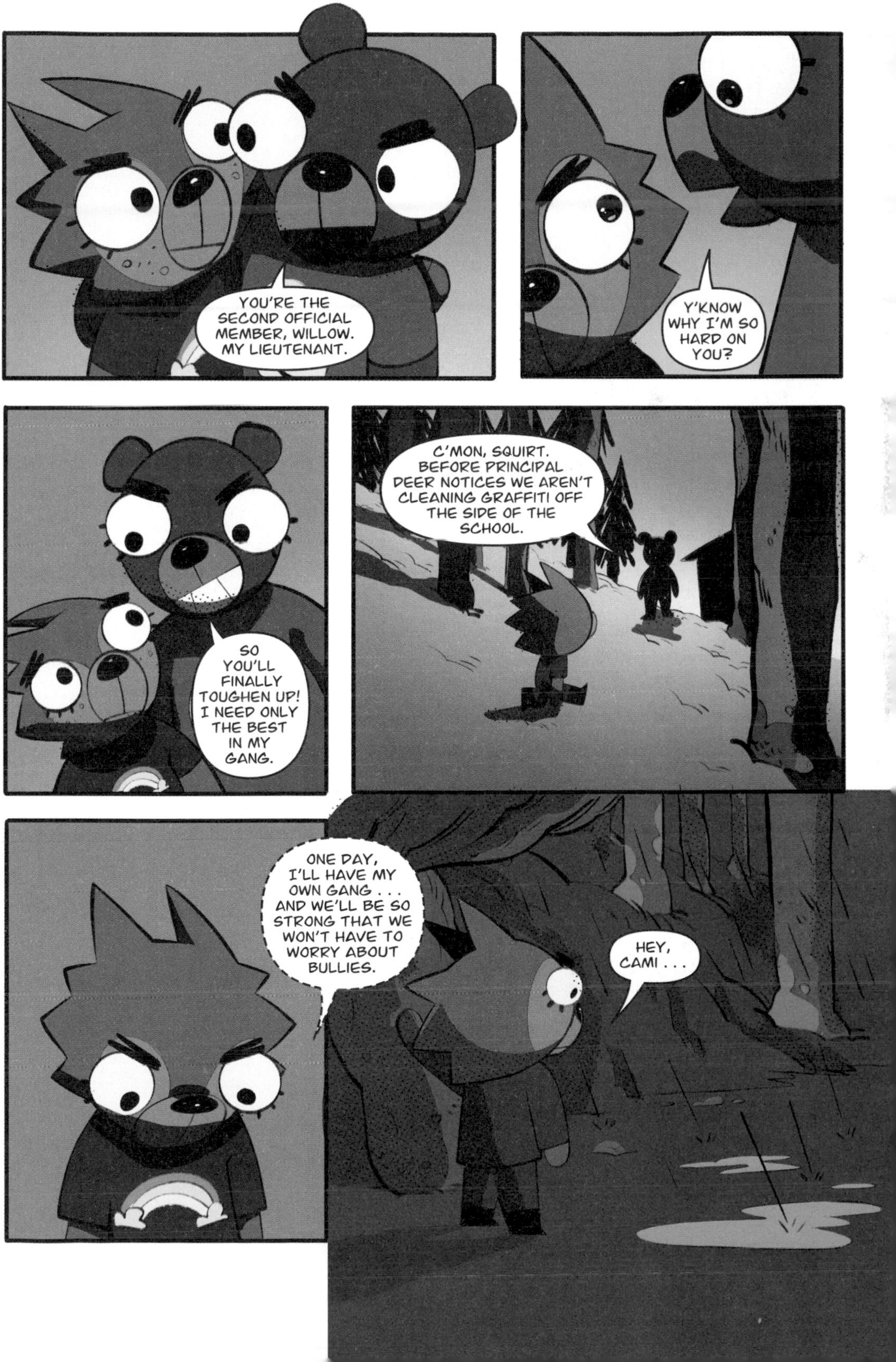
YOU'RE THE SECOND OFFICIAL MEMBER, WILLOW. MY LIEUTENANT.
Y'KNOW WHY I'M SO HARD ON YOU?
SO YOU'LL FINALLY TOUGHEN UP! I NEED ONLY THE BEST IN MY GANG.
C'MON, SQUIRT. BEFORE PRINCIPAL DEER NOTICES WE AREN'T CLEANING GRAFFITI OFF THE SIDE OF THE SCHOOL.
ONE DAY, I'LL HAVE MY OWN GANG . . . AND WE'LL BE SO STRONG THAT WE WON'T HAVE TO WORRY ABOUT BULLIES.
HEY, CAMI . . .

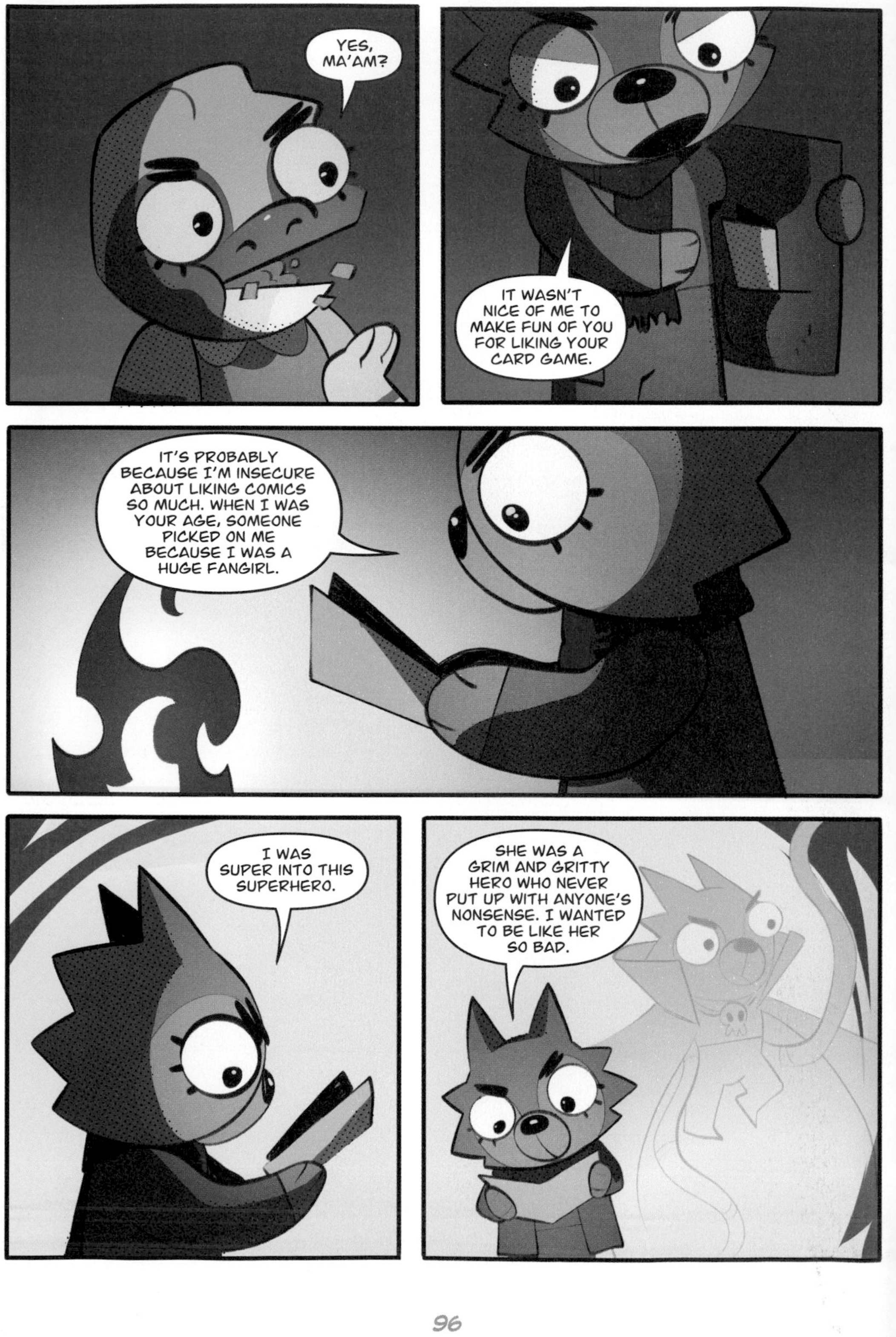
YES, MA'AM?
IT WASN'T NICE OF ME TO MAKE FUN OF YOU FOR LIKING YOUR CARD GAME.
IT'S PROBABLY BECAUSE I'M INSECURE ABOUT LIKING COMICS SO MUCH. WHEN I WAS YOUR AGE, SOMEONE PICKED ON ME BECAUSE I WAS A HUGE FANGIRL.
I WAS SUPER INTO THIS SUPERHERO.
SHE WAS A GRIM AND GRITTY HERO WHO NEVER PUT UP WITH ANYONE'S NONSENSE. I WANTED TO BE LIKE HER SO BAD.

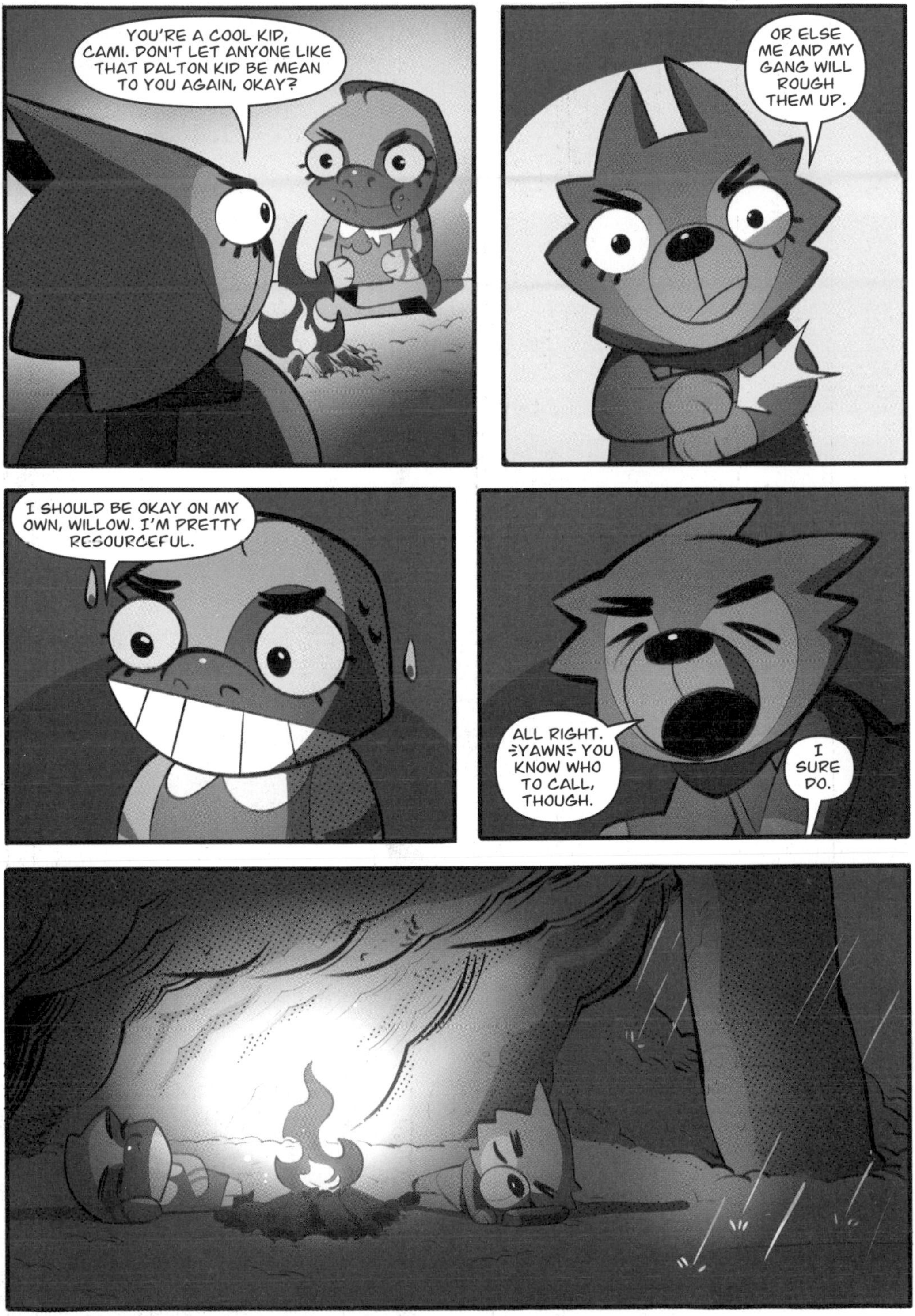
YOU'RE A COOL KID, CAMI. DON'T LET ANYONE LIKE THAT DALTON KID BE MEAN TO YOU AGAIN, OKAY?
OR ELSE ME AND MY GANG WILL ROUGH THEM UP.
I SHOULD BE OKAY ON MY OWN, WILLOW. I'M PRETTY RESOURCEFUL.
ALL RIGHT. =YAWN= YOU KNOW WHO TO CALL, THOUGH.
I SURE DO.

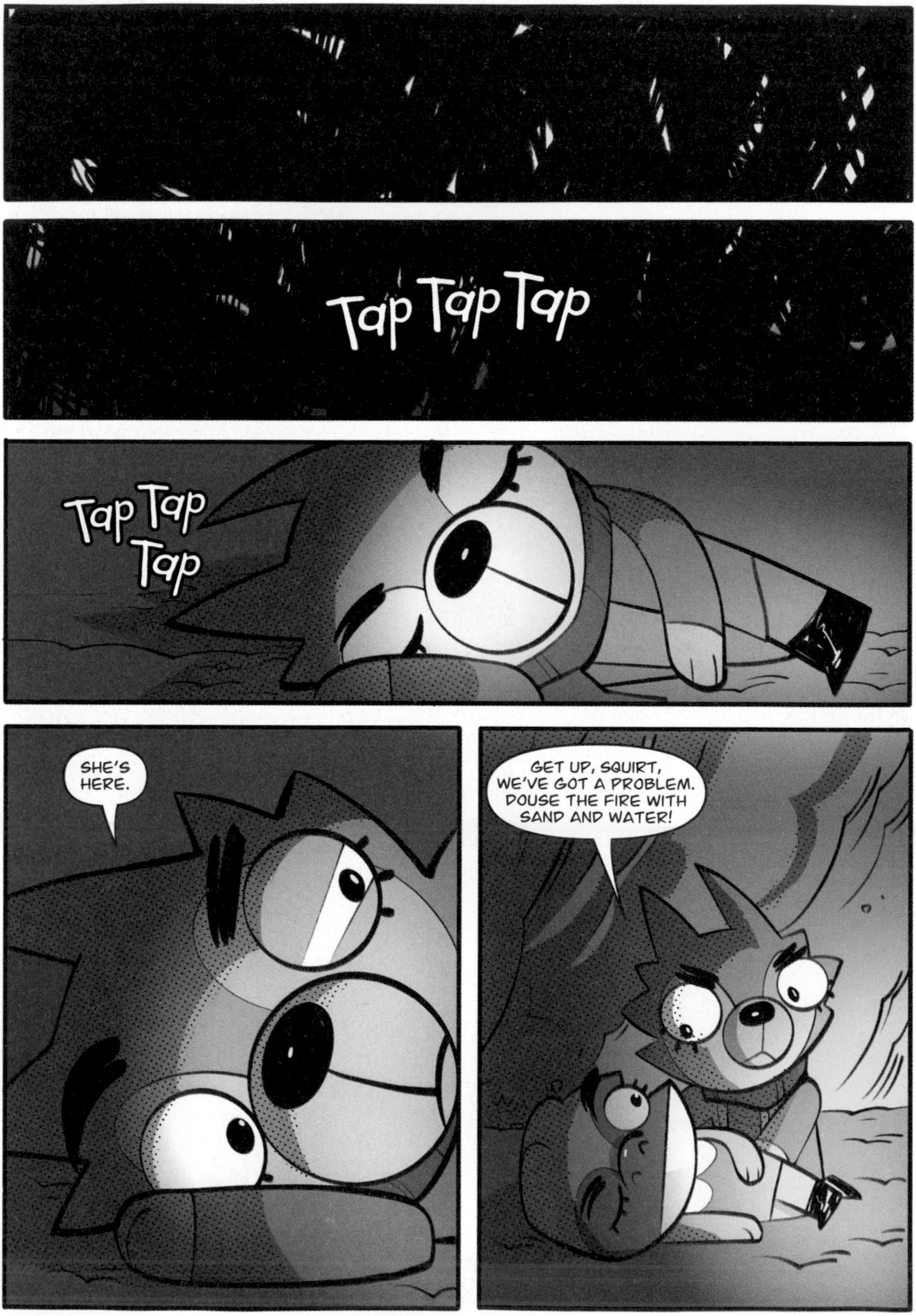
Tap Tap Tap
Tap Tap
Tap
SHE'S HERE.
GET UP, SQUIRT, WE'VE GOT A PROBLEM. DOUSE THE FIRE WITH SAND AND WATER!

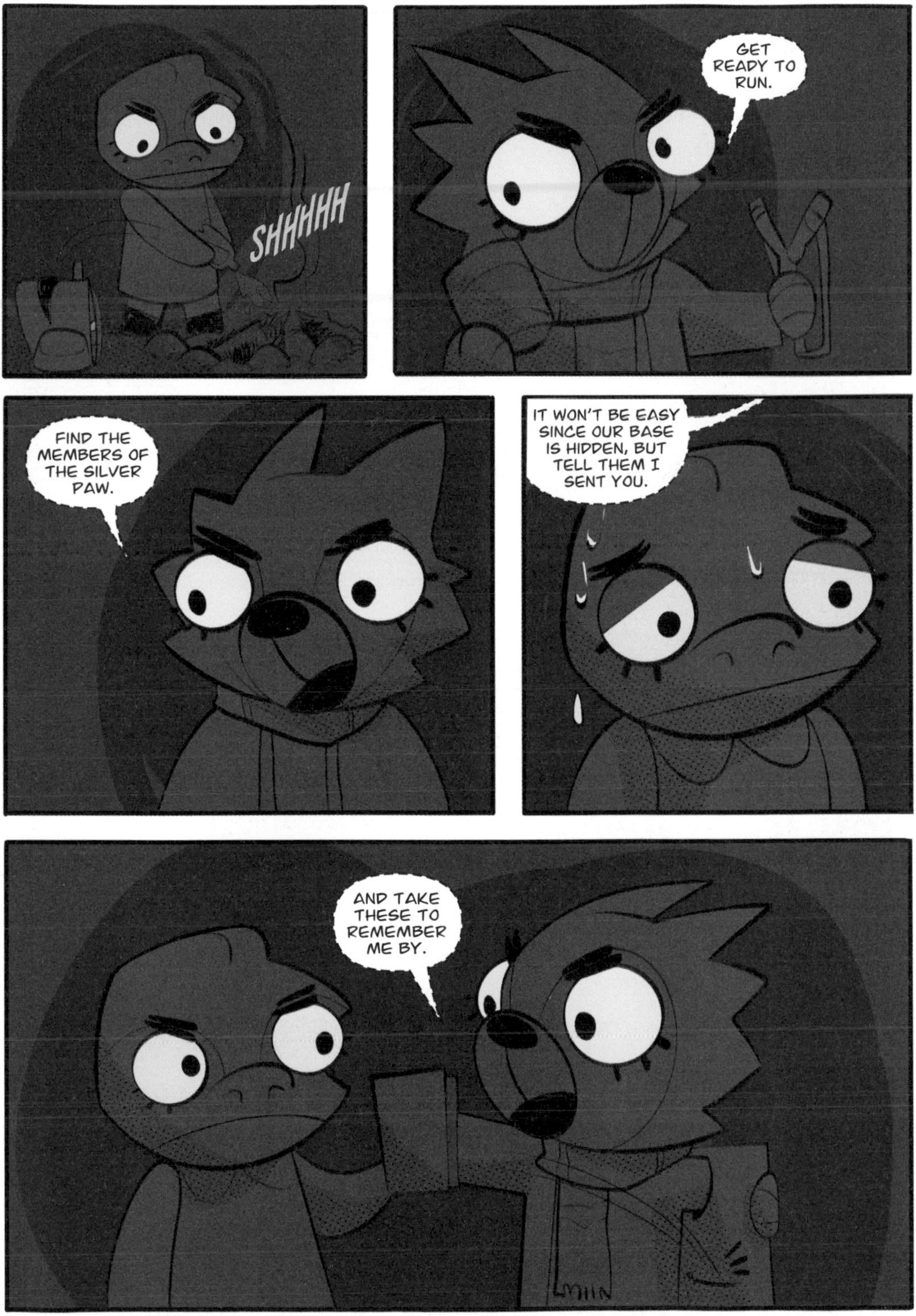
SHHHHH
GET READY TO RUN.
FIND THE MEMBERS OF THE SILVER PAW.
IT WON'T BE EASY SINCE OUR BASE IS HIDDEN, BUT TELL THEM I SENT YOU.
AND TAKE THESE TO REMEMBER ME BY.

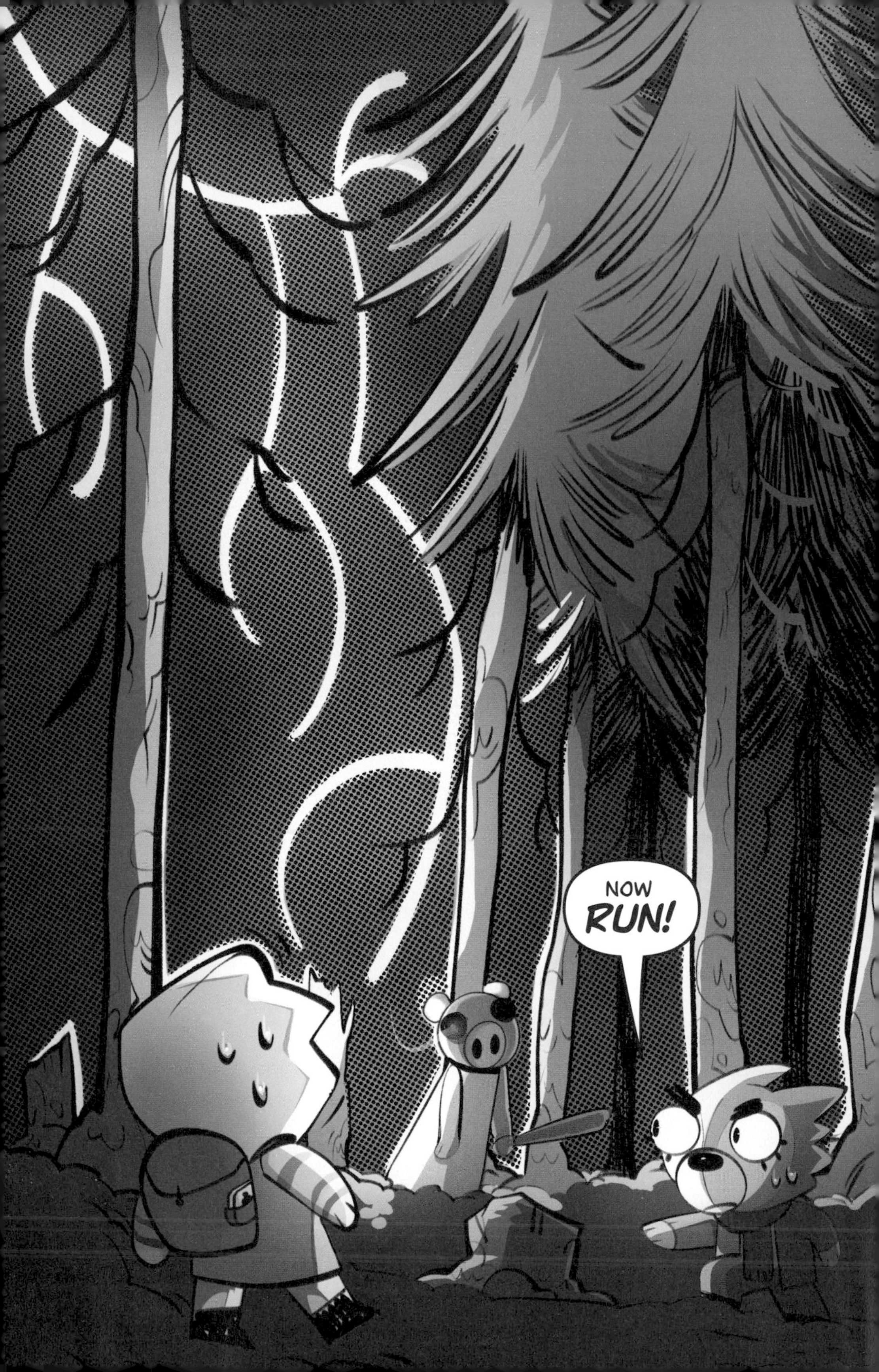
NOW
RUN!

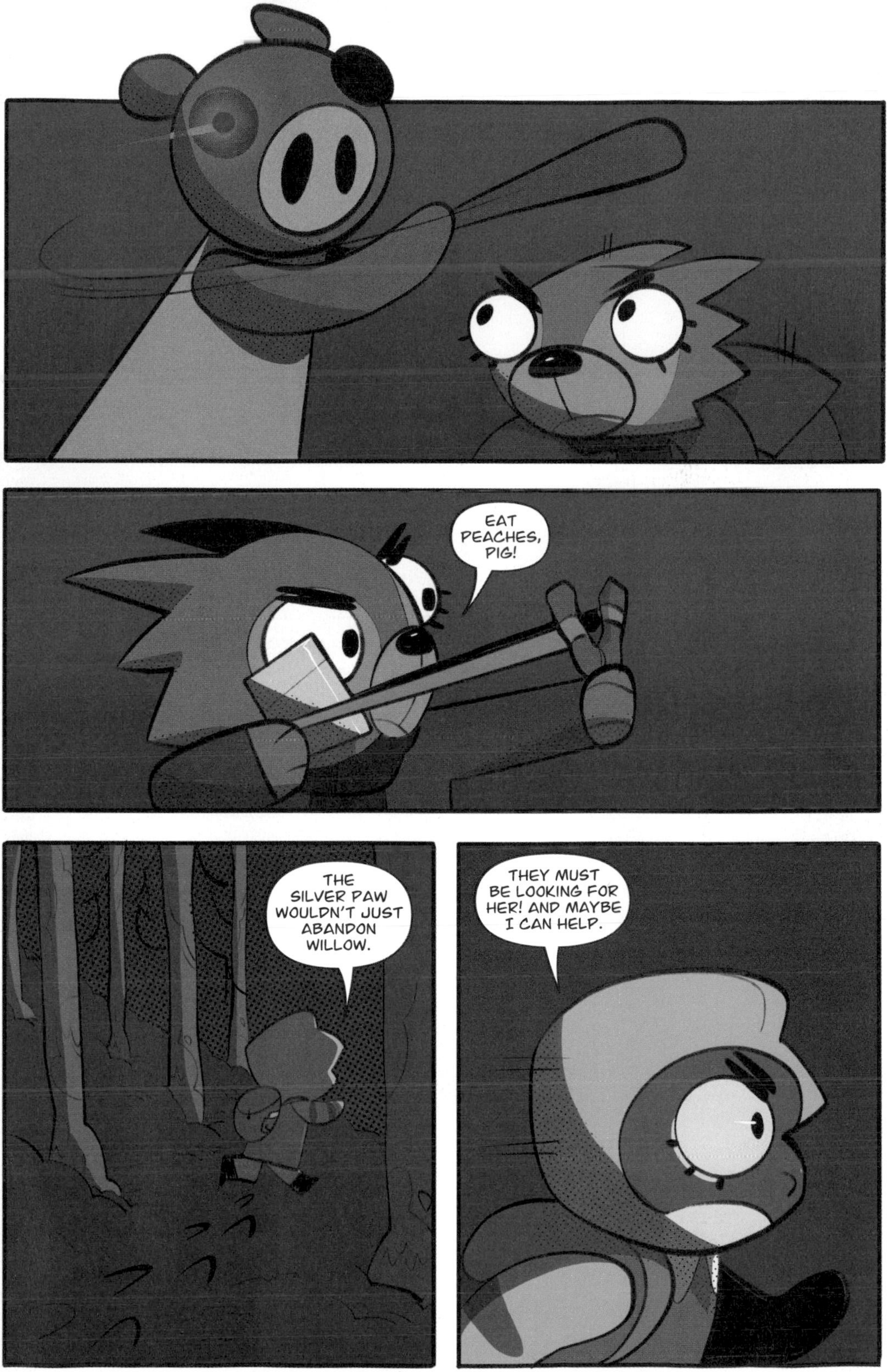
EAT PEACHES, PIG!
THE SILVER PAW WOULDN'T JUST ABANDON WILLOW.
THEY MUST BE LOOKING FOR HER! AND MAYBE I CAN HELP.

Survival Tip for Middle School #8 - Getting Help

If you are lost in the wilderness and don't have a phone, there are multiple ways you can signal someone for help.

Don't panic! Panicking keeps you from thinking clearly about the situation.

Three of anything is the international symbol that someone needs help. (Rule of threes!)

Use three fires spaced out to signal that you're not just a camper. Occasionally add wet leaves to make it smokier.

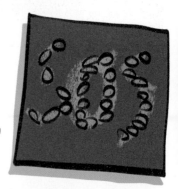

If searchers are flying by, it's easiest to see wide-open areas. Use lighter rocks on dark ground to form words like *SOS*.

Use extra fabric items you have to make flags that wave in the breeze.

Blowing a whistle three times is also a signal that someone needs help.

Flash a light on shiny surfaces, causing them to flicker back and forth.

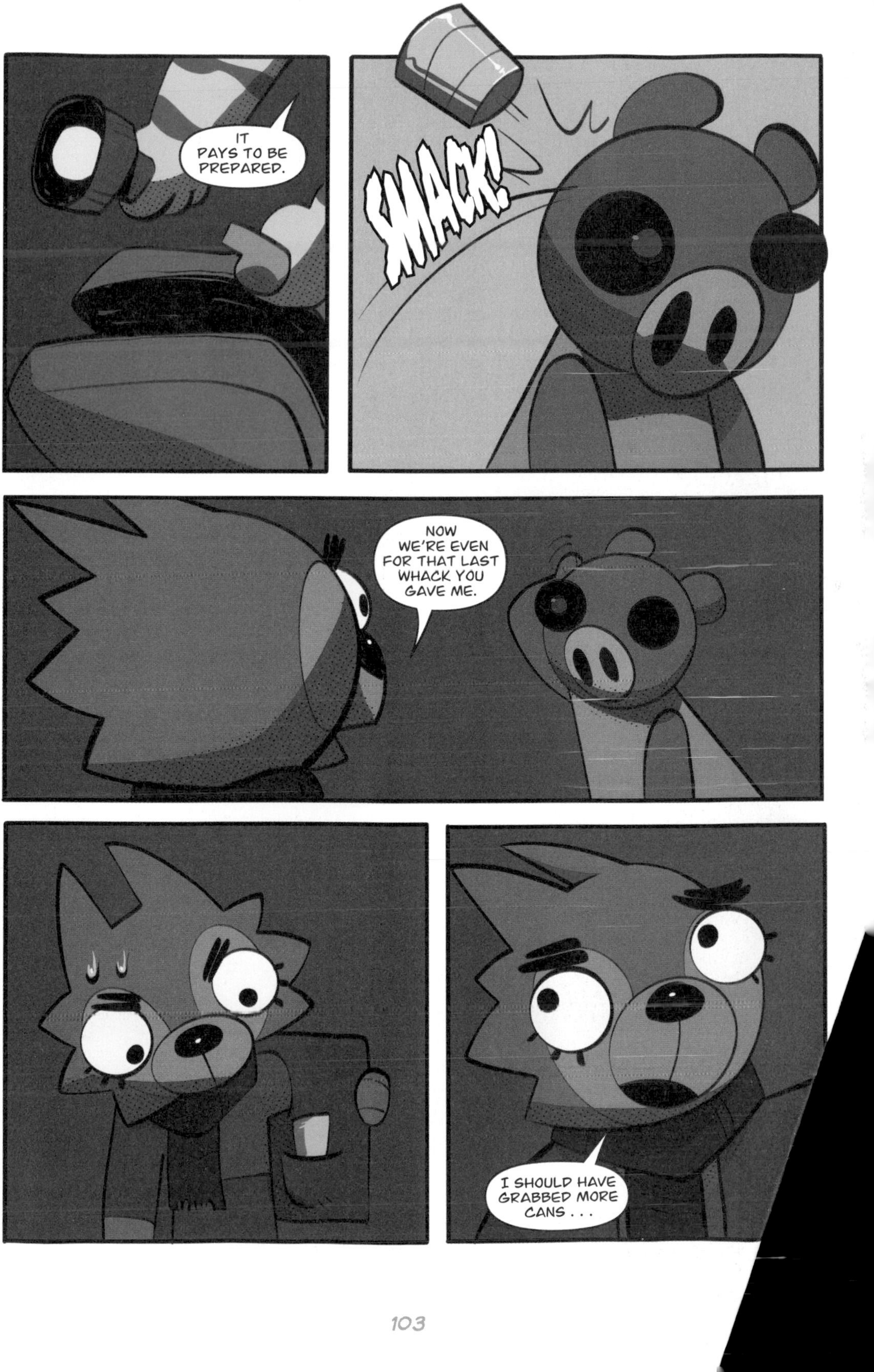
IT PAYS TO BE PREPARED.
SMACK!
NOW WE'RE EVEN FOR THAT LAST WHACK YOU GAVE ME.
I SHOULD HAVE GRABBED MORE CANS . . .

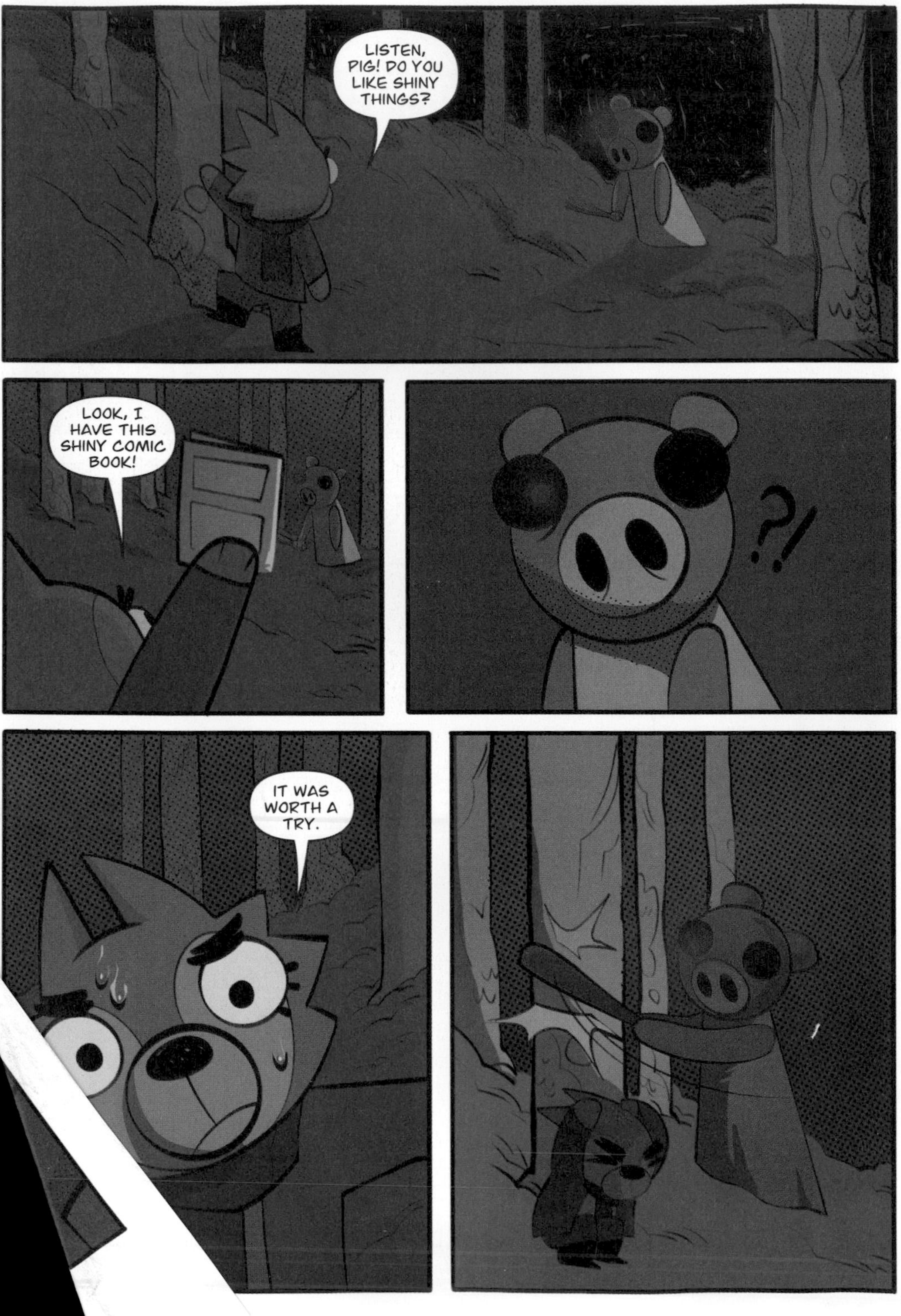
LISTEN, PIG! DO YOU LIKE SHINY THINGS?
LOOK, I HAVE THIS SHINY COMIC BOOK!
?!
IT WAS WORTH A TRY.

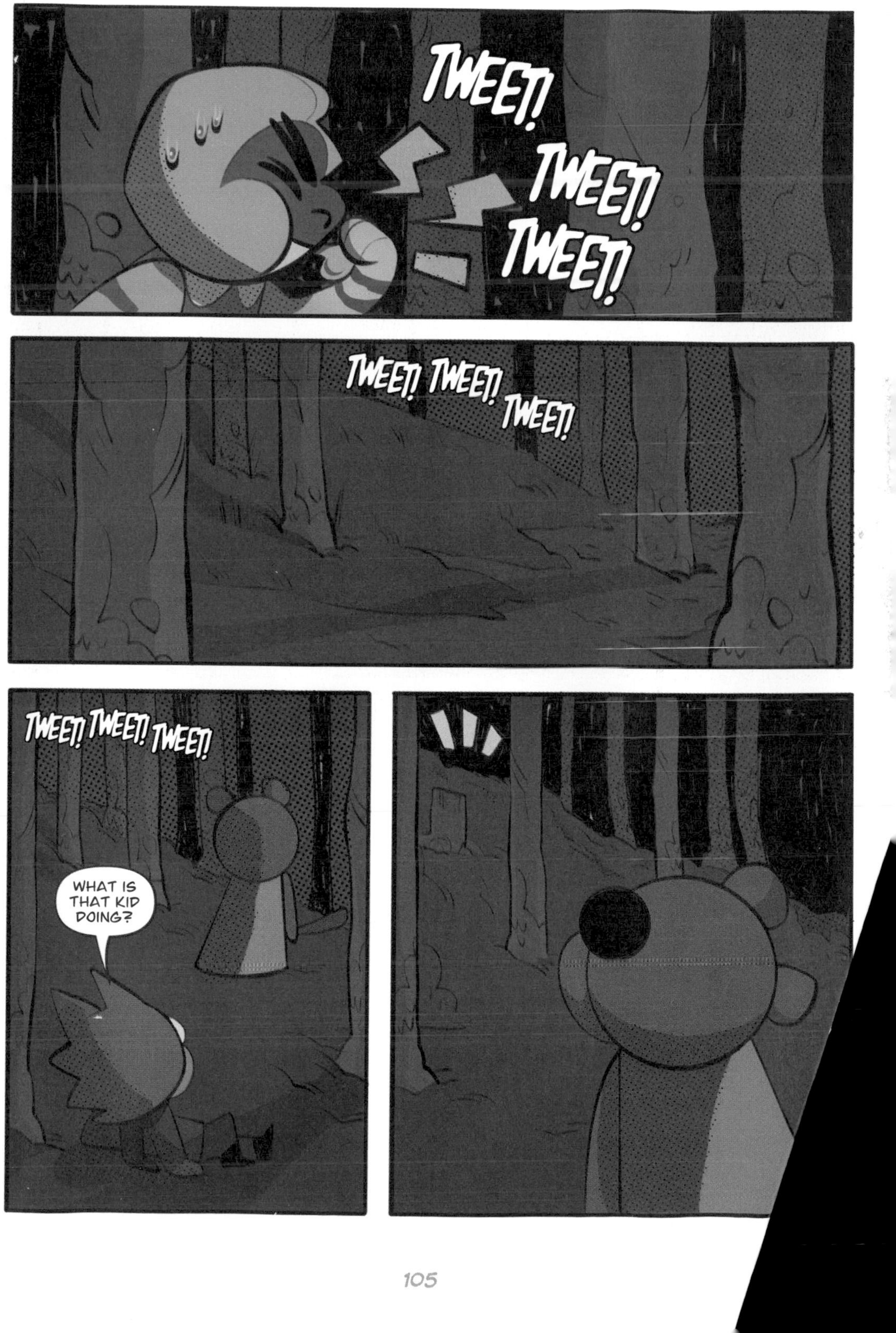
TWEET!
TWEET!
TWEET!
TWEET! TWEET! TWEET!
TWEET! TWEET! TWEET!
WHAT IS THAT KID DOING?

WAIT! PAY ATTENTION TO ME!

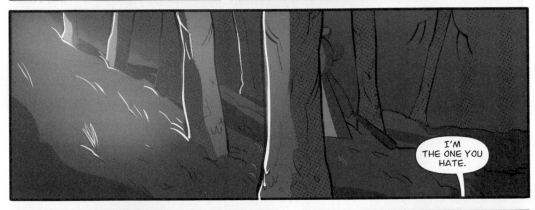

I'M THE ONE YOU HATE.

KEEP ATTACKING ME!

DON'T GO AFTER THE KID!

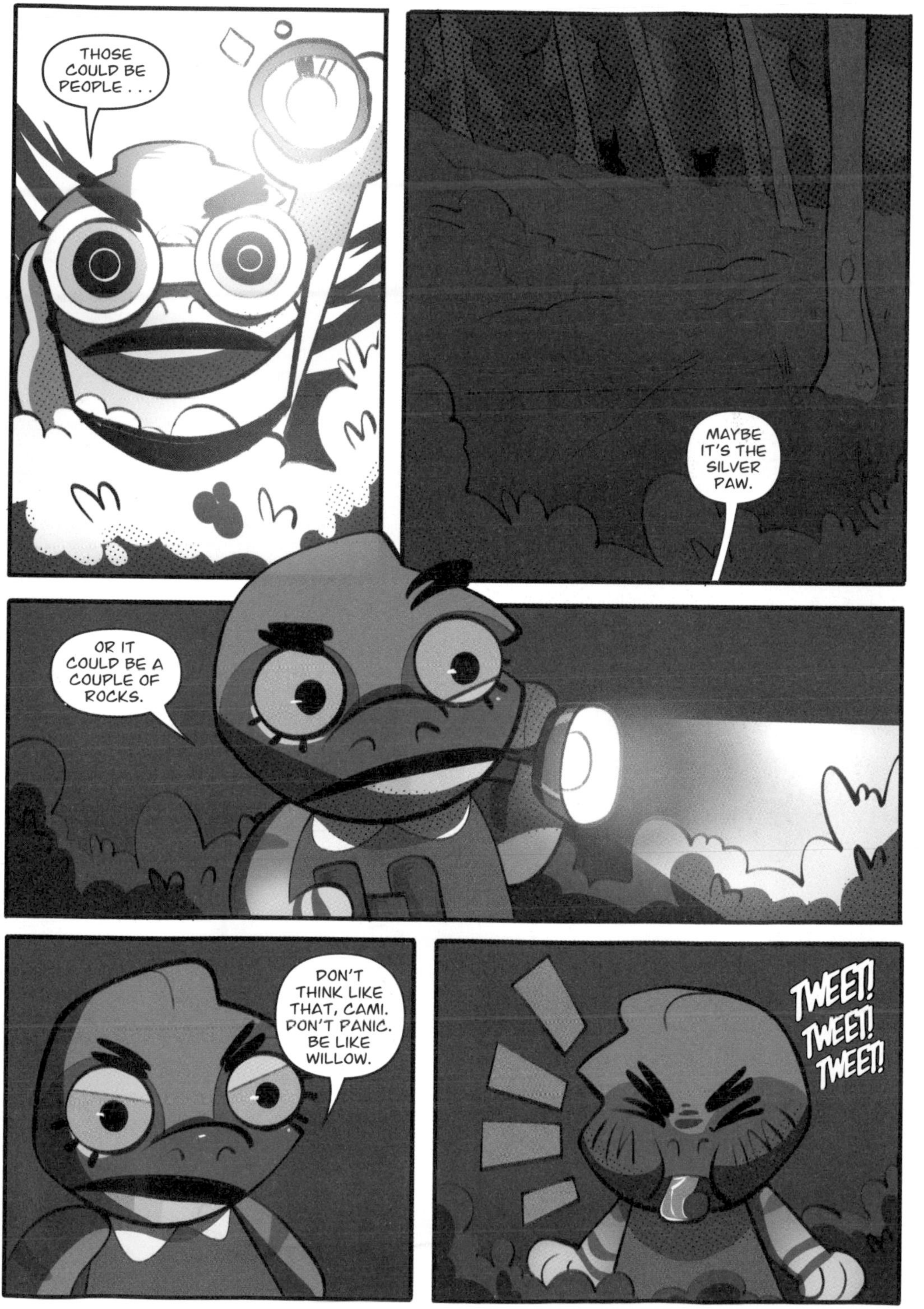
THOSE COULD BE PEOPLE . . .
MAYBE IT'S THE SILVER PAW.
OR IT COULD BE A COUPLE OF ROCKS.
DON'T THINK LIKE THAT, CAMI. DON'T PANIC. BE LIKE WILLOW.
TWEET! TWEET! TWEET!

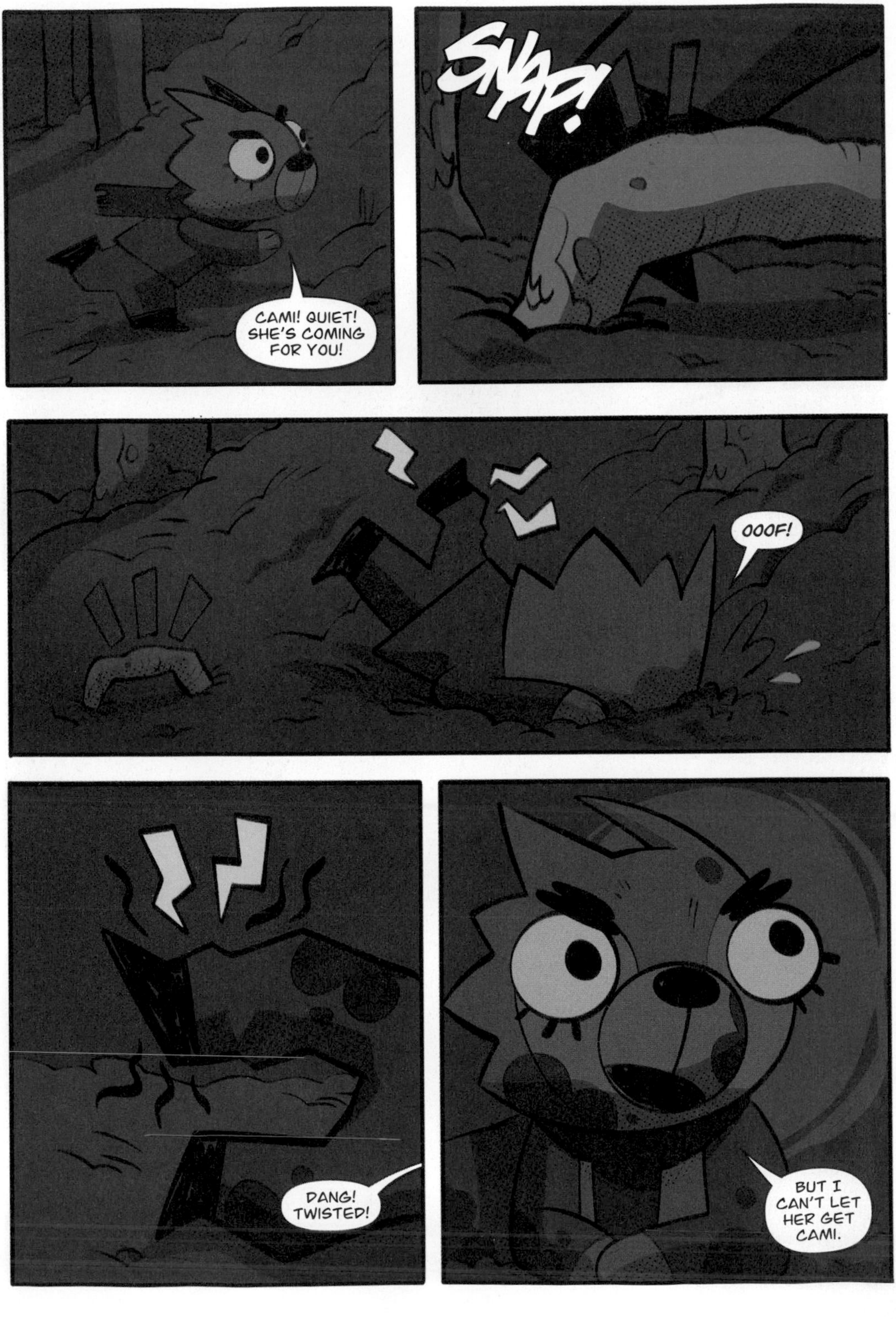
CAMI! QUIET! SHE'S COMING FOR YOU!
SNAP!
OOOF!
DANG! TWISTED!
BUT I CAN'T LET HER GET CAMI.

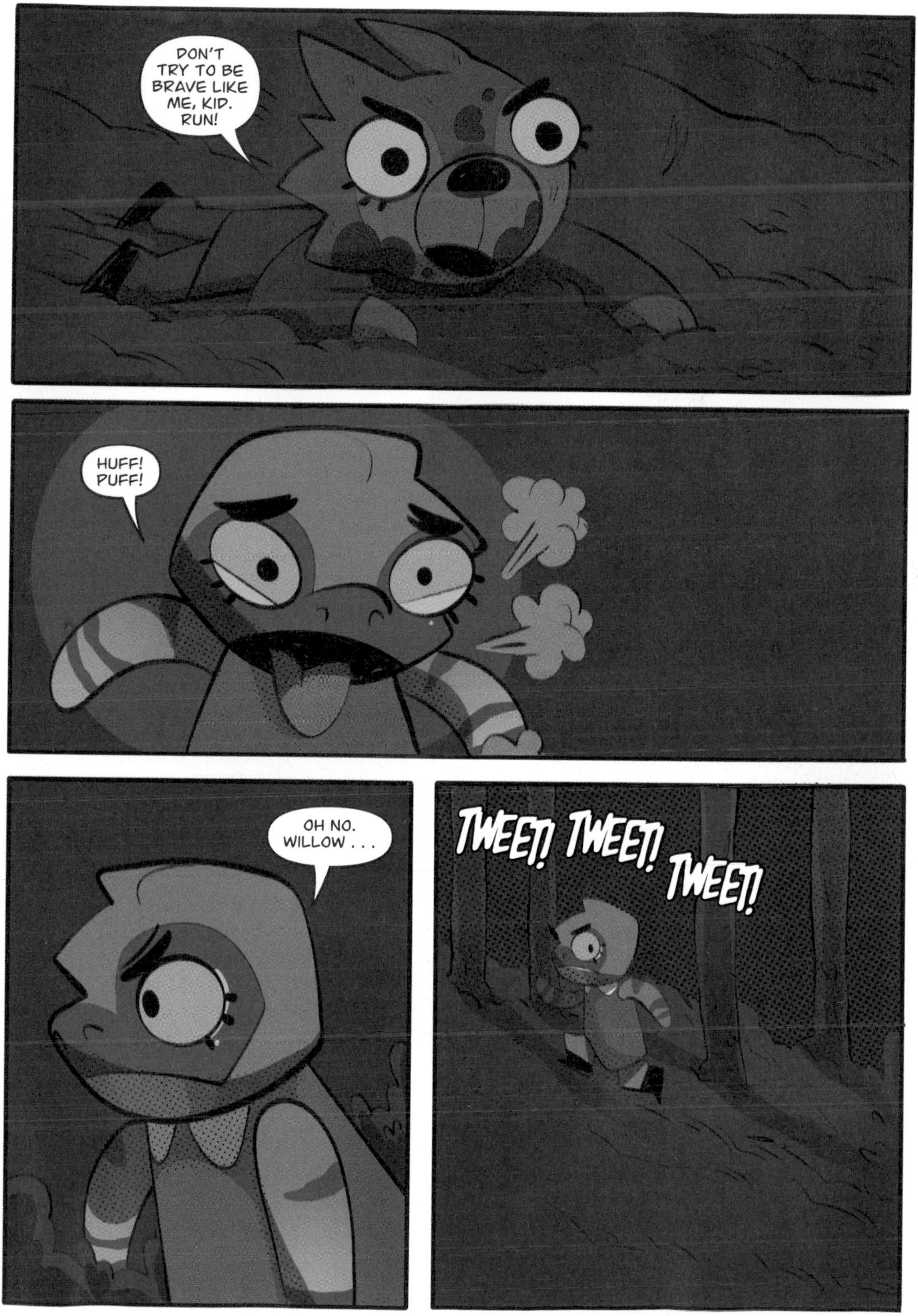
DON'T TRY TO BE BRAVE LIKE ME, KID. RUN!
HUFF! PUFF!
OH NO. WILLOW . . .
TWEET! TWEET! TWEET!

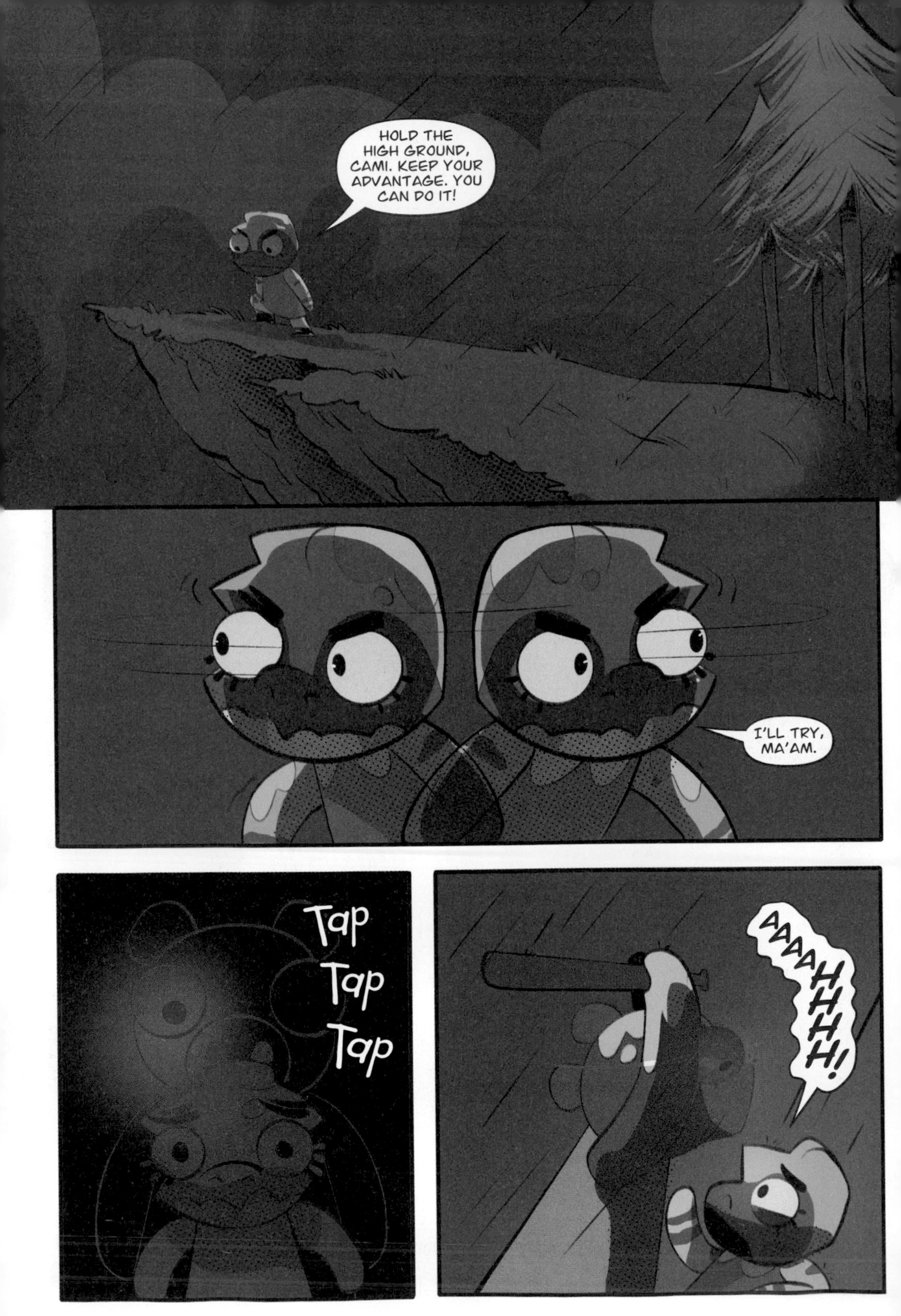
HOLD THE HIGH GROUND, CAMI. KEEP YOUR ADVANTAGE. YOU CAN DO IT!
I'LL TRY, MA'AM.
Tap
Tap
Tap
AAAAHHHHH!

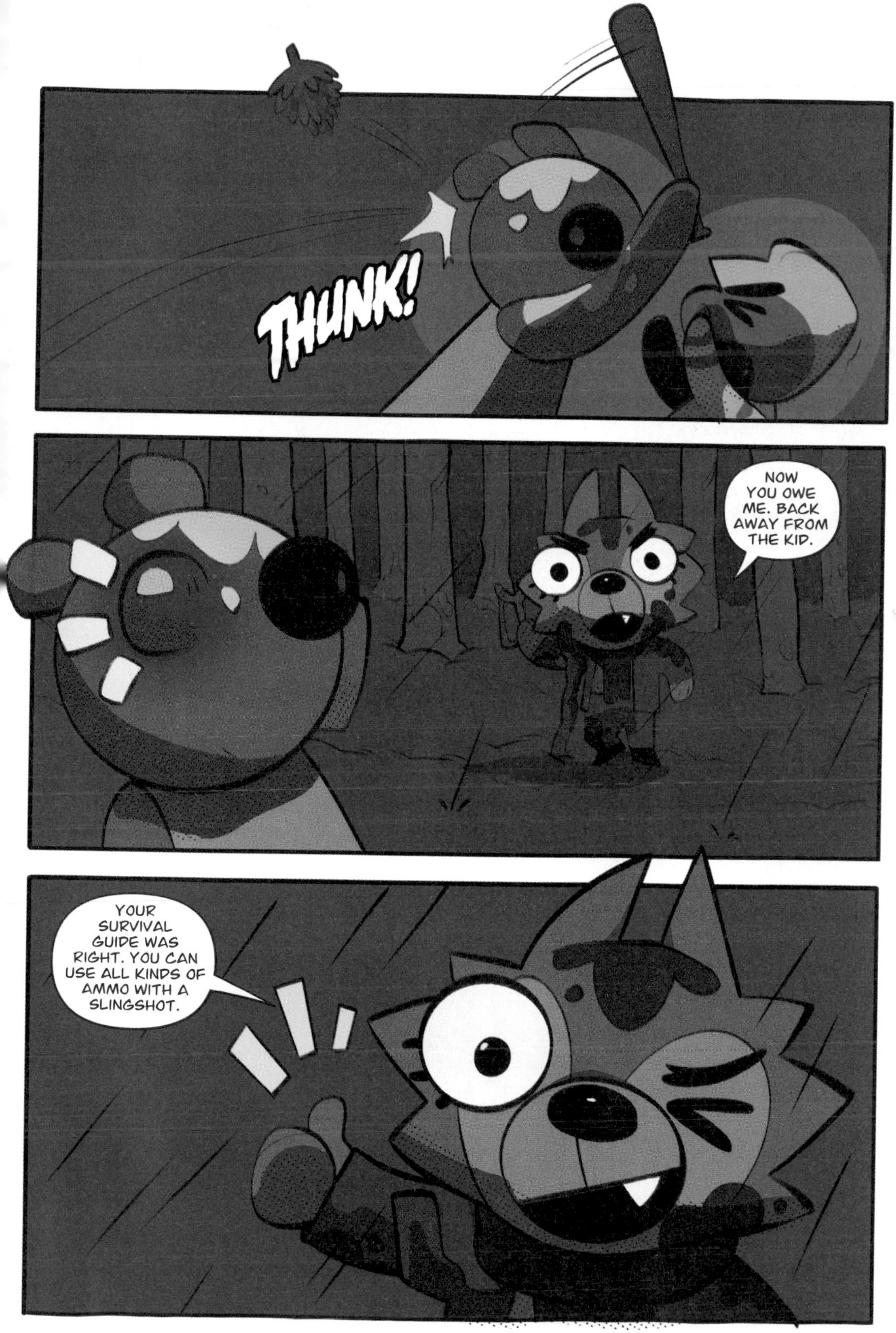
THUNK!
NOW YOU OWE ME. BACK AWAY FROM THE KID.
YOUR SURVIVAL GUIDE WAS RIGHT. YOU CAN USE ALL KINDS OF AMMO WITH A SLINGSHOT.

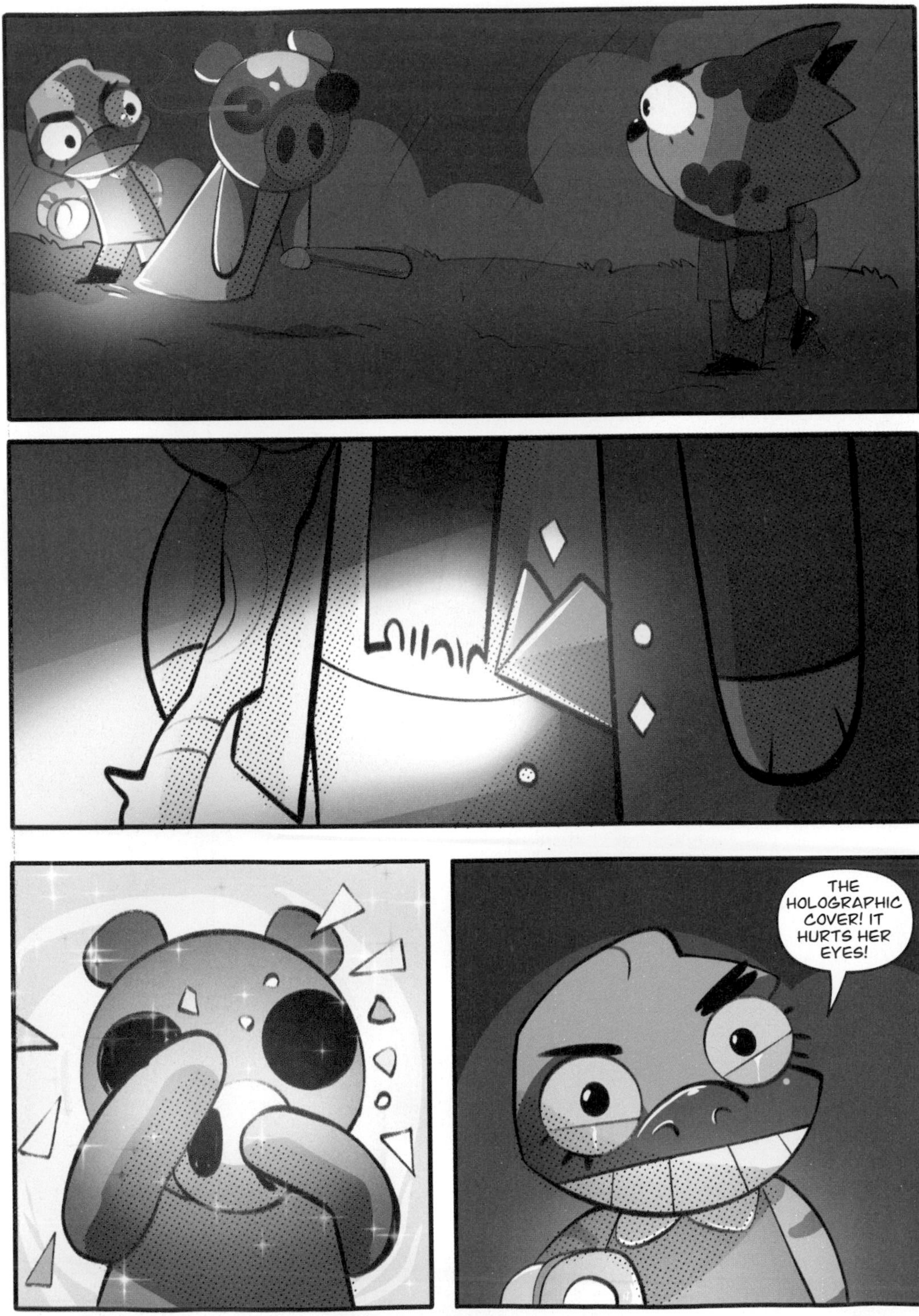
THE HOLOGRAPHIC COVER! IT HURTS HER EYES!

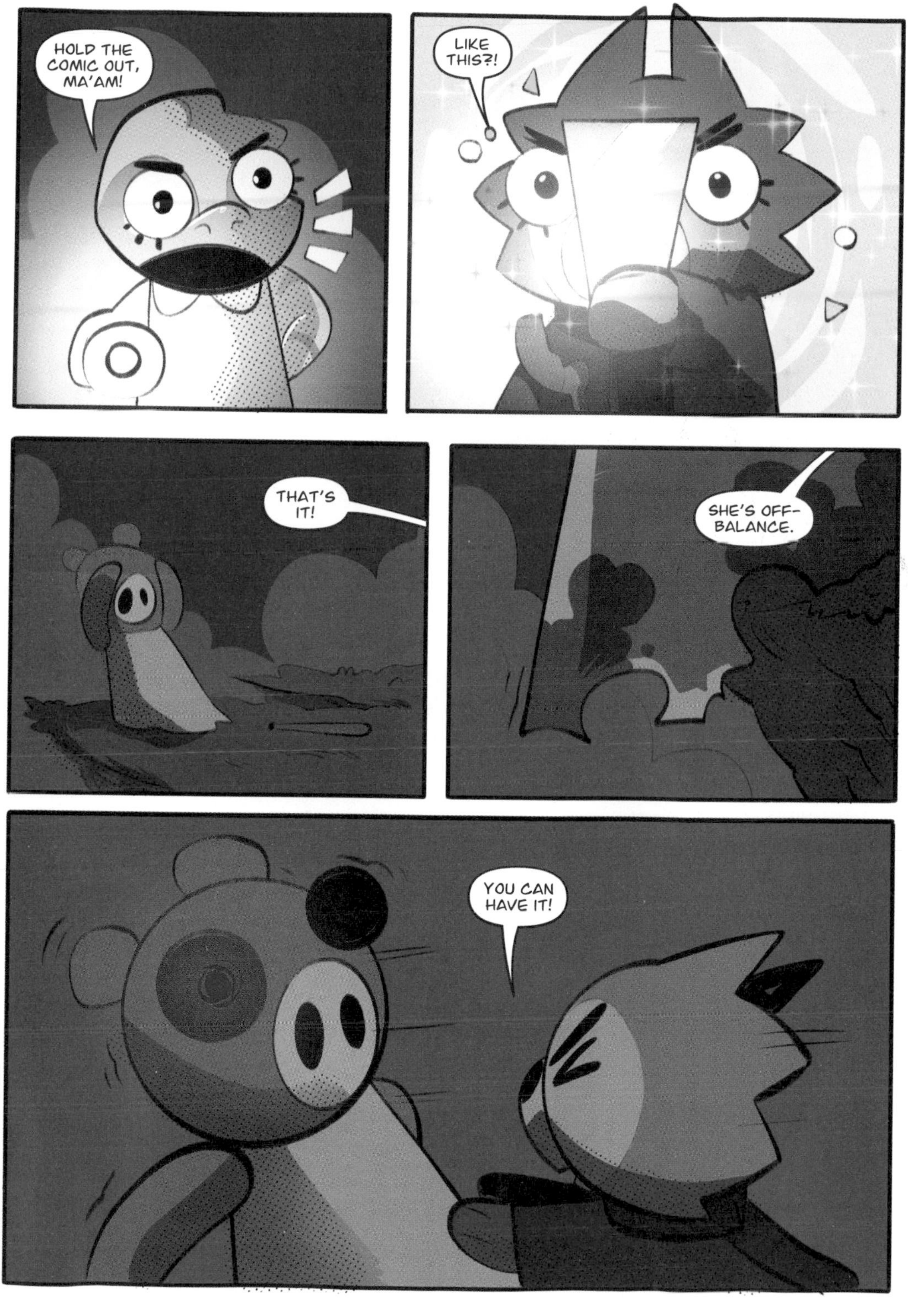
HOLD THE COMIC OUT, MA'AM!
LIKE THIS?!
THAT'S IT!
SHE'S OFF-BALANCE.
YOU CAN HAVE IT!

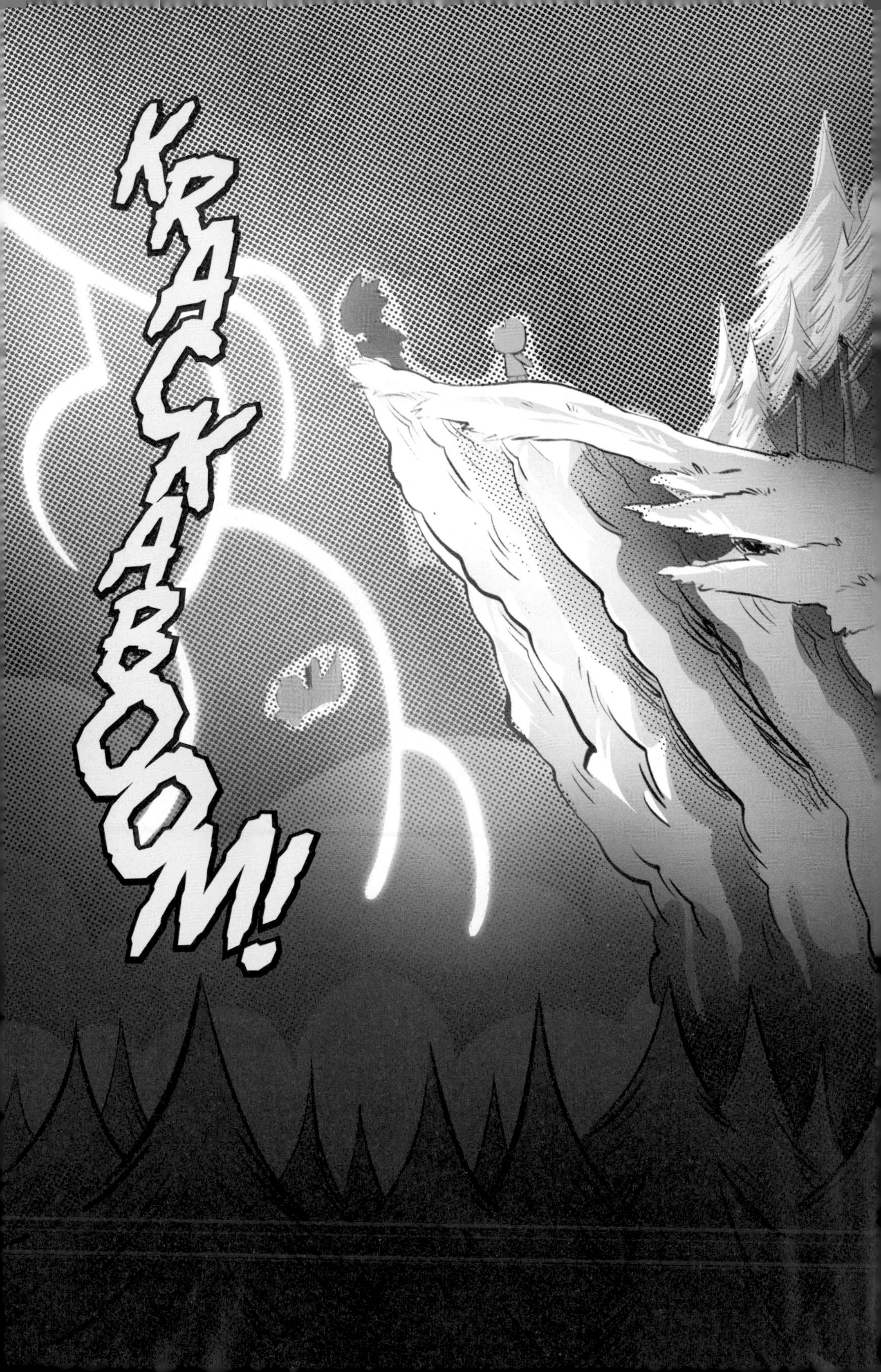
KRACKABOOM!

IT'S OKAY, CAMI. I'VE GOT YA!

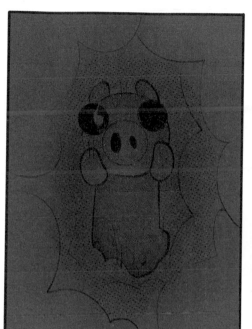

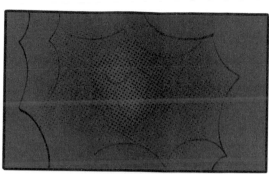

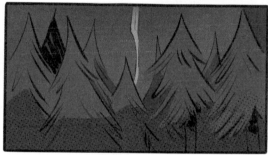

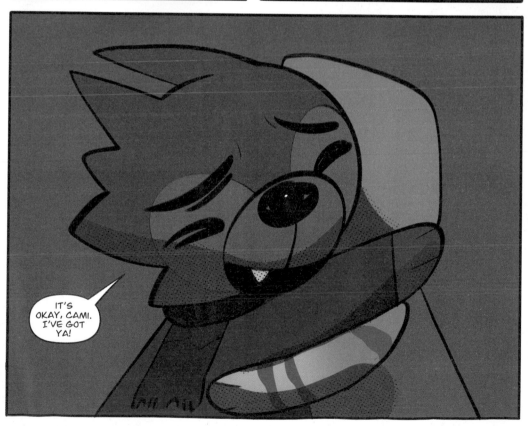

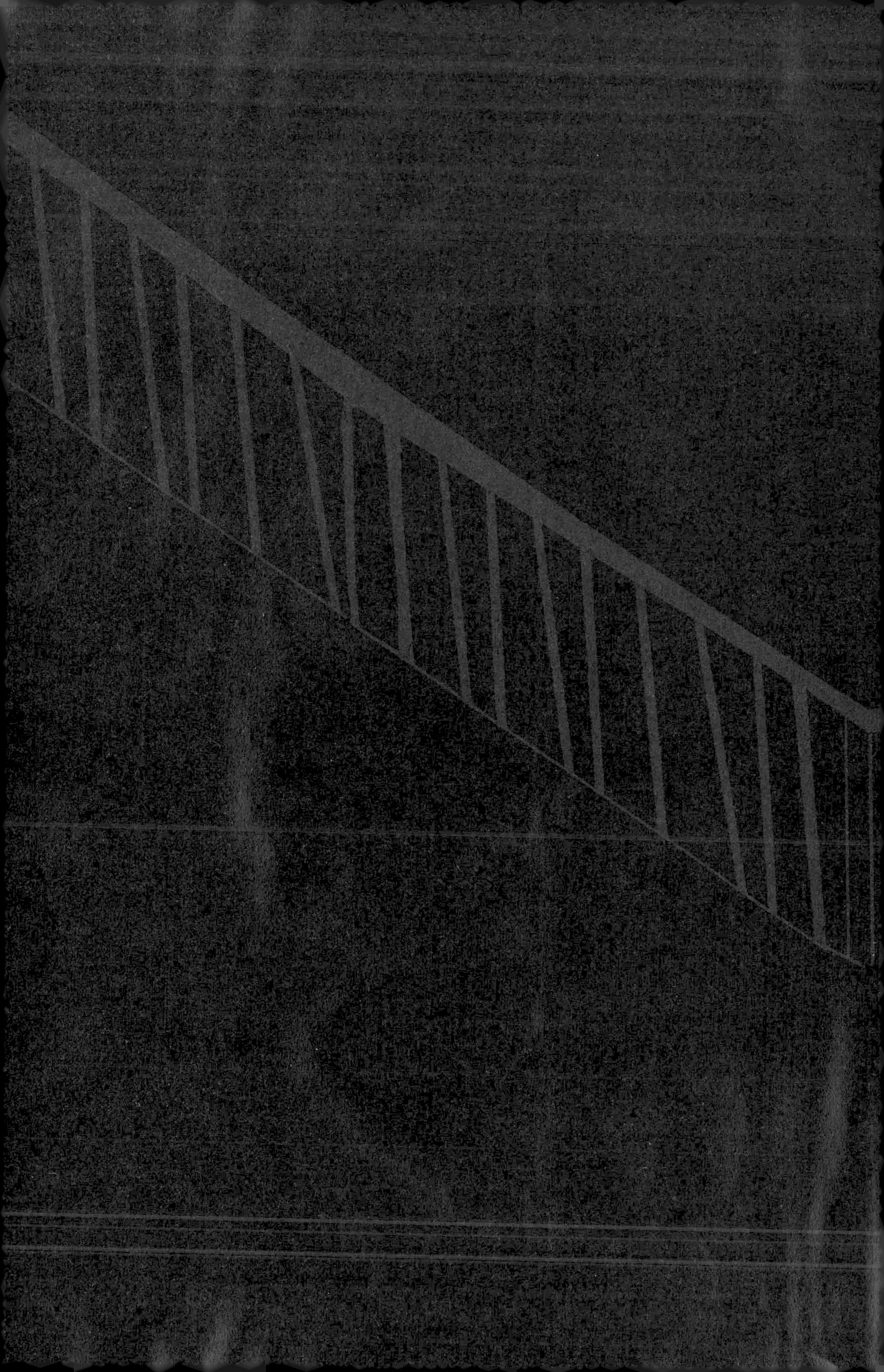

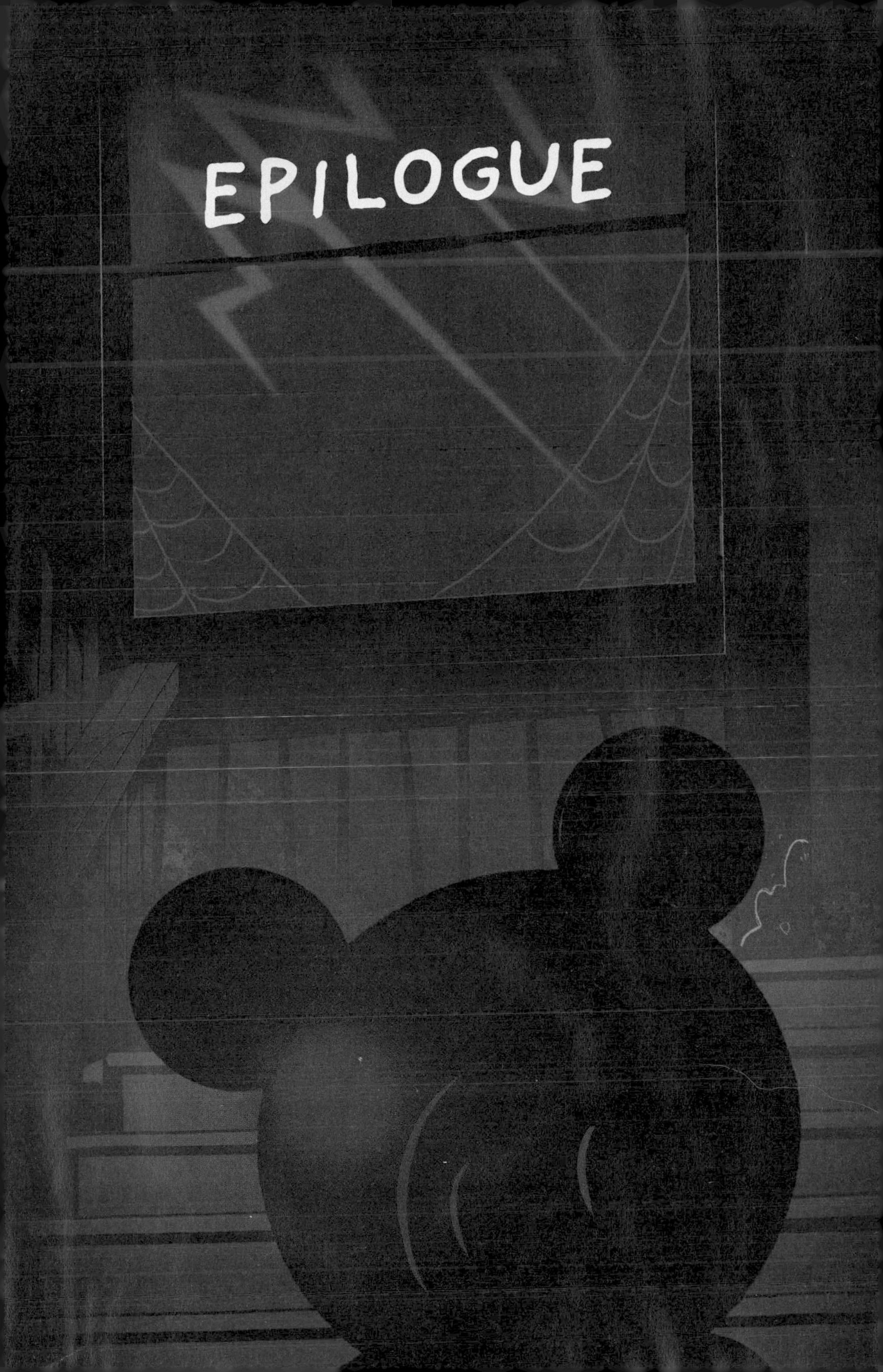
EPILOGUE

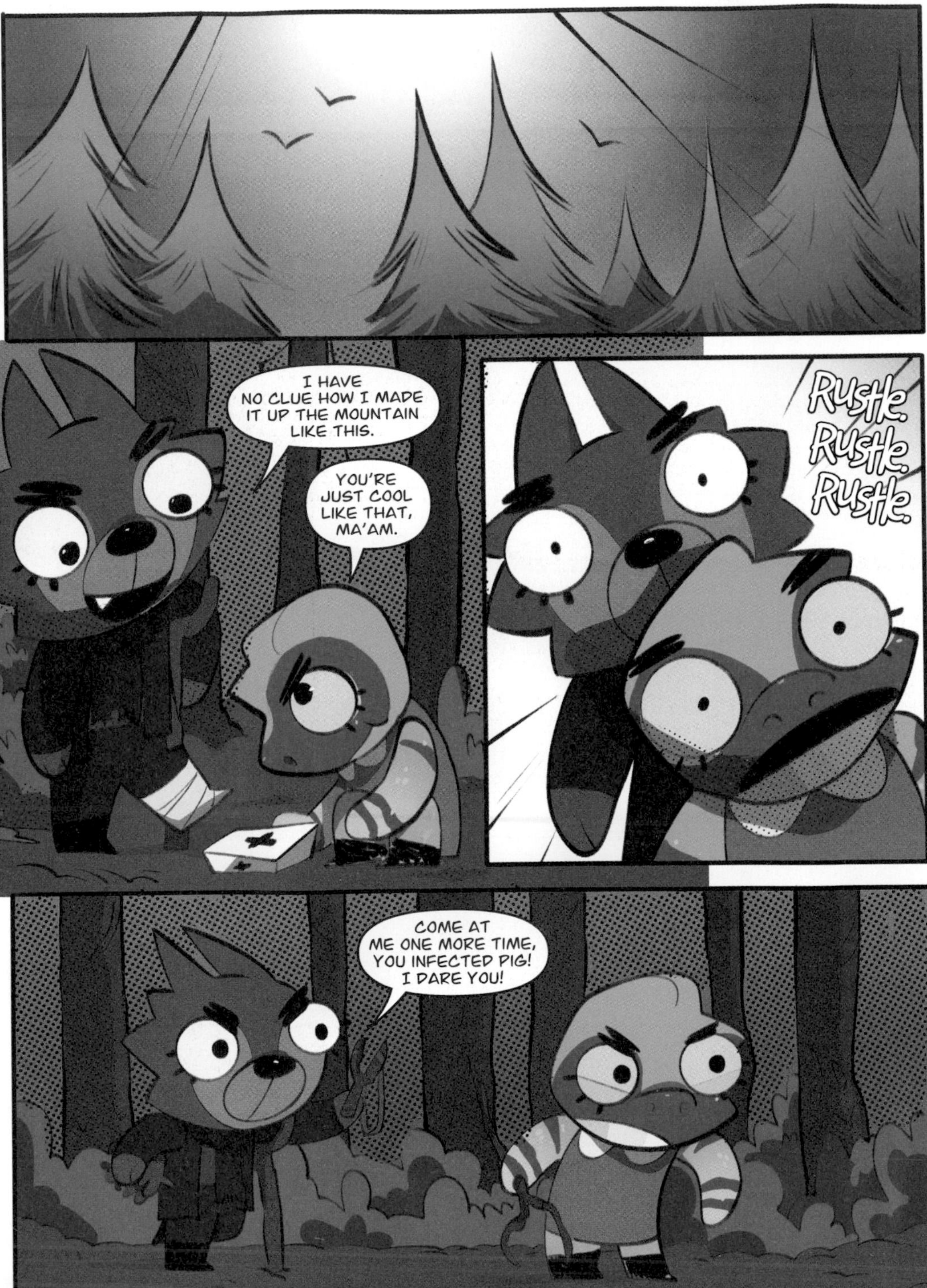
I HAVE NO CLUE HOW I MADE IT UP THE MOUNTAIN LIKE THIS.
YOU'RE JUST COOL LIKE THAT, MA'AM.
Rustle. Rustle. Rustle.
COME AT ME ONE MORE TIME, YOU INFECTED PIG! I DARE YOU!

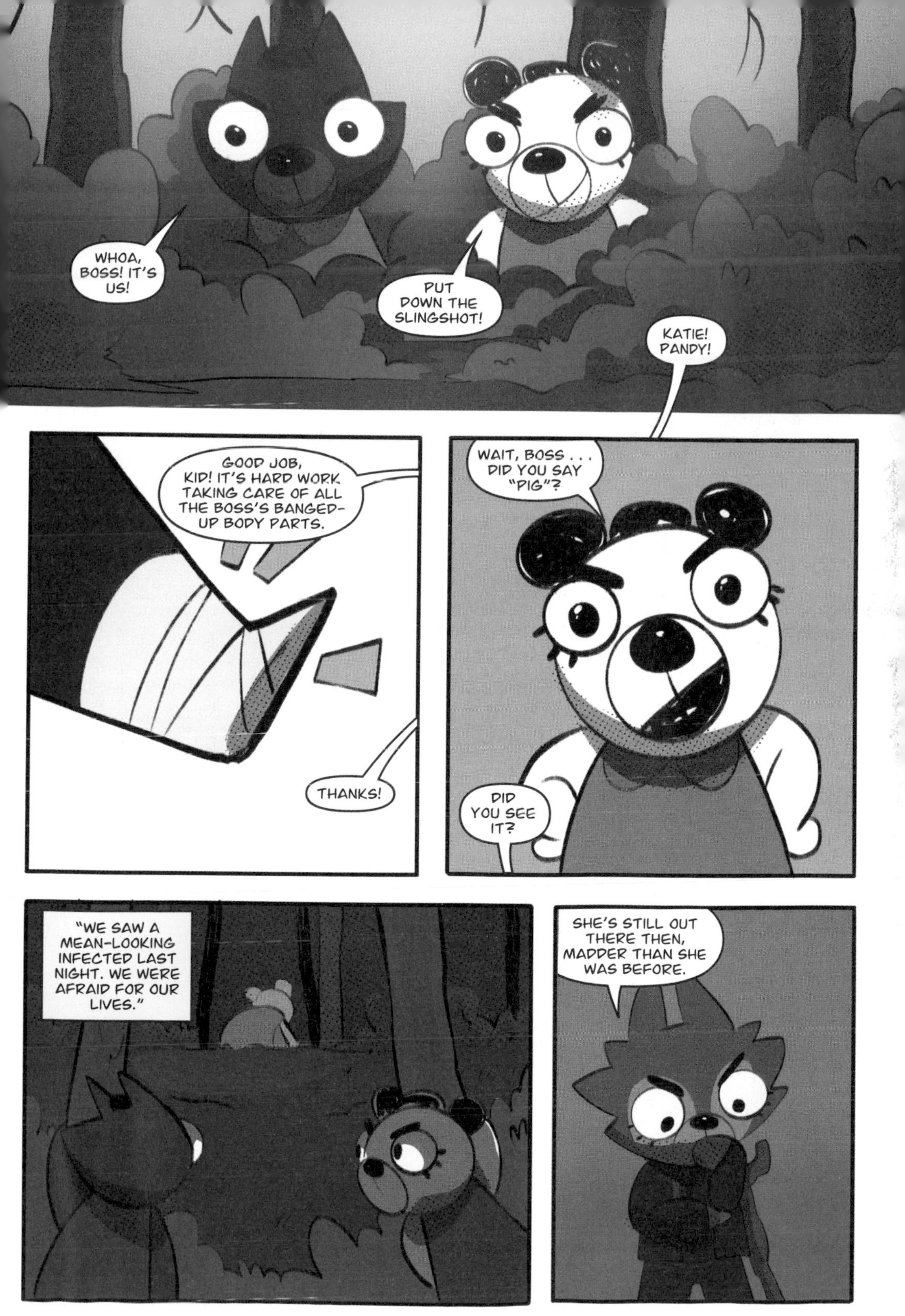
WHOA, BOSS! IT'S US!
PUT DOWN THE SLINGSHOT!
KATIE! PANDY!
GOOD JOB, KID! IT'S HARD WORK TAKING CARE OF ALL THE BOSS'S BANGED-UP BODY PARTS.
THANKS!
WAIT, BOSS . . . DID YOU SAY "PIG"?
DID YOU SEE IT?
"WE SAW A MEAN-LOOKING INFECTED LAST NIGHT. WE WERE AFRAID FOR OUR LIVES."
SHE'S STILL OUT THERE THEN, MADDER THAN SHE WAS BEFORE.

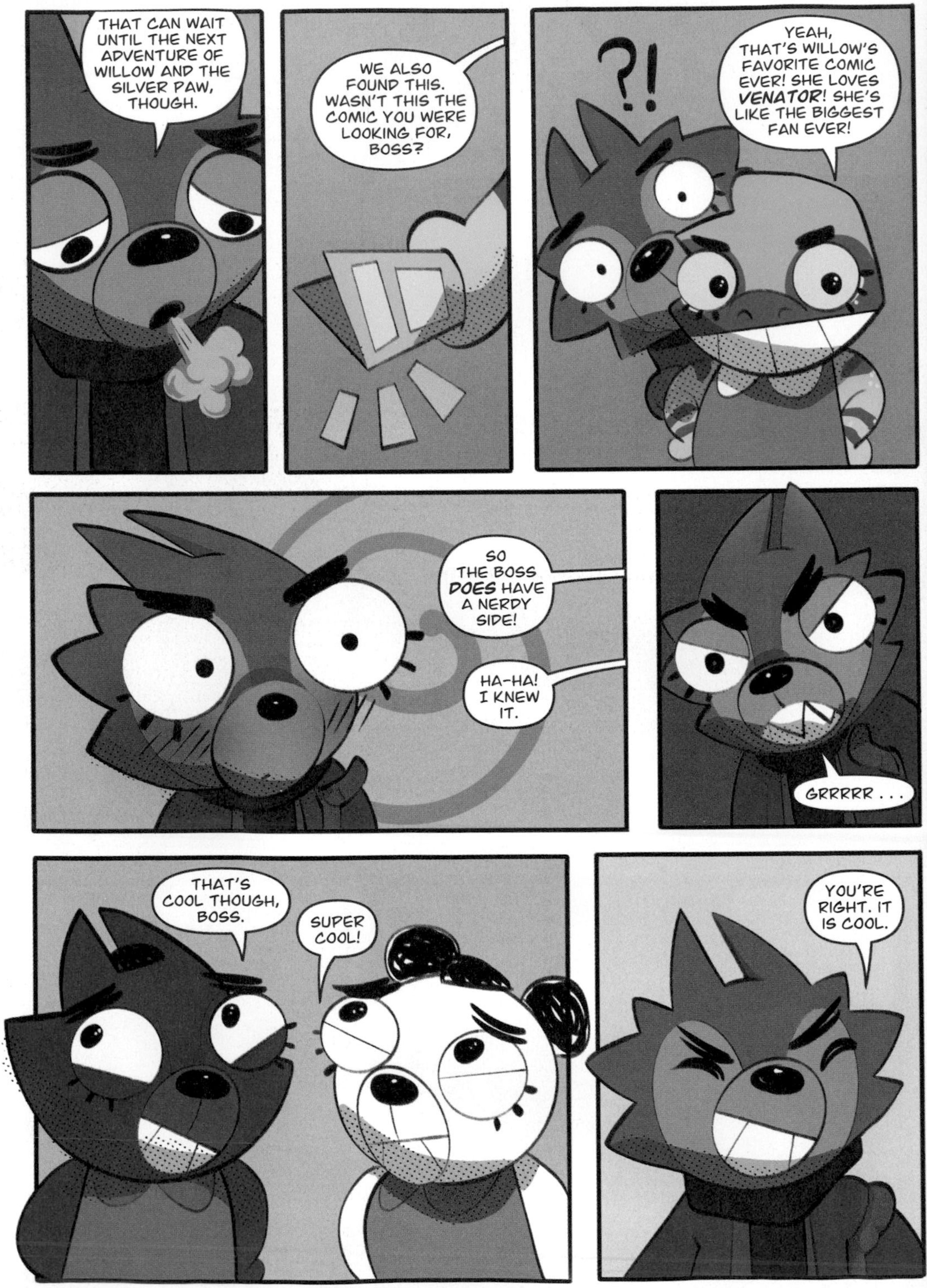
THAT CAN WAIT UNTIL THE NEXT ADVENTURE OF WILLOW AND THE SILVER PAW, THOUGH.
WE ALSO FOUND THIS. WASN'T THIS THE COMIC YOU WERE LOOKING FOR, BOSS?
?!
YEAH, THAT'S WILLOW'S FAVORITE COMIC EVER! SHE LOVES VENATOR! SHE'S LIKE THE BIGGEST FAN EVER!
SO THE BOSS DOES HAVE A NERDY SIDE!
HA-HA! I KNEW IT.
GRRRRR . . .
THAT'S COOL THOUGH, BOSS.
SUPER COOL!
YOU'RE RIGHT. IT IS COOL.

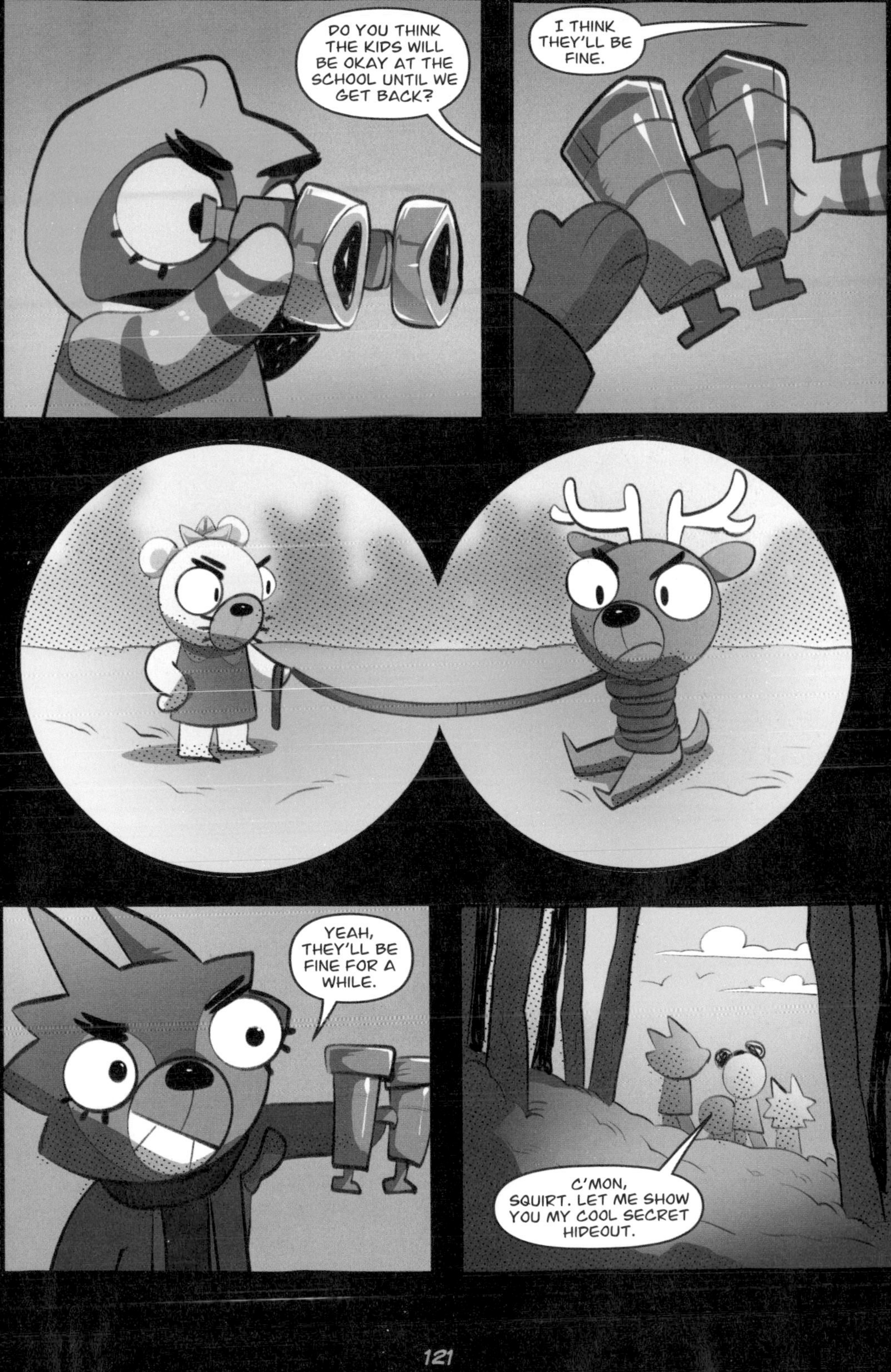
DO YOU THINK THE KIDS WILL BE OKAY AT THE SCHOOL UNTIL WE GET BACK?
I THINK THEY'LL BE FINE.
YEAH, THEY'LL BE FINE FOR A WHILE.
C'MON, SQUIRT. LET ME SHOW YOU MY COOL SECRET HIDEOUT.

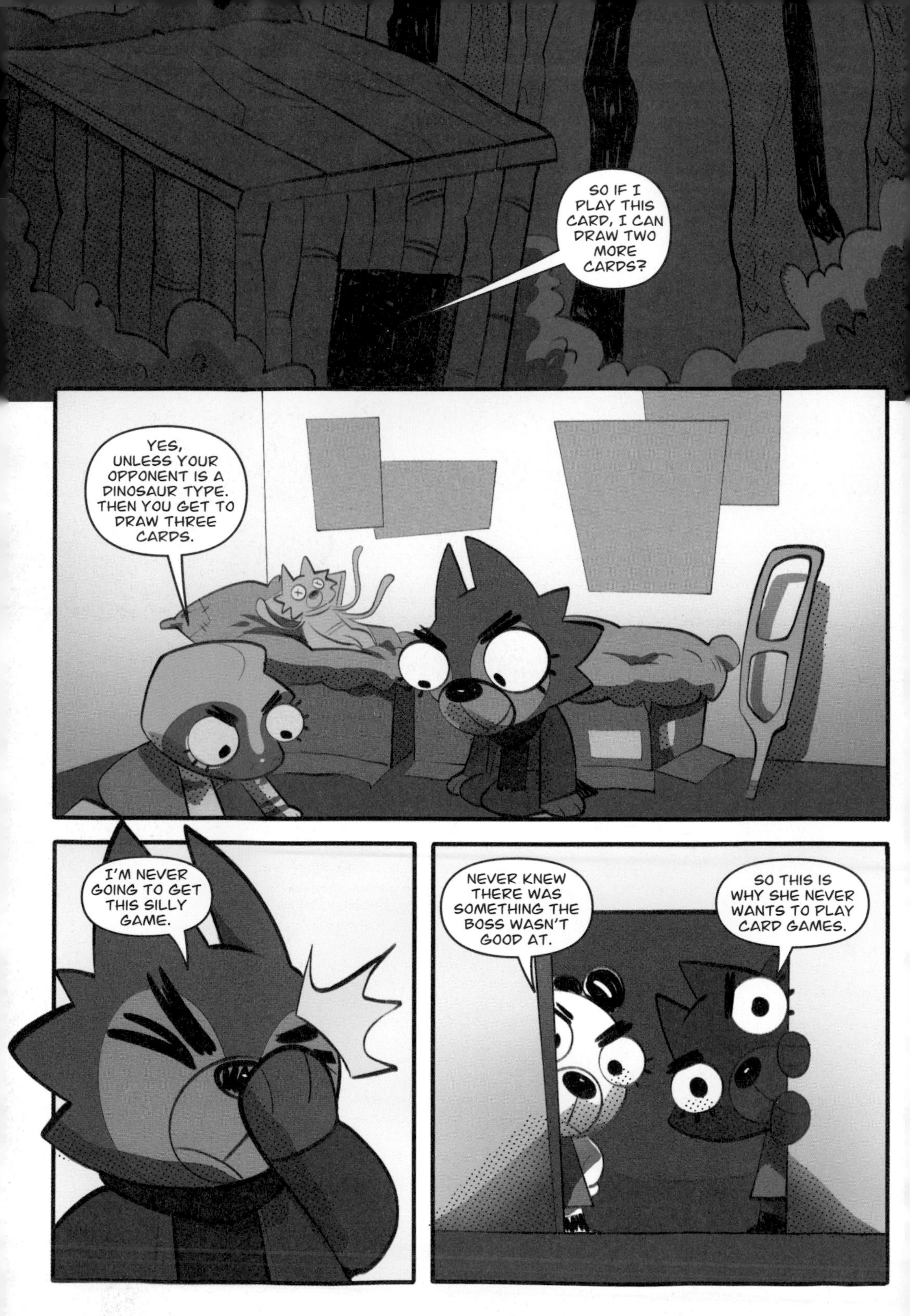
SO IF I PLAY THIS CARD, I CAN DRAW TWO MORE CARDS?
YES, UNLESS YOUR OPPONENT IS A DINOSAUR TYPE. THEN YOU GET TO DRAW THREE CARDS.
I'M NEVER GOING TO GET THIS SILLY GAME.
NEVER KNEW THERE WAS SOMETHING THE BOSS WASN'T GOOD AT.
SO THIS IS WHY SHE NEVER WANTS TO PLAY CARD GAMES.

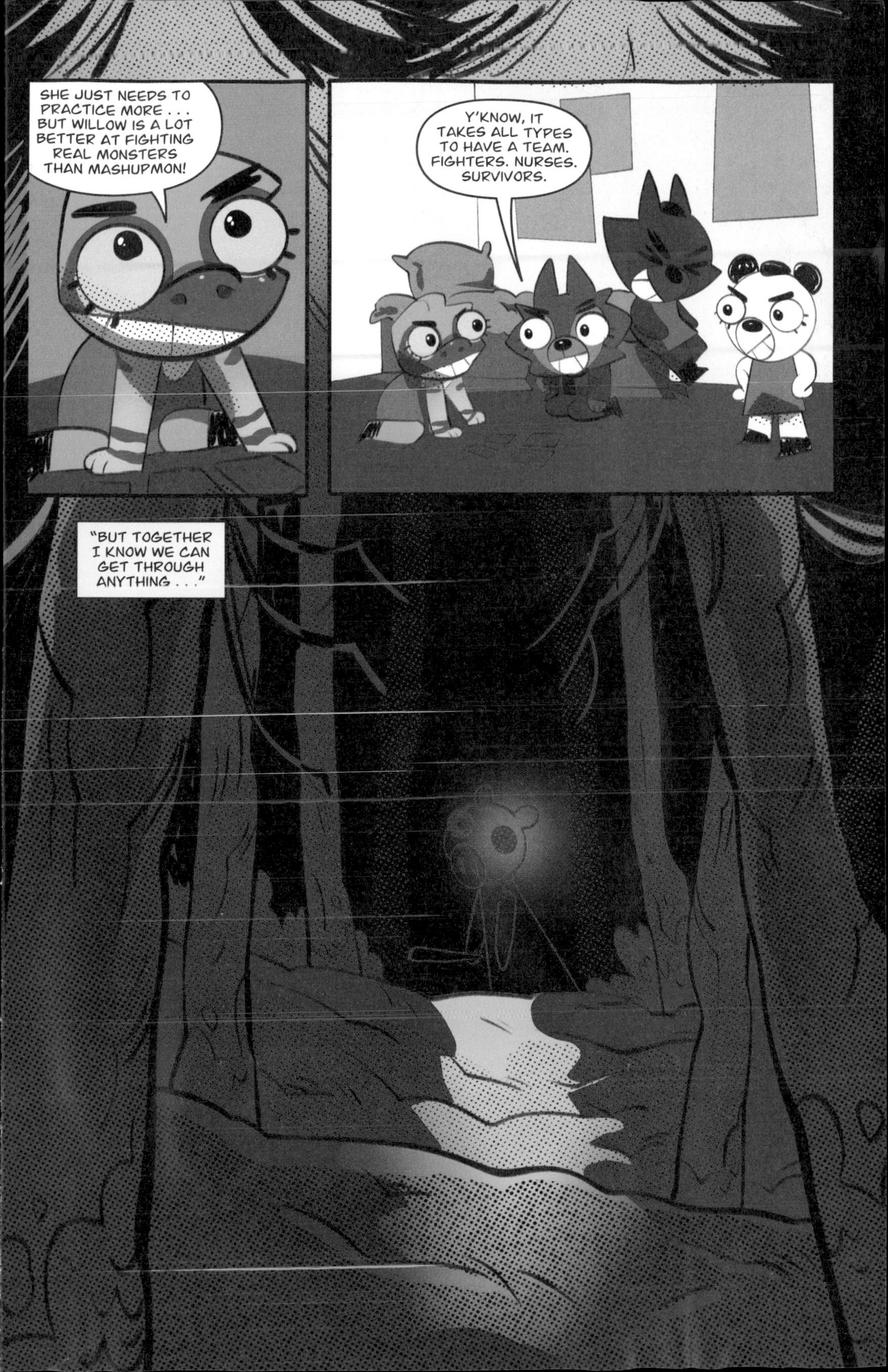
SHE JUST NEEDS TO PRACTICE MORE . . . BUT WILLOW IS A LOT BETTER AT FIGHTING REAL MONSTERS THAN MASHUPMON!
Y'KNOW, IT TAKES ALL TYPES TO HAVE A TEAM. FIGHTERS. NURSES. SURVIVORS.
"BUT TOGETHER I KNOW WE CAN GET THROUGH ANYTHING . . ."

PIGGY COVER SKETCHES

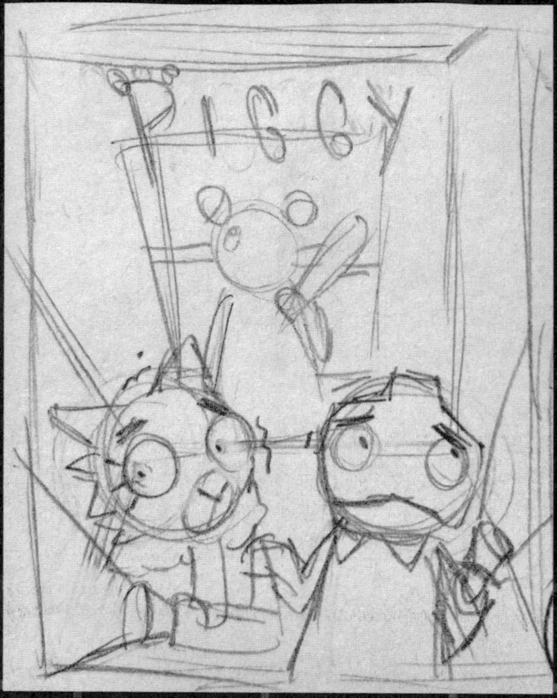
PIGGY

1) Initial Cover Thumbnail Sketch

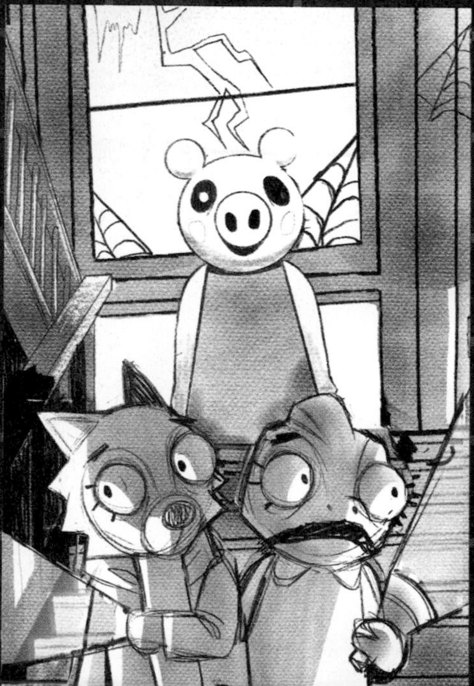

2) First Cover Sketch

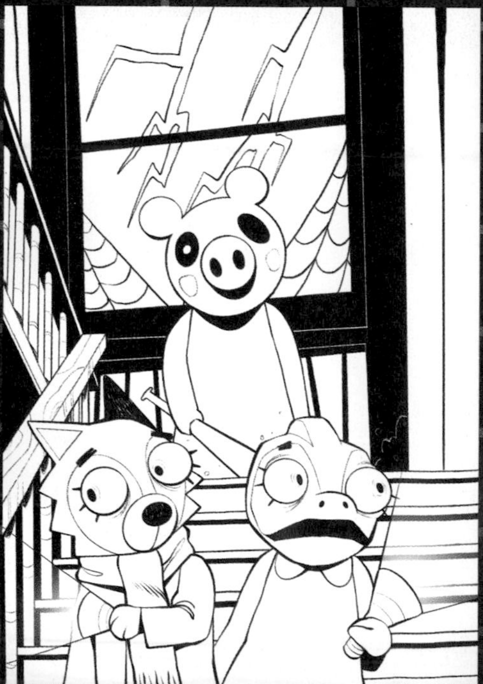

3) First Cover Inks

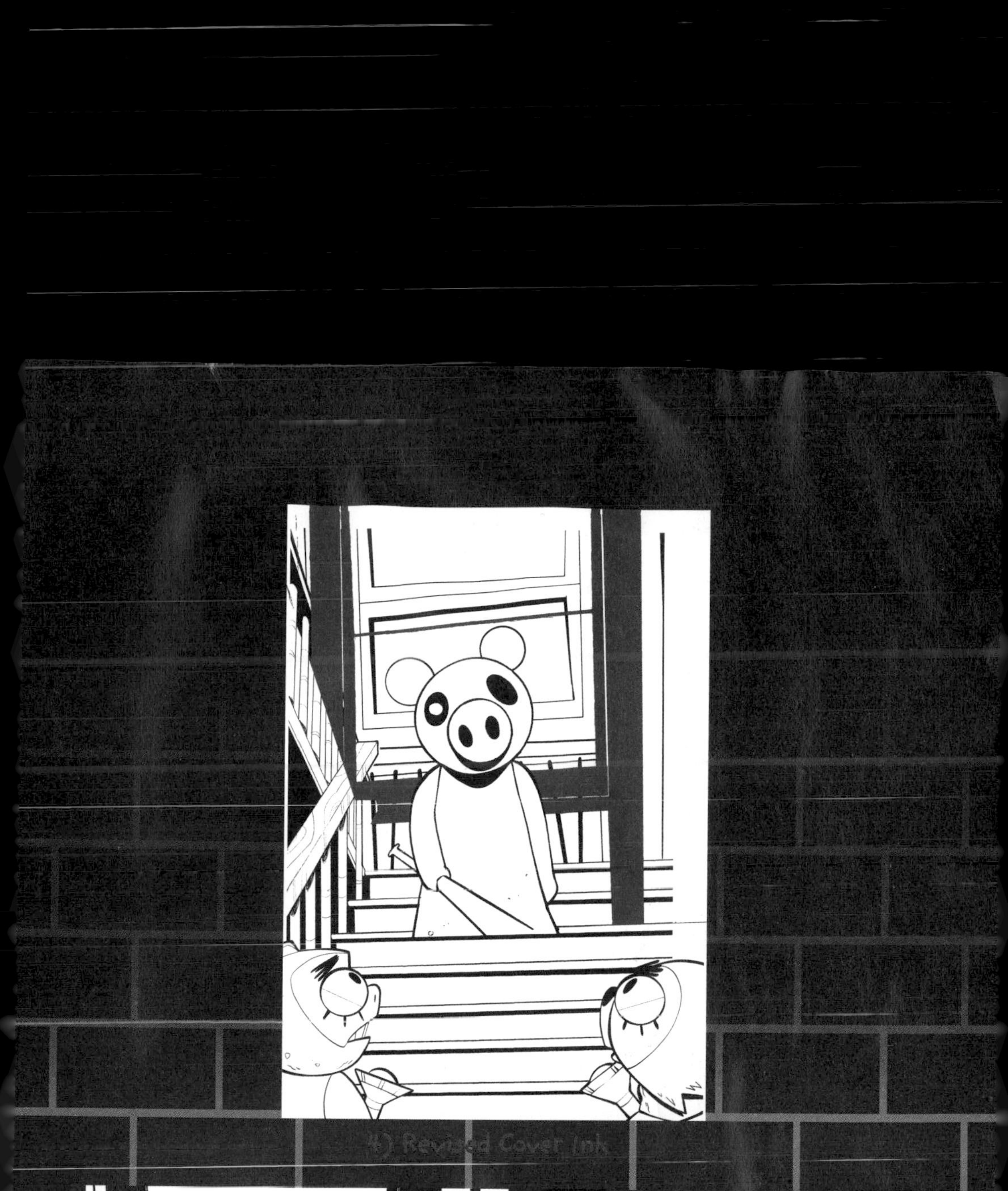

4) Revised Cover Ink

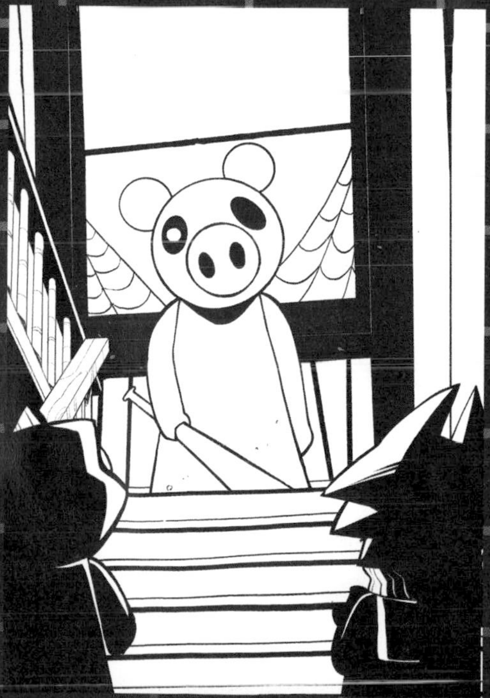

5) Final Cover Ink

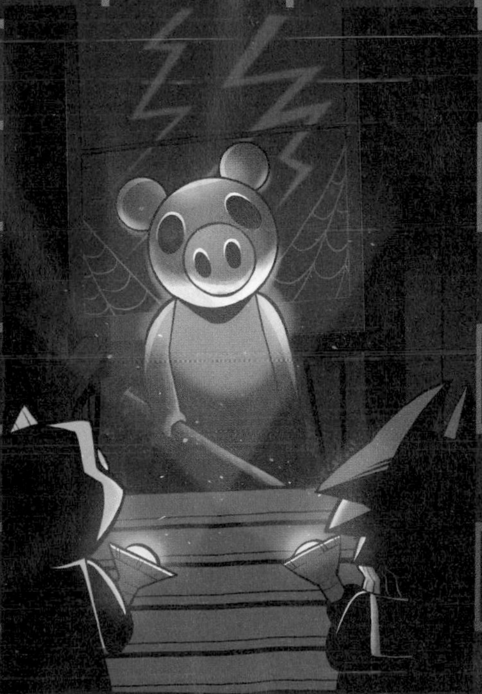

6) Final Cover with Color

PIGGY CHARACTER STUDIES

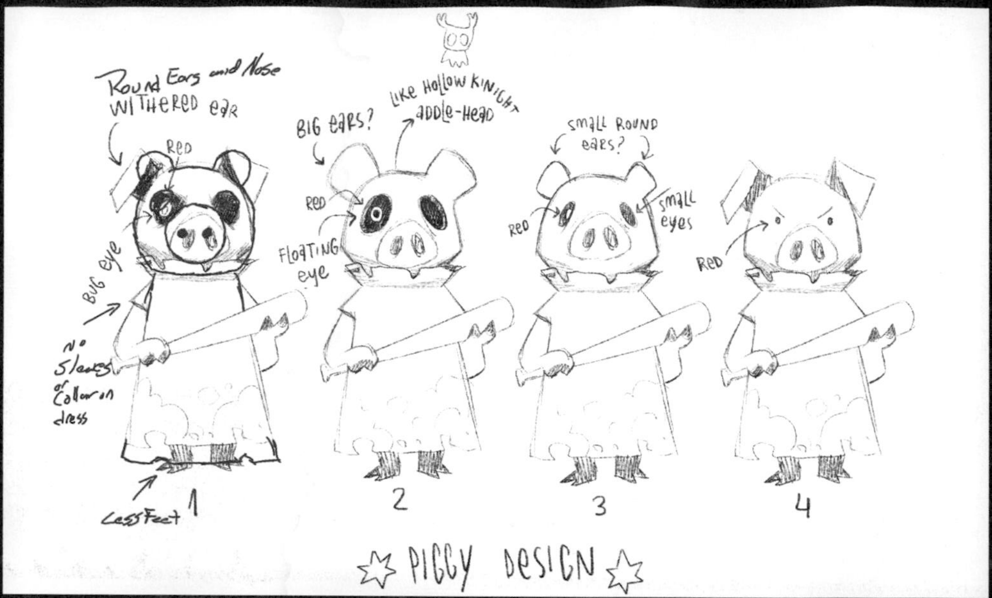

Round Ears and Nose
WITHERED ear
Red
Bug eye
No Sleeves or Collar on dress
Less Feet
1
BIG ears?
LIKE HOLLOW KNIGHT
ADDLE-HEAD
Red
FLOATING eye
2
SMALL ROUND ears?
Red
SMALL eyes
3
Red
4
PIGGY DESIGN

Initial Piggy character studies with art direction notes

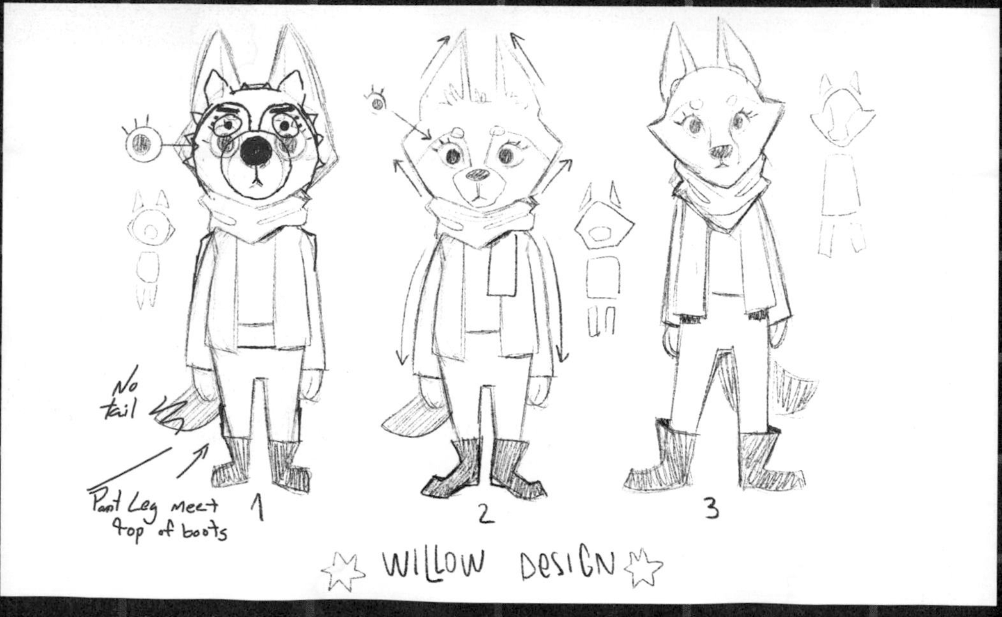

No tail
Pant Leg meet top of boots
1
2
3
WILLOW DESIGN

Initial Willow character studies with art direction notes

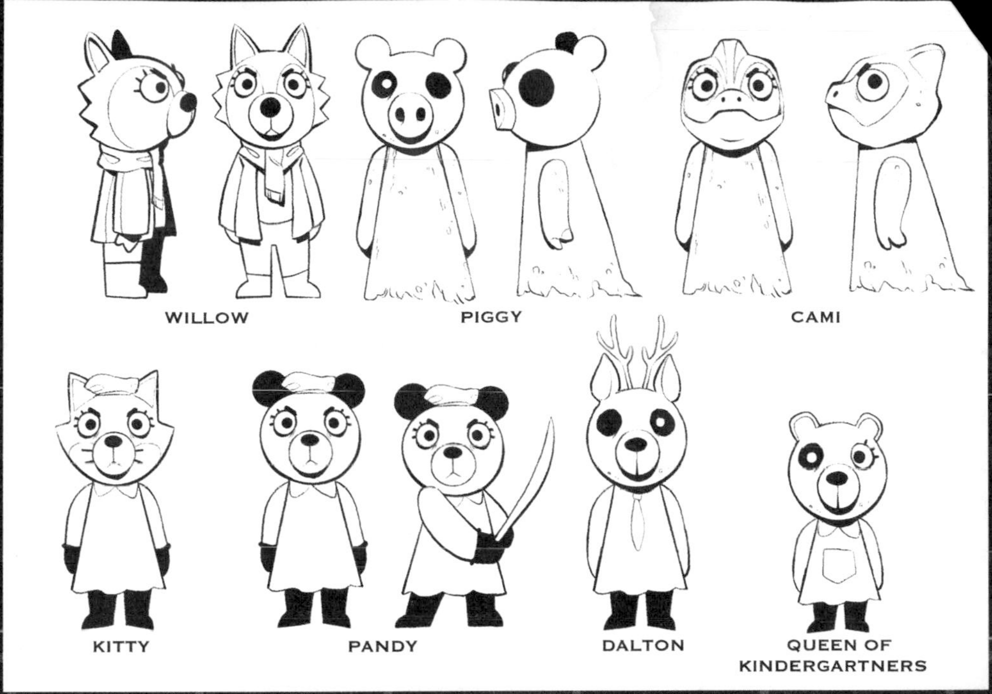
WILLOW
PIGGY
CAMI
KITTY
PANDY
DALTON
QUEEN OF
KINDERGARTNERS

3) Piggy character inks

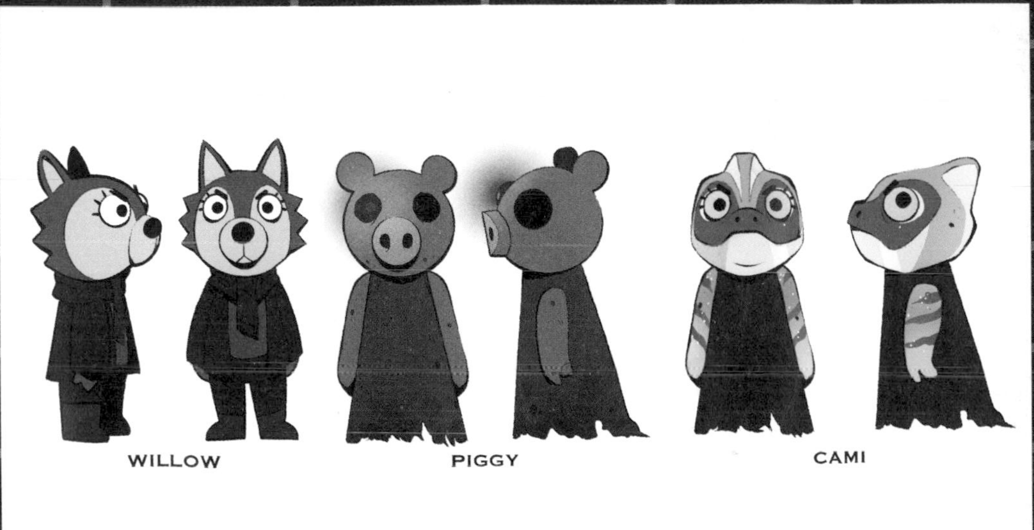
WILLOW
PIGGY
CAMI

4) initial character color studies

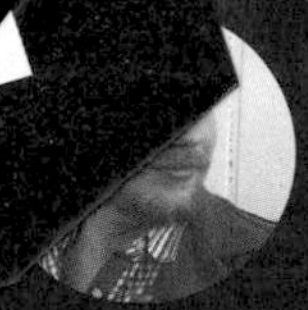

Vannotes is a writer, cartoonist, and educator based out of Idaho. Their work includes the *Spy Ninjas Official Graphic Novel: Virtual Reality Madness!*, *Bendy: Crack-Up Comics Collection*, and *Piggy: Permanent Detention*. They received their bachelor of fine arts degree in comic art from the Minneapolis College of Art and Design and their master of fine arts degree in creative writing from Eastern Oregon University. In their free time, they read way too many comics and play far too many video games.

Learn more about Vannotes at **vannotesbooks.com.**

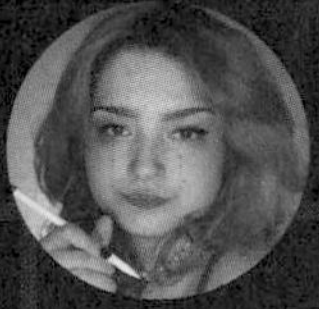

Malu Menezes is a Brazilian freelance illustrator and comic book artist who works as a designer, finalist, and colorist in several editorial and comic productions. Before entering the comics business, Malu worked for three years illustrating textbooks, covers, and personal commissions, soon after she worked for two years as a tattoo artist of authorial illustrations in small studios in her hometown, Manaus–Amazonas, Brazil. Malu likes indie digital games, reading comics when there are no new games available, and getting new tattoos, of course.

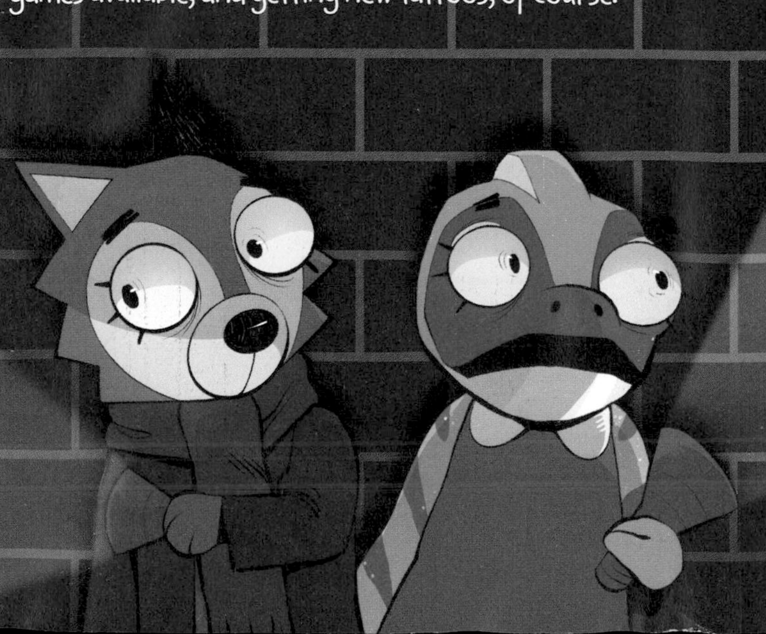